Second Chance

AN AGENT MELANIE WARD NOVEL

Kate Mathis

POWWOW
PUBLISHING

PowWow Publishing
P.O. 31855
Tucson, AZ 85751-1855 U.S.A.

Printed in the United States of America
First Printing July 2011

Library of Congress Control Number: 2011901704
Mathis, Kate.

Second Chance - Book Two: An Agent Melanie Ward Novel / Kate Mathis - 1st ed.

1. Female Spy – Fiction. 2. Mystery – Fiction. 3. Thriller Romance – Fiction
4. Humor – Fiction. 5. Adventure – Fiction. 6. Melanie Ward – Fiction.
7. Suspense – Fiction. 8. An Agent Melanie Ward Novel – Fiction
9. Sequel to Living Lies – Fiction 10. Terrorists – Fiction. 11. Basque – Fiction
12. Spain – Fiction 13. Espionage – Fiction

ISBN-13: 978-0-9819789-6-3
ISBN-10:   0-9819789-6-7

Book design and composition by PowWow Inc.

for
Frank and Laura

PROLOGUE

Lying to the Board was nothing to lose sleep over. He'd done it hundreds of times. Finn rehearsed in front of the mirror – Hugh would be in attendance and he had to look good. The gist of his story was a bit fantastical, but no more so than Ward accusing *him* of having a hand in her kidnapping.

Finn smiled at himself, his blue eyes twinkling in that way that made the Board trust him. It wasn't just that his father was Senator Hugh Parker and on the Board … *no,* Finn thought, *they love me.*

"And why not? I'm adorable." He said aloud with a wink at himself before heading out.

Driving to the meeting he played the events in his head, visualizing them exactly as his story went. He'd been abducted on July 4th for a formula that he'd obtained. When he wouldn't succumb to their torture, they went after his successor, Melanie Ward, and she immediately crumbled like a cookie. The second she called the chubby techie dude and ordered him to upload the formula he knew they were both dead.

There was no way to save Ward – though he tried – her mouth had hammered the nail in her coffin.

At the end the events had unfolded quickly. He believed Ward had been shot. He was tossed into the back of an SUV. The barn they'd been held in exploded. After a few miles he managed to over take the driver, breaking his neck. That's when the SUV flew over the ridge and flipped to the bottom of the ravine.

Finn's forehead gleamed by the time he'd finished performing the reenactment … The Board was riveted.

"Hook, line and sinker," Hugh whispered in the parking garage. "Nicely done, son. Your medical release is in and the Agency is eagerly awaiting your return. I've had the doctors hold Ward for a solid two weeks." A shadow passed over his grin.

"Problem?"

"No, there's just one doctor I'm going to have to deal with … pain in the ass. I'll have to decide how to get rid of him … a malpractice suit or I suppose I could allow him to retire. We'll see." Focusing back on Finn, he added, "Nothing for you to worry about … just get back in there like you own the joint. Because, really, we do."

It's a good day, Finn thought.

CHAPTER 1

"Hello," Melanie said, sliding her fingers through Adam's dark hair. "You're a thousand miles away."

"I'm sorry," he answered, the distant look clearing as he shifted on his pillow to face her. "I feel useless here. Well," he smiled, "not exactly useless. But I should be out there protecting you. You haven't forgotten that there's a madman gunning for you, right?"

"I think you're overreacting," Melanie said. It had been two weeks since Finn Parker, her fellow agent, had captured, tortured and failed in his attempt to kill her. "I've known Parker for years and that he got as close as he did to eliminating me was dumb luck."

"That attitude is what scares me." Adam sighed the growl at the back of his throat punctuating his disapproval. "Look, you'll be going back to work in a few days, your ribs are nearly healed … I haven't heard you curse in three days and I can't hide out in your bedroom forever." Gently squeezing her fingers he continued, "I don't *want* to leave you but…"

"I know what you're thinking and I don't like it. It's too dangerous and it's unnecessary."

"It's not." There was nothing defiant or wavering in his tone. "But I swear if it starts to feel risky, I'll get out."

"You think you'll get out, but what if you can't?" she asked, pushing herself up, despite the slice of pain in her ribs. "My resources are limited if you get into trouble."

The creases in his forehead eased. "Babe, I won't need rescuing." He caressed her shoulder. "I'm going to be fine. I know these people – I was one of them."

"I don't like it, Adam."

"I'll be in and out. You won't even notice I'm gone." He smiled. "If this were one of your missions you'd do the same thing."

"It's not the same thing."

"Right, it's more important. It's about your safety. I don't know Finn, but he didn't strike me as the kind of guy who's going to let this drop."

"Have you already made up your mind?"

He nodded.

"Would you tell me if there were an argument I could use to change your mind?"

Without hesitation he locked his gaze to hers. "If you said you'd stop loving me."

"That won't happen." Melanie said, clamping her bottom lip between her teeth. She couldn't believe she was going to sit back as he retreated into his old life. Her stomach churned, "I feel sick."

"Everything is going to be all right," he said gently, pulling her close. "You're a quick healer." He brushed his lips over her mending face, her lips, her eyes, cheek. "I love you, Melanie. Nothing bad is going to happen to you or to me, I promise."

Pulling away she looked directly into his green eyes that looked as if they'd been created by thousands of dazzling emeralds.

"I'm going to hold you to that promise."

CHAPTER 2

Sweat slid in currents down between his shoulder blades and the side of his face. It was useless to try wiping it away. South America was hotter than he remembered. Progress had not reached this side of the world. It'd been twelve years since he'd last driven this dirt road that cut into the heart of the jungle. Time here had stood still.

At the base of Hector's compound the heavily armed militia gave him a moment of trepidation. Masked with the cold authority of an assassin, he approached the men.

How many old-timers would still be on the payroll? He wondered. Terese was the only safe bet. After a brief exchange and terse words over walkie-talkies, the steely-eyed gun-toters allowed him to pass.

The dense foliage spilled out onto the narrow lane. Adam drove without emotion, mentally checking out as he'd done when he was Hector's right-hand man. It was an automatic response to being back. The sense of being in control was undeniable, a rush of invincibility. *Was this how I always felt?* He was surprised at how quickly the arrogance returned and how comfortably it fit.

The lane bent and climbed opening at the top to a magnificent view of the palacio, a white mansion jutting over the edge of a cliff. The rental car fit snuggly between two mud-stained Hummers. Feeling a presence, he looked over his shoulder and his breath caught – standing beneath an archway to the gardens, was Terese. She was as beautiful as ever with her dark hair tumbling down her back. She looked like a flower in a rose-colored dress.

"It *is* you!" she called before breaking into a girly, high-heeled dash.

"Hello, Darling," he said, the way he always had to the woman he could never have. "I heard about Hector."

Terese was in his arms, pressing her face to his chest. "I am devastated. Not surprised, but heartsick from the loss. You know what a big personality he was … now the house feels empty."

"I am so sorry." The words choked him. He was sorry, *but Hector gave me no other choice.* Adam pushed away the memory of that moment – having to choose between Hector and Melanie. He had killed his mentor to save her life, and now … he dropped his face into Terese's thick, silky hair and wanted nothing more than her forgiveness.

"I know you are." She patted his chest. "If only you two could have reconciled before…" Terese looked away and he gave her time to recover. "Come inside. The boys are starting the celebration without us."

"Celebration?"

"Of course! I am so grateful you're here. I don't trust most of those ruffians with Hector's business. And the ones I *do* trust don't have the brains for the operation." She linked her arm with his, leading him to the house.

"Terese, I'm only here for a short stay. Definitely not to take over the business."

"Why not? It's your birthright. Hector thought of you as his son." She waved him off. "Doesn't matter, but you haven't told me how I look."

Adam smiled. "Beautiful. You haven't aged from the day Hector introduced us."

"Ha! Still the charmer."

"Possibly. But it's the truth."

Rowdy laughter bellowed from the house. Adam knew the owner of that throaty, foghorn laugh. The shouts turned to an uproar as he and Terese entered. The blast of reception was startling and Adam had to take a step back.

The teasing came with rough embraces. The overwhelming sense of belonging brought an ache to his heart. He hadn't been prepared for such a homecoming.

"You've gotten fat, my friend," said a bald man whose waist was double his height.

"Have I?" Adam looked down.

"Remember how sickly he was? Like a little girl."

"No," Terese chimed in, interrupting their bellows while hanging onto Adam's arm. "Leave him alone. Besides, I remember *he* was the one who always got the girl."

"Mother Terese, still to your rescue."

All in good humor, Hector's original band trickled in and everyone was fair game for the ridicule. The alcohol flowed as freely as did the exaggerations.

These men were bad, yet Adam couldn't help but feel he was

among friends.

The party hadn't ended when he staggered to his old room and passed out on the bed.

⤫

Consciousness arrived with a skull-piercing headache. He willed his arms to move, reaching to verify he was not bleeding from a head wound, and bumped into a person stretched out along his side.

"You've become a light weight."

"I thought I'd gotten wiser," he smirked, squeezing his eyelids. "I haven't drunk like that since I left this place."

"We haven't stopped."

Terese moved, and her long hair swept across his bare chest. Adam opened one eye to see how much of him was exposed.

"Don't worry, your virtue hasn't been compromised. I kept my hands to myself," she laughed, running her sharp nail down his chest as she floated out of bed. "Come, let's have breakfast."

"Can't." Adam used his thumbs to place pressure on his forehead.

"Suit yourself." She pranced out of the room. "I had your bag brought up ... it's by the dresser."

"Thanks," Adam groaned. *What are you doing here?* The taste of alcohol clung to the back of his throat. *Hector*, Adam called out silently, pushing back the well of moisture that rose to fill his eyes, *what have I done?*

He couldn't deny the kinship he had with these people. They were his family.

Courage to face the day came from a shower and a shave. From there he was free to roam the house. The living room had been emptied from the impromptu party – not like the old days, when drunken bodies would be strewn out across the rugs, draped over tables or curled up on chairs.

But the rest was just as he remembered, elegant with expensive antiques around every corner. Adam grinned, recalling Hector's legend that his palacio was built upon ancient temple ruins. Hector had been a great storyteller, with the talent to talk anyone out of the shirt off their back.

After his self-guided tour he found Terese outside, beneath a covered veranda overlooking the pool.

"Hey," he said, pulling out a patio chair and planting a kiss on her cheek. He glanced over his shoulder at the lawn that had served as Hector's driving range. If he closed his eyes he could see him with clubs knocking balls over the low sun-baked stonewall – beyond was a straight drop to the Atlantic.

"Drink this." Terese slid a glass of milky beige liquid in his direction.

"Is this *the remedy*?" He gritted his teeth as he tipped it down his throat, "Has nothing changed around here?" The drink was Terese's famous cure for hangovers, but the joke was that the foul stench was the real prevention.

"Would you do me a favor after you eat?" She waved over a young woman to bring a plate of food.

"Anything."

"Go through Hector's office. A couple of the others have tried to get into his computer but couldn't get past the security. It would be such a help."

"Who's taken over his affairs?"

Terese shook her head. "After you left he didn't trust anyone enough to prepare them. He always thought there'd be tomorrow."

"I'll see what I can do, but it's been a long time."

"Thank you." She delicately laid her hand over his. "It is such a comfort having you around."

"Terese," he cautioned.

"I've been lonely."

"You're Hector's wife."

"In case you haven't noticed, Hector isn't here. Even before he…" she fluttered her eyes, "we were living separate lives."

"You know I've always found you attractive, but…" He needed her to trust him. He needed her to stop hitting on him. And was about to let her down gently when she looked at him with her big brown eyes when something inside stirred. *Maybe,* he thought, checking out the sliver of exposed thigh. *No! I'm not like that anymore.*

"We won't worry about this now," she said, breaking his thought and dismissing his refusal. "Eat."

Adam devoured the plate of huevos rancheros with potatoes as he soaked in the sun.

"Did you miss us?" she wanted to know as she leaned her head back, relaxing.

"I'd forgotten." He said honestly, finished off his orange juice.

"I'm glad you came to pay your respects. I wondered if you would or if you'd even know he died." She smiled sadly at him. "Are you ready?"

Adam nodded and followed her along the familiar halls.

"Hector always said you'd be back." She said, unlocking the office. A soft, musty, cave-like cool breeze blew through him when she opened the door and flipped on the lights. "I'll leave you alone," she said, shutting the door behind her.

"Hey, Old Man," Adam sighed into the emptiness.

Above the desk, where there had once been a framed photo of the two of them on a deep-sea diving trip, now hung a painting of his family.

"You fucked up," he said softly taking in the surroundings. He paced the room, grazing his fingers over the things that had meant so much to Hector. "God damn it! I loved you."

There was no answer. No fight or resolution.

Adam could do nothing to stop the flood of memories. He sat in the desk chair and felt Hector's presence. Emotions ran hot and cold as his thoughts jumped from one escapade to another. He lost track of time in the windowless office and was startled when the door opened.

"How's it going?" Terese asked, peeking her head into the room.

"Hasn't. I've been thinking."

"Oh, *mi hijito*," she consoled. "Nobody loved the man more than I did, but truly ... he was a pig." She sat on the desk, facing Adam. "You had every right to leave, he was stealing from you. Hector would've cheated, lied and stolen from his own mother."

"I know."

"You've gone soft." She shook her head. "Not good for this line of work. Who melted my cold-hearted businessman?"

"Time."

"Well, don't let those guys out there see you like this. They'll attack."

"I have regrets…"

"Fine. Just don't let them show. Your reputation is what keeps you safe – there are those who would kill to take Hector's throne but won't dare now that you're back."

"I'm not back."

"Just unlock that information and we'll figure the rest out later."

He failed three times before Terese left him alone. With her gone, he set to work. Hector had once explained his pattern for passwords – Bible verses.

Adam picked through the desk drawers. In the top was five cell phones lined up, turned off and unplugged. Buried in the bottom drawer he found the photo of them with the 60-pound Marlin he'd caught off the coast of Florida.

"That was a good day," he said out loud, releasing a weight from his shoulders. "I'm sorry, but I've got things to do here and I can't have your ghost following me around. If you're going to strike me down … then get it over with." Adam waited, listening to the creaking of the old house. "I am sorry, man. I'll set someone capable up to run the business and take care of Terese and the girls. We won't be even, but it's what I can offer. Okay?" he asked searching the ceiling for a sign. Feeling better, he opened the easel on the back of the frame and set the picture on the desk.

Adam stared at the keyboard before trying again. And offered up his thanks when the security page vanished, leaving him with full access to Hector's secrets.

Pages of e-mails scrolled down the screen. Hector was inundated with spam. Adam sent out a brief message to clients – announcing he was back for the time being – and deleted the rest. The assassin line of his business had been downgraded after Adam left. There hadn't been anyone able to take his place … but there were still major clients that hired for that service. Hector had been taking those assignments himself and had recently started training a new shooter.

According to the books, gun-running profits had boomed.

"Are you ready for dinner?"

"Is it that time already?" He stretched back in the chair and checked his watch. Looking up he noticed the transparency of Terese's strapless, billowy dress. *Christ, she's relentless.* "Let me just close up here," he said.

"You got in! Oh, I'm so happy. I knew you could do it." Her laugh was that of church bells chiming around the room. "You are not only the most handsome man in the whole country but you are smart as well."

CHAPTER 3

"Agent Ward." Ben Jackson smiled, a rare smile. "How are you feeling?" he asked jumping from his seat to scoot the chair out for her. It was her first day back.

"Better. I guess." She lowered herself keeping her abdomen as vertical as possible while trying to look casual. "You can stop worrying."

"I didn't say a thing!"

"Ben, you've been my boss for a decade and I'm pretty good at reading people. Especially you."

"Fair enough." He nodded, apologetically, "And you look much better than the last time I saw you. Something to take the edge off?" He asked, already pouring her a scotch.

Melanie smiled. "How're things here?"

Ben grimaced sideways at her through his wire-rimmed glasses. "Controlled. But what did you do to my file cabinets?"

"We went digital." The two weeks before her abduction she'd

slipped into his job while he mourned the loss of his wife. During those two weeks she'd updated his system.

Ben tightened his thin lips and shook his head. "I guess I shouldn't complain, but dammit Ward … I liked my manila folders. And I can't get this darn thing to work." He lifted a touch screen remote control. "Why do you need so many televisions?"

"It's easier than flipping between the different news channels. Sorry."

"Oh, forget it. I suppose it's time I move to the twenty-first century. But I'm an old dog, remember." He scratched his head and looked at her. "I'm starting you off on light duty. I'll give you a couple of cases to monitor and see how that goes."

"You do realize last month I was doing your job."

"And you hadn't been kidnapped and nursing broken ribs."

Melanie shrugged.

He shook his head. "Two cases, monitoring – nothing more."

"Fine. For the time being." She gave in, having more pressing issues on her mind. "Can I ask about Parker?"

Ben didn't break eye contact as his mood darkened. "Now that you're back there is going to be an inquiry. You know he's saying you abandoned him after he risked his life to free you."

The knot in her abdomen tightened.

Ben sighed. "The point is, your stories are dramatically different."

"And if he were anyone other than a Parker we'd be on a level starting field." She shook her head, straining to keep control. Every muscle in her body tensed. Ben's concern was clear in his pale blue eyes.

Her sides ached and she felt her pulse throbbing at her wrists where the shackles had cut to her bone. Melanie looked up at her mentor, who was looking down at her with an identical intensity.

"How are you?" she asked, noticing the bags under his eyes. He was still counting in weeks since the death of his wife.

She'd noticed sometimes now, when he walked, his head jutted forward and his back was faintly bent. She felt guilty for being a source of distress.

"The nights are the hardest," he whispered.

"I'm sorry. I'm not making things easy for you."

CHAPTER 4

In the two weeks during her medical leave, Finn had regrouped his fellow agents. They were eating out of his hands, desensitized to Ward's accusations. But the anxious, gnawing feeling grew stronger as her return grew closer. *I've told my side of the story so many times I could totally pass a polygraph*, he thought, convincing himself. "So, bring *it* on, Bitch."

His bravado didn't stop the acid in his stomach from bubbling up when she entered the room and their eyes locked. Well, her one eye, anyway – the other, the one he'd hit, was still partially ringed with purple. Absently Finn rubbed his knuckles, grateful those bruises had gone unnoticed.

He'd never had the slightest inkling of fear toward Ward, but restrained behind her brown eyes was a fury he hadn't expected. He knew Melanie Ward to be a model agent. She'd never taken a bribe or skirted the law for her own benefit. It was what he counted on, her good behavior. But the burning behind her eyes bordered on crazed.

Sweat began to form at his hairline, behind his neck, armpits and the back of his knees.

"Hello, Agent Ward," he said, walking straight up to her.

"Don't think you're going to get away with it," she said, her voice hushed enough for only him to hear.

"I've heard about delusions that can occur after a traumatic event. I've spoken to my father about hiring on an additional therapist solely for you." He knew he shouldn't be grinding salt in her wounds, but it was just so much damn fun.

"She's a lunatic," he exploded to his father. "I swear, she's liable to shoot me. You've got to do something!"

"Can't. The Board handed accountability completely to Jackson. They want me to wash my hands of the situation."

"Great. She's going to kill me."

Hugh's laugh echoed across the wireless universe and came in loud and clear. "Ever think you deserve it? Frankly, I'm impressed by her restraint."

He felt his ears burn and managed a weak retort to his father's indifference. "This isn't a joke."

"Then you'd better smarten up."

"What do you mean?" Finn hated having to ask.

"Think about it."

"Just tell me!" Finn whined.

"What part of your DNA is Parker? Have you no foresight? Jesus." Finn's backbone crumpled onto itself. "Use her lunacy to your advantage. It proves she's erratic, irrational – Christ, what more do you need? She's handing her weaknesses to you on a silver platter."

"Oh," Finn nodded, "of course."

I'm Ward's Achilles heel. And he knew his weapon of choice – you can't underestimate the power of a single wink. That well-placed, private gesture could send her into a very unfashionable straight jacket.

Smarten up and be unafraid, he repeated. Knowing Ward could smell his fear was what he abhorred most – that his weakness was exposed to her.

She was stronger than he was, everyone knew it ... Hugh knew it. She'd been strapped to a beam and beaten, yet she hadn't yielded, there'd been no look of fear. Damn her! The heat of hatred burned blue flames inside of him.

CHAPTER 5

Melanie looked through the mini-blinds of the conference room as it filled with the usual crowd. She could feel the change in the weather. Autumn had arrived right on schedule. Her bruises had healed but it was the infection eating at her soul that wouldn't mend, keeping her awake at nights.

Ben, standing at the head of the table, reported on the progress of open cases. Melanie, to his direct right, sat patiently, trying to stay interested and ignoring Finn sitting across the table with his condescending leer. The first weeks had been unbearable.

Eight weeks wasn't nearly enough time to forget what he'd done. His account was that he'd escaped the night she was found out in the woods. He had given the Board an outlandish, fabricated tale of his ingenuity – overpowering the driver of the Suburban and surviving a plunge off an embankment. The fall was fatal for the driver, whose prints were clean and whose dental identification suggested he was from a country with antiquated oral care. It was preposterous and now it'd become another tool to pick at her scabs.

The Board took fifteen minutes to authenticate Finn's story before allowing him back into the Agency. Mostly, she could overlook Parker's existence – if he'd just keep his fucking mouth shut.

She hated Finn Parker, hated the Board that let him get away with lies and was disgusted by the agents who were too frightened to acknowledge the truth.

She'd lived 33 years without needing a word more intense than *hate* – but these past few months had exposed the gap in her vocabulary. With a fiery passion she detested Parker – and he returned the sentiment.

The stare downs were new – since her return to work.

I could kill him and claim temporary insanity. It wouldn't be a lie, I feel truly insane. Ready to break at the slightest ... wink ... *he did not just wink?!*

"What was that about?" she asked, her audience forgotten.

"Me?" Finn asked innocently. The deepening of his grin only enhanced the sparkle in his blue eyes. "I didn't say anything. Did any of you hear me say a thing?"

Melanie fumed. He hadn't *said* anything, he'd winked. Now the sweetness in his voice was luring the others into believing she was nuts. Mustering every ounce of strength not to rip the dare off his taunting face, she took a breath. It was classic Parker to antagonize in a seemingly non-threatening manner and she'd fallen for it – again. She was angry with herself for having been sucked into his sick, twisted vortex and made to look like a fool.

"Agent Jackson, did they check Ward for psychological trauma?"

"I'm holding on here, Parker, but give me one more reason and I swear..." Melanie's voice came through clenched teeth.

"Outside!" Ben's voice boomed. "Both of you!"

Melanie needed air anyway. She'd felt the depletion of oxygen as everyone in the room gulped it down when she'd confronted Parker. Melanie pushed away from the table, taking her folder and ignoring the stares. She'd heard the rumors. Finn Parker, with his boyish good looks, could be persuasive. Mike had even informed her of a bet among some of the braver agents about who would win this war. She wasn't the favorite. A handful thought she was nuts, others thought she was being vindictive, and a few at least considered the possibility that Finn had a hand in her kidnapping.

Melanie strode down the hall toward her office. It was clear she needed to cool down.

"You're pathetic, you know."

His voice sent ripples down her spine. She spun around to confront him, her gun jabbing into his ribs. She wasn't aware that she'd drawn her weapon – but there it was, her finger firmly on the trigger. A split second later she felt the barrel of his gun pressing under her breast. Their eyes were locked, their positions were locked and neither was giving in.

"Give me a reason," she said, glaring in his demon eyes. *Just shoot him*, she thought, her index finger tingling.

"Put those guns down," Ben ordered as he passed them in the hall, "or I swear, I'll shoot you both myself."

She held the stare, daring him.

"Do you see this, Ben?" Parker pleaded, his voice showing the slightest waver. "She's crazy. We cannot have her carrying a piece – if you hadn't showed up she'd have killed me."

"I still may," she whispered.

"Shut up," Ben spat. "I've had it with both of you."

Melanie grinned.

"Ward!" Ben said, the vein in his neck leaping out of his skin.

Melanie turned without a word. Her pounding heart echoing in her ears, she strode down the hall to her office.

CHAPTER 6

She made me look like a fool for the last time, Finn raged, taking it out on the gas pedal. *A gun. She'd actually pulled a gun – I bet I'll have a bruise*, he mused, rubbing the sore spot on his bottom rib, *but I was just as fast as she was … or almost*. Hugh's instructions were clear: "Wait nine months to retaliate".

"I've waited long enough," he decided, flipping through the pages as a childish fear clutched his abdomen. He was going against Hugh.

Behind a brick in the mantel of his 17th-century, three-story Victorian, Finn had found a lock box dating back to the original owner. His felt giddy as he fingered the cool compartment and pulled out his little black book.

Wouldn't Ward love to get her hands on this, he thought with a chill as the spine of the notebook cracked open to the right page.

From an untraceable cell phone he kept with his book he made the call, leisurely leaning back in his desk chair. He didn't worry about being overheard – he'd spent over a hundred grand on this room, soundproofing and adding satellite interference along with the extra insulation. It was impossible for anyone to break through the security. *Money well spent*, Finn thought, *for complete peace of mind*.

The strange voice answering his call gave Finn a start. He chuckled under his breath at the absurdity. *Of course, it couldn't be Hector*.

"Ingles?" Finn asked, though he was perfectly capable of conversing in either language.

"Of course." The voice was unmistakably American and sounded irritated.

"Have you taken over for Hector?"

"Who is this?" He demanded.

Finn pictured the man from the barn – the one who'd allowed Ward to walk away. The one Hector had trusted. Finn's pulse picked up it's pace.

"Finn Parker," he said, shrugging off the uncomfortable feeling of exposure. "Surprise you?"

"Yeah, you did. I've been wanting to speak to you."

"Really?" The momentary concern gave way to intrigue.

"I'm waiting on your final payment. Your contract was completed and yet … there've been no arrangements for the final installment. Did you think just because Hector's dead that you could slip by without paying?"

"No, but…" His heart hammering out of rhythm, he sputtered out the first excuse that came to mind, "The job wasn't completed."

"Like hell."

"You missed the target." Finn's rage caused him to punctuate each syllable. "Ward got away!"

"The female agent was never part of the agreement. I have the contract in my hands. Seems as though the deal revolved around retrieving the disc. With that satisfied, the contract is complete."

"Bastard."

"Well, if it wasn't to pay up, what'd you contact me for?"

"To finish the job. Ward's death *was* part of the equation and you won't get a dime until she's six feet under."

The voice on the other end laughed. "You think you're going to sneak that in for free?"

"It was part of…"

"I just read the communications. Agent Ward is noted as a benefit, not a stipulation."

"This is ridiculous. I'm not paying you until she's dead. Listen Hombre, do you know who I am?"

"Yes, which is another reason why you should be more amiable." The threat behind the words wasn't lost on Finn.

"My father…"

"I'll tell you what I can do for you. It's not giving you a hit for free, especially an agent of the government, but I'll give you a good price. Prelim analysis has already been done."

"How magnanimous."

"Take it or leave it."

"So, you're in charge of Hector's operation? You? Do they know that you killed him?"

"It's how it works in the wild, isn't it? Strongest takes over the pride."

Finn sighed. "If I'm going to have to pay, then I might as well shop around."

"Knock yourself out. But I'd be weary of those online assassin sites."

"Sarcasm won't gain my trust. Why should I pay you more for a job that you screwed up? You missed."

"Wasn't aiming. Think it over. I'll expect final payment by Friday."

The phone clicked dead on the other end. Finn's heart was clogging his throat. He hadn't seen this coming. That money was long gone – Finn looked regretfully at his over-priced watch … a platinum Audemars Piguet. *God Damn It!* He couldn't return the timepiece and there weren't many places he could dig up that kind of cash. *You're a Parker.* He reminded himself and with a curt nod he knew he'd figure it out.

CHAPTER 7

"May I?" Ben motioned to the empty chair.

"Am I going to be scolded?"

"Yes."

"Then no, you may not," she said, sitting up straighter in her chair.

"Tough," Ben said, his red-streaked eyes droopy. "What the hell are you thinking? And don't tell me you're not – that won't fly."

Ben wasn't a regular in her office. Usually she was summoned to his – he looked too big for her cramped workspace.

He settled in with a sigh. Only his eyes moved beneath a furrowed brow that had recently become a permanent expression. "I'm not going to lecture you," he said, folding his left hand into his right to create a large fist, "but you can't lose control in the middle of a briefing."

"I know." Ben was right. "But to have to sit across from him. He tried to kill me, Ben. Literally kill." Melanie sucked in a double breath and held it. They'd been over this so many times that Ben didn't have to be there, she knew his lines as well as her own. "If you let me take him out back and shoot him this could be solved."

"Not funny. One more outbreak and I'm sending you on assignment to Siberia."

Melanie laughed. Siberia was definitely 'old school'. These days there were much worse places to be sent. She was hungry for a case of her own. Ben had kept her prisoner, attached to the computer or training new recruits on the art of retrieving fingerprints. "I'd gladly take an assignment anywhere. Including Siberia."

"I got your medical release this morning."

"Really?" She'd been waiting for the doctor's green light. "I'm ready. Anything. Just send me out. This waiting around," she motioned with her palms up in the air, "can't continue. I could kill him."

"That bit of information you should keep to yourself. How can I send you out? You're a loose cannon." He sat quietly, observing, thinking, considering.

"Only toward Finn."

"A medical release doesn't mean you're emotionally ready. If you were to agree to see a shrink," he started, but apparently he was tired of that conversation. "Let me sleep on it," Ben said, rising from the old chair. He was graceful, never seeming to have the joint pain or stiffness found in most people his age. But then again, she wasn't entirely sure *of* his age – for all she knew he was only a few years older than she was.

"I really need to get out of here." She continued to plead her case. "I haven't been stuck behind a desk for … well, ever. I'm not built to do nothing."

Ben was nearing the door when he turned to scrutinize her behind his glasses. "How are you coming on the cases I gave you?"

Melanie huffed and rolled her eyes. Her case load could be

summed up in one word: baby-sitting. "You can't actually call them cases. Twenty years ago, maybe..."

He raised his hands to stop her. "I'll let you know what I decide tomorrow."

"Thanks."

She waited until the sounds of his footsteps were a memory before continuing her drill on Parker. She'd watched the bastard's every move for the weeks since she'd been back. But Finn was laying low.

Her tabs on him had taken hours to design and install. She'd tested the limits of her electronic stalking abilities. Her pride was the alarms attached to particular words spoken or typed on his cell or computer. But 'tee time' and 'lunch' were not in her scope of objectives and the days passed quietly.

"I can wait, too." She told her empty office.

Everything about him inflamed her loathing, including his stalling. But Parker wasn't her only obsession. She ran list after list, cross-checking data of unsolved professionally linked murders, searching for Adam.

Hired hits were not uncommon. Untraceable ones were.

Bypassing torture, poisoning or overdose and drowning – she was only interested in shootings. Specifically, clean, long-range targets, possibly high-profile people with zero evidence left behind.

During the weeks he'd cared for her, she'd avoided the topic of his past, not ready to delve into the depths of his previous life. What she did know was that he'd been highly paid – his hits weren't the average adulterer – and he wasn't wanted by national or international agencies.

In Melanie's research, she stopped short of searching for him specifically. She didn't want to start a chain reaction that led to his arrest and one never knew who might be snooping.

With the halls quiet, her coffee cup empty, she finally looked up from her computer screen. The only sound was her own fingers clicking on the keyboard, which she'd long since ignored.

Time frames and demographics had narrowed her search to a few hundred. She leaned back to take a breath and digest her new facts. Her stomach churned as she read the list of names with heavy eyelids. Closing her eyes brought no relief. Snapshots of each person on the list flashed in slideshow procession. She stopped on the British professor who was killed by a single shot while washing dishes. The case hadn't been closed but left with only one piece of evidence – the killer had laid belly down on a tree limb in the neighbor's yard. Melanie studied photos from the scene – the precision and creativity of the trajectory seemed impossible.

Mentally she placed Adam on that branch, cold eye to scope, finger on the trigger and no emotion in his heart. Her breath came rapidly and her lids flashed open.

It was all in her imagination and yet it felt real. *You're overworked,* she told herself, slapping her cheeks lightly to shake off the rush that'd come with the hallucination.

Her thoughts about Adam came splintered. Why hadn't he made contact? He'd promised, but eight weeks? *Too much time has passed,* her worries mounting by the day. *He knows what he's doing,* had been her reply to her frazzled nerves.

If Adam had been anyone else … they'd both be dead. She lived because of who he was. And he was an assassin. Or had been. But benefiting from the lives he'd taken was a burden too heavy for her to carry.

Melanie shut down her computer and made herself comfortable on the couch. The light from her computer screen flickered before going dark and leaving her alone in the square office not much bigger than the average prison cell.

She tried to remember why she stayed at this job. There had never been any semblance of balance. Finn's father, Senator Hugh Parker, was on the Agency's Board of Executives and as long as he remained, Melanie would always be fighting for equality.

She kicked off her heels and allowed her mind to wander back to that pivotal day when she stood tethered to a beam, knowing her time on earth was about to expire. It was the day she'd learned the truth about Finn – and the truth about Adam.

Finn's evil core had been exposed. He'd salivated at the prospect of ending her life, and he would have succeeded had Adam been the average chef from San Diego. His bright green eyes had turned dark, flat and cold. Her body flinched thinking about those dead eyes glaring at her. In those moments she'd believed he intended to kill her. She'd made her peace with God and though she wasn't ready to die, she accepted her fate.

In some ways it had been a relief knowing how it was going to happen. She'd never held on to delusions. Espionage was dangerous and it wasn't the first time she'd dodged a tricky situation. But this time she'd not only invited peril in through the front door she'd also allowed it – and him – into her bed and heart.

Melanie felt a shiver and reached under the couch for a spare blanket. She was no longer tired, her mind had been unleashed. She didn't want to relive the stale air laced with the smell of dust and gasoline, picturing family and friends she'd never see again. Her blood had streaked down her forearms from torn wrists and the fear had been paralyzing. She'd only been able to give the slightest of nods to her executioner.

The memories of those hours had not faded and once she opened that door she couldn't stop their momentum.

The pain had been expected, she'd been shot before. And though she doubted they'd be generous enough to kill her instantly, she had held her breath in anticipation.

There was no feeling with the first shot. *A quick death?* But a moment later the second shot was fired – hitting hard, not a bullet, – more like a brick. Melanie reached for her face, expecting it to be gone, and instead found herself on the ground, coughing up dirt.

It wasn't until she was outside – being carried by Adam, the barn in a ball of flames and Finn fleeing – that she realized he was rescuing her. He'd eliminated the two accomplices – one of them his old teacher and friend.

She always breathed a sigh of relief when her recollections brought her to this point. She welcomed the relief and joy of being saved. She and Adam had parted that night – she had been taken to the agency's clinic and treated for her injuries, Adam had disappeared into the forest.

There had been no choice, really. She had to ignore the fact that Adam had been an assassin capable of … stop … She loved him. He'd saved her. He was her hero.

Guarded theories poked at tender moments she'd shared with Adam. How could she forgive his past? Ten years of her life had been devoted to eliminating bad elements from civilization. Why was he special, because he'd rescued her?

Captives fell for their captors, patients for their doctors, lonely women for notorious inmates – it was not a new phenomenon. But was it the same? Melanie knew that her parents would be grieving the loss of their daughter if not for him. She was plagued by emotions she couldn't understand ... did it matter why she loved him? There was no turning back. She'd fallen.

"Ugh! I've got to get out of here!" she told herself, grabbing her running shoes. Taking an easy pace on the treadmill she scoured through options until, reluctantly, gave into her best answer. Trish. Melanie's gorgeous, outrageous, foul-mouthed friend whose boyfriend, Jason, happened to be tight with Adam. Trish's gossipy ways usually worked against Melanie ... maybe this time would be different.

Jeez I'm desperate, she thought as she dialed.

"He's in London." Trish paused. "Didn't he tell you? Someone he knows is opening a restaurant."

"First I've heard of it," Melanie said. Sticking as close to the truth (as possible) was her policy, and it hadn't failed her yet.

"I told Jason! I should've listened to my instincts and called you. But did I? No. Why? Because he told me to mind my own business – well, screw that! Seriously, you didn't know?"

"Trish, don't you think I'd remember that conversation?"

"Did you break up with him?" she accused.

"We're working out the logistics," she said, knowing how lame she sounded. "Hey Trish, let me call you back. My boss is here." She could hear Ben talking with her assistant, Jane. Before his wife's death she'd never seen him striding his long angular strides through the corridors, in the kitchen or gym. Now he was everywhere.

"Good morning," Ben said, leaning his head into her office. "I've come up with a small assignment for you. Don't go and get too excited. I'm talking about a little investigative work."

"Investigative?" She grimaced – slang for sifting through documents and mountains of crap.

"It gets you out of the Manor," he said, and she sighed. "There's a factory in Wisconsin…" Melanie stopped listening – her attention turned to the vibrating phone still in her hands. Deftly flicking through her password she opened the file. Ben continued speaking, "… make sense of a few leads…"

Finn had just confirmed last minute hotel and flight reservations to the Big Apple. Tipping back in her chair she could see him at his car in the parking lot.

"A factory in Wisconsin sounds fine," she answered, coming back to his conversation.

"Really? It's just field work," he clarified at her sudden acceptance. "I didn't mean to make it sound glamorous."

"Oh, you didn't. But if you've got background have Judith send it over. I'm leaving tomorrow."

"Why do I have the feeling I've just been duped?"

"What you have is perfect timing," she corrected. "I've got to pack, so …"

"Ward, whatever you're concocting …" He shook his head and paused. "Just be smart."

CHAPTER 8

"Good morning, Agent Parker," Adam said from a poolside lounge chair.

"Did you receive the transfer?"

"Ten minutes ago. I called to thank you for your business and…" Adam had to tread delicately here. "…inquire as to the status of your next venture."

"This is a secure line," Parker snorted. "To answer your question, I'm still interested in ridding my life of Agent Ward."

The line was silent, each thinking about what that would do to their lives.

"Look," Parker said, ready to move on with his plan. "You screwed me over last time and you're not the only game in town."

Playing his part, Adam let out a deep, rumbling laugh. "Agent, do you think it wise to be so vocal about hiring a hit man? It's not like you're shopping for a car."

"You obviously have no idea the depths of my contacts. I'm

practically invincible."

"Care to test that out?"

"The way I figure it," Parker went on as if Adam had said nothing, "you owe me."

"I'm not sure if you've got a giant set or if you're ignorant. But I like you, Parker. Can't say why. Maybe it's just your lucky day."

"So you'll do it? Great." He said without stopping to ask what kind of luck he'd generated. "On paper it looks more difficult. I know her and can get her out in the open anytime, anywhere. I'm doing a test run this week in New York. You could do it then!"

"Hold on, Little Man. I haven't agreed to a thing. Besides I'm not offering a freebie. And I am not a thug off the street. When I get done it'll never get back to you. No embarrassment, no questioning, no accusation. Clean."

Parker sighed. "Send over the contract."

CHAPTER 9

"Am I interrupting something?" Melanie asked as she entered Mike's communication headquarters.

"No," Tom and Mike said in lying, guilty unison.

"Okay," she said, now certain they were up to something but not curious enough to push the issue. She looked to Mike. "I need a favor."

"You look all lit up," Mike said, rolling his chair back to his computer station.

"Yeah," she grinned, feeling the electricity. "I'm going to need a new phone." She squatted down beside him for a private conversation. "One without the locator."

Mike's bushy brows pulled in and he shot her a glance of weary caution. "Why do you always do this to me? No. No, don't try that … and don't say anything. We both know I'm going to end up giving you the damn phone, then sweat over it for days until you bring it back. The Agency isn't big on rogue agents and what if you get into trouble?"

"I'm safer with another phone. In the meantime will you go over my old one and reset the diagnostics? Make sure the thing hasn't been compromised."

Mike was already digging through his ring for the right key. "I don't know how you get me to do these things for you. You're not my wife and yet I do whatever you say. Kind of makes me mad."

"You'll forgive me." She smiled, patting his cheek.

"We're only friends because I know beneath that thick layer of rudeness there's a sweetheart wanting to come out."

"If that's what you want to believe." Melanie laughed, stood and looked at Mike, his bald spot widening along with his waistline. "We're friends because you're cool and I trust you. Not to mention you're a bad-ass wizard on the computer."

"I'm funny, too," he added, flushing as he tapped on the keyboard. "And handsome, you forgot handsome. It's my eyes."

"Okay, you're funny, too."

"Ouch, and here I thought we were bonding."

"Just get me the phone."

"Jeez, give me a sec. Even the – what did you call me? – Master of All Technology needs a second."

Three minutes later he handed her a new satellite phone.

"Remember to keep it turned off when not in use. Keeps you off the grid," he said, tilting his head side-to-side, "sort of. So," Mike's smile looked more wily than cheerful. "If you're going on official business maybe you'd be interested in some new tricks."

"Why am I suddenly afraid of you?"

"There's this girl in R&D – she's real cute and she's brilliant, but can't get anyone to test out these new goggles…"

"Pack me a pair and whatever else she's got. But if I explode or lose my vision, I'm holding you responsible."

"Thanks. I really like her and seriously, she's going to freak. You're like her idol."

"Great. I'm happy to help out your love life. Just have the equipment sent up to Jane in like ten minutes."

"I will. Thanks. Be safe. I'd hate to have to explain your disappearance to Jackson."

"Will do, Master." She said, feeling free.

With Finn out of town, Melanie monitored the foot traffic of the Manor and just after midnight she broke into his office. It was three times the size of hers. Knowing she turned down this particular space didn't ease the grudge. His furniture, artwork, stuffed pheasants were purchased to impress. Melanie's hands itched to uncover the hidden treasures within Finn's sanctuary.

20 minutes later she placed the area rug back in its spot. "There's nothing here," she concluded, after rummaging through the entire office and bathroom.

Dropping into one of the lush seats, she chewed on the disappointment while reading the titles of books behind his desk. It didn't make sense. There were no personal signs of Finn anywhere in his office. *Even I have a couple of photos,* she thought concentrating on the absence of personality in his workspace.

Her apartment in the Manor was no frills – a bath, a bed and a dresser. She sat in the dark and considered the implications that possibly Finn had a real hiding spot. In her attempts to gain access to his home there had been one room she couldn't penetrate. At first it appeared to be natural interference, but when thermal, satellite and audio surveillances failed … a thought crept in … *Had he installed a protective barrier?* She wrangled with the notion. It seemed ambitious for Finn, but it would explain matters.

Melanie had avoided interaction with Finn as much as possible, he was evil for sure … but clever? She'd have to mull that one over, it seemed impossible but maybe Finn wasn't the complete dolt she thought he was.

The next morning she confirmed her ruse flight to Madison and headed for the train station. New York was thrilling as she traveled with a current of mid-day pedestrians to a moderate hotel across the street from the one where Finn had spared no expense.

The Agency had his location on GPS and Melanie piggybacked on its technology to monitor his movements. It wasn't long before he met up with a woman dressed in a black pantsuit, outside the building. Finn's demeanor, rigid back and serious expression suggested the meeting was all business.

Trailing in their wake, she watched as the pair entered a building of newly renovated condos. Listing after listing, Melanie tagged along behind, losing interest with each stop. He was apartment hunting.

Waiting for him outside a building, Melanie cursed herself right along with Finn. *I'm dead if I lose my instincts. I thought for sure he was up to something.*

"Melanie?"

Startled, she jumped and whipped around to verify Finn was still inside the building and out of earshot. Then turned back, ready to kick the crap out of someone – someone with a slightly crooked smile and eyes the color of smooth milk chocolate.

"Holy shit! It *is* you." He stood, jaw dropped, a mere six feet away.

"Danny?" she said soundlessly after just having the breath knocked out of her.

People flowed through the gap between them but their eyes were locked. In seconds, ten years vanished and she was a college girl in love with Danny Ashe.

"Melanie Ward."

Her body rattled each time he said her name, sending a warm, anxious thrill through her veins. She took a tentative step forward, hoping he wasn't an apparition of her over-worked brain.

"Wow, I'm speechless. Look at you." His grin widened as he shook his golden hair, which was darker than before. The way he looked at her ... came directly from her college-girl dreams.

"I can't believe ... I'm surprised..." She didn't finish her thoughts out loud. *To run into you – after I'd stopped looking.*

"I know," he said, his enthusiastic nods helping her feel less foolish. "Look Mel, I've got to fly, but have dinner with me."

"Yeah, I'd love to," she answered, sounding completely cool.

"Great, I'll pick you up at six ... Are you living here?"

"Hotel," she said, giving him the name and address.

He smiled at her again, his eyes caressing her face. "I've been thinking about you a lot lately. Tonight then. Six." He leaned forward, placing a quick peck that burned into her cheek. "God, I can't stop staring. I must look like a complete idiot."

"Not even close," she assured him, thinking exactly the opposite was true. A few extra creases around his eyes and a couple of laugh lines at the corner of his mouth had added maturity to his sexy, boyish charm.

It wasn't right that her heart betrayed her, but to its defense the reaction was automatic. His smile had always revved up her heartbeat, which was recovering from its flurry of rapid palpitations to a clumsy pounding.

"Maybe by dinner I'll have recovered my senses," she coughed.

His burst of laughter caused her to flush a color she hadn't reached since college. "I feel the same way," he said, turning to leave.

"Um, Danny," she called, catching him before he was too far away. "I have a boyfriend." Her voice carried, echoing off pillars and walls.

Immediately she was embarrassed, even before Danny's laugh roared back to her. He waved and was gone. *That was stupid*, she thought pressing the tips of her fingers into her forehead. Melanie stood on the sidewalk, having completely forgotten where she was.

Taxi horns blasting jolted her back.

Crap. Still holding her hot dog she dumped it in the trash and slipped into a bookstore to wait for Finn. The wait was short, two minutes before her phone buzzed alerting her that Finn was dialing out. She attached to his link and from the shop window she could see that the vein from his eyebrow to his hairline was throbbing and he was cursing into his cell. Melanie grinned, sorry for the unlucky schmuck on the other end.

"... Yes! She should be here ... hiding somewhere," he turned casting his gaze like a net around his surroundings. "I know she followed me."

"You're wasting my time."

Melanie's throat clamped. That deep, husky voice belonged to Adam.

"It's not right. Fucking Wisconsin?" Finn retreated and retraced his heavy steps.

"You might not be as important to her as you believed. Why did you think she'd follow you?"

Finn growled. "I found a bug in my office. I figured it was her who planted it. She's always sticking her nose where it doesn't belong."

"Guess you figured wrong."

Goosebumps rushed to attention from the top of her head to her toes.

Finn snarled. "I can't take another day. Damn it!" He raised his fingers to his lips and blew out a sharp whistle. "And I've been reconsidering our agreement. She knows what you are and now, you'll never get close enough to get the job done."

"No fear. I have a way with women. They all think they can change me." She heard the amusement in his tone.

"Yeah, well, what if she got to you and now you have a thing for her. How do I know you didn't let her go on purpose?"

"You don't. My life is none of your damned business." Adam's calculated voice was authoritative. "You pay me half up front and the rest when I get the job done. Simple."

Finn blew a frustrated sigh into the receiver. "Okay, but this had better get done. What do I need to do?"

"Not a thing. You've purchased the all-inclusive package. I'll be in touch." Adam said, ending the call.

Finn had set a trap, hired Adam … she felt sick … to kill her.

Though almost too horrified to learn any more, she reluctantly connected to Finn's next call as he hopped into a cab. He was canceling dinner with the mayor and booking a flight home.

The last few minutes had jarred her out of the notion that Finn was a transparent playboy. He was more dangerous than she'd ever guessed.

It's Finn, she thought to counter the prickles of fear that were threatening to take hold of her. And then there was Adam. Most of her – didn't believe a single word he said to Finn. He was protecting her. It was the superior tone in his callous voice that was haunting her.

She'd walked three blocks out of her way before realizing her error and turned back.

"Something on your mind?" Danny said, falling into step with her outside the revolving doors of her hotel. "I hope it's me."

She looked up with a start. *How could she have forgotten?* "Sort of. Am I late?" She glanced at him making certain he wasn't just her imagination and not liking the fact that he spotted her first. She was slipping.

"Actually, I'm very early," he confessed. "I was useless at home so I thought I'd catch up with you. This is an interesting choice for a place to stay," he said, nodding toward the worn lobby with a faint smell of chicken and burnt popcorn that she hadn't noticed earlier.

She couldn't go to dinner with Danny. Somehow she was going to have to cancel ... but, how?

"Which floor?" His face scrunched with distaste.

"Four."

He tapped the circular button twice before punching it to light up. "If you're having money problems, Mel, I can put you up in a better place."

"It was the location that attracted me, not the price. But thanks." Her smile was nervously pinched. She was having difficulty keeping her emotions in check. "Danny, I don't think I can have dinner tonight."

"Fasting?" he grinned, stepping inside the elevator.

"No." She smiled.

He looked at her with a skeptical gaze when the cage jostled. "Maybe we should have taken the stairs." Danny's brows were tightly knit, scrutinizing every piece of ripped wallpaper and every carpet stain.

"It's got atmosphere." She defended, staring up at him. "Danny…"

"Yeah?"

In that one look she knew there was no way she'd break this date. "I've thought about you a lot over the years."

"Me, too, you."

She changed as quickly as possible into a pair of jeans and it wasn't until they'd found a quiet corner booth in a neighborhood bar that she finally was able to breathe. They ordered a pitcher of beer and made small talk for a few minutes.

"So, why aren't you married?" Danny sipped his drink.

"Who says I'm not?"

Lifting his left hand, he pointed to the indention on his ring finger. "No ring. I expected you to have been hitched a long time ago."

"I guess I've been too busy with work."

"Did you know I was married?"

Melanie nodded. "Saw it on your rugby teams website. Right after you'd gotten engaged." She broke a pretzel in half and brushed off the salt. "Where's your ring?"

"We divorced last month." Danny swallowed the last half of his beer. "She left me," he said, waving at the barmaid for another round. "Apparently, she hasn't been in love with me for a long time and found what she was looking for in Paolo Russo."

"The race car driver?" *With the quintessential Italian reputation?*

Danny threw up his hands. "What is it about that guy? Why does everyone know who is?"

"I watch a lot of news."

"Did you see he was getting married in a week?"

"No." She bit her lower lip before asking, "He's marrying your ex?"

Danny nodded.

Melanie could feel the wall of sorrow build up around him. "I think he ranked pretty low his last couple of races," Melanie offered, hoping to cheer him up.

"Shame. Probably exhausted from nailing with my wife." He looked up guiltily. "Sorry."

The husky woman, all in black, running the bar – not Elvira black with cleavage and lipstick, but Johnny Cash black, with a snap front shirt and jeans – came to their table.

"Here, honey, I thought you could use a couple of shots," she said, her gravely voice adding 20 years to her appearance.

"You must be a mind reader," Danny said gratefully.

She winked. "Call me if you need anything else?"

"I want to hear about you and that boyfriend you shouted about." A slow grin appeared on his face.

"I didn't shout. I," she laughed, "I got nervous. Shut up."

"Tell me about him," he slid one of the shot glasses in front of her. "What does he do, where'd you meet?"

Melanie leaned back into the shadows to hide her blush. "He's a chef and we met over the summer. His name is Adam. I ... what?"

"Just wondering if you're happy?"

"Yeah, I think so."

"But you don't know?"

"My life is complicated."

Danny grimaced. "Still?"

"Yeah, still, and this has been a really strange day. Running into you and then ... work has been ... killer." She blew out a pent-up breath, nothing she could say about work. "So ... here with you and this little shot of tequila is exactly what I needed."

"Since the divorce I've had time to think and you've come up," he said, as they reached for the lime wedges. "Bottoms up," Danny said, handing her the salt shaker.

"Oh, yeah?" she asked, licking the salt and swallowing. Her eyes watered. It'd been months since she'd worked on her tolerance level.

"I was hoping you hadn't changed." He was staring at her and the volume of his voice dropped.

Her heart caught and the occasional background noises, clattering glasses and low talking faded. Melanie saw only Danny.

"Have I changed?"

"Nope. It's weird how I feel ... like no time has passed. Like I'm still crazy in love with you."

"Danny," she warned. He was on dangerous ground.

"I know. Of course, but inside," he placed a flat palm against his chest, "I feel the same."

She couldn't go there.

"You're lonely, missing your wife and you've created this memory of us." How many times had she been told that her recollection of Danny was 99 percent fantasy?

"Maybe," he sighed. "I thought that after the divorce – you know the final signature – that she'd be out of my system. I love her and I hate her. Is that even possible? But it's Avery I worry about."

"Avery?"

"Our daughter." Melanie was slow to process while Danny kept on talking. "She's six. And just like her mother, good and bad. Before we had her, Lauren and I talked. I didn't want to put a kid through what I went through. And now..." He shook his head.

"Wow, you have a kid. You're a dad." She squinted to see him differently. Responsible. In all her dreams she'd never pictured Danny as a father. Never occurred to her, and now she was trying to reformulate her image of him.

"That's where I was going today. To sign papers allowing Lauren to take Avery out of the country for the wedding."

"Let me see the pictures," Melanie smiled, holding out her hand, wiggling her fingers.

Danny grinned boyishly, and reached inside his breast pocket and pulled out his cell. Avery's bright blond hair was cut in a short bob and blue eyes held no resemblance to her father but her smile was pure Danny. She flipped her through a dozen frames.

"She's beautiful."

"Thanks," he gazed ruefully at the picture. "What a mess, but enough about me. How are your parents?"

They laughed. She felt the swoosh of time, as they reminisced right through the dinner reservation Danny had made at an uptown restaurant. Instead, they ordered burgers and fries with the beer.

"I just got a place in the city, not too far from here," the implication clear in his glossy gaze.

"I'm still in DC, same place even," she said, dodging the invite.

"No!" He shook his head. "No wonder you don't mind that crappy hotel."

"You judge too quickly." The alcohol was smoothing out her nervous jitters. "And just so you know … that hotel has one of the best views in the city."

"What? A view of the hotel across the street?" Danny shook his head, sighing out a laugh. As their eyes locked the atmosphere thickened. "Does the boyfriend know how lucky he is?"

"Danny," she sighed.

"Sizing up the competition."

He looked at her from across the table, the cockiness draining from his expression. Three months ago she'd have killed for this opportunity.

"I used to keep an eye out for you every time I stepped into the city," she admitted, unable to resist his pull.

"You stopped?"

"You were married." The hint of sadness slipped into her tone. "It took me a long time to get over you." She didn't care to disclose how long.

"Now you have?" He ran his fingers through his hair.

"Mostly." She whispered, the truth slipping. "But there isn't a contest. I'm with Adam."

"Okay, but you were the one who mentioned fate earlier. Maybe it's fate that brought us together again. I bet Rita doesn't like him as much as she liked me."

"At my age my mom would love any eligible prospect. Last summer she was willing to hook me up with a woman."

"Your mom is a card." He laughed. "Look at us."

"I know. We're all grown up. How did so much time pass?"

"I have no idea. But I'm young with you. How's Trish?"

"Settling down, if you can believe that."

"I met up with a couple of my rugby teammates from college last year ... they've aged, bald or balding. I almost bought a box of Rogaine on my way home."

"I'm afraid to think what you'd do with your hands if you lost your hair," she mused.

He lifted his brows. "Really? You've got a dirty mind, Mel."

"You're not losing your hair, Danny." She laughed freely. "Truth is, you've gotten better with age."

"Not too beaten up?"

"Tell me you're not worried about wrinkles."

"I'm back on the market and since you aren't – there are women I've got to impress."

He laughed as she mildly punched his shoulder. "Jerk."

"Sucker."

"I think you've had enough alcohol." She said.

It was after midnight when they switched to coffee.

"Is he the jealous type?" Danny asked, taking her hand as they walked back to her hotel.

"Doubt it," she thought about Adam and wondered how much he'd mind Danny hanging around while he was away. She withdrew her hand from his.

"Change your mind?" The move was smooth, his arm draped over her shoulders as he whispered in her ear. The tingle of his breath caused a small quake and Melanie bent her head to cover her exposed neck.

Six hours of reminiscing had erased the years apart, almost. Her heart started knocking roughly, again, as the elevator jostled them up to her floor. He lingered, his fingers caressing hers.

"Are you going to invite me in?"

"No." She cringed because it was impossible that this idea wasn't impossible.

"You know you want to." His breath was soft on her neck.

"No, if I wanted to I would." It was almost true. "Good night," she whispered, chewing on her bottom lip, her blood rushing in her eardrums.

"Goodnight, Mel."

His cologne was strong, standing so close that his foot was between her heels. His warm breath, blowing against her cheek, was intoxicating. Her body felt heavy, drowsy as she lifted her face to look him in the eye.

Sliding his jaw against her skin, she knew she should stop him but … couldn't. He kissed the corner of her mouth. She didn't protest and he inched his lips until they were pressed fully against hers.

"I can't do this," she shook the haze from her brain, leaving the memory of his lips.

"I'm sorry. I know you're with someone else … I got carried away. I'm sorry," he said, stepping back further from her and running this fingers through his hair.

"Goodnight, Danny." She smiled. "I had a great time."

"Me too. I hope you'll go out with me again." He looked truly remorseful. "I mean it, next time you'll have to beg *me* for a kiss."

The green light on the key card lock gave the all clear. What she wanted was to retreat into the darkness, lay across the bed and drown in her guilt.

"Goodnight, Melanie Ward. Make sure you lock your door."

"I will." Melanie exhaled a heavy, weighted gust of pent-up air.

What the hell was that? She shivered in response. *That was trouble.*

CHAPTER 10

Inside her room, Melanie took a moment at the door with the pretense of latching the metal bar. In actuality she needed the time to regroup, settle her hormones and cool the fire.

Before she turned to face the blackened room she knew she wasn't alone. There was a stir in the air. She felt it. Her gun from her purse was already in hand, she listened while scanning for an inconsistent pattern in the darkness. Her pupils dilated, letting in the scarce light. She fixed upon a shadow, deeper than the rest of the room, in the farthest corner.

"Was it a nice kiss?"

The tension released from her body. "Adam."

She nearly leaped over the bed to reach the shady figure. He didn't move and she recognized his tense pose – squared shoulders, arms crossed – too late. Her arms were already flung around him.

"Adam," she whispered, closing her eyes and pressing in close, feeling suddenly safe. She tried to capture the usual scent of rosemary or citrus but he smelled metallic. "Hold me," she ordered, moving away only enough to assist in uncrossing his arms and wiggling back in close.

His hands went to her back and for a moment she thought he wasn't going to forgive the kiss. Then his grip hardened with his fingers digging into her and his face dropping into her hair.

"Melanie," he breathed and chills ran through her.

"I can't believe you're here," she said when he let up enough to allow her to breath.

"Disappointed?"

"Stop!" She pulled out of his embrace. She couldn't see his face, it was difficult to scold a shadow. "I've been desperate for you. God, that sounds stupid but it's been weeks, Adam. Months." She pressed her forehead into his chest.

"And I find you with not just another man but with *him*."

He was jealous.

"I thought your fantasy guy would've been taller."

"You are taller," she said, tilting her face until her cheek pressed against his heart. Steady, rhythmic.

"His cologne is all over you," Adam grumbled.

"We can fix that," she took his clenched fist and led him to the bathroom.

With the lights off, she ran her hands over his chest, unbuttoning his shirt then tugging the tails out of his pants and pulling it off his broad shoulders.

"How many shirts did you have to wear?" she asked, when she got to the T-shirt.

His fingers went around her throat, forcing her to look up into the darkness. She gasped at the aggressiveness of his kiss.

"You grew a beard!" The course hair pricked her skin. She had to see, and leaned to flick on the lights. "Adam," her body sighed with joy and relief. "Hi," was all she managed to say.

"Hi," he said, leaning back against the sink basin.

She saw him, everything all at once. His dark hair shaggy and uncombed, beard covering his jaw, black T-shirt and cargo pants with combat boots.

"I should be mad at you," she said, wanting to be angry.

"I should be mad at *you*," he retorted. "You're the one on a date with your ex."

Melanie smiled, tip-toed up to him took his prickly face in her hands. "I love you. Thank you for being jealous. It's sweet but we both know you're the only one for me."

She wasn't startled by the kiss. And she was no longer in charge. Adam undressed her with one hand while the other turned on the water for their shower.

❦

He lay on his back, she on her side, resting her head on his shoulder – her arm draped across the taut muscles of his chest and her legs entangled in his. Adam's body had changed in two months. It was more than his six pack had increased to eight, it was his entire body … skin pulled smoothly over rigid, hard muscles.

"Are you going to tell my why you showed up tonight?" she asked, hoping he'd come clean about his involvement with Finn. "How'd you know I was here?"

"I watch you … sometimes."

"I don't think you followed me." *Not possible, I haven't lost that much skill.*

"Finn called, told me you'd be in New York." The lump caught in her throat, as it had this afternoon when she'd heard both voices on the line. "I'll explain when it's safe."

"At some point over these two months … you could've called."

"Not worth the risk." He kissed the top of her head.

"I've missed you."

"You were fine."

"You assumed."

"You're strong," was his answer as he lifted her arm and slid out from beneath her to the edge of the bed. Melanie watched him search for his clothes.

"You're leaving?"

"Have to. It's nearly dawn." He pulled his T-shirt over his head.

"But…" she wanted to protest, to remind him … "You just promised to explain!"

"When it's safe. It isn't, Mel." He shook his head, tossing his hair, which was curlier than she'd ever seen. "Right now it's not safe for us to be together. I shouldn't have come here … to you."

Melanie sat up and reached for her phone. The ability to scramble airwaves was standard, even her new phone had the capabilities. "You shouldn't be here because you're working with Parker?"

He finished putting on his shoes and twisted to look at her. "What do you know about that?"

"We need to talk."

"Not here. Not now."

"If we work together…"

"Our connection will just get in the way. I promised I'd take care of it."

"He hired a hit man," she said, as if he didn't know, "to kill me."

"And if I hadn't gone back he'd have hired someone other than me. Going back was the right decision."

"But…"

"No buts." He interrupted not letting her put her thoughts into words. "Tonight should never have happened. Makes it harder to leave." He zipped up his jacket – if this was 'harder,' she couldn't tell.

"Adam, you cannot just leave." Melanie's throat tightened and she felt dizzy as he moved swiftly through the room. Physically she was no match but she put her body between him and the door. "Please," she begged, forgetting for the moment who or what she was. "You promised."

"Melanie," her name sounded pitiful. His hands were cool as he took her shoulders and easily moved her out of his way. He paused for a fraction of a second and then, without looking back, he was gone.

CHAPTER 11

"What the hell did I just do?" Adam's question echoed off the empty stairwell. He dragged his fingers through his untrimmed hair. At the first landing he stopped, fighting the urge not to rush back to her room. He changed his mind three times before hurdling over the railing to the flight below.

His heart ached. Pain as real as if he'd been knifed. He'd felt this before, but it'd been a very long time. He'd forgotten how much a heart could hurt.

The beard was itching as he pulled up the collar of his jacket to cover any identifying facial features.

Damn it! He punched the fire escape doors, slamming them against the outside brick. *Luckily old hotels are lax on security,* he thought, *probably one of the reasons she chose this place. Maybe I should stay.*

"She's a liability," replied his darker half.

The alley was vacant as he hunkered down into his coat, hands in his pockets and mind elsewhere.

Change of plans, he thought, rounding the corner. *You're not as in control as you believed.*

CHAPTER 12

Groggy from lack of sleep, Melanie waited with a crowd of business folk for an early train to D.C., catching up on a day's worth of messages. Of her college friends she had been closest to Carla but over the past few months she'd been turning to Trish. Each had left "what's up?" messages and her mom had called twice to say hello.

Melanie called Carla first, knowing she was too wrapped up in her own drama to ask questions.

"Mel," Carla exhaled. "I'm so glad you called back."

"What's wrong?" she swallowed a lump of panic.

"Everything. Everything. It's Ted, he's going to lose his seat. Oh, Melanie, I don't know what to do."

"Slow down and explain."

Carla's husband, Ted, was running for his second term as a U.S. Congressman and was being creamed by a used car dealer, Salvador Luhan. In the midst of Carla's trauma Melanie saw her chance – an opportunity to leave all her troubles behind, jump on a plane and escape under the guise of helping Carla and Ted.

Her feet were in D.C. for less than an hour, not even bothering to stop by the office. She set her sights on Luhan, a 44-year-old self-made multi-millionaire. With a first-class seat and her computer on her lap, she began researching. Luhan had started out poorer than dirt. He was born to migrant workers at a wide spot in the dusty road of Gadsden, Arizona, which, according to the Census 2000 was home to 953 people. In this border town just outside of Yuma, the Luhan family made a living through the local agricultural economy, mostly picking lettuce but occasionally moving to citrus or grain.

At nineteen, Sal lost his father, Manuel, in a tractor accident. The official report cited Manuel for carelessness, holding him culpable and freeing the farm of any blame. His arms had been severed while baling hay and he'd bled to death under the searing Arizona sun. In his decades on the job it was his only infraction.

With his two older brothers, Sal had left the farm days after the funeral in a worn-out, formerly gold metallic Chevy conversion van they purchased for $250. The boys made it to San Diego, where Salvador hustled their first job loading and delivering boxes – using that van. And, thus, establishing The Luhan Brothers Moving Co., for months the multi-purpose vehicle served as both money-maker and living quarters.

Four years later Sal sold his third of the business, borrowed five grand and purchased his first used-car lot in downtown San Diego. A decade after that Luhan Motors had grown to ten lots and was expanding into Los Angeles County.

He was living the American Dream, a successful businessman with two ex-wives and a ranchito in the hills of Escondido. A recent photo of Sal showed him standing at a podium, looking very far from his roots, in a white dress shirt with a red striped tie, pumping his fist in the air. He represented the masses. He was hope.

Melanie came away from the research thinking Ted Bradley was in big trouble. *This used car salesman,* she thought, *had better be hiding a hideously dark secret.* He was a media darling, while Ted had squandered precious airtime defusing the backlash from a $1,000-a-plate fund-raising banquet.

She leaned back her head, pinched the bridge of her nose and closed her eyes. In that fraction of a fraction of a second, her defenses dropped and her troubles rushed in. Adam, Danny ... *Don't think about them,* she scolded when Finn's face appeared in line after Danny's. She couldn't help but add him as the unwanted, third man in her life. Melanie sighed, rubbing her face. *Going nuts in a meeting? You're borderline insane, Mel.*

She opened her eyes and sighed, flipping forward to the next file. *Good thing you've found a diversion.* She was fascinated by Sal and curious about his dirty little secrets. But to do political damage they'd have to be big. No penny ante crimes – drugs, prostitution or embezzlement – people were bored with those. So many questionable choices made by elected officials recently, the American population seemed to be impervious to scandal. Simple adultery wasn't shame enough for a resignation. Sal would have to be smuggling Mexican nationals in his trunk and then selling the underage girls to star in kiddy porn to ruin his chances for Ted's seat.

Seemed highly unlikely but ... well, *I hope not.* She stopped herself: She was becoming a Luhan supporter.

Tapping into the Agency's intel, she pulled up Sal's financials: tax returns, investment and rental properties, bank statements for both business and personal accounts. In her world nothing was sacred.

If Sal was dirty she was going to find out. And if by some miracle he wasn't …

Sal was doing all right, expanding his array of dealerships into the high-end luxury market. He had a ten-acre ranch named Lechuga Linda with stables and corrals, a 5,000 square-foot house and a six-car garage.

From the San Diego airport she drove her rental car through the choked evening rush hour, finally giving up and exiting the bumper-to-bumper aggravation. Sleepless nights were catching up with her and she found herself having to concentrate to drive. The hotel off the freeway was convenient. The balcony to her room faced north, and leaning against the railing she could just make out the exit ramp to her parent's house. Abandoning her thoughts of a shower, she stripped to her underwear and collapsed on the bed.

It was dark when she awoke. Somewhere a television was blaring. Melanie stretched out on the bed. Her stomach groaned. It was late, room service had ended and the mini bar held only bottled water.

She dressed in dark clothing, pulling the ponytail through her baseball cap and grabbed her bag. The eerily silent hallway to the elevator reminded her of The Shining and she was happy to be rewarded with a single ding, like it had been waiting for her.

She was hungry but the best she could say about her burrito was that it was hot and the drive-thru was fast. Driving while eating hadn't yet been banned and she was taking full opportunity. Melanie parked her rental beside a bristly shrub at the bottom of Luhan's hill. The land was raw California desert: large, craggy rocks and sandy ground with parched undergrowth just waiting for the summer fire season.

If she'd intended to break into his house, it hadn't been conscious decision. It was part of the job – digging for the truth. So what if it was illegal? Most things she did for her job were.

The smart ones could hide their bad behaviors well. Sal was smart. The need to label him as bad or good was strong, not just for the Bradleys, but for her.

In her car she pulled a black fleece sweater over her T-shirt and settled the strap of her messenger bag across her chest. The quarter moon was at her back as she picked her way through the desert shrubbery. Shoulder-high creosote bushes pulled at her sweater as she worked around prickly pear cacti and loose rocks.

Near the peak of the hill was a two-foot block wall topped with five-foot wrought iron stakes, and beyond that was a manicured landscape. She hunkered down, her back against the base of a mesquite. The long two-story ranch style home had porches on both levels with a heavily tiled roof.

Melanie lifted the night-vision goggles Mike's girlfriend had designed. They were weighty, but after a few minutes of playing around with the buttons she was impressed. Melanie adjusted the sights to track the level of energy that ran like a blue stream through the house to the electrical box that was set on the side closest to her.

Making her move, she scaled the iron fence that kept small wildlife from intruding while still allowing for a view of the desert landscape. Reconfiguring the alarm system by bypassing the automatic call to the police she cut off the electricity altogether. Stepping back she checked the flow of electricity – the house was dark.

At the back door she reached into her bag and removed her next set of tools. The French doors were more décor than security; the lock was simple. Entering the house she reset her goggles to night vision and activated the digital camcorder.

Melanie made rounds through the bedrooms, Sal and Becky in one and a little girl in another. All deep in sleep, she moved to Sal's office.

Standing inside the doorway, she saw that the space was clear of clutter and free of a computer. Behind Sal's desk was an expansive bookshelf. The books were non-fiction of the "How to get ahead" variety. Pictures on each shelf were of Sal, shaking hands with influentials – actors, civil rights pioneers and politicians, the previous president included. There were the ego shots – Sal on a horse, on a boat, with skis, with cars, at storefronts. He was everywhere. Then the awards: Little League plaques, Man of the Year, thank you for your support, top dealership, most sold, Number One dealership eight years in a row, dedicated citizen. Melanie would have shaken her head at the sheer narcissism of the room but it would have affected the video.

His desk was less self-congratulatory: a picture of Sal and Becky, the young girl and a teenage boy who wasn't in the house.

She checked the drawers, the electrical outlets, but no laptop, no cords – nothing except file folders. Her stomach knotted. Luhan wasn't old enough to have banished technology.

Shit.

Off the grid, as Mike would say. Briefly, she flicked through the colored hanging files with disdain. She looked around the room. No one in a powerful position was this squeaky clean. *Think, Mel, think.*

Inside her goggles the timer was ticking off the seconds of wasted time. On impulse she adjusted the sights and ... hallelujah chorus ... the room lit up. The walls were alive with current streaming to an oil painting: a ranch scene with rolling hills, cattle and a cowboy on a horse.

The rest of the room was dead, but this painting was being supplied energy by a separate generator and it was heavily electrified. Melanie popped the painting free of its latch and uncovered a safe behind. Removing the combination panel she studied the mechanism and removed tools from her bag. In less than thirty seconds the steel door swung open.

Locked away in Luhan's fireproof vault was an account register, Melanie flipped through the pages, making sure the camera got a good shot. There were deeds and cash but stashed in the back corner was a mailing envelope. The seal was broken and inside was a pre-paid cell phone. She popped open the back and removed the chip, then stuck the phone back inside the envelope. She scanned the return address, a resort in the Bahamas dated this past March.

Checking the room, she made sure she'd missed nothing of importance, then pressed her ear to the door and checked for a heat source. All clear.

From atop Luhan hill, Melanie paused. Then sun's rays were already peeking over the distant low mountain range. Her adrenaline rush was fading as she jogged back to the car. She drove to her parents' house in La Jolla thinking about the mysterious cell phone and the hidden register.

Quietly she climbed the stairs to her old room.

"Annie?"

She was caught.

"Hey, Dad. I didn't mean to wake you," she said, hugging him.

"What a wonderful surprise. Your mother is going to be thrilled."

"I had a couple of days … Carla's been having troubles with the campaign."

Roger nodded. "Figured we'd see you around sooner or later. How's Ted?"

Melanie shook her head.

"Well, Ted's a good guy."

"Honey!" Rita embraced her. "I'll make us some coffee."

"How about we go out for a cup? Just let me get changed."

When she returned downstairs Rita had already brewed a pot of sludge.

"Did you see this?" Rita asked, lifting the San Diego Union-Tribune's front page. From the cupboard she pulled down a tankard of a cup, filled it with coffee and handed it over to Melanie.

Melanie shrank from the dark liquid and took the paper.

Sal was ahead by double digits. Dueling photos showed Sal speaking in front of a crowd of thousands, Ted speaking in a garden with a dozen tables of women in wide-brimmed hats.

Sal was by the people, for the people and (ethnically) of the majority in Ted's district.

Unless there was something outrageously damning on that cell chip … Ted was going to be unemployed soon. She chewed her lip, thinking about how she'd approach Mike about obtaining the information. She swallowed the coffee without thinking. The choking and spraying the counter came immediately.

"Melanie!"

"I'm sorry," she gasped, rushing for paper towels to clean up the mess and wipe down her face.

"Have you lost your mind?"

"Momentary lapse," Melanie agreed. *Why else would I have drunk that?*

"The news about Ted is depressing. And I don't like that Luhan character," her mother said, sponge in hand.

"You seem to be the only one."

"I know, it's like he's cast a spell over the community. Before this summer he was hawking cars ... doesn't anyone remember those terrible commercials? Outfitted with feathery boas, dancing with stripper girls, yelling at the camera? I hated those. Now he's in the same league as Ted?" Rita tossed her head side to side in utter disgust.

"That all changed ... when?"

"When he became a big hero. Don't you remember?" Her mother looked flabbergasted. "It was all Sal all the time on the news stations after he tackled that terrorist with the bombs. It's like the media adopted him and he started wearing suits, dyed his hair and stopped those awful, sexist commercials."

"You're sure about the timing?"

Rita gave Melanie an odd look. "Pretty sure. Why?"

"Just curious."

CHAPTER 13

Adam sat in the back of the limo, cold as stone with Hugh and Finn Parker opposite him. His beard, a trucker cap and the upturned collar of his army jacket protected him from recognition. Finn had seen his face months ago but at the time he'd paid little attention to Adam.

"Scotch?" Hugh asked, clinking the ice in his glass.

"Thanks, no." Adam said, the colored contacts irritating slightly. "What's so important that it couldn't have been handled over the phone?" The impatience in his voice was backed by his icy stare. Men like Hugh Parker thrived on intimidation. He wasn't about to be bullied.

"There's a misunderstanding between you and my son." Hugh said, leaning back casually, his grin meeting Adam's bored expression. "Agent Ward's extermination was part of the original deal we had with Hector."

Adam dug into his inside coat pocket and removed a folded eight-by-eleven sheet of paper. "The contract says nothing about Ward." He handed the evidence over to a scowling Hugh.

"Well," the Senator hummed, "It was implied."

"I'm not arguing this with you." Adam said, tapping on the glass between them and the driver. "Drop me off here," he said when the phone beside Hugh rang.

"Never mind, just keep driving." Hugh set the receiver down and stared across the dark space.

Adam sat back, dropping open his jacket exposing the Glock strapped to his belt.

"Now don't get excited," Hugh's crooked grin appeared as he took in the threat. "The real reason I asked to meet you was two fold. I really don't care about the money," he said, waving his fingers at the triviality of the dollar. "What I want to know is that you are able to take down the girl. Finn tells me she was your target before Hector captured her … is that correct?"

"Yes."

"And eliminating her now is not a problem?"

"It's a job that pays. No room for sentimentality."

Hugh hummed, nodding as he appraised the assassin. "And am I also to understand you were once friends with Hector and now after ending his life you have taken over his business?"

"What's your point?"

"My point," he said dryly, "is that I could use a man of your talents in my organization."

"Sorry, I'm a free agent," Adam said as he shifted his gaze to Finn, who'd remained silent the entire time. "You can't offer me anything I don't already have."

"I don't think you quite grasp the extent of my interests. Everybody wants something and I would venture to include you in that broad category. Here is what I'm proposing." The old man leaned forward, the scent of his cigar heavy on his breath. "I have aligned a wide range of people from every walk of life, on every surface of our planet and we all work for each other. An 'I'll scratch your back and you'll scratch mine' system. Whatever you need, can be done... no matter the scope. As payment, at times, your services will be requested. There will be no reason for you to hide, no reason you can't live in normal society ... no one will ever be seeking you and you will always be guarded from the law."

Jesus.

Seductive wasn't enough of a word for that offer. Adam allowed the lump that had risen in his throat to stay put. It was important not to give Hugh a hint of how close he'd hit the target. The man was offering him freedom – the one thing he wanted that he couldn't get himself.

"Oh, don't make a decision now." Hugh's smile was cryptic. "Think about it." He pressed a button on the intercom beside him and the limo pulled over. "I'm sure you can find your way home from here."

"Don't forget you have the Ward business to carry out first," Finn added, then sat back in the shadows after a look of reprimand from his father.

The driver opened the door and Adam slipped through. "I'll be in touch," he said. The fresh air did little to clear Hugh's voice from invading his head. *Sanctuary.* Adam walked quickly through the streets, pushing away the temptation. How long had it taken to perfect becoming invisible? Even in San Diego, when his life was as close to normal as it ever had been, he still found himself keeping up the habits of a criminal.

Hugh was the devil.

Only the devil traded in souls. Now his, or whatever was left of it, for his greatest desire. Freedom. *For* a price.

I'd have to live as an assassin. Adam shook his head, dislodging the idea. *Melanie would never go for it*, he thought before remembering how he'd left her. Now he swallowed down the lump, *she wouldn't take me back, anyway.* He was alone. The decision was all his.

CHAPTER 14

"What do you think?" Finn asked his father. He was a tough man to read and Finn had given up trying when he was a kid.

"Didn't you see him?" Hugh cackled, sending a shiver of fear up through Finn's vertebrae. "If there's one thing I'm good at, my boy, it's reading people. The answer is yes. He'll join, he won't be able to resist."

Finn nodded as if he'd seen any shred of what his father was talking about. To his blind eyes the assassin had seemed cool, unflinching, but who was he to disagree?

"He'll take care of Ward then, you think?"

"Why would you question that?" Hugh barked, his cheery mood vanishing.

"I just thought," he stuttered, "he might have had feelings for Ward, that it wasn't an act. I mean, well, he didn't kill her…"

"Don't be a fool. That man," he pointed to the door, "is a professional. Better than Hector. We're lucky," he said, his smile returning. "He's going to make us a lot of money."

Good, Finn thought, his shoulders dropping. If that's what Hugh thought then there was nothing to worry about. He took a sip of his drink and gave a mental toast. *Adios, Agent Ward.* And he smiled.

CHAPTER 15

"Hey, Trish, would you want to see Carla with me?" Melanie asked after apologizing for not having given more notice to her visit.

"That itty-bitty woman is scary. I swear she busted my balls last time I tried to have a conversation. You're on your own, unless..." Melanie could feel Trish's grin.

"What?"

"You spill the dirt on you and Adam."

"I guess I'm on my own." Melanie smiled.

"You're a dirty player, you know I'm dying here. Well, then, I won't be able to tell you what Jason said about Adam."

Melanie wanted to hold out ... but... "Okay, but not because I believe you know anything. I just don't want to go alone."

"Sucker! I'll pick you up in a bit."

Two hours passed before a burgundy Porsche squealed at her curb.

Trish looked exhausted as Melanie, reluctantly, took the passenger's seat of Jason's beloved car.

"Does Jace know you're driving his car?" Melanie asked, leaving the door open, afraid to commit to being a passenger while Trish sat behind the wheel.

"Please, like he'd care."

Her normally pale completion was pallid and fevered.

"Trish, don't you know how to drive a stick?"

"I got myself here, didn't I?"

"Okay," Melanie said, strapping herself in.

Trish sucked in a breath and fired up the ignition. They lunged, stopped, lunged and stopped for half a block.

"You should keep a set of neck braces in here," Melanie said, bracing her foot to the imaginary brake on the passenger-side floorboards. "Slowly take your foot off the clutch and with the same delicacy, please, lightly press down on the gas."

"Like this?" she asked. The car jerked and stalled.

"No."

"Shut up," Trish said. "Crap, look at me, I'm sweating like a pig."

"Give me the keys." Melanie held out her hand.

"No way can I trust Jace's car with a stranger."

"Stranger?" Melanie snarled and swiped the keys out of the ignition. "Move over." She ran around the car while horns honked and Trish scooted to the passenger seat. "Where are we going?"

"I'm weak with hunger. It took all my energy to get to your parent's house. Can we eat?"

"Your call."

"OG's."

The salad buffet used only locally grown organic foods and was priced as such. "Since when did you go organic?" Melanie asked.

"Jace," she said, twisting her mouth. "He's environmentally

conscious. Whatever that means. Besides, I like lettuce." Trish stabbed a leaf. "Not that I'd mind a little animal flesh mixed in … grilled chicken or salmon. And please don't say a fish isn't an animal because I truly don't give a shit."

"Wow, it was simple question," Melanie puffed, baiting Trish. "You and Jason are doing well?"

"Still hot and heavy. You'd know if you'd ever let me give you details," she joked. "Truth is Mel, I think I love him. Like, *love him*, love him. It feels terrible. I saw all the stupid trauma you went through and hell if I'm going to wind up like you." She looked up. "Sorry, but you know what I mean."

"You have such compassion," Melanie said.

"I don't worry that he's going to leave me, but he's a professional athlete and you know their reputation." She sighed. "So many women throwing themselves at the players. He's just a guy. How can I expect him to be faithful?"

Melanie shrugged. "He loves you."

"You don't think Tiger loved Elin? Ugh! It's too much trouble. I'm sick of love. I never understood how you felt. Now I'm scared to lose him. But if he ever fucks another girl I'll kill him."

"I have no idea what to say to that."

She shrugged. "It's just a fact, Mel. How are things with Adam?"

"Um."

"No! You promised to spill."

"I don't know what there is to say."

"You shoved him away, didn't you? Damn it, Melanie."

"Hold on. I didn't shove anyone away. Jeez, you're as bad as my mother."

"Well, you've sort of got a bad history with men. Okay, so, here's where you tell me how fantastic Adam is and how he mumbles love poems during…"

"Trish. You are so annoying," Melanie laughed.

"Have you talked to him lately?"

"Define lately."

"I swear you can make anything complicated. Your problem is that you're too uptight."

"Maybe."

"And FYI, I like your mom, she's got a pair the size of cantaloupes."

"Lovely. Can we please focus on Carla?"

"Unless you know a good shrink, I think she's a lost cause."

"Have a little faith," Melanie advised.

"When was the last time you had a conversation with her? She's a nut. And it's only going to get worse when Ted loses. I know I'm a bitch, so don't bother with the look."

"We'd better go," Melanie said, picking up the check. "I've got the family dinner at five and I was already warned not to be late. Cheryl and Bruce have a Lamaze class…"

"God, are they still pregnant? What is Cheryl, part elephant? She must be huge."

Melanie wondered how it must feel to be able to say anything that came to mind.

The Porsche was a dream to drive, slipping way past speed limits without notice.

"Jesus Christ, where'd you learn to drive?"

"NASCAR," Melanie smiled, thinking about that summer.

"Don't tell me, whatever. I don't care. Anyway, you're so lucky you live across the country. I mean it wasn't bad at first when Carla was suffering in silence." She giggled. "Sounds bad like that but I swear if you were here you'd be ready to smack that little pixie down.

"It's the Sal Luhan thing. And I hope you like that name because you're going to hear it about five hundred times. Not just Sal but both names – Sal Luhan – and when she's really stoked, which she always is nowadays, he becomes Salvador Luhan." Trish sighed. "I counted one night how many times she said his name – you know, in an hour how many times? Take a guess."

Melanie hated these games.

"Seventeen."

"Nope. Higher."

"Twenty-four."

"Higher."

"Just tell me."

"You are no fun. One more guess," she taunted.

"No."

"One more."

Melanie looked at Trish, her hair longer, still blonde but no more curls. She didn't want to guess, but she already knew who was going to win.

"No."

"Please?"

"Fine. Fifty-three."

Trish's expression dropped. Melanie grinned, she'd guessed right.

"Well, yeah," Trish was less enthusiastic. "That averages to almost one a minute but truly it was worse because Car cried for like fifteen of those minutes." Trish paused, "but she did sob his name once or twice."

"Car cried?"

"Sucked major, let me tell you."

Melanie prepared herself for a distraught Carla as she pulled the Porsche through the gate of 12-foot high hedges and parked behind two silver CL class Mercedes coupes.

"Looks like she's got company."

"Uh oh," Trish groaned. "I think those belong to Ted's family." She looked over at Melanie. "Maybe we should come back some other time."

"Chicken," Melanie said, pulling to a stop.

The Carla who greeted them at the door was very different from the one they expected.

"Melanie! I can't believe you came all the way here for me!" Carla sprung up and down on the balls of her bare feet.

Melanie pressed her hands to the sides of Carla's face, squishing down the abnormally unruly curls, and looked directly into her dilated pupils. "What did you do with Carla?"

"Chopped her up into little pieces and ate her," Carla laughed wickedly. "Come inside." Trish and Melanie exchanged glances and followed Carla inside the Bradley mansion. "Can I get you something to drink?"

"I'll have whatever you're having," Trish laughed, "but make mine a double."

"I've had almost two bottles of beer and I didn't even use a glass," Carla whispered. She led them to the north wing. "I've been bored stiff hanging out in the parlor. I'm no longer needed, since The Triad arrived." Leaning a hip into a section of the paneling she unlatched a rotating bar hidden behind the wall. "It took me five minutes to figure out where the bottle opener was." She took out two Stella Artois and turned toward them. "Would you like them in glasses?"

Melanie took her beer in the bottle and tried to settle into the stiff

Queen Anne chair. The room was immaculate, with a striped sofa, wall-to-wall silk Oriental rug, and above the mantle a portrait of Carla and Ted with Ted's parents looming over the seated couple.

"Who's The Triad?"

Carla rolled her eyes. "Ted's family. They came in last night and immediately took over my sunroom. They're in there now." She crumpled onto the stiff couch, tucked her bare feet beneath her rolled-up jeans and swigged a mouthful of beer.

Melanie and Trish shared a glance, both stunned into quiet observation.

"They're planning." Air quotes and a gagging sound accompanied the word 'planning'. "They think if they employ their antiquated methods they can beat Salvador Luhan. But the truth is," she glanced over her shoulder and leaned in to whisper, "Ted's going to get his skinny ass kicked. Have you seen Salvador Luhan's campaign? Genius. Catch a terrorist and become an immediate hero." She leaned back and raised her bottle in a sloppy toast. "Ted's limo driver could have smashed into that car, what does that prove? Wrong time? Wrong place? All sorts of wrongs lining up, single file, I've been there plenty of times. But none of my wrongs ever miraculously turned out so darn right." She was talking with her hands and Trish grabbed the beer before it spattered out of the neck.

Trish sat on the corner of the cushion. "The election isn't over, anything is possible. Have faith."

Melanie rolled her eyes. Trish had stolen her words.

"There's no question, Salvador Luhan was a blessed man." Carla burped at the end of man.

"Oh, excuse me," Ted appeared in the doorway. "I didn't know you ladies were here."

Ted looked exactly the same – impeccably dressed with every hair in place and a smile that stretched across his entire district.

"We're just here to support Carla," Trish nipped.

"Well, it is always nice to see you." He turned to Carla, "It doesn't feel right not having you in the room. Would you please join us?"

"I'm not interested in having all my ideas shot down."

Ted's discomfort was obvious as his jaw set. "I've talked to them. We need to be unified if we're to prevail. When you're done here…" he said, leaving the request to speak for itself.

Carla nodded.

"Thank you. Um, Melanie would you have a moment?" he asked.

"Sure." Melanie followed him out of the room, and as she left heard Trish tell Carla, "That was nice. I thought you said he was being a prick."

"I'm not sure where there's an acceptable place to speak," he said, his eyebrows shifting as he glanced to the front doors.

"What are we talking about, Ted?" Melanie asked, using her voice to advise caution and not liking the direction of this conversation.

"What else? Luhan." He punched his fists deep into his pockets. "I have an idea about what you do … I hear rumors in the halls."

Melanie shook her head. "You can't believe everything you hear."

"I know, and I don't. But I'm at the end of my rope and it seems I've crossed the wrong man."

Reaching into her pocket she distorted the airwaves and lowered her voice. She didn't need an inflammatory story about Ted hitting the newsstands. "Is there something I should know?"

"Nothing scandalous, I assure you." He looked frightened by the mention. "About a year ago Senator Parker asked me to co-sponsor one of his bills. After I checked it out I told him that I couldn't in good conscience put my name on such self-profiteering garbage."

"And how did the Senator take the rejection?"

"Not well. He promised to end my career and hung up the phone." Ted paled behind his tan. "He's avoided me ever since. And needless to say I've given him the same latitude."

"You think it's Parker behind Luhan's success?" Melanie pictured the Father of the Year award in Luhan's office. It seemed far reaching, even for Hugh.

"I do. His race is too clean, we can't find anything on him."

"Maybe there's nothing to find."

"Everyone has something."

"Do you?" she asked.

Ted sighed and leaned back on his heels. "Everyone else."

"I'll see what I can do ... but no promises."

"Thank you."

"Don't mention it. Seriously." She smiled.

Trish was at the bar, blending, when she returned to the parlor and Ted went back to his family.

"This summer Ted was a shoe-in." Carla quickly wiped a tear from her cheek with the back of her hand and moved on to adjust her earring, fooling no one. "I really shouldn't have any more to drink."

"Margarita?" Trish asked, offering glasses. "This one I made without alcohol." She handed it to Carla. "The problem with Ted is he's too perfect. Take Sal. He's Mexican and can relate to..."

"Trish I really wish you'd stop being so offensive," Carla snapped.

"What?" Trish asked, looking at Melanie for clarification. "What did I say?"

"He's Hispanic," Carla corrected in a hushed tone. "You can't go around propagating stereotypes."

"Isn't he Mexican? Because I think that's how he describes himself – I read it in the Union-Tribune."

"I think we've gotten off point," suggested Melanie, the mediator.

Carla talked and sipped – spilling her concerns about Sal Luhan. Melanie tried not to, but couldn't help counting the number of times Carla said the name. It was a ticker inside her head – 15 … 22 … 34…

"And now Ted's parents are here." Carla squinted while keeping one eye on the door, ready to flee.

"I thought you liked the Bradleys."

"I put on a good show."

It was the hiccup that gave her away. "I swear, this is all going to be my fault … somehow. My fault Ted's not…" she looked over her shoulder and in a hushed giggle said, "… not Mexican."

Melanie turned to Trish's shocked expression and asked, "Did you get the virgin?"

It took a couple of beats of confusion before Trish took a sip of her drink and smiled.

"I like the sound of that, I got the virgin," she tossed her head back and chuckled.

Carla's lids were droopy. "Oh," she exclaimed and started to giggle again. "I get it. You got the virgin because you like sex."

"Is she for real?" Trish asked, checking out Carla's empty glass. "She's tanked on one sissy drink?"

"That plus two beers. I doubt she's had any liquor in years."

"Hey, Car," Trish moved into Carla's line of sight. "How's Ted in bed?"

"Trish! Come on!"

"What? You know you want to know."

Melanie ignored Trish and got up to search for a coffee pot.

"I can barely remember," Carla piped in the Southern drawl that was usually barely detectable but now was clear. Her guard was down. "It's been months. But from what I remember…"

"Car, shut up," Melanie said, angry with Trish. "Why do you do that?"

"Sorry."

"Could I get another one of these?" Carla asked, licking the rim of the glass.

"No. You're drunk, Car." Melanie took the glass. "Where's your coffee pot?"

"Impossible. I only had one beer."

"I thought you said two," Melanie straightened her out.

"Lied," she chuckled. "Didn't want you to think I was a light weight."

"You're worse than a light weight. How's it feel?"

"I like it. And I don't want coffee, Mel. Besides, we have a cappuccino machine and I don't know how it works."

"Have it your way," Melanie couldn't hide her irritation.

"We're going to lose anyway, what's the point? Truthfully I should be grateful to Salvador Luhan." Melanie marked off another mental tick. "I'm tired and sick of my life revolving around Ted."

This was shy Carla didn't drink, the alcohol was liberated her tongue.

"I'm considering a divorce. His family is involved in all of our decisions – like some damn democracy where I haven't got a vote. Did you know they made him get a vasectomy? Yeah," she nodded and suddenly her face dropped. "*They* wanted us to wait to have children and *they* didn't trust … me. So, snip, snip." Her elbow fell off her knee as she made scissor fingers.

"No way!" Trish exclaimed. "Christ, they're like mobsters. And Ted goes along with it?"

Melanie stayed quiet. It wasn't helping Car to trash her in-laws and it wasn't the worst family dynamics she knew about. Still, they were assholes and for the first time she was lumping Ted into that category.

"He hasn't got a choice. The Triad's got him by the extra … by the extram … extren … they've got him by the balls."

Carla glanced over her shoulder for the hundredth time, almost as many times as she'd spoken *his* name.

"Why do you keep doing that?" Melanie asked. She had run a quick sweep – it was clean.

"Oh, I don't know, I'm paranoid. I mean I don't think they'd have me knocked off … unless it gave Ted a double-digit lead." She snorted.

"Carla," Melanie found herself stuck at the beginning of her rebuke.

"I don't get it, what's the big deal? It's not like he's running for president," Trish said, shifting her gaze from Melanie back to Carla. "Is he?"

"You didn't hear that from me," Carla said, shrugging her shoulders.

"Oh my God, really?! Wow, this is so cool. Can I go to the inauguration?" Trish was on her feet.

"Sit down," Melanie commanded. "I think you're getting a little ahead of yourself. Ted is down in the numbers, remember?"

"Right." She sat back down on the coffee table. "So, what do we do?"

"We toast Salvador Luhan." Carla raised her glass.

"Don't give up," Trish urged.

Melanie could tell Trish was mentally picking out gowns.

"They were going to let him reverse the vasectomy next year. It's part of their plan. The White House in twelve years. They didn't want him to have old children but a ten-year-old would give him stability in the minds of voters. A family man. It's all planned out. But now…His parents are mad – I heard them raising their voices. Ted said he didn't want to be in anyone's pocket and he could win the election clean."

"Is Ted dirty?" Trish asked, without innuendo.

"No," Carla pressed the tips of her fingers into her temples. "He has people who handle the unpleasant aspects of the job."

"Hello." All three women were suddenly focused on the figure looming in the doorway. "I don't mean to intrude," Ted's sister said, her presence feeling more in line with a horror movie.

"Ruth, you remember my friends Melanie and Trish."

"Of course, how nice to see you again," Ruth purred. Her bottle-blonde hair was pulled up into an old-fashioned up-do and sprayed with a lacquer until the whole thing shined.

Melanie smiled. "How nice of you and your parents to come and support Ted and Carla."

A frown of puzzlement swept her expression before she grunted a brief agreement. "Have you any club soda, Carla dear?"

"Let me find some," Ted said, bumping past Ruth to the bar.

"So, Ted," Trish started and Melanie held her breath. "Have you ever considered planting a sex tape?"

The rest of the room quieted.

"Sex tapes of Luhan?" Ted asked, curiosity in his squinty gaze. "Do you know something we don't?"

Trish paused for a beat. "Actually, I was thinking of your sex tapes. You know, add some spice to your personality. I think you'd be more relatable to regular people." She looked from one aghast face to the next. "Okay, well, maybe not. Just a suggestion. Mel, are we about ready?"

"I think so. Ruth, Ted," she gave a nod before giving Carla a hug. "Sorry to have kept Carla from your strategy meeting."

Ted was the first to speak. "How about it, Dear? We could use your input."

"Wouldn't miss it. Bye-bye, Mel. Thanks."

"I'm only a phone call away."

"Me, too," Trish chimed in.

Melanie grabbed Trish by the wrist and towed her out to the Porsche.

"Can I speak now or are you going to shush me again?" Trish asked indignantly.

"I just wanted to get out of there." Melanie said, firing up the car. "Shut your door."

"Jeez, you're so bossy. But wasn't that fun? God, that Ruth is a piece of work. Creepy. Ha! I want to do it again!"

Melanie tore out of the driveway, eager to get to work on uncovering Luhan's secret, especially if it had something to do with Hugh Parker. "I can take you home or you can come to family dinner," Melanie grinned.

"Thanks for the offer but ... I'm going to pass. I've got some toilet scrubbing to catch up on."

"Had to ask."

"Do you really think Ted's family has the presidency in their sights?"

"I think every politician has it on their mind."

"I feel gross, like I need a shower."

Trish rambled on as Melanie drove with more on her mind than Ted Bradley for president. Reaching Jason's house a scream tore her out of her reverie. Trish leapt out of the car before the brake had been pulled and tackled Jason over a short hedge and to the ground. Melanie parked behind the yellow cab as the driver was yelling out the window.

"Hey," Melanie said, jogging to the car and knocking on the back window. "Can you give me a lift?"

"This guy hasn't paid me yet."

"I'll cover it." Melanie was already in the back seat, peeling off bills to get the driver moving. "See you guys later," she called out the window, sighing as Trish ripped open Jace's shirt.

"I should carry a video camera, the things I see," the driver murmured. "It's always the rich ones who stiff you out of a tip. That guy rolling in the grass is a famous ball player. I could put that on YouTube."

"Don't be a pervert."

"Pervert?" he barked, staring at Melanie in the rear view mirror. "I drive this damn car all day long – my testicles are numb from the bouncing. I wish I were a pervert."

Melanie's phone rang, a number she didn't recognize.

"Melanie here."

"Melanie here? That's your greeting? What ever happened to Hello?"

"Who is this?" she laughed.

"Your friendly etiquette coach. How are you?" Danny asked.

"I'm good. How are you?"

"Great. Hey, would you be up for another dinner?"

"I absolutely adore dinner." Her heart gave an annoying skip.

"I have not been able to stop thinking about you," he said, his cheerfulness unmasked. "I even dug up some old photos. I'll bring them when I come down. You won't believe how young we were."

"It's hard to imagine," she said over a wave of nostalgia.

"Is the day after tomorrow too soon?"

"Perfect," she said, her throat closing up.

"Good, because I was worried that maybe you were pissed at me for kissing you."

"I'm not, but…"

"You don't have to remind me … I've got competition."

"Danny."

"Later, Mel."

"Bye."

The phone went silent but she could still feel his essence hanging on.

"Lady, we're here."

Melanie looked out the window to the dimming sky behind her parent's house and stripped off an extra bill for the man with the bruised testicles. "Right, sorry."

"Thanks. Don't forget your cell," the driver said, nodding to the silver phone beside her.

Jason's.

"Honey, you're early," Rita called from the kitchen. "Bruce and Cheryl are watching TV with your father."

"What's going on in here?"

"Dinner," Rita said, stirring a pot with a wooden spoon.

"Smells good." Melanie looked around, there were no dirty pots and pans, only a bowl on the counter.

"It does, doesn't it?" She lifted her brows in two smooth movements. "Your friend, Adam, sent me information about a class a few months back. He's very sweet."

"Mom," Melanie shook her head. "You know I'm not going to tell you anything. You'll blow it out of proportion, get your hopes up and then be crestfallen when I'm not married in a year."

"Marriage?"

"I'm going to get Dad." Melanie placed a kiss on her mom's cheek. "I love you."

She'd left two messages for Jason at his house and one on Trish's cell. A phone is like a diary. It was a moral dilemma. It wouldn't be right to break in, Melanie knew, but … it burned in her left palm. Trish's voice replayed to shroud her judgment. 'He calls Jace at least twice a week.' Melanie cursed, paced her room and finally plopped down onto the corner of her bed. Ready to cross the line. There was nothing to break into … no security. *Foolish civilian ball player*, Melanie thought, sliding through his texts.

Adam's untraceable number was listed in Jason's address book.

CHAPTER 16

"How was your trip?" Jane asked, rushing from behind her desk to take Melanie's luggage.

"It was fine. How are things here?" Her distracting few days felt much longer.

"The same. Agent Jackson has asked that you call when you arrive. Everything else I've been forwarding to you."

"Great. Thanks." Surveying her office, all looked serene. She dropped her computer bag on the desk and went to see Ben. She'd skipped out on the Wisconsin gig but it was so menial that it might not have registered.

"Agent Ward, come in," Ben said, frowning at her from over his wire-rimmed glasses. "I'm glad you're here, I think I broke this..." The remote sat flat on his open hand. "I liked my file cabinets," he grumbled.

"I can put in an order to have them brought up, they're in storage." Melanie offered as she reprogrammed the remote. "Though, for security, I had the contents shredded. Here you go," she said, handing him the remote.

"It's just that I always thought I was keeping up with technology. I hate to think I'm getting old."

"How's the memory?" She asked with a grin. "Did you forget you sent me to Madison or are we ignoring it?"

"Forget that you disobeyed an order?" He barked out a laugh. "I'm not nearly that old."

"Why aren't you yelling at me?"

"To what end? Madison was a waste of time, anyway. But Ward," his voice dropped, "don't ever do that again."

"I won't," she answered. It was enough of a reprimand. "Have you got a real case for me?"

He handled the remote as if it were a dead rodent, placing it on the edge of his desk. "I do have a real assignment for you. And you *are* going," he said with a stern look. "A handful of Basque dissidents have been holding monthly meetings. Nothing raucous but … they aren't especially known for their civil obedience. It's a good assignment for you. Gets you out of town and if there's anything to the complaint I know you'll ferret it out."

"Thanks, Ben."

"Judith has a digital file." He picked up the remote with determination. "I know this has been difficult for you. And even with the occasional blip you've handled the situation well."

"Thanks," she said, now embarrassed at her recent behavior. "I'll pick up the information on my way out."

I'm going to Spain, she thought with a new purpose to her step. Giddy, she slipped the drive into the USB slot, launching a tutorial on Spain's Northern Region – geographical information, a brief history and a copy of the phone call that triggered her trip made by Andrea Velez, a woman from a village thirty kilometers south of Bilbao.

Melanie listened to the transmission a few times before calling Andrea.

"Andrea Velez?" Melanie asked.

"Yes?"

She introduced herself.

"I've been expecting your call," Andrea said, her breath coming out in deep pants.

"How did you get our number?" Melanie asked. It wasn't published and the call had come in directly.

"My father, Antonio, brags about how he was an American Spy for a week and a day, ten years ago. I found the number to your organization in a box at the bottom of his closet. He would never call." She sounded nervous and was speed talking.

"Okay, tell me what's going on that you think we need to become involved?" Melanie typed in Antonio Velez's name as she spoke. There were situations when someone off the street would be useful as an informational gathering tool. It was rare, but it happened.

"My brother and others are very excited about a man who's arrived. He's promoting the Basque separatist movement." Andrea slowed down. "I hope it is just my imagination and this call was unnecessary. I've been to a few meetings and before that I paid little attention. I can't help much, I'm sorry."

Melanie probed and unearthed a few extra details.

The next meeting was Tuesday night. Andrea would introduce Melanie as an American friend. Though tensions had been steadily escalating, Andrea thought Melanie, with a few carefully placed lies, would be welcomed.

"I'll be there Monday to have a look around."

"It's probably nothing."

"Either way I need the number to a nearby hotel."

"My aunt owns an inn across from the church. I'll let her know you'll be here for a few nights. Her name is Begonia and I work at the counter next door."

She had a good feeling about this case. There was an angle of intrigue wrapped in a shroud of excitement. Melanie replayed the tutorial, paying close attention to the region's cultural values and history of oppression.

She couldn't tear her eyes away even as she answered her phone.

"I'm so sorry I'm late."

"It's okay," she responded looking at the clock on her computer. "There's no problem. We can do dinner another time."

"No, I'm in D.C. now. I'll pick you up ... or we can meet somewhere."

"Are you okay?"

He sighed. "Better now, just missing you."

"Danny, your charm doesn't work on me anymore."

"That doesn't stop me from enjoying flirting with you."

"Knock yourself out, then. I'll meet you at your hotel and we'll go from there."

"Better be quick – I might be wasted by the time you arrive."

"Too bad for you, because I had plans you can only enjoy sober."

"Really?"

"No. Damn, you're easy."

"One of my better qualities," he chuckled. "We could gorge on room service, watch pay television and order in a masseuse."

"Or ... I could wear my running shoes and we could check out the gym."

"That won't work for me … We could poison ourselves with tankards of alcohol until we wake up in a different hotel completely nude, having done the unimaginable."

"Add two foreigners and a handful of monkeys and you've got a deal," Melanie added.

"You are such a tease."

"I'll be there in 20 minutes and I like the workout plan."

"I'll meet you in the lobby. I'll be the one with my heart on my sleeve, drink in my hand and not wearing running shoes."

"Order me one of whatever you're drinking."

Careful not to be followed, Melanie used the service entrance to exit the Manor and jogged to the hotel cutting through the park.

At the hotel she slowed, aware of the bustle of business travelers, tourists, valet attendants – nothing out of place. The low hum of the lobby was interrupted by a few who were vocalizing their affairs with a bit too much volume. Melanie's attention slid over these pretenders to the potential scouts. Satisfied she edged toward the lounge, cursing Parker under her breath for the umpteenth time.

The lounge was set in the corner of the building, enclosed in tempered, tinted glass. The room was as she expected; exposed and unprotected. And by the angle of the gaze of every woman in the dimly lit bar, Melanie knew exactly where Danny was seated: at a round, snug table for two, studying the brown liquid in a glass he rolled between his palms.

Melanie's breath caught.

The tails of his shirt were hanging out of his trousers, the tip of his collar was awkwardly bent inside the neck of his shirt and his hair had fallen over his eyes. He was undeniably gorgeous. The tortured look worked well on him. Approaching, she felt the urge to fix him.

"Hi!" he said, looking up from his drink, a small grin replacing the slump of his shoulders. "Where are the slutty heels?" he asked, standing to drop a soft kiss on her cheek and pull out her chair.

"You started without me," she answered, smelling the alcohol on him and taking her seat.

"Only a couple of shots. What can I get you?" He waved over the bartender.

"I thought we were hungry."

"I was hungry, wasn't I?" he asked, and she nodded. "They probably serve food here."

A menu was brought over and he ordered for them.

"You are a sight for sore eyes," he said, staring at her. "Lauren never understood me the way you do. I haven't stopped wondering about us since we ran into each other," Danny said, pulling his right ankle to his left knee and fidgeting with the cuff of his pants. "Before then I was a mess."

"I can't imagine that," she said, scanning his turned collar and ringed eyes.

"You're sweet." He swept his fingers through his shaggy hair, causing her heart to stagger.

He lifted his eyes and he gazed at her from behind heavily drooping lids. It was obvious Danny was still in love with his ex-wife. She was trying to come up with a diplomatic way of asking what'd happened to cause this spiral.

"Lauren is getting married this Saturday," he said, reading her thoughts.

"I'm sorry."

"She's sending Avery back to me on Sunday. She's with me for two weeks."

Melanie was unprepared.

"This stinks. She's getting rid of our daughter for her damned honeymoon." Danny pounded a fist on the table, causing the dishes to rattle. "You're staring at me like I'm on a suicide watch."

"I'm concerned. I've never seen you despondent."

"Sort of sucking the fun out of the room, aren't I?" The slightest of crinkles played across the corners of his eyes.

Melanie shrugged. "I can handle it."

"You sure? Because I've got a favor to ask." He sat up straighter. "The only times I haven't been miserable are the ones I've spent with you." He fidgeted nervously. "I really need a friend, Mel. Not someone reporting my every move to Lauren or hiring strippers trying to get me laid. I just cannot deal with that right now."

"We'll always be friends."

"I know, but what I'm asking is if we can hang out … a lot … over the next few weeks or months. I don't want to cause trouble with the boyfriend, but I need you."

"Definitely we can hang out." Her offer was tinged with a doubt that vanished with Danny's grateful expression.

"Seriously?" he asked, the crease ebbing.

"Danny, I'd love to hang out with you, for as long as you like or need. And I'm glad you mentioned Adam because … you and I are friends."

"I'm not expecting more. I know I've been coming on strong but I'm not ready for a relationship. It's just a reaction to a situation I can't handle." His shoulders sagged. "But, thank you, you have no idea how much this means." He swallowed, nodding his appreciation.

Melanie bit down on her lower lip. "You haven't mentioned

your job."

Danny shrugged. "I work from my computer, investing – turns out I'm pretty good, too, even in this market. It's perfect. I get to spend time with Avery. Or I used to." He took in a deep breath, "I used to get her ready for school, make her lunch and hold her hand all the way to the school gate. Now I get weekends."

Melanie reached for his hand.

"Anyway," he sighed although the corners of his mouth turned upward. "I almost forgot, check these out." Danny pulled a white envelope from his inside pocket and slid it across the table toward her.

"Pictures?" She breathed out a 'wow' of amazement as her college self beamed up at her from the Pacific Beach pier. Danny's cheek pressed against hers but only the left side of his face could be seen. He'd taken the picture at arms length, misjudging the angle. These were taken before the stale perfection of digital cameras made it effortlessness to abort the imperfects. A decade later this flawed picture with Danny laughing, showing his one silver filling, was wonderful.

Tilting the pictures for both to view, she pointed out her favorite jeans, the books they carried and the people in the background. The two of them were always together, front and center.

"I had this, too," he reached inside the envelope and took out a birthday card she'd given him.

Melanie read her words. Her flowing handwriting sent an ache straight through her heart. "I think I might have been in love with you," she said, placing her loving words back into the envelope. Exactly where they belonged, hidden and shut away.

"It worked out perfectly because I felt the same about you." His droopy gaze focused on her and Melanie's throat clenched as she battled the rush of emotion. "Mel, you were my first love."

There was nothing to say. She stared at him, Danny Ashe, older and wounded. How in the world was this going to work?

Dinner arrived and they ate in comfortable silence. Melanie rode the elevator up to Danny's floor, refusing to cross the threshold to his room.

"Want to come in?"

Melanie shook her head. "Will I see you tomorrow?"

"You bet," he said, sticking out his hand for a goodbye shake, making her laugh. He shrugged, "since I can't kiss you."

Her intention had been to go back to her crappy apartment, but there was too much going on beneath her skin. Melanie jogged, taking the long way back to the Manor. Out of breath, she raced up the flight of stairs before unlocking her office and dropping to the vinyl desk chair.

CHAPTER 17

"Morning, Mike."

"Hey! How was the trip?" he asked from behind his newly acquired giant monitor.

"Um...," she had to think for a moment – what trip? "Fine."

"Did you use the goggles?"

"Oh, yeah, your girlfriend has got talent." Melanie said, wheeling a chair closer. "Let me know what else she's working on. What's the word on Finn? I can't seem to track him down today."

He shifted in his seat, "She's not actually my girlfriend."

Melanie sighed. "Well, she's got talent if not taste." Melanie patted his back. "I'll put in a good word for you if that'll help. Now, about Finn? He hasn't been around all day and..." she stalled, unwilling to reveal her extravagant means of keeping track of him.

"Assigned a case. I thought you were, too."

"Yeah," she answered, her thoughts flittering over to Spain.

"Finn left right after speaking with Jackson."

"Do we know where to?"

He didn't have to say a word. Exasperation was all over his face. She was going to have to tread easy. "Sorry," she smiled toward the massive monitor. "Mike, why do you need such a large screen? I hear they sell eyeglasses everywhere these days."

"Isn't it awesome? True, if I look at it directly I go a bit nearsighted and I have to roll the chair back a few feet ... but it's cool, check this out." A pad on his table controlled the screen. With a waggle of his fingers the images responded. "I'm setting it up for voice activation, now. Sweet, right?"

"Okay, that is pretty cool. Can I try?"

"If you think you can figure it out, go for it." Mike wheeled himself out of the way.

Melanie rubbed her hands together, cracked her knuckles and typed quickly.

"You're getting it!" From her side she felt his nod of approval. "Hey, wait. What are you looking for?" Mike asked, quickly moving to peer over her shoulder. "Jesus, Melanie. No wonder you're such a great spook."

Melanie smiled. "Well, you weren't going to tell me where Finn was headed."

"Because I didn't know." He shielded his eyes from the screen. "That's classified information!"

"Santa Barbara." Melanie read through the details. Offshore drilling. Combatants, threats, dates, times and names. Looked legit. "Thanks, Mike. Though I guess we could've just traced his cell." She leaned her head back on the ergonomic chair and felt Mike's frustration blow through her. "But then we wouldn't have known the purpose ... still," she sat back up, "we don't know that's where he is.

How long to pinpoint his *exact* location?" Danny's name appeared on her caller ID. "I need to take this," she said before hurrying off, "but keep up that trace."

"How's the hangover?" she asked, amused.

"Ha! I woke up clearer than I have in months. I had a dream about you."

"As much as I'd love to hear about it, I don't want to know."

"It was an innocent dream, we were driving ... someplace."

It was with a mixture of thrill and dread that she flirted with Danny. Ancient memories and 10 years of absence had shaped him into a specimen of near-perfection. And the *near* was only because she was realistic, not because she could actually pinpoint any actual flaw. If radiant light followed him through the streets, streaming down from gaps in billowy clouds illuminating the golden highlights in his hair, she wouldn't have been surprised.

This new, older Danny was still funny, attentive and incredibly sad. Sorrow clung heavily to the air around him. Through it, he found occasion to laugh and was able to make her feel comfortable.

I can control this, she reminded herself whenever twists of guilt flickered in from her subconscious. *There are no romantic motivations.*

"Mel?" Mike asked from his chair across the room.

His worried look stopped her short.

"Danny, I've got to go, but dinner, right?"

"Same time, same place."

"Okay," she answered, absently ending the call. "What have you got?"

"I don't think you're going to like it."

Just what I need, more bad news.

"He's in San Diego."

Just like that blood rushed from her extremities, leaving her chilled. "Exact location?"

"Pacific Beach. Mean anything to you?"

Adam. That's what it meant.

"Yeah, it means he's checking up on me."

"You don't think he'll try anything with your family, do you?"

"No. He hires people to do the dirty work. He's gathering information."

"You aren't going to do anything ... stupid, are you?"

"I hope not."

Melanie shut the door to her office and tried the cell number Adam had given her. Again. This time she didn't get the pleasant woman's voice instructing her to leave a message. It was a man who informed her the number was no longer in service.

Frustrated, she wanted to hurl her phone, hear the smash and watch it shatter into a dozen pieces against the wall.

Take a breath, demanded the rational part of her brain.

He'd abandoned that number without warning. She shook with worry and anger. It was the not knowing that was causing the insanity. He'd left no choice. She hadn't wanted to use the number from Jason's cell.

He won't be happy, she thought, staring at the number. *But you need to stop caring about what he thinks.*

He'd discarded her on purpose, changed his number because of her. She distorted the frequencies in her office, prepared her trace and hit the green go button.

"Jace, man, I was going to call you."

Melanie had used Jason's number as a router, listing him on Adam's caller ID.

Her innards quivered at the sound of his deep voice. Melanie sucked in her breath, grateful he was alive, but … "It's not Jason." She could hear his silent swear.

"Melanie." Other than the frostiness to her name there was zero emotion in his voice.

Refusing to feel foolish turned out to be a challenge.

"I'm going to have to learn not to underestimate you," he said. "How've you been?"

"Parker is in Pacific Beach. I don't know what he can find but thought you needed to know." Her words rushed out. Ready to drop the line as soon as possible.

"Shit, he'd better not fuck up my place." He sounded fierce. "Sorry, there isn't anything to find but thanks for the heads up." His voice softened. "You didn't answer my question."

"What do you want me to say? I'm fine." She wanted to tell him she hurt, that *he* was hurting her, but couldn't.

"Good to hear."

Melanie looked around, crazed. "I'm lying."

"That's okay by me."

She closed her eyes. "I'm fine if you say you're safe."

"Then you're fine because, I'm safe and in control. Don't you think I've thought through every other option? I never wanted to wind up back here."

Melanie quietly pressed keys on her keyboard – receiving satellite images. South America, a small costal village, she zeroed in tighter to a mansion on the edge of a cliff. It was beautiful.

"If you hate it so much, then come home." She hid her alarm at the armed guards pacing the perimeter – she adjusted the angle, taking in the men on the roof and surveillance cameras.

"I don't hate it. It is what it is. You've got your life and now I've got mine."

"No. I'm not accepting that, we're in this together. I'm not giving up on that." *There he is!* Her breath came in rapid short pants. He was leaning against the wall of the courtyard facing the edge of the cliff, wearing a pair of dark blue swim trunks. He looked handsome and healthy. The wind tossed his dark hair off his forehead, his beard was trimmed and his bicep flexed as he held the phone to his ear. He was as beautiful as the scenery.

"Sorry. Doesn't work that way. I'm going to take care of Parker. But after that we need to acknowledge our differences."

"Which are what?" she asked as a thousand miles away he turned away from the sea.

"Babe."

"I'm not going to let you just walk away," she threatened.

"I already have."

"Damn it! Please don't..." Her chest hurt, "push me away. I can do this if I know you're coming back." She spoke quickly, feeling as if it may be her last chance with him. "I need you to reach out for me, Adam." She didn't care if he heard the desperation in her voice. She couldn't control it at the moment.

"Melanie," he said with sympathy. "I want you to live a long, happy life."

"I want that, too," she interrupted. "With you. *With you.*"

"Okay," he sighed, rubbing his eyes with his free hand like he was getting a headache. "Okay, baby. I'll figure out a way to make it work. You'll have to be patient."

Melanie nodded, somehow feeling worse.

"I'll call you," Adam said.

"Thank you," she answered weakly. "I need you to call."

"I will. I'll call. Goodbye, Mel."

"Bye," she said, but he was already gone. Melanie watched with dread. She knew she'd lost him. Adam stared down at the phone in his hand. Her heart rate quickened. She wanted to see something in his manner that would give her a glimmer of hope … a sign that hinted to his pain, that this wasn't what he wanted, that he still loved her. Melanie focused hard at her screen, looking for any trace. But he simply stared out over the ocean, his jaw set.

He was right there, in front of her. Her heart swelled, there was no denying what he did to her. Adam looked up and she smiled, he was tan and as handsome as ever. An expression of turmoil clouded his face as he pitched the phone over the barrier and off the cliff, down to the rocky sea below.

In her chest, her heart cracked.

From her angle, his gaze was dark and his shoulders slumped. Then two men approached on the landing and changed everything. His mood lightened and the three men went inside, leaving Melanie alone to ache.

She searched the rest of the fortress on the hill and the village at the bottom.

"Agent Ward," Jane's cautious voice came through the intercom.

"Yes?"

"You have a visitor, Daniel Ashe."

"Okay, I'll be right down," she said, distracted. Though she looked, Adam didn't emerge again. Melanie scanned the security feed. With her office secured and her sweater in hand, she glossed her lips quickly and said goodnight to Jane.

Danny was standing with his back toward her, apparently studying the framed propaganda posters for the fake company. There was a flicker of guilt as she appreciated the way his T-shirt stretched across his broad shoulders to hang loosely down to his jeans.

"Hi," she said, bumping her shoulder against his.

"There you are." Every one of his features lifted to create his casual smile. "That's some rent-a-cop you've got guarding this place." He nodded in direction of the guard.

"Engineers are working on some new technology. Very hush-hush," she said, catching his infectious smile. "I thought we were meeting at your hotel."

"We were. But I thought I'd surprise you. Are you ready?" Melanie nodded and he held open the door for her. Locks of the vehicle at the curb disengaged. "I rented a car."

"Where are we going? I'm not sure if you're aware but I'm not a big fan of surprises."

"Too bad. I am." Danny slid behind the wheel. "Tell me about your day. What did you do?"

This simple question stopped her. Her normal was not normal.

"Checked e-mail, bought a Snickers from the vending machine ... those are the highlights," Melanie lied.

"That's terrible, Mel."

"Well, what about you?"

"Took a swim, worked out, made some calls," he looked at her with a hint of embarrassment. "I've reconnected with my agent. He says there could be work for a middle-aged wreck of an athlete."

"Or, he could use you." She said.

"That's what I'm crossing my fingers for. Maybe I can do some endorsement work. Is that crazy?" Not waiting for a response he plowed on, "I did a little shopping."

"Not crazy but ... Hey, this is my apartment," she said as he pulled the parking brake. "I thought we were going someplace."

"This is someplace. I'm cooking dinner." He was at her door in a flash, fishing a key from his pocket. "I hope you don't mind but ... your key was not very well hidden. Above the door jam in a small nook, same as 10 years ago."

"Danny," she started, not sure which words were going to take shape.

"Don't say anything, Mel. I can see it in your face. I'm sorry. I was restless and I tried running but ... well, I ended up here."

"It's okay, you're always welcome. Whether I'm here or not." She squeezed his arm. "What's for dinner?"

"Hamburgers and tater tots," he was grinning. "I got popcorn and a couple of movies, too, but I didn't notice a TV."

"It's upstairs, you can help me bring it down."

"I bought a Foreman grill but tell me that your oven works."

Melanie shrugged. "Not positive, and I hope you don't mind standing while you eat. No chairs." Melanie said under crimson cheeks. *I'm really going to have to do something about this place,* she thought, embarrassed.

"I, myself, have always been a fan of patterned shag carpeting. Besides you have plenty of room, where most people keep cluttered objects like furniture." He yanked the grill out of its cardboard container. "Let's get this baby fired up."

While Danny grilled, Melanie scavenged what she had to create an informal dinner on her living room floor. Using books to stabilize the wine glasses, she laid out the blanket from her bed and they sat cross-legged to eat their burgers and baked-to-a crisp tater tots.

"Your bad day didn't have anything to do with me, did it?" Danny asked, groaning as he pushed himself up to his feet. "I can't believe how out of shape I am." He balanced all the plates in one hand, carrying them to the sink.

"Who said I had a bad day?"

"Nice try. You can't lie to me, Mel. I hear the strain in your voice. Is it the non-jealous boyfriend?"

"As it turns out, *Adam*," she annunciated his name, "wasn't as okay with you as I'd thought he'd be." Her stomach churned. She blamed the charred tater tot she'd eaten on a dare.

"Yeah, you're gullible. If you were my girlfriend there's no way I'd be okay with your ex back in the picture."

"I see that now," she nodded, thinking about how many other problems separated her and Adam.

"Should I leave?"

"No. You're not the only one who could use a friend."

"I feel bad." Danny said.

"You and I are friends, just friends." Danny groaned and went for his jacket. "We're not friends?" she asked, raising her eyebrow.

Danny moved in, his face inches from hers, gaze piercing. "Aren't there moments," he whispered, "when you remember how it felt to be naked with me? Don't," he moistened his lips nervously, "you wonder how it would feel to kiss me? How I would taste? If it would be the same as you remembered?"

Melanie was breathing heavily. She'd been ignoring these thoughts.

"Me being here is a temptation. Could you resist me? If I kissed you, really kissed you? I could seriously mess things up with you and Adam."

Her mind was muddled. He was too close, talking about things she'd been pushing away. "I don't want you to go. But I don't want to lose him." She stared up into his chocolate eyes. The stare lasted a full minute as each sized the other up.

"Don't leave," she finally said, "Don't talk about kissing and don't leave." Her voice cracked and she cleared her throat waiting for his decision.

He looked at her with concern for a full minute before taking off his jacket.

"Where's the TV?"

Between the two of them they wrangled the 32-inch flat screen down the stairs, arguing most of the way.

"Mel, I've got it. It's not heavy if you'd get out of the way."

"I can carry this, Danny and it's you causing the problems."

"God, you're a pain," he said setting the TV on the brick hearth.

"Not if I get my way," she said, sitting next to him and leaning against the wall.

"Ever think you've lived alone too long?"

"I'm going to get some pillows." She climbed back up the stairs and slumped down on the corner of her bed. She took a moment to acknowledge the dull, pounding of pain and sadness. Two breaths later she grabbed the pillows and went down to watch a horrible slasher movie.

"I still don't know why you like these movies. They're so predictable," Melanie said to distract from an awkward scene of girls romping around a wooded cabin in their matching panty-and-bra sets while another couple had sex in the top bunk.

"We watched them because you liked them," he said.

"You're delusional. Why would I be interested in girls being stabbed? You liked watching their bouncy run."

"Did I? I was a horny bastard, wasn't I?"

"Yes."

"Well, I wasn't alone, remember?"

"Please!" Melanie rolled her eyes. "You had a whole line of girls before me."

"Yeah, but I was at my most rigorous with you – and you kept up." They stared at each other. "Are you having a flash back, too?"

Melanie nodded.

"I'd better go." Danny said, jumping up and kissing the back of her hands before leaving.

Her sad apartment felt pathetic after he left. She wandered around with nothing to do. Danny had washed and dried the dishes, taken the scorched remains of potatoes out with the trash and refrigerated the veggies.

Melanie lay on her bed with all the lights off and stared at the empty space above her head. Finn was nosing around her hometown. Adam was cavorting with assassins and Danny was back. How had this happened?

Her eyes snapped open with the thudding of someone tramping into her apartment.

"It's just me, Mel." Danny called up the stairs.

She didn't know anyone who treaded heavier than Danny. He moved with the carelessness of one who's never been hunted. Pulling open her bedroom door, she saw it was bright – it was morning and she felt as though she hadn't slept a wink. Squinting down at him she tried to think of a polite way to ask.

"Couldn't sleep," he answered before she could formulate the question.

"I'll be down in a minute." She felt groggy. Her shower was hot and the vanilla oil Trish had sent eased her mind and stifled the coffee aroma.

He was pouring a cup when she drifted downstairs. "Good morning."

"Morning, where did you get the coffee pot?"

"The cupboard," he pointed to one on the bottom. "I noticed it and a bag of dry roast in your freezer last night." His gaze narrowed and he took a guess. "The boyfriend?"

"Adam."

"When do I get to meet him?"

"I have no idea." Melanie took a sip. "But nice job with the coffee," she said, raising her cup.

"I remember it's practically a food group for you."

"Still is. It's embarrassing. I feel like I've been stagnated for 10 years as the rest of the world evolved and changed."

"You're sleeping with someone who isn't me. That sounds like change enough. Though I am beginning to wonder where this guy is or if you made him up to keep me begging."

Melanie chuckled. "Yes, it's my evil plot to torture you."

"I'm heading back home this morning." His tone was cautious. "Don't give me that look. I've got to go home sometime."

"Not today."

"It's no big deal."

"Right, so you no longer care Lauren is getting remarried this afternoon?"

Danny shrugged. "Not a thing I can do about it. What's the point?"

"We can be in the Caribbean in three hours, stop the wedding and be drunk by midnight. What do you say? I'm game if you are." And she was, knowing the company jet was always ready at a moment's notice. "Who knows, it could be fun."

"I'm up for the drunk part," he said with a smiled. "But I'm done with Lauren."

"Plan B it is," Melanie said, having already decided upon a diversion. "We need to get your workout clothes and head out. Don't ask."

"This is going to be painful, isn't it?"

What Melanie had in mind was a four-story rock-climbing complex an hour outside the city. It was for serious climbers – no bright plastic hand and foot holds lining a smooth wall. A simulated cliff – Melanie had laughed the first time she'd heard that, but with the safety harnesses she could stretch her limits under supervised conditions.

"Holy shit, Mel." Danny was strapped in, standing arm's length from the wall, gazing toward the ceiling. "How the hell am I supposed to start?"

"Search for cavities in the rock," Melanie said, dusting her hands with chalk, stretching above her head and pulling herself up by an extended piece of shale. Using her feet, she pushed her body high enough to dig her fingertips into a slit. "You can't fall, you're hooked up."

He wasn't convinced, even as he progressed from inches to feet off the ground. Melanie looked down at him as he worked to maintain a minimal distance between them. *Still as competitive as hell,* she grinned, at least his mind was off his troubles.

Circumnavigating the building and reaching the top, he relented. "You win, Mel. I'd throw my arms up in surrender but I've lost feeling in them."

He was still complaining in the car as he tried to change the radio station.

"I'm picking you up in an hour," she threatened, dropping him off at his hotel and laughing as he used his backside to shut the car door.

"Jesus, you're trying to kill me. I'm an old man."

"If you say so, but dinner and shit-faced drunk is the agenda for tonight."

"I'm starting to rethink the drunk part. Rain check?"

"Hell, no. Take a hot shower, you'll feel better. I'll see you in an hour."

Danny nodded. He did look like he'd aged a bit since that morning.

She followed her own advice and changed into a snug deep blue dress, whore heels and a generous amount of eyeliner.

"Wow!" Danny sighed, stepping back into his room to look her over. "Come in, you look gorgeous. I'm almost ready. Do I look okay?"

"And you look rested. How is that possible?" she asked, looking him over in his loose-fitting jeans and gray T-shirt beneath a black blazer. "You were in pretty bad shape when I left you."

"I soaked in the Jacuzzi until my skin was ready to peel off and decided against the getting drunk thing." Danny turned to face her. "I had a breakthrough day and I'd rather not ruin it by blacking out for the evening. I feel so great. I'm not sure if it's because it's over, she's married, or if it's because of you. But I'm ready to put my life back together."

"I can tell."

"And there is one more thing," he said, his voice deep and serious. "I want you back."

Stunned, she didn't move though she thought she'd shaken her head.

"I'm ready to fight for you."

"I'm not ready to give him up." Her answer was barely audible. She hadn't told him or admitted that Adam had let her go.

"Where is he?" He looked around as if Adam should be in the hotel room.

"Doesn't work that way," she said, repeating Adam's words. "I don't want to hurt you, Danny."

"You love me." Danny brushed away a strand of hair.

"Yes, but..."

He shushed her. "How about we go dancing?"

It wasn't a question. He'd already made plans. And even, hours later, as he dropped her off at her door, he was still dodging the relationship conversation.

"Thanks for today," he said, placing a peck on her cheek, his crooked grin claiming victory.

"Danny..."

"'Night." He said, taking the key from her hand and unlocking her door. Then jogged through the dim night back to his car he stopped to blow her a kiss.

"Crap," Melanie said, locking herself inside her apartment.

CHAPTER 18

Danny called before he took the afternoon train home. By then Melanie had already been at work for hours.

"I'll have Avery for two weeks and then she's in Italy. And I'm free for the next two."

"Danny, can we please talk? You're complicating us."

"Beautiful, we're already complicated."

Melanie sighed. "I know, but…"

"I promised I wouldn't interfere when you were with him."

"You know Adam's out of town."

"Mel, I'm not going to force you to do anything." He chuckled. "But I won't stop you when you say you want me, too."

"Ugh, you're giving me a headache," she said, pulling her fingernails from her forehead.

"You've got two weeks to get used to the idea. Bye, Melanie Ward."

"Yeah, bye Danny Ashe." She couldn't stop herself. The reply was a reflex.

Of all the bad timing, Melanie grumbled to herself as she stared out over her desk, seeing nothing. *You've got things to do*, she thought angrily, snapping out of her daze. *Check on him one more time but then focus on Spain.*

The enormous house was in an inconvenient spot. Though it sat atop a hill, the back three-quarters was concealed by the dense rainforest that threatened to engulf the entire fortress. The only exposed areas were the lawn next to the swimming pool and patio that faced the ocean, where she'd found Adam that first time.

The Agency had every resource at its disposal, and yet she continued to bump into limitations while drilling into the confines of Hector's mansion. Audio had proven to be the most challenging. Unless she were on the line, as she had been with Adam, static interfered with cellular transmissions. She couldn't alter the waves from white noise to conversations.

Most of the traffic on the two-lane dirt road from the village was Humvees patrolling the gates. Militants armed with M16s stalked the grounds. Hidden within the trees a sentry would emerge to inspect a truck and occasionally rough up the driver.

What the hell am I doing? Melanie asked herself over and over. *If I could just talk to Adam.*

"Hey, you." Trish sounded entirely too chipper.

"I've got a favor to ask." Melanie thumped her forehead as she said the words. She hated involving Trish – the outcome was never good.

"Name it, Kiddo." She giggled. "There's an old man, actually he's not old at all but he always calls me Kiddo and amazingly I kind of like it. So it's my new expression … It's not an expression, is it?"

"Trish," Melanie took in a deep expanse of oxygen. "I need your help. I don't know what's going on with Adam. He's not answering my calls." She could feel the queasiness from her stomach beginning to surface.

"No way. Oh Mel, what can I do?"

"I have to talk to him."

"Of course you do."

"When he calls Jason – God, I hate to ask this – will Jace have him call me?"

"Hell yeah, anything. He'll call you, I swear." Trish stopped talking for a minute, "Consider it done."

"Thank you," she sighed, throwing her bag in the overhead compartment.

Melanie flew the first commercial flight from Reagan National to Bilbao, Spain. Her first dip back into the proverbial espionage pool, investigating a group of disgruntled Basque. Being Spy Melanie was like shedding a layer of troubles. Stepping out without the burdens of life and starting new. No longer Melanie, just some form of her was exactly what she needed.

At the airport she rented a miniscule vehicle and drove the 30 kilometers to the little town of Balmaseda.

It wasn't late but darkness was thick as Melanie crossed the bridge into the small town. She'd memorized the town square and drove the multitude of narrow, deserted one-way streets around the open plaza to the inn. Though she couldn't see the 15-century cathedral, she felt its presence, grand and looming over the town square. A row of two-and three-story buildings sat across the cobblestone lane. The dim light from the few open doors was gobbled up by the intense blackness. The only activity was from the café, where Andrea worked.

Begonia of Begonia's Pension was seated in one of the embroidered chairs in the second-floor lobby wearing a faded housedress when Melanie arrived. The building and its owner creaked and moaned like they both were from the 15th century.

Melanie followed the direction of Begonia's crooked finger to her sparse room. A full-size bed took up most of the space but along the walls were a dresser, a sink basin and a pair of French doors that faced the church. Stepping up she peered over the fenced, 4-inch ledge that Begonia had sold as a balcony. Cigar smoke wafted up from the boisterous crowd at the café below.

She took her appetite down to greet Andrea and make her first impression with the residents who would be inviting her to their meeting. The group outside was too involved in their conversation to notice her. Inside, the café was bright with the scents and sounds of a restaurant. The glass bar-like counter on one side was vacant and tables and chairs along the other held a handful of couples who stopped talking to frown at her as she entered.

Melanie plastered a pleasant expression on her face and called out a friendly, "Hello."

Wiping her hands on an apron a young woman with brown and pink hair pulled up into a ponytail and lipstick the color of boysenberries came out from the back room.

"Andrea?"

"Si?" Andrea's ready smile faded, replaced by a look of anxiety.

"Soy Melanie, de America," Melanie said.

Andrea recovered but the strain showed through her eyes. "Yes! I am so glad you are finally here. I've been watching for you all day." Her smile returned and she was around the counter in an instant, embracing Melanie and planting a kiss on each cheek. "You must be hungry. Have a seat." Andrea was a speed talker, even in her broken English, but she ushered Melanie to a stool at the counter.

Melanie liked Andrea Velez instantly.

"You had a good trip?" she asked absently, nervously concentrating on selecting food from the display. "There is a local meeting tonight, in about an hour," she whispered, placing a plate of tapas in front of Melanie.

"Am I invited?"

"Of course. Eat and then we go."

Melanie climbed into Andrea's aluminum can and they drove 15 minutes out of town, up a mountain pass to a stone house. Half a dozen cars were parked in the front yard and smoke billowed from the chimneystack.

"If there is a leader in town," Andrea's crooked her head toward the house, "he lives here. The Celaya family has been here for generations and is respected by everyone. This gathering is to unite us locals for the big meeting tomorrow, in Vittoria." She yanked on the emergency brake. "My parents think I met you online. I don't like betraying them. These people here tonight are my friends standing up for equality," Andrea said, pulling at the rubber band and shaking out her hair. "But, this new man…" She stopped and Melanie could feel the concern. "There's something dark about him."

Melanie had already gotten a taste of the tension from the argumentative group outside her balcony. This meeting was more like a family party. She was introduced, each cheek kissed by everyone gathered to discuss politics. The house was small, without enough chairs, so people sat on the floor by the fireplace. Food was spread across two kitchen tables: a quiche, pork strips, fresh bread and bottles of home-brewed wine.

"Eat, Melanie," Andrea's mom said, having great difficulty with her name.

Slipping into cover as Andrea's friend was effortless. These people weren't terrorists, organized and filled with vengeance. They had lists of grievances but their plan to circumvent the law was to fly the Basque flag at all civil buildings.

It was after midnight when they climbed back into Andrea's car.

"Well, what do you think?" Andrea asked. "Those are not a group of rebels."

Melanie could feel the woman's anxiety as she waited for a response. "I agree."

Andrea's posture immediately relaxed. "Oh, thank God, you see that, too." She whooshed out a sigh.

"We'll see what happens at the meeting tomorrow night." Andrea nodded but she looked pale. "It's going to be all right. You did the right thing by calling."

"We'll pick you up at eight tomorrow night – it's about an hour drive and the meeting is at nine-thirty," she said coolly, stopping near the door to Begonia's.

"I'll be ready."

"I'd like to show you around town during the day. You could meet some more friends, see who we are."

Melanie smiled gently. She was tired. "That sounds wonderful."

Grateful for her exhaustion, Melanie sunk onto the bed and didn't stir until mid-morning. She woke stiff and sore and with a desperate need for her toothbrush.

Soft sunlight shone through cracks in the shutters. Curious of her surroundings, Melanie opened the doors to her balcony. Breathless, she stood in awe. The magnificent cathedral of San Sabistino was less than 30 feet away. Built out of limestone mined from a local quarry, a light rain had caused it to glimmer, deepening the yellow and peach hues. It was nearly impossible to believe that something so beautiful and enormous could be compressed into the small space of the plaza. Erected centuries earlier, now it postured directly across the street from a row of shoddy 20th-century buildings. Melanie couldn't believe how oblivious she'd been the night before.

Tearing her gaze away she inspected the rest of her surroundings. An octagon-shaped newsstand was in the southeast corner of the plaza. Clear plastic had been strung up along the two open sides and Melanie could just make out the color of human flesh behind the tarp. A line of school children laughed and skipped through puddles and the neighboring buildings had opened their shutters to the damp autumn day. She could imagine the square packed with people during festivals with colorful flags and flowers.

Taking advantage of the momentary crack in the clouds, Melanie laced up her running shoes and was diverted at the first whiff of a bakery. She ordered a croissant and a black coffee and enjoyed the culture before exploring the quaint town with graffitied walls, sidewalks and billboards.

She jogged along the riverbank, taking photos of the markings and realized she needed to bone up on her Eskara – the Basque language. It was difficult to decipher. And it occurred to Melanie that it was *the* language of rebellion. It affixed the most forgotten letter in the alphabet to the forefront: the usually shy, ultra-confusing letter X. Eskara is the 'Screw You' of languages.

But the city didn't feel at all hostile. The locals were friendly, the streets were clean – other than the graffiti. When she bumped into some of the people she'd met at the party, it was comfortable.

At the inn, Begonia was back in one of the old embroidered chairs, her silvery hair up in a chignon, her tiny body covered from neck to knee by a coarse, gray dress. She dropped her knitting when Melanie walked in and smiled. "How do you like our city?"

"Very nice," Melanie said, sitting beside the woman. "What are you making?"

"This?" She lifted the yarn. "A blanket. The town is expecting three births in the next few months."

"It's a small town that can keep track of births."

"Most of us can trace generations of ancestors in this part, we are a family. Oh, a few we'd like to get rid of, but … what can you do?"

Melanie nodded, thinking more about the Agency than her actual family.

A few minutes before 8 the rowdiness from the street caused her to poke her head out the window. It was her ride. Andrea's father was behind the wheel of a 70's throw back van loaded with at least six more people than it could comfortably hold. Andrea was sticking waist-high out the sunroof, waving for Melanie to come down.

"Will I fit?" Melanie asked. Windows were cranked open to free up space for the arms and shoulders that were hanging out. The suspension was shot by the weight of the passengers and the tires were riding way too low.

"Plenty of room."

Ducking her head down Melanie squeezed herself in – limbs and torsos parted like the waves in the movie The 10 Commandments. But within seconds the gap closed and she was drowning in a sea of bodies. Skin against skin with sweaty strangers.

Antonio honked his way out of town in tempo with the fight song going on inside the vehicle. The rally was getting an early start.

"I'm sorry I didn't see you today. I kept calling but Begonia said you were either sleeping or out."

"It's okay. Thanks anyway – I think I got a good idea of the town. It's nice." Melanie said, pulling herself over a fraction of an inch.

An hour later Melanie's shoulders were pulled in so tight they were nearly touching and her muscles were cramping. Andrea had somehow ended up on her lap and Melanie had to keep knocking Pedro's hand off her thigh.

Fortunately, Antonio was pushing the vehicle to a respectable speed across the well-maintained toll road and they were nearing city lights. Melanie twisted to catch glimpses of suburban sprawl with trashy yards, broken-down cars and cinder-block buildings enclosed by chain-link. A European ghetto.

Cold air rushed in from the open windows, helping Melanie stay conscious in the pit of bodies.

Antonio slowed, spun the van off the road and abruptly accelerated to hop the curb and park among a battalion of aged vehicles.

"Sorry, sorry," he apologized to his cargo that had smashed heads on the ceiling and en masse landed back down on the stiff, coiled seats.

The van joined in with the chorus of complaints.

Melanie pushed Andrea off as the doors opened and the group exploded from the van. She tumbled out onto the front steps of an abandoned church. Stretching, she took in her surroundings: rusted scaffolding along the side of the building with boarded-up windows and fallen ladders. Through the gaps in the haphazardly nailed boards an orange glow filtered to the dirt. There was a buzz in the air. In a herd-like procession people made their way toward the entrance. Her adrenaline spiked like she was arriving at The Garden right before an event.

"Look at this crowd," Pedro griped. "We're going to be stuck in the back."

"This is the biggest yet." Ganix Celaya's eyes were lit with excitement. "We are on the verge of something great. Can you feel it?"

The Balmaseda ensemble gathered at the steps when one of the guards stopped them with a Popeye forearm against Ganix's chest.

"What are your credentials?" he asked.

"I'm Ganix, from Balmaseda. We've been invited to these meetings for months."

The guard eyeballed each person. Melanie erased any emotion from her expression and stood beside Andrea, the least menacing of the bunch. Finally the man nodded and stepped aside. Melanie managed a sideways glance at the man as she passed and her feet nearly failed. She recognized him.

Getting lost in the crowd was easy. Nobody paid attention to her as the familiar feeling grew, the cool calm of being a spy spread through her veins. Melanie grinned and accepted the rush like an addict.

It was standing room only for the 400 people packed into the gutted church. There were no longer pews or adornments, leaving the hallowed ground barren and unfulfilled.

Where the altar should have been, a platform had been erected – a sheet of plywood set atop blocks. Melanie wedged her way closer to the front. Her heart beat violently in anticipation.

From somewhere in the bowels of the mob, a soft murmur of chanting began to grow. Amplifying and pulsating, it traveled through the building as though it were alive. Melanie felt her own pulse fall into rhythm with the movement as a deep voice boomed from speakers.

A dark haired man walked on stage and beamed at his followers, raising his hands in a spurious call for quiet. "Thank you, my friends," he hollered, sending another eruption through the crowd. Chanting and arm pumping continued for an additional minute.

Melanie hadn't realized she was holding her breath until he spoke.

Stunned elation filled her as she stared at the thin man who was supposed to have died a year and a half ago, splattered into oblivion by an explosion inside his car ... an explosion planted by The Agency's tactical rivals. *Thugs*, she thought. But here he was a man simply known as Henry. Her gaze moved to each of his four henchmen, recognizing two who had been with him in his previous life.

Henry, wearing a blue sweater vest over a button down striped shirt and black chinos at the base of the Pyrenees inciting a relatively passive group of people. His voice was smooth and monotone, his eloquent and poignant words started out tame. He praised their predecessors. His dialogue was slow to shift, hardly noticeable, but the words began to take on a sharp edge. Talk of true autonomy and the sacrifices needed to achieve such a goal. At the current pace their great grandchildren might benefit ... but were they willing to wait that long? His men vocalized their dissension with a boisterous "No!" Were they willing to hand over their rights to the Spanish government? "No!" More voices joined the chorus each time he posed a question.

Melanie studied the faces around her, mostly round, older men bald beneath caps or berets. She could feel the blood pressure rising in the room and hoped someone besides her knew CPR. This place was a heart attack waiting to happen.

Henry, she thought, mentally shaking her head and wanting to laugh. He was a master with words, inflaming the pain of unhealed wounds and repressions. Melanie slipped outside while the entire room was entangled in his spellbinding snare. Two men were standing at a barrel fire, warming their hands and laughing while the roar erupted once again from inside.

She dialed. "Ben," her voice was low, "we need to talk."

"Ward? Is that you?"

Startled. "Jack, why are you answering Ben's personal line?"

"Ben has decided he wants to be more hands on, and that includes trips to Asia." Melanie could feel Jack annoyance. He was unused to Ben's antics, so they were still confusing and cumbersome. "He's forwarding all calls to me."

She laughed. "Congrats. Well, you're going to want to take a seat for what I'm about to tell you. Ready?"

"On the edge of my seat," he said, cynically.

"Remember Henry, the head of the R.I.E.?"

"Difficult to forget a man who can convince 1,200 people to collectively commit suicide. What about him?"

"He's pulled a Humpty-Dumpty and put himself together again. Reassembled as a motivational speaker." Melanie ambled around the parked cars, stopping beside a shiny black sedan. She tucked the phone against her shoulder, looking around the windshield and undercarriage for a digital readout attached to the car's computer system.

"No shit! Is that even possible?" He asked, now totally involved.

"Apparently."

"What is it like being you? I cannot believe your luck. You get a nothing assignment and pull out the dead leader of the terrorist community."

"I don't really think terrorists belong to a community."

Jack sighed. "And I'm stuck in this shit-hole office. Okay, so what's your plan?"

"I've pegged his car so Mike can track his movements. I'm going to finish the rally to deter suspicion then U-turn and track him from Balmaseda. Henry. Can you fucking believe it?"

"No. I wish I were with you."

"Can we extradite him? I'd rather you get the jet here and we bring him in quietly. I wouldn't think we need papers, he's already dead, right?"

"Alone? You think that's a good idea?"

"I'll have to wait and see what I'm up against. Unless..." she paused, wondering for the first time what responsibility Jack held. "Unless it's your call now?"

"Not mine. I'm just a seat warmer until Ben gets back. But don't lose him, I could call in the troops ... you're going to need back-up." Jack paused. "If it *were* up to me I'd make sure the fucker was obliterated. He's bad, Mel. That you ran into him before..." she could feel Jack shaking his head.

"It's not luck, Jack. It's Ben. He's got a sixth sense." Melanie smiled, she felt good. "I'll let you know, but at this moment I'm not anticipating any radical move. Patch me over to Mike, will you?"

"Good luck, Ward."

Finding a receptor, Melanie aimed the red laser of her phone at the sedan and waited for Mike.

"Hey, I need to relay some information I retrieved from a vehicle. Can you check that we have its position and attach a GPS monitor?"

"Give me a sec," Mike said, the usual tapping of keys in the background. "Okay, I've got the data. It's going to take me a minute to triangulate the signals. I'll call you right back."

Melanie rubbed her eyes. She was going to have to go back to Balmaseda with Andrea to maintain her cover ... that meant a minimum of two hours before she could get to Henry. There was no way for him to know he was being tracked and Mike was the best – it wasn't perfect, but it was damn good.

"You *are* the master, because that was lightning fast," she said, answering her phone. "Are we up and ready?"

"Um, it's Adam."

Melanie stood at the top of Spain, the wind knocked out of her as her mind whirled, trying to shift back to civilian mode.

"Mel?" he asked softly.

"I wasn't expecting you," her breath faltered as she spoke.

"Really? Because Trish is punishing Jason until I call you. No sex. Personally I think Jace can outlast her … but I promised, so, what is it you wanted?"

What did she want? She couldn't remember. Her heart pounded – and she was beginning to sweat out in the cold. *Should I lie and ask about Parker?*

"You're calling so Jason can get laid?" She asked, stalling.

"What difference does it make? I'm calling."

"Wow, okay." She sank down, hiding between the cars. "I wanted to find out what was going on."

Adam sighed. "You already know what's going on."

"Please," rubbing her forehead she said, "I don't have time for puzzles." She sounded angry. "Remember you promised you'd come back if things weren't going well?"

"It's going well."

"NOT for me. It isn't going well at all, *for me*." She lowered her voice and for a silent second she thought she'd gotten through to him.

Clearing his throat he whispered, "I'm … I'm with someone else."

"That's bullshit." She swallowed as a tingling sensation crept along her skin. He remained quiet and when she spoke again her voice was even. "You wouldn't do that." If she'd been aware of a conscious thought she'd have been disturbed by the sudden calm that overtook her.

"You give me too much credit."

"Who is she, then?"

"You don't know her." He grumbled and she could see him, jaw clenched and cold eyes distant. "I knew her from before. Her name is Terese. She gets me … the real me. I don't have to pretend around her."

Melanie weakened, having stopped listening after the name. "Hector's wife? You're fucking Hector's wife?"

"How … how do you know who she is?"

Melanie clenched her chattering teeth so hard they hurt. "Jesus, Adam. What are you doing?"

"Exactly what I've been trained to do."

"No, listen. I've got to finish something here and then I'm coming for you. I'm going to get you out." Her heart hammered to get out of her chest.

"You will not do any such thing!"

"You promised," she breathed.

"What is the word of an assassin worth?"

"I trusted you." Sucking in the cold air, Melanie, swiped away moisture from her cheek.

When he spoke again, his voice had less of an edge. "I belong here."

She shook her head. "You're wrong. Besides what happens if they find out about Hector?"

"Only two people who know about that," his reply was clipped.

"Jesus Christ! Did you just threaten me?" Her blood ran icy through her veins.

"No! No, that came out wrong. I would never hurt you."

"What's the word of an assassin worth?" she asked.

It had been a threat and they both knew it … whether he'd instinctively spoke as a survival technique … he was changing.

"Melanie," Andrea called from the doorway, "the rally is ending. I don't want us to be separated."

Draining the emotion from her voice, she covered the receiver and called back. She had only a couple of minutes to clear up the tangle of troubles with Adam. Turning back to him, she said, "We're not over."

"Fuck, Melanie, are you on a job?" he snapped.

"What does it matter?"

"It matters," his voice lost its deep menacing quality, "because it isn't safe. Why the hell did you take my call?"

"Your number was blocked … I thought you were someone else … I would've answered anyway. I needed to hear your voice," she said, fighting to remain in control.

"Are you in danger?"

Melanie sighed. "I don't know," she said, feeling nothing. The tears had dried and the place where her heart should be felt as empty as the abandoned church.

"God damn it! Where are you?"

"You know I can't tell you that." She looked up to see Andrea at the door waving her urgently back indoors. "I love you and I thought we did understand each other. I thought that was part of our bond." She didn't know what more to say and there was no more time. "I've got to go. Thanks for calling."

"Melanie, it's foolish to hold onto me. Move on."

She nodded, her facial muscles clamped.

She jogged back inside the room, dazed and numb. Andrea had already retreated a few feet in and stood on her tiptoes to hear. Melanie lingered at the entrance. The volume of the crowd rose to a fevered pitch.

"Andrea," she tapped her shoulder, "Hey, I'm not going back with you. The van is too crowded … make an excuse for me." Melanie had no definite plan.

"What's this?" Andrea asked.

"The key to my room. I'm paid up and I've got what I need in my bag." She nodded to her messenger bag across her shoulder.

"You aren't coming back?"

"Not sure." She shook her head, exasperated. Having no energy for creativity she stated the first lie that came to mind. "I met a couple of old friends and I'm hitching a ride with them."

Andrea nodded, looking confused, and when she turned to look at Henry delivering his final push, Melanie disappeared.

She felt raw. Scraped to the bone. Listening to Henry spew poison turned her emptiness to rage – against the charismatic insurgent and the gullible masses. She stepped back into the night not really knowing what she was going to do. Only that she had to remove herself from the temptation of taking out Henry right then and there.

The wind had picked up and the cold was cutting through her jacket. It felt good. Her words with Adam were already pushed into some dark recess of her mind. Moving along the parked cars she stopped where she could keep an eye on the sedan and broke into the one nearest the exit.

She had no tools. No gear to help with eavesdropping, tracing or surveillance … nothing but a cell phone, her hands and her gun.

Henry and his men burst from the rear of the church, laughing and congratulating each other on their success.

Bastard, Melanie swore under her breath. Maybe if Henry hadn't cocked his head back, or maybe if the men hadn't slapped each other on the back she wouldn't have done it. But she did.

Yanking out the wires beneath the steering column, she ignited the engine and threw the car into reverse. Henry and his cohorts, too entertained by their own magnitude to notice they were being followed, fled the parking lot, unaware. Through the small streets she raced behind them, struggling to keep up as she pushed the oxidized silver car as hard as it could go. The screaming agony of metal on metal made her regret having to shift gears as she steadied the wobbly steering wheel.

Shit! She slowed enough to dig her phone from her pocket and answer the damn call.

"Yeah?" she shouted over the noise of air whistling entering through seals around the windows.

"Okay, I've got the vehicle tagged. It's going like 200 kph."

"I know, I'm following them. Well, trying. I should've been more choosy about the car I borrowed but ... damn! It's about to drop the transmission. Hold on," she transferred her phone to her shoulder. Giving her the use of both hands.

"What happened?"

Melanie grunted and took a sharp turn. "You don't want to know. I'll call you when I'm done here."

"Done with what?"

"Saving the planet. I'm a superhero, didn't you know?" Mike stayed quiet. "I'm in the middle of a car chase." She'd missed a turn, slammed the car into reverse and swung around. "I'm a little distracted. I'll call you later."

"You're driving and sounding like you're having a breakdown. Who pissed you off?"

"Great, let me grab a pillow and we'll have a conversation on your couch."

"I'm going to link you up with my tracking."

"Aren't you listening? There isn't one bit of technology in this tin piece of shit. There's no linking. Mike, I'd really love to stay and chat, Shit! They turned. Fuck!" She sped past the car as it pulled into a concealed driveway. Killing the weak flickering headlights of her car, she backtracked on the silent road twice to get a feel for the space before idling off the side. "You still there?" She asked picking up the fallen phone. "No? Good."

Exchanging her phone for her gun she did the math: Henry plus – she would assume – four well-trained, dangerous men and a dark house.

The night was cold and still. Craning her neck out the window, the stars littered the sky and the moon cast bright shadows over the brushy terrain. Melanie pushed her car to the base of the driveway to block the exit and jogged along the side of the long drive.

Keeping to the edges, her breath escaping in pillows of fog, she approached the vehicle. Henry sat beside the driver and the other three were in the back seat. Pressed against the rear tire she summoned her alter-ego before stepping up to rap on Henry's window.

A full two seconds passed before the laughter stopped.

"Hi," Melanie smiled when the window opened. "I was at the rally tonight."

"You've got a groupie," the driver said, making the men howl.

Henry settled his gaze on Melanie and raised his hand. His men stopped.

"Do I know you?" he asked, his brows pulled in so close they nearly touched.

"No," Melanie said, sharing a silent communication with Henry. His deep-set eyes took in the information without a trace of anxiety.

"Who are you?"

"Unimportant. What matters is that currently we have a couple of options," she said. Her fingertips caressed the texture of her gun, loving how the weight was balanced in her palm.

"I see only one," he said.

A blast cracked and Melanie bent to look inside his window. Henry had fired off a shot from his small-caliber directly in line with her abdomen.

"Bulletproof." Using her pistol she thumped twice on the outside of the door, where the bullet was lodged, and smiled. "Lucky me."

"What do you want? Money? Information?" He glared at her through hollow, cavernous eyes.

"Both sound good, but for the moment I'll take you. Get out."

"Bullshit." He glared. "What are you morons waiting for? Kill her!" His yell cut into the quiet night.

The driver was clumsy with his weapon and Melanie sent out two rounds, taking out both of his hands. Within that second a bullet, from the house, ricocheted off the top of the car, missing her only because Henry had kicked open his door with enough force to knock her to the ground. The men were no longer laughing but firing from all directions as she disappeared into the thorny brush that lined the drive.

"Don't let her escape," Henry ordered. "She recognized me."

Melanie settled into the dark, blending with the night shadows.

Stupid, stupid, she thought but even as she scolded her situation she felt good. Happily, pulling in a lung full of dusty air.

Henry shouted out threats and promises as she checked the two full magazines stored in the side pocket of her cargo pants. She slid out of her hiding spot, behind a lagging member of Henry's posse. Grabbing the back of his jacket she drove the barrel of her gun up under his ear. "Drop the weapon," she commanded.

The man was obstinate, reaching out to grab her off his back. Melanie rammed her boot into the back of his knees, buckling him down into a praying position. *Son of a bitch*, she thought as the man hollered out in pain. Twisting his gun arm to his spine, she hunkered down behind the bulk of the man and fired off rounds at the figures; one running toward her and the other behind the car door. Adjusting her aim to allow for her odd angle she heard one body hit the ground hard and the scream of another as her human shield shuttered. He'd taken two bullets in the chest. He slumped forward and the weight of him tipped her with him. Losing her balance she rolled to the edge of the drive.

With long strides she flew over the soft, mulchy terrain to the back of a corrugated tin shed 10 yards from the house. Leaning against the small structure, panting, she peeked around the corner to an obstructed view of the back porch. As she watched, the pallid yellow lights blinked off, flickered back to life and finally died, leaving the world washed in the colorless gleam of the moonbeams.

Melanie recalculated her odds. Two men had been eliminated and two injured … with one being the driver who was no longer a threat unless he could fire off a gun with his toes. Over her shoulder was an unknown, a silent threat inside the dark house.

Changing out her clip, she made her move, gliding forward when a high-pitch shriek ripped through the tranquil night. Melanie didn't wait for the first bullet, her belly already pressed to the cold ground.

Melanie could see the side of the house where a woman, holding a long-barreled shotgun was shooting high and indiscriminately. Melanie waited for the woman to reload before jumping to her feet and sprinting the short distance to the back door. From the second story she heard the lookout yell out her location. Backing up against the thorny lattice, from the corner of her eye she caught a movement at the edge of the porch.

Melanie fired once. The woman hit the wooden steps with a hard thump and slipped to the gravel.

Melanie climbed the brittle crisscross frame up to the porch roof. Henry's eyes glowered from the darkened window, light glistened from the muzzle of his pistol. He and Melanie fired in sync. She lost her footing, rolled and scraped her arm on the gutter as she fell.

Favoring her gun arm, she twisted in mid-flight and landed in a privet hedge. The wind knocked out of her and her arm burning, she coughed and shook off the dizziness. Blinking until her eyes cleared, she crept to the front of the house.

At her feet lay the woman with the shotgun, her face to the ashen gravel, her legs strewn over the bottom three stairs. Stepping across her body Melanie gingerly swung open the front door. A warm draft of heavily scented air escaped from the otherwise still house.

The bare floorboards creaked with every step, effectively ending her stealth strategy.

"It's over," Melanie yelled into the darkness. She paused, straining to hear any response. "Come out and you won't be hurt."

Keeping her back to the wall she climbed the stairs to the quiet second floor. At the top of the stairwell were four doors, all closed.

Taking a deep breath, Melanie cleared each room, on guard for an ambush at any moment.

In the last room she checked, the drapes waved in the light breeze and Henry lay motionless at the base of the bed. She checked for a pulse but he was dead.

Stashing his gun in her pants at the small of her back she moved swiftly downstairs. The kitchen was the last area to be checked. She entered off the living room and from the corner of her eye she felt the energy of a living person. Plunging to one knee she fired off two rapid shots.

Melanie flicked on the lights and saw a woman on the floor, wounded but rising up on her elbow. Under her body was a baby. Melanie's heart lunged as the woman put the gun to the baby's head.

"You did this," she gargled, blood spilling from her lip.

"No!" Melanie screamed, putting three more bullets into the fallen woman, who collapsed, smothering the child. Kicking the gun out of the woman's hand Melanie gripped her shoulder and hauled her off the baby.

The infant's blue dress was covered in blood and she was limp as Melanie gathered her into her arms. Melanie's heart lodged in her throat and her hands shook as she turned the baby over and looked into the glass eyes.

Her mind shifted from horror to relief. "It's a doll," she shouted. "It's just a doll." Tears spilled over her eyelids as she breathed. She drooped to the linoleum, exhausted. The woman's body to her left and the doll still in her arms, Melanie lowered her head and cried.

CHAPTER 19

He'd made the call from a rocky inlet at the bottom of the cliff, the safest place at the palacio. Adam had used one of the secret escape routes Hector had built from his office and bedroom out to the sea.

Speaking with Melanie had been harder than he believed it could be. After the call, somehow he'd found himself on the steps of the village church, looking up at the stained glass window. A long time ago, he'd known the priest but that man had been old back then.

The flames of the candles swayed as he entered the cool church. He kneeled in the weathered confessional waiting for the tattered curtain to slide open.

"Forgive me, Father, but it has been 20 years since my last confession."

"What brings you back, my son?" the man on the other side wheezed and coughed.

"Padre, is it really you?" Adam said, squinting with his fingers seizing the filigree that separated him from the old man.

"The good Lord hasn't seen fit to take me home, yet. It's been a long time since you've been across from me. Please, tell me what's on your mind."

"You remember me?"

"I remember." Said the shaky voice.

Adam sighed in relief. "My life brings me back." The priest was patient and waited for Adam to speak. "I don't know what to do or why I'm here." He stopped, hoping the advice would come without more explanation. It didn't. "I hurt people, Father. I didn't mean to but it happened and she's so…" he trailed off. "I belong here. I feel like I've returned home … and she's too good … she belongs to the world that I left. I don't deserve to even consider keeping her … I'm evil, Father."

"I've prayed for you all these years that you had found freedom from your demons. I will continue the vigil." The priest's soft voice was melodic. "I don't believe that you are evil. After you left, Señor Hector," Adam saw the shadow as the man crossed himself in respect for the dead, "sought out my counsel. He loved you and we prayed together many times. In the end I believe he had forgiven himself and he'd forgiven you."

A lump lodged in Adam's throat, blocking his airways. He choked back the sob. The padre's words were meant to be uplifting, he knew, but… "I haven't forgiven me."

Adam lowered his head into his hands.

"Then that is what I will pray for."

"Father there aren't enough prayers in this world to rid me of my sins."

"We can always try. Anything is possible with God by your side."

Adam didn't believe in a world where God was by his side. He'd never been before.

Reading his thoughts, "God loves you." Said the holy man from behind the little window.

With his eyes downcast, he wanted to be accepted and forgiven. He wanted to be a whole person. The incense was making his head feel fuzzy. "No good has ever come to the people I've loved. I am incapable of love," Adam whispered.

Closing his eyes he replayed the conversation he'd just had with Melanie. He'd hurt her. His heart died a little in that phone call. *I'm not good enough for her but maybe Ashe is*. Adam was startled by the truth in his thoughts and the silence hung in the rich air. "How about my penance?" he finally choked out.

Outside he felt numb, watching the trucks zipping by. Religion didn't make him feel any better. He dragged his fingers through his overgrown hair struggling for inner stillness.

"Look who's here," a voice echoed from the street.

Adam glanced up at a truckload of his friends. "Where are you going?"

"The bar to get drunk," the driver said.

"Now that's what I'm talking about."

The man in the passenger seat hopped into the back and Adam took his place in the front.

CHAPTER 20

"I may have caused a bit of trouble," Melanie said after Ben's assistant, Janet, forwarded her call. Melanie's foot rammed against the floorboard of the stolen clunker. Her official story of the evening included everything except her sobbing on the floor and Adam's phone call. She'd shoved that to the back of her mind to deal with later, or forget entirely. "One got away … but he was injured." She'd found the fourth man by the shed, peppered by shotgun pellets.

"Body count?" Ben asked when she'd finished.

Melanie blew out a huge sigh. "Four men, two women."

"And you're positive it was Henry?"

"I took DNA samples from all the dead, video and snapshots. I'm about an hour below the French border" *and I'm in a stolen vehicle, which I'll ditch before crossing*, she decided.

"Not a good time to be caught as a spy," Ben gargled out the obvious and Melanie snickered. "Right," Ben sighed, his mind elsewhere, "never a good time – I'll send a clean-up crew in before notifying the authorities."

"I've got a side trip to make before heading back to the Agency," she said, gritting her teeth against the car that was about to lose a steering wheel.

"No, I want you back home. I won't rest until you're safely at the Manor." Reading her thoughts he added, "That's a directive, Ward. No worming around – first flight non-stop. I'll be waiting, I'm on my way home as we speak."

"How was Asia?"

"Don't try to distract me, Agent. Straight home."

"Understood. I'll notify you when I have details on the flight." She cranked the heat to full blast in attempt to restore feeling to her fingers. The coughing engine strained under the added responsibility. "*Piece of shit car*," she said, accidentally breaking the knob.

"Okay, Mel," she resorted to speaking in order to distract from the cold, but her breath came out in vapors. "Damn!" she blew on her fingers. *What a night*, she thought as the sun began to brighten the clear sky. *Don't think about it,* she advised her exhausted self.

Battling with the car and the chill was an effective diversion. And the feeling that if she stopped even for a moment she'd break, was too strong to ignore. There was too much to do, and there was no time for a breakdown.

"Excuse me, ma'am." Melanie, blurry-eyed, squinted, first at the woman's hand jostling her shoulder and then up into her face. Her phony smile faltered. "You're going to have to put your seat in the upright position. We're landing."

She'd slept the entire flight. Her head was hazy, the left side of her body ached and she wondered about her ribs. She rubbed circulation back into her face.

It was going to be a long day of inquiry and celebration. According to Mike the party had already been arranged in the conference room.

She stared out the window. She was supposed to be feeling delight. *All I feel is beaten up*, she thought as the plane bounced onto the runway, brakes squealing to a stop. She hooked the strap of her bag over her shoulder and took her place towing her luggage in the slow-moving line. Her chest lightened slightly at the sight of Ben.

"Hi, Boss," she said. "What are you doing here?"

"I was in the neighborhood," he said, taking the bag and jiggling it. "It's empty."

"Almost. I bought a few souvenirs at the airport. Can't board an international flight without luggage, especially with this face." She pointed to the small, pink swell on her cheek. "I left most of my stuff with the informant, she's about my size." Taking his arm, "Did you have fun getting your hands dirty with agents in the Orient?"

"I won't believe what they say about you if you don't believe what they say about me." Ben said, though his expert eye was evaluating her.

"You okay?" She noticed the bagginess of his suit. "Didn't they feed you over there?"

"Been keeping busy. I must say, I'm pleasantly surprised to see you in one piece." The crinkles around his eyes and lips deepened as his mouth curved into a smile.

"Why wouldn't I be?"

"Ward, you refused medical treatment. My guess was because you didn't want to be told you couldn't fly."

"I refused because I'm fine. But *I must say*," she laughed as she mocked him, "I am feeling the love." He smiled and gently squeezed her sore arm. "Hey, are you checking my pulse? Wow, you're sneaky! I really am okay." They stopped walking long enough for their eyes to meet. "So, I'm not exactly *okay*, but I am a quick healer."

"You got Henry." His eyes twinkled and Melanie felt the elation ripple under her skin. It was the bliss that came after a successful mission.

"I did."

Ben put an arm around her shoulder and gripped her tightly. He was proud and she knew it. "Let's get back.

"I had arranged a conference. I wanted you to go over the incident in detail with the other agents. Explain how this opportunity presented itself and how you took advantage of the situation."

Melanie groaned. She hated these meetings where she was supposed to dissect her thought process.

"It's a learning experience for the newer agents. But hold your grumbling. I was out-voted."

"Really? Since when do you put anything up for a vote?"

"We're having a party instead."

Melanie groaned again.

Their car was waiting at the curb, Marcos holding open the door. He nodded a quick acknowledgement as she clumsily fell into the back seat while trying to protect her side.

"A party?" Melanie asked.

"Complete with cupcakes and punch."

"Sounds festive," she said, sarcastically, not looking forward to the part she was going to play. "Any way to avoid it?"

"I'm glad you asked." Ben smiled devilishly and knocked on the window that separated them from the driver.

"What trap did I just fall into?"

"I'm taking you to the clinic." He put up his hands to ward off her complaints. "See, this is why I didn't trust anyone else with this task. You'd charm your way out of going to the doctor. You have a way about you."

Melanie looked out the window. "I always thought I was closer to annoying than charming."

"Both, actually. But it works for you."

Melanie leaned her head back and closed her eyes, "Yeah, well, it's not working now. I feel like shit."

She went into the clinic with a willing spirit, napping during the X-ray and changing back into jeans as soon as she was free to move about.

"Hello, Ms. Ward, I'm Dr. Monroe."

Melanie shook his hand. "Yeah, where's Andy? Dr. Young." She added as Dr. Monroe squinted at her chart.

"Oh, retired or private practice, not really sure," he said without looking up.

"No," she said, disappointed. She'd known Andy for years – and he knew her – she was not in the mood to break in a new doctor.

"That's what I heard." He shrugged.

Melanie took another look at Dr. Monroe. Late twenties, wedding ring, receding hairline – she gave him two years before he shaved his head entirely. "You have catsup on your smock."

"Lunch. Would you mind leaning back?" He gestured behind her where the exam table angled up.

"Actually, I do mind. Sorry."

"You have a nasty set of bruises. It must be painful," he said, smacking his lips,

"It's not."

"Okay, then."

"Okay, then, what? That's it?" Melanie asked, confused. "I realize I'm a bit jet-lagged but ... are you even a doctor?"

The catsup-stained doctor sat on the round, wheeled stool and rolled up to her, face to face. "*Andy* may not have told you about *me* but he left extensive notes about *you*." He looked at her with eyes so dark brown the pupil was indistinguishable. "You have no internal bleeding, no life-threatening injuries and you're not going to follow any advice I give you ... I don't see any point in wasting your time or mine. I simply wanted to see the mark."

Melanie studied Dr. Monroe, his perfect olive complexion, long lashes and laughed. "All right, Doc, you want to see the bruise?" He helped her lean back, putting a couple pillows behind her head and lifted her T-shirt up over her bra. His fingers were cool and gentle pressing along the edges of the purple marking on her side.

"It's ugly but it's healing and there is hardly any inflammation around your ribs ... If I wrote out a prescription would you take it?" he asked, helping her back into a sitting position.

"Not unless it says I should avoid office parties."

"Well, you should stay away from dancing." He said, helping her off the table.

Melanie was at the door, curious. "So, what does my file say ... you're just letting me off like this?"

"That you're stubborn and never do as instructed." She nodded, uncertain. Turning to go, Dr. Monroe added with a grin, "Don't worry, yours isn't the most interesting."

"You're not telling me something I don't already know." She left the room still considering her take on the new guy. "Hey," she said, "you waited?" Ben was in a plastic chair reading a health magazine.

"You thought I wouldn't?"

"You're a busy man."

"What's the verdict?"

"Jet lag," Melanie said as Ben fell into step along side her.

"Sounds like your diagnosis."

"Ugly was the official term but no internal bleeding … just another day at the office."

A deep groan escaped from his throat. "I should've gone in there with you."

"Next time."

"Where've you been?" Mike asked, breathlessly. "I couldn't keep them off the cupcakes. Really they're more like vultures than humans." He said, loud enough for all to hear.

"That's okay, I'm supposed to stay off sweets," Melanie said, patting his back. "Thanks for trying."

"Good to see you, Ward," Jack said, grinning and bending down to give Melanie an unexpected hug.

"Thanks."

"Agent Ward is here," Mike called out to get the party started. Melanie turned to plead silently with Ben.

"Are you sure you don't want to come out with us?" Jack asked as a dozen people left the Manor to continue the party at an after-hours club.

"I'm positive."

"Great party, Mel!" Mike said, his goofy grin crooked as he stumbled with two thumbs up.

"You're taking him?" she asked, shifting her gaze back to Jack.

"I'm sticking him in the car and having Marcos drive him home. How'd he get drunk, anyway?"

"Champagne."

Jack snorted at the feebleness of some men and pushed open the doors. "Tomorrow."

That wasn't so horrible, she thought, taking the elevator up to her office. Recounting the events she only excluded losing it in the kitchen, and had told only Jack about the doll.

"Shit, a doll?" he'd said. "That's just creepy."

Melanie shivered at the thought of those blinking eyes and pushed the macabre out of mind by waking up her computer. Seemed like ages since she'd checked on Parker. *One more day won't matter*, she reasoned as her fingers plugged in the longitude and latitude of the house on the cliff.

When the image cleared she was crashing a party. Colored lights trimmed the patio and a big bonfire burned in the grassy yard beside the pool. Tables and chairs had been set up along the porch and luminarias floated on lily pads in the blue water.

She zoomed in on one laughing face after another, paying particular attention to the women. As she narrowed down her choices for Terese, her gut rolled with nerves and jealousy, the intense desire to know – while knowing she'd be better off leaving it alone.

There was no shortage of beautiful women – Melanie's breath quickened as she turned to the men. There were one or two handsome, younger men who must be getting all the action. Because as a whole, it was a collection of perhaps the most unattractive men ever assembled – a prominent display of belly fat, bulbous facial features and unusually short limbs.

You're going to have to stop doing this. It's not healthy, Melanie sighed as she shut down her computer without finding Adam.

She pushed through the door of her Manor apartment, wanting only a hot shower and a set of clean sheets. She stopped as her boot crunched down on a manila envelope that had been slipped under her door. Melanie's name on the front was in Mike's robotic scrawl. He'd mentioned a present earlier but she'd envisioned a new gadget, an app for her phone or some chocolaty delectable, not paperwork.

The item was too heavy and she knew she couldn't handle anything of importance before a shower. Flinging the package onto her bed, Melanie stripped and ignored the mirror. *These bruises will heal – just like the others*, she thought, testing the temp of the water as her phone rang.

"Hello?" she said, reluctantly twisting the handles to stop the flow of hot water.

"Can you speak or are you still on the job?"

Adam.

"I'm in D.C.," she said, feeling a new kind of low and sinking down to the edge of the tub.

"I was worried."

"Yeah, well, I'm not your problem anymore *and* I can take care of myself. Been doing it for years." She heard the sounds of laughter erupting in the background. "At a party?"

"Dia de los Muertes."

"Sounds festive."

"Look, I'm sorry."

"For?"

"That phone call."

"No sweat." She said, cutting him off, not knowing if she could handle hearing more. "It's late and I'm tired." *My body aches and I can't do this.*

"I'm trying to apologize."

"Unless you're apologizing for something major ... I don't want to hear it."

Adam breathed hard into the receiver for the second time. "What's major? Because maybe I am."

"Leading me on, making me believe lies, for having an affair ... all of that, Adam, all of that is major."

He didn't hesitate. "Yeah, I am sorry for all of that."

Melanie nodded, tears pricking. "Okay, consider yourself heard. Your guests will be wondering where you ran off to..."

"Suppose so." His voice softened. "I know you'll take care of yourself so I'll leave you with goodnight."

Her lips were clamped. Unable to speak she nodded and ended the call with silence. Sitting on the cold porcelain tub, leaning her head against the tiled walls she felt drained and overwhelmed by the crushing sadness of that weird conversation.

Even her favorite pajamas weren't enough to comfort her to sleep. Propping two pillows behind her back she tore open Mike's gift. The papers were clipped together, a small stack of less than half a dozen sheets. Melanie tipped the envelope and Salvador Luhan's SIM card tumbled onto the bedspread.

Melanie couldn't continue to fool herself into believing she would find sleep and it was – sort of – a reasonable time to rise. Before coffee and a doughnut she went to find Ben.

"You look at home," she said, entering his office. Jack was sitting behind the big desk looking disgruntled.

He looked up at her with two gray streaks beneath his eyes and managed a thin smile. "Don't be jealous. It's really not much fun."

"I know." She'd been Ben's sidekick for years. "I think you are a good fit. Ben needs someone stable, and lately I'm like a lightning rod." She took her usual seat. "Where is he?"

"Good question. Gone. Somewhere. He keeps getting these ideas in his head and then, whoosh." Jack tried not to roll his eyes. "He's gone and I'm stuck here. Anyway," he sighed, "you should've come out with us last night."

"What time did you get in? You look like shit."

"Thanks. I was in bed by one. I can't believe I used to do that every night." Jack laughed. "I think it'll be my last free night for awhile."

"Yeah, well, I'd trade places with you." Before Jack could process and start the litany of questions Melanie continued, "If it's all right with you my sister-in-law is due any day and I'd like to get back to San Diego."

"Ben might have other plans for you."

"Like what?"

"Like Finn," he said, his eyebrows raised and the smile stretching across his face. "He's still in Malibu. Dicking around with the protesters."

"And what? You want me to go and bring him back? I don't know if you've noticed but there's some animosity between me and Parker."

"Your name was thrown out there."

"Then throw it back because sending me is not a good idea." Melanie shook her head. "I'll do whatever you want but … you've got my number." She reached the door and turned. "When I get back if you could keep both Parker and me busy I'd appreciate it."

Jack pulled his head back, surprised. "You've always said keeping Finn away from an assignment was best for humanity."

"That's still true, but keeping him occupied is best for me. See ya, Jack."

Melanie lifted her bag over her shoulder and headed to the below-ground garage where Marcos was ready to drive her to the airport.

CHAPTER 21

The usual feeling of homecoming didn't greet her as the plane touched down. Regret and disappointment clouded the beautiful blue sky as she headed east on Interstate 8, toward Luhan Motors. There was no point in putting off the inevitable; Salvador Luhan was about to have an especially bad day.

He was no hero.

Mike had broken into the SIM card she'd captured from the cell in Luhan's safe, printed the numbers and transcribed the texts. The phone had been activated in April. There were only three numbers associated with this cell: Sal's office, his girlfriend Becky and a prepaid, untraceable number. But it was the messages that did the damage, four succinct texts. Three dealt with the 'incident,' arranging a time and place, agreeing upon a dollar amount and directions to wire the funds to an offshore account. The final instruction was disposing the phone by smashing the device and dropping it overboard on a deep-sea fishing venture.

Parking in a visitor space of the distinctive circular glass building, Melanie shifted her sunglasses to the top of her head and adopted a new personality – one without remorse for Luhan's fall, without pity for the man who seemed to have such potential.

She rushed through the lot in an effort to avoid the hungry commission-based sales agents. Inside the showroom from the ceiling and upper balcony flew *Luhan for Congress* banners and the shiny new cars on display were already outfitted with Luhan bumper stickers. The lobby, though nearly empty, was abuzz with energy.

Climbing the curved stairway that mimicked the architecture to the second-floor offices, Melanie spotted Sal inside his glass cage.

"Can I help you?" he asked, sounding more perturbed than helpful when Melanie let herself in and took a seat.

"I'm wondering if you know that your office is being bugged," she asked, already scrambling the airwaves. "Curious," she said, analyzing his expression, wondering if he was the one bugging his own office, for security reasons. "Makes no difference, just gives me less time." She sat in the ultra modern leather chair in front of his desk.

"What the … who the hell are you?" His dark eyes narrowed and his bushy brows tugged in close, separated only by a crease. "I've seen you," he mumbled.

"See, I knew you'd remember. But it only adds to my disappointment." Melanie tsked as Sal leaned forward. Now he was curious.

"Independence Day!" He pointed at her then touched the tip of his nose. "You were at the party with Javier." He leaned back, his laughter full of relief. "I think he's on a test drive but I can't help you, anyway. Javier is my employee but he does what he does."

Melanie snorted. "Javier is great." They'd sort of dated over the summer. "But this isn't about him. It's about you."

"Me?"

She nodded, holding eye contact. "The problem is, Sal – may I call you Sal?" He nodded and she continued. "The problem is that I like you. I was rooting for you. Slime ball politicians are a dime a dozen, but you ... I could imagine you making a change, doing good work. Maybe if you'd gone about it legitimately ... you probably would have been eaten alive but you'd been able to look yourself in the mirror. Now?" She shrugged. "We need to discuss your withdrawing from the race."

"Ha! You're crazy," he barked, nervously.

"Your valiant rescue was staged and I have the evidence."

"I don't know what you're talking about." Luhan said with trembling lips.

Melanie reached into her back pocket and unfolded a copy of the transcripts, smoothed them out and slid the papers in front of Sal.

He looked at the first page, his face pulled back in a grimace and his color drained

"How did you get these?"

Melanie shrugged one shoulder.

"You broke into my home? That's illegal!"

"Really? That's your defense?" she asked. "I did feel kind of bad about it at the time ... now I'm just pissed."

"What do you want? Money? When I'm in Congress I could do favors."

"Why does everyone always think I want money?" She looked down at herself. "Do I really come across as a gold digger?"

"Then what is it?"

"Law abiding representatives? Too much to ask?"

"I have friends in high places. They can do amazing things," he said, his voice faltering at the end.

"There are no friends in politics and no one is above the law."

"Except you."

"I guess." She laughed, he was following along.

Salvador stared at her, the muscles in his shoulders slackened. "I knew you'd come, not you but someone like you. I told him but he said he had everything covered." Sal shook his head.

"Who told you?"

"You're the detective – you figure it out." He grunted before retreating into thought.

"The election is in six days – I'll give you three days to step aside citing personal reasons. If there's no word from your camp on day four, I go to the media. I can promise that no one will be standing beside you." Melanie stood and spoke again from the door, "Look around, Sal, you're not doing badly here. Consider this a blessing in disguise. Politics is a nasty business."

From the vantage point at the top of the stairs she could see Javier striding across the lobby. He looked exactly the same as in her memories, languid and sexy with slick, jet-black hair tied back into a stubby ponytail, bronzed skin and an easy grin. Recollecting her cataclysmic summer was not high on her to-do list. But Javier had helped her survive those two months of turmoil. Moving like molten lava between the new cars, he led a woman, his fingers splayed across the small of her back, to his office.

Melanie's smile was unconscious, the heat of the memory rushing up her collar. *That woman is in for a treat*, she thought, skirting the salesmen toward the front doors.

Over her shoulder she caught Sal pacing, speaking animatedly on his phone. She'd left his life in chaos and felt nothing. No remorse, no guilt. Settling her sunglasses back on the bridge of her nose she exited Luhan Motors.

The familiarity of her hometown complicated her internal dialogue. She needed down time from the bravado of Spy Melanie – of knowing more, ruling the situation and forcing an opponent to succumb.

Melanie weaved her way through the tidy, narrow streets of La Jolla trying to grapple between bad-ass secret agent and regular Melanie.

"Hello?" she called out, already knowing her parents weren't home. Her mother's presence was larger than one room, filling the house with energy. Today it was vacant.

Dialing her dad's cell, Rita answered. "Hello?"

"Hey, Mom."

"Melanie, what are you doing at the house?"

Melanie smiled. "I got a couple of days off and I'm not sure that'll happen again for awhile and I wanted to … be here in case the baby is born."

"Wouldn't that be something? Well, I can't really talk now. Your Aunt Pauley is in the hospital … She thought it was a heart attack but turned out to be angina." Melanie could feel Rita's irritation. Aunt Pauley was always coming down with something that, fortunately, turned out to be nothing. "Just about everyone is here, so, we're going to visit for awhile. There's food in the fridge."

"Have fun. And say hello for me," Melanie set the handset back on the charger and took stock of being alone. Delighted with her freedom she trotted up the stairs to bed.

Nowhere on Earth did she sleep more soundly than in her lavender bedroom. Showered and tucked between the sheets she fell instantly out of consciousness. It was dinner time when she woke.

"Hey there, sleepyhead."

"Hi, Dad," she said, embracing him at the bottom of the steps. "I love that bed."

"Everything all right? You haven't gone and quit your job again, have you?" He laughed and set a gentle elbow in her ribs.

"Mom made you ask?"

"If we don't ask we may never know. But, seriously, are you okay? You look tired."

"Groggy. And work is fine. Actually I'm hoping to be busy pretty soon." Melanie nodded toward the kitchen. "Is it safe?"

"Lately, yes. But we'd better go have a look."

"I could go back to bed."

"Oh, no you don't," Roger said, wrapping a strong arm around her shoulder and leading her into the kitchen. "Look who I found loitering in the hall."

"Honey!" Rita exclaimed, the creases between her eyes disappearing and shifting to the corners of her upturned mouth. "I think I may have fouled up the defrosting the chicken."

"Don't worry about it," Melanie said, giving her mom a kiss. "How's the coffee?" Turned out, it was bad, too.

Rita was busy and Melanie took the opportunity to dial Trish.

"Kiddo, you in town yet?" Trish answered.

"I was kind of hoping you'd be over that phase by now," Melanie said, leaning back on the newly refinished rocking chair. She tucked her feet beneath her and pulled the blanket tight around her. She'd been putting off this call, she was tired of thinking about Adam.

"Spoil sport." Trish's high, chipper voice dropped an octave. "How are you?" she asked melodramatically.

"I'm fine," Melanie groaned, not having energy for the big production Trish wanted.

"I've squeezed out tidbits of information from Jace. I'm going to pick you up and we're going to get toasted."

"Tonight?" The winter sun had been camped below the horizon for hours.

"Why not? It's only ten."

The sharp prickling of a headache played at her brain as she weighed Trish's offer. "I've sort of given up alcohol. How about you come over here?"

"What?!" Horror filled her voice. "God, tell me you're pulling my leg. Why would you do that?"

"To prevent becoming a blithering idiot for one."

Trish humphed. "From blithering to boring. Fine. But I still want to go out. There's that little trendy college meat market by your parents." She sighed. "I'll pick you up in twenty."

Her lack of clothing options dictated her choices: jeans and a T-shirt layered over another long-sleeved T – *which Trish is going to hate*, thought Melanie as she strapped on a pair of gladiator heels.

Hanging in the closet was her favorite jacket. She held her breath as she rubbed the soft camel-colored leather, bending back the corner to inspect a small burgundy colored stain. Her heart skipped a beat. She'd knocked into a waiter carrying a single glass of merlot and doused Adam from collar to cuff while she'd walked away with nothing more than the spot.

Melanie shoved the jacket back and pulled a heavy cable sweater off its hanger.

"Hi, You!" Trish sang out as Melanie ducked into the passenger seat of Trish's Mini Cooper. "What are you wearing?"

"I didn't bring much. Besides, all my new clothes are for summer."

The cabin light was only on for a moment before she shut the door … she didn't want to stare but … Trish had dark hair.

"Summer clothes are *not* new," she said, pulling away from the curb without looking in the rear view mirror. "You so sad over Adam?" Trish asked, cocking her head and protruding her lower lip.

Melanie sighed, leaning her head back. "I've been really busy and haven't had much time to think about it. But I like the dark hairdo."

"I'm blonde again tomorrow," she said, flashing a grimace in the mirror. "Jace has some really cute friends – we'll get you drunk. You'll feel better after you've had sex with a stranger." Her voice took on a breezy, chipper tone.

Melanie laughed. "Thanks, but I don't have time this trip. I was hoping Cheryl would have the baby while I was here."

"I can't believe it takes so long to produce a baby. Jesus, I am never doing that." Trish said, cutting across two lanes.

"I didn't know we were talking about you," Melanie grasped the door handle and pressed down on the imaginary brake.

"It's Jace, he's so damn domestic I think he's the fucking girl in this relationship."

"And you're what? The sailor?" Melanie asked, holding her breath as Trish whipped around in a U-turn.

"Ha! Sometimes I call him 'the little woman.'" Trish laughed as she tapped the front fender into a meter and stopped. "Oops."

"How does Jace put up with you?"

"Blow jobs," she laughed with a wink. "I've got this thing I do with…"

Melanie cut her off. "How about you save that piece of information?"

The bar was above the restaurant and the chilly sea breeze was warmed by space heaters. The crowd had assembled mostly downstairs to hear the live band but with speakers and thin ceilings or floors Melanie and Trish got the full benefit of the music. The unabashed Trish bribed a couple at a table for four, for the price of two beers, to scoot over and make room for them.

"Lovely, thanks," Trish said, whispering over to Melanie. "A new favorite word, lovely. You're the one who said it to me, remember?"

"No." Melanie grinned and ordered hot tea and fried mozzarella sticks.

"Seriously, you're not drinking? Because I've also got a new favorite drink," she smiled at the waitress wearing a logo half-shirt and shorts and tossing rude remarks at the patrons that everyone seemed to think were hysterical. "Don't you love this place?" Trish asked, after ordering a tequila sunrise and pulling a stray brunette curl back into a clip. Catching Melanie's gaze, "I don't know what I was thinking."

"You've been blonde for ... ever. And what's with all the new sayings, favorite drinks, words – what's going on?"

Trish shrugged her thin shoulders. "Jace wants to buy me a new car. He doesn't think mine is safe enough."

"For you or the rest of San Diego?"

"When did you get so funny?" she asked sarcastically then turned harshly to the extra woman at their table. "Do you mind?" She'd obviously been listening, having tucked a tuft of hair behind her ear. Trish rolled her eyes at Melanie. "I think I'm scared. He's moving so fast. He talks marriage, kids. Jesus he talks about retirement."

"Don't ball players retire at 35?" Melanie asked, before seeing the crazed look in her carefree friend. "So, ask him to slow down."

"I've tried. He doesn't know how – he's really happy," she said, a small smile curving the ends of her lips. "I'm happy, too. But I'd be perfectly content to keep things status quo. Not him. He wants to make an honest woman of me."

Melanie was struck by curiosity. "How does it feel? To be loved like that?"

Trish's porcelain complexion shaded. "It's nice. Wonderful. I mean, I've never been committed to anyone for it to matter but ... I trust him. He told me he'd kissed the last lips he'd ever kiss." She leaned into the table squishing her breasts so they nearly spilled out of her dress. "How can he say something like that?" She reached for Melanie's hands, her eyes wide. "I don't even look at men anymore, but to *never* kiss another soul? How can I live with that?"

"What are you going to do?"

Trish leaned back. "Marry the bastard." Trish's eyes followed the waitress, calling out, "Excuse me."

Melanie's phone buzzed in her pocked, and she took a discreet glance and grinned. Danny. Turning her back to Trish, who at the moment was ordering another drink, she slipped off the stool.

"Hi, what're you doing up so late?" she asked, glancing at her watch.

"Mel, I had an unbelievable day."

"Unbelievably good?"

"Not good, great. I've been working on my resume and website when my agent, Bill, called. Sports Nation is looking to change their programming, adding a daily segment. God, Mel," he took a moment, "they'd already narrowed their search to 10 but ... somehow Bill got my tape to them and now I'm one of the top 11 candidates."

"Danny!"

"I know. Amazing." He was laughing. "This is because of you."

"What are you talking about? You did it."

"We did it, then! I've got an interview. Then they'll whittle down to the top four and I don't know any more beyond that."

"Are you preparing?"

"Preparing, well, I just found out, but I've got a suit."

Melanie knew better than to laugh. "Danny you're already gorgeous. I'm talking about studying up on the company, its mission statement, demographics."

"Christ, I hadn't even thought about it. Do you think everyone is doing that? Because they've got a couple of days ahead of me."

"E-mail me what you know of the company, who you're going to meet with … whatever Bill knows – I'll do some research for you. You're going to be great," she said, looking up into Trish's wide blue eyes.

"Who are you flirting with?" she mouthed.

Melanie shook her head, trying to ignore her. "I better go, and you should get some sleep."

"I don't think I'll be able to."

"Where's Avery?"

"Oh,. I sent her with her grandmother to Italy. She was hating having to spend two weeks with me – so I figured, let Lauren deal with it."

"Danny, I'm sorry," Melanie said, realizing her mistake a moment too late.

"Danny who, Mel?"

"Is that Trish?" Danny asked.

Melanie stared at Trish and answered him. "Yeah, it's Trish." Her heartbeat thudded fiercely, causing her hand to tremble as she covered the receiver and whispered – Danny Ashe.

"What the Freak!!!?"

"I take it you hadn't told her I was back."

"You heard that? No, I hadn't gotten around to telling her yet."

"Did Adam know you were seeing Dan? Is that why he broke up with you?"

"Wait, when did you break up with Adam?"

Melanie was caught in dueling conversations. "Can I call you back tomorrow?"

"Just answer me. Are you and the boyfriend broken up?"

Melanie closed her eyes. "I'm not sure. Can we please talk later?"

"Sure, good luck. She sounds pissed. And Mel, I'm sorry."

"No you're not."

"That you're hurting, I am."

"See ya." She disconnected and set the phone on the table between them. Then took a second to catch her breath so she could explain. "Danny and I are friends. Nothing romantic."

"Give me a break," she snapped, cutting short each word. "This is Freakin' *Danny* Ashe we're talking about. Of course there's *something* going on. Please. When were you planning on telling me?"

Melanie shook her head. "There wasn't a plan. But..."

"You can't trust that guy. Remember how he just flat out dumped you?"

"I don't remember it *exactly* that way."

"Well, I do!" Trish thought for a moment. "Actually, I only remember the first time he dumped you when we were graduating but then you got back together and ... I just know I hate him because you were completely miserable and cried whenever anyone said his name."

"Trish…" Melanie searched for a way to explain.

"You're still in love with him," Trish said, her gaze penetrating Melanie's skin.

"Not like before." Melanie justified the previous weeks, having reunited with Danny.

"Adam knew you were seeing Dan?" Trish asked with her lips puckered, daring Melanie to lie.

Instead she nodded slowly.

"Damn. You needed to initiate damage control right away."

"There was no damage. Adam's gone for his own reasons and none have to do with Danny. Adam *knows* Danny and I are…that we aren't…" there was no right way to word it.

"Duh, Mel." She smacked the heel of her hand to her forehead. "He left you before you could choose Dan over him."

"No. That isn't possible," Melanie started as Trish cocked her head with an expectant expression, frozen for a moment. "Is it?"

"Yes. He *knows* how you feel about Dan. And it isn't harmless." Trish said, imitating Melanie's speech pattern.

"He also *knows* how I feel about him."

"Men have egos, dummy."

Melanie stared blankly at Trish. "He saw Danny kiss me. I feel sick."

"Holy Mother of bad news. Shit, Mel. I was going to say that you could fix this but…" Trish sighed and looked around as she conjured up a plan. "Okay," she said, finally coming back. "You're going to have to put an end to Dan." Melanie froze, deciphering what Trish was proposing. "Stop seeing, talking with or even thinking about Dan."

"It's not that simple." Melanie said, staring at the cheese stained napkin. "Adam's already found someone else."

Trish's jaw slackened. "Not possible."

Melanie nodded. "I think it's what he does. He hops from girl to girl. Maybe it's the chase or maybe he gets scared. Think about it. You thought he really liked Gigi."

"That's different. He left her for you."

Melanie raised a brow. "Now he's left me for someone else."

"God, Mel. No." Her brows knitted into a hard expression of perplexity.

"It's okay." She tried on a fake smile that didn't fool either of them.

"You seriously don't think it was because of Dan?"

"He was pulling away before Danny arrived," she said, unable to look up. "I feel like such a loser. I can't believe I resorted to begging him to stay when he never even loved me."

Trish wrapped her arms around Melanie. "There must be some mistake."

Melanie shook her head against Trish's shoulder. "He never loved me, Trish."

In bed Melanie stared up at the glow-in-the-dark stars and replayed the evenings conversation. Trish had been surprisingly helpful.

Lust doesn't last, had been one of her simplified explanations of life. And admitting, "I'm prone to lust. You know that. The longest I've kept a man around was for…" Trish tilted her head, calculating, "six weeks. And he was my favorite but then," she shrugged, "he got boring. I got what I wanted then I threw them away without looking back. The worst were the needy ones." She shuttered.

"How is it different with Jason?"

Trish's smile was as much of an answer as her words. "I want to be with him, all the time. I don't mind when he calls 10 times in a day – half the time he's returning my call. I don't look at other men. Hell, I don't even see other men, Mel, it's different."

Melanie rewound the conversation and played it over ... stopping to probe the edges of Trish's meaning, to apply it to her situation. Wondering if it was her lack of experience with men that had her confused. Could it be that it was lust she felt for Adam? She thought she was in love but each time she tried to mark that box, love came up short. Lust seemed to be the victor.

She gave up. But Trish's second topic had been even more taboo and had been aimed directly at her relationship with Danny.

Don't go there, Mel, she advised. *Just roll over and go to sleep.*

"That looked like a nice kiss," Adam had said after catching ...

Told you not to go there, the voice in her said, smugly. Melanie pulled the pillow out from under her head and pressed it against her face, but it didn't stop the memories.

Her argument with Trish had been one-sided, she defending and Trish saying nothing, shaking her brunette curls with each new excuse.

Adam had been jealous that night ... and it was the first time he'd suggested they separate ... Her heart began to flutter anxiously ... But! He'd left in the first place and had vanished for weeks without a word.

Melanie felt queasy.

"Annie?" her dad said, sticking his head in the door. "You awake?"

"Unfortunately."

"John's son can't make tee time so we have an opening for a single. Interested?"

"Yeah. I'll be down in a minute," she said, jumping at the chance to escape her revolving mind.

"The car is idling on the drive and I've already thrown your old clubs into the trunk."

Melanie lay motionless for an additional moment. She knew better than to ask the time; it was never too early for her dad to be up for a round of golf.

"Come on, Annie, we're already late," Roger said, tapping his knuckles on her door.

She dressed in the same outfit she'd worn the night before, minus the heels – those she exchanged for tennis shoes.

"I grabbed one of your mother's coats – it might be brisk out there for awhile."

"Thanks." Melanie stretched her muscles. "Dad!" she said, sucking in the damp air as he opened the front door.

"This? Oh, it'll burn off," Roger said, cutting a path through the cloud of fog that clung to the ground.

Melanie couldn't help but laugh. The street lamps were like lighthouses guiding weary travelers, or passionate sports enthusiasts as the case may be. She shrugged into her mother's jacket – it was a bit more than brisk.

"Breakfast," he nodded to the white paper bag on her side of the seat.

The inside of the car was steamy and smelled delicious. "Burritos?"

"Chorizo," he grinned, "and a cup of coffee. It isn't one of your fancy ones but it's hot."

Melanie placed her face right into the steam, absorbing the aroma into her lungs. They drove inland, listening to the radio and munching on breakfast. Over the set of hills the first rays of light appeared in the distance and the fog was already lifting, refracting the morning light to a golden glow above the roof tops.

"I'm going to drop you and the clubs off at the front then go around and park. You remember John, right? Go find him, we don't want to miss our start time. Can you manage both bags?"

"Yup, I remember John and yup, I can handle two bags," she said, the car already stopping at the loading zone. "Just pop the trunk." Her bag was light, she didn't have a full set of clubs … Her dad's was a different story – they weighed a ton.

"Go, find John."

Melanie hauled both sets of clubs over her shoulders and half jogged inside the iron gates, where she immediately ran into John.

"They're here," he called out and waved to a man standing beside what looked like a hut. "Good morning," he smiled, turning back to her, relieved. "Just in time. They give your spot away if everyone isn't here on time," John explained while reaching to take the load off her shoulders.

"Did we make it?" Roger panted as he approached at a jog.

"We're up next," the big guy John had waved to said as he approached.

"Annie, have you met Bob?"

"No," she smiled. "Hi and I'm Melanie," she corrected, shaking his hand before he began calling her Annie. "You're younger than most of my dad's friends." Bob was tall, over six feet with a Red Sox cap.

"He joined the practice a couple of months ago," Roger said.

"Congratulations. Pediatrics?" she asked, wondering if his size scared the tiny patients.

"Yeah, with a physical therapy background. You're dad is great, by the way." He smiled.

Melanie's grin hadn't faded. "I think so, too. But hasn't he given you crap about your hat?"

Bob laughed. "I take two strokes because I'm wearing it."

"He likes you," Melanie joked. "Otherwise the payment would be a lot higher."

"We'd better get a move on," Roger grumped, hurrying them along. Golf was serious, she knew. Roger and John lifted their bags. "Since John's heart attack, no cart, we walk."

The course was manicured to perfection, the wet grass crunching beneath their feet and the dew glistening like diamonds clinging to each blade. The sky cast a silvery haze through the valley, the coniferous trees added fragrance to the crisp morning.

"Why don't we, at least, use those handcarts for the clubs?" she asked by the third tee. The extra weight was holding the early-morning chill at bay, but chaffed her shoulder.

"The effort is good for the heart."

"Dad," Melanie said after a few minutes of silence. "Can I ask you something?"

Roger stopped, adjusted the weight of his own bag and regarded her with a solemn expression. "You can ask anything."

"It's not bad," she smiled, "we can walk." Melanie tugged at his bicep. It took another minute of silent strides for the conversation to start back up. "When you met mom, how did you know she was the one?"

Even looking at her feet Melanie could feel her father's amusement.

"The one what? Who gave me food poisoning, twice? Or the one who gave me two beautiful children?" He snorted out a chuckle, lost for a moment in his private thoughts. "Okay," he started, regaining his serious tone. "Marriage isn't love at first sight or happily ever after … It's work. It's caring and loving each other. It's never losing the respect." He shook his head. "It's complicated."

"So there was no lightning bolt?"

"We were young, that was our lightning bolt. Beyond that … I just got lucky."

"Yeah, that's not all that helpful," Melanie said, bending down to check the angle of her ball to the flag.

She was shooting par on the seventh hole when she brought up the subject again. "Were you scared standing at the alter?"

"Terrified. Until I saw her … then I looked at her father and started to sweat."

"Grandpa wasn't so bad."

"Hmmm," was his comment.

"Jason's asked Trish to marry him. She's worried."

He nodded, waiting a few beats then asked, "What happened to that man you were dating, the one who could cook?"

"I thought we were talking about Trish."

"Were we?" Roger smiled and handed her a club.

Melanie approached the ball, checked her stance and her grip, and swung.

"Nice shot," he said as they watched the ball sail over the fairway.

"Thanks."

"He seemed like a nice fellow, the chef."

"Did you meet him?" she asked.

"He came by a few times back in July, I think, after you went back to work. Helped your mother out with a couple of easy-to-prepare dishes. I gained a few pounds that month."

"Yeah, well, I hope she wrote down the recipes."

He caught the gist. "That's too bad. We gave him a copy of my mother's personal cookbook to recreate. I was looking forward to seeing what he could do with it."

"I'm sorry, Dad. Maybe we can find someone else to..." she couldn't finish her suggestion, Roger was already weakly agreeing. "Sorry."

"Honey, I just want you to be happy."

"Me, too." Melanie sighed, her thoughts flickering to Finn and his search for an assassin. "I ran into Danny Ashe," she confessed, nervously.

"Hmm."

"Yeah, he's getting a divorce," she added, watching her father line up his shot. Waiting for the swing ... "Perfect," she said as the ball disappeared in the patchy sky.

Conversations with her dad were different than with her mother, drawn out and cautious. With Rita it was rapid fire ... quick and heated with emotion.

"Dad, what should I do?" she asked, unable to wait, biting her lip.

"Hit the ball at the bottom of the club head. It'll give it the lift it needs to make the green." He posed and gave a mock swing with his club to display what he meant.

It wasn't the advice she was looking for but ... her ball flew and landed feet from the flag.

"You could've gone pro," he said, clapping her back. "But we'd better get a move on."

She took off her mother's jacket, tied it around her waist and was beginning to enjoy the game. For the remaining eleven holes she shied away from delicate subjects – obviously, her dad wasn't ready to deal with relationship questions.

"Roger is always bragging about you," John said. "He's very proud."

"Is he?" Melanie glanced over at him. "Thanks, that's nice to hear."

By the nineteenth hole she was out of chit-chat and though she wasn't hungry, breakfast was part of the social affair. The tables were filled and the men all knew each other. Roger paraded Melanie around, introducing her.

"I've been thinking," Roger said as he tossed her clubs into the trunk, "that you should remember how it felt when Dan left you. I wonder if you can trust him."

His words were out of the blue and Melanie was surprised by his candor. "Trish sort of mentioned having the same problem with him and I get that, really."

"Well," he said with a tone that suggested he'd stepped in as far as he dared. "Whatever, you decide, Honey, your mother and I support you."

"I appreciate that."

They were home before noon and the gentle sun had made its way through the clouds.

Melanie enjoyed the precise balance of October weather from the back patio. The picnic table in the backyard was shaded by the orange tree with droplets of sunshine streaming through the gaps in the leaves. Melanie opened her laptop and researched Sports Nation. The list of interviewers Danny had e-mailed was a starting point. She busied herself – delving deeper into the organization than she'd intended and leaving most of it out of her response to Danny.

"Did you have fun this morning?" her mom asked, leaning on the sliding glass door, her voice filled with humor. "Since you went out with your father maybe tomorrow you could come with me to my woman's group."

"Thanks but I'm on the last flight out tonight. But," Melanie continued while shutting down her computer. "Would you want to go visit Cheryl with me? I was really hoping she'd have had the baby …" she shrugged.

"That's a great idea, how about we take her something?" Rita said, tapping her nail on her chin as she thought. "Nothing with caffeine. Maybe one of those strawberry smoothies."

CHAPTER 22

In her window, Melanie's reflection stared back at her as the plane sailed along in total blackness. She dissected the image and no matter the angle, she wasn't proud of what she saw. She was losing herself in the chaos. *But that's what this trip is for*, she thought, answering the questioning look of her likeness in the window. *It's not about Adam. It's about regaining order and control and saying goodbye. It's about me.*

He doesn't want you.

The thought choked her and filled her chest with longing. He'd made it profoundly clear ... he was with Terese. The dynamics of that relationship was ... she didn't know what to think. *He* had insisted on going back. God, she was tired of thinking but she couldn't stop. And now she was nursing a new thought. *Maybe Terese was unsettled business.* Melanie banged her head against the wall of the plane.

You could have a normal life with Danny. She left her forehead on the cool plastic.

Melanie laughed. Danny's idea of being prepared for the interview was having a suit. He'd been sweet, so grateful for the information she'd sent and said he was cramming before his meeting in the morning.

He was naïve and trusting and that could be exactly what she needed. When she was with him it felt as though she were in an invisible safety net and her violent, sad world no longer existed.

The annihilation of civilization was never the first or the hundredth thing on his mind. He never chose a place to sit in a restaurant based on the proximity to an exit. He was attentive and loving and could cause a shiver down her spine with a single, sexy look.

Danny's pro/con list was heavily loaded on the affirmative side – 9 to 1. The solitary con belonged to Adam.

Another airport, another rental car ... this is it. Once you get this out of your system it's back to the real world. Where all you have to worry about is Parker. Melanie smiled, it was late and the thought felt too ridiculous to be true. Signing the credit receipt for the hotel she added, *another hotel.*

"I can't believe you're doing this," she mumbled to herself, slipping the key card into the slot of the unmemorable airport hotel. There was so much she didn't understand about Adam and if she was going to solve the puzzle she needed to start at the beginning.

Out of habit she switched on the television before passing out

Circling the campus twice, she took in the brick-and-mortar, utilitarian 1950's sprawl and was reminded of her high school days. The field was neatly planned with two outdoor stadiums, tennis and racquetball courts, two baseball diamonds and the red oval track had a long jump in the center. This was a school dedicated to athletic over achievers.

Less attention had been paid to the parking lot with its narrow lanes and poorly angled spaces that forced cars to take up more than their allotted room. Melanie killed the ignition in a no-parking zone directly in front of the double doors.

She climbed the steps and her fingers tugged the brass patina handles, opening up a world of linoleum tile and florescent lights. A flimsy wooden sign asked that all visitors sign in at the office with arrows directing the way.

Shiny yellow tile, shoulder high, lined the hall past the office door until the lockers began. Promotional banners above the lockers endorsed team spirit and announced the time and date for the Harvest Festival. Mixed in were propaganda posters depicting the dangers of bullies, drugs, sex and firearms. At the bottom, added in black Sharpie, was the name and number of the school counselor and a 24-hour anonymous hotline to call if you felt suicidal or knew of someone who did.

She tried to place Adam among the decorated lockers and low ceilings. She couldn't. He was too mysterious, too big for something so familiar.

Stopping at the trophy cases, she searched the overconfident faces for his, read the placards for his name. But the cases were packed with statues, team photos – she gave up and pushed open the windowed door to the office. The bell above the door broadcasted her entrance.

The length of the room was cut in half by a chest-high counter, a barrier between the faculty and the riff-raff.

"Can I help you?" asked the elderly woman with short, silver hair.

"Hi, I'm looking to replace a yearbook."

"Gloria, could you help her?" the older woman asked, returning to her paperwork.

Gloria peeked up from behind a monitor and smiled as she approached. "We're only supposed to sell books to students, were you a Falcon?"

"Yes," Melanie said, going along with it and telling Gloria the year she was looking for.

"No way! Really, that was my class, too. I thought you looked familiar! Don't tell me. I'm good at this."

Melanie wanted to squirm under the intense scrutiny but smiled, raising her brow in challenge.

"Rose Gowen?"

"You are good at this! Haven't I changed?"

"A little but your eyes are the same … except for losing the huge specks. You don't recognize me, that's okay." She pointed to her chest, "I'm Gloria Evans. Well, Gloria Kapinski now."

Melanie squinted her eyes, tilted then shook her head. "I'm sorry. I don't remember. But I fell down a few months ago, lost some memory. Kind of why I wanted my old yearbooks."

"Oh, you poor thing. No one ever remembers me anyway. In high school I was going for invisible." She reddened and pulled at the ends of her wispy brown hair. "We don't carry extra books. I can order them but it'd be over a hundred bucks apiece. Would you like to look through the school's copy, even use the copier if you'd like?"

"I'd appreciate that, thanks."

Two minutes later, Gloria returned from an adjacent room, grinning.

"Here you are," she laid four books on the counter. Cracked the latest open to a specific page and pointed to an awkward girl with frizzy brown hair and blue-rimmed glasses. The teenage girl's closed smile stretched ear to ear and there was a studious, shy quality about her.

Melanie took in the similarities between her and this stranger ... Gloria was right about the eyes, her own senior picture hadn't been much different.

"Bad perm," Melanie chuckled and felt a twinge of pity for the girl.

"You think you looked bad? Here I am," Gloria tossed back a half-dozen pages, swiveled the book so both could see and rested her finger on an overweight girl with bangs that fell nearly to her chin. Even the curtain of hair couldn't hide a most furious case of acne.

Ouch.

"Well, you look great now."

"Thanks, took years to drop the weight. I took this job as a sort of therapy, to rid my scolionophobia. That's the fear of school. It's not too bad, now." Gloria flipped the glossy pages, her hip pressed to the counter while Melanie did the same on the opposite side – their faces only inches apart over the book.

"Wait!" Melanie said, throwing her hand in to stop the page.

"Adam Chase," Gloria said with a dreamy quality to her voice. "Who wasn't in love with him?"

A line of boys, their arms linked across shoulders in a masculine chain of youth. Adam stood in the center, staring straight into the lens, ready to take on the world. Her heart leapt. It'd been months since she'd seen that smile, though then it was different. Carefree.

Adam's dark hair was combed forward, covering his forehead, muttonchops converging to his chin.

"He was nice ... well, for a jock," Gloria said wistfully. "He ran into me once, I dropped my books and he picked them up."

"These were his friends who died? God, they were so young." Melanie's finger glided over the image of the boys. A powerful, foreboding moment, captured on film.

"After the accident Adam wigged out and disappeared. I heard he attempted suicide. Horrible to think of him like that ... he was IT, he had it all." Gloria shook her head at the shame of it, flipping the page. "I wonder what he's doing now. Oh, here's Kristin, his girlfriend," Gloria said, dragging her finger to a very blonde cheerleader suspended in the air, her pom-poms flaring. "And here." This pose was a seductive glance over the shoulder, the waves of her long hair cascading over her shoulder. "And here." Kristin was everywhere flaunting her beauty. The glint in her eyes said it all.

Adam and Kristin, a perfectly matched pair.

"Did you like her?" Melanie questioned.

"Kristin and me ... we're different species."

Gloria, in control of the page management, pointed out a couple of shots with her in the background. Rose had been fourth in their graduating class, missing out on cum laude by a hundredth of a point.

"Well, I'd better get back to work," Gloria said as if waking from a trance. "A couple of pages were added to the back of the yearbook to memorialize each of the students who died. You can stay and look or I could make copies."

"I'll just hang out here for a few minutes. Thanks, Gloria."

"I hope you get that memory back. Though I wouldn't mind

forgetting most of my high school days."

Melanie drove, distracted, back to the airport, reality momentarily suspended from the ancient tragedy. The memories of her own past tingled at the surface.

Every high school has an 'Adam,' that one guy that every girl and most boys are in love with, the alpha male whose charisma stretched past the student body to the faculty. In her school it was Kevin Kincade. His name, surrounded in hearts, decorated her notebooks and her daydreams. Kevin had sandy blonde hair and blue eyes, and it never mattered that he had tiny teeth or freckles. A track star since junior high ... *he* was the reason she'd joined the team freshman year. The same year he bypassed track for wrestling. She and about two dozen other Kevin devotees, also known as Kev-iacs, were devastated. Only three showed up for practice the following day.

Whatever happened to Kevin? She wondered as she pulled the rental car into a return slot and her phone buzzed.

"Hola Jack," she said, parking in the stall, scooping up her bag from the back seat with the phone cradled between her shoulder and jaw.

"There are a few executives who want to talk to you about the Henry matter."

Melanie sighed. "Am I being questioned again?"

Jack's voice held a hint of amusement. "I think they want to give you a gift card to Applebee's."

"Tell them to keep it," she said, jumping on a shuttle.

"Mel," he warned.

"Henry is old news."

"You need to learn to play the game, Ward."

"I played the game for years, what good did it do? Parker breathing down my neck, nearly puts a bullet in my head and … what? Nothing. Fucking nothing. Screw the game."

"Hostile much?"

"Did you get someone to check on him?"

Jack snorted. "Yeah, he's partying with the celebrities."

Tension, she hadn't realized she was carrying, eased.

"How long can you let him goof off?"

"I was going to haul his ass back in today," Jack said.

"Any way to let it simmer for a few extra days?"

"Ward, would you tell me," he sighed, "never mind. But if you knew … let me try this again … what the hell is going on?"

"Nothing." She snorted. "Sorry, Jack, it's the best I've got for you at the moment. Even if there were something no one would believe me and your hands are tied."

"Crap," he blew out a long, whistley breath.

"Don't worry … just keep Parker busy." Melanie tipped the driver and checked the big screen for flights to Knoxville. "My flight's boarding … catch you later."

Descending over the vast landscape, roads cutting through miles of undisturbed country, Melanie wondered if life here were as peaceful as it looked. The nerves in her stomach tightened. She was about to delve deeper into Adam's history. The only family he had left – his mother's brother, Rob, and his wife Rebecca. All she knew about them was what Adam had told her. They owned a ranch 20 minutes outside Knoxville and had three grown daughters.

She parked her third rental car beside the road just feet from the extended drive to Robert Holt's country home. From the road the big white house was picturesque, with big trees shading the asphalt drive.

"Now or never, Mel," she said aloud. The two-story, plantation-style home had a big porch with columns and a wooden swing. Gnomes and resin deer stood guard around the steps, feeders and birdhouses hung from branches of the aged oak that shaded the east side of the house. She straightened her hair and checked her face in the rear-view mirror. *Can't make a good first impression with food stuck between your teeth*, she thought, slipping out of the car.

"You lost?"

Melanie swung around toward the voice. A moment earlier the yard had been empty. She smiled at the approaching cowboy in a faded flannel shirt, dark jeans and a pair of roughed-up boots. Behind him was a modern-looking barn with sheet metal siding, big enough to house horses, trailers and an RV.

"Hi," she said, pushing down the nerves that were making her hands shake.

"What can I help you with?" the man asked in a deep, gravely voice that matched the weathered lines that criss-crossed his face and the silver strands that invaded the dark hair at his temples.

"I'm here about your nephew, Adam," Melanie said, dazed and certain she was speaking to Robert. His deep green eyes that sparkled in the sunlight like jewels were exact replicas of Adam's.

"He's not here."

"I know. My name is Melanie Ward and I ... well, I was a friend of his." She took a step closer, her heels crunching on the decorative rock beside the driveway. "Please, I have questions." Melanie held her breath, intimidated by Robert's familiar eyes.

"There isn't anything I can tell you," he said in a tone that held no hint of regret.

Melanie held her breath. She'd hoped not to be shut down so quickly. "I understand, but I've come a long way and…"

"Listen," he said, putting out his hands, a mannerism she'd seen Adam use a dozen times. "I don't know you and I haven't heard from my nephew in a month."

"Rob?"

Melanie looked up on the porch to a woman in an apron with a large mixing bowl in one arm, hitched up on her hip.

"It's nothing, Bec, just go back inside," Robert said, cutting off any more questions with his tone and shooing her with a wave.

Melanie locked her gaze to Rebecca, her last possibility. Her words had to be convincing. They came out quickly and pleading. "My name is Melanie Ward and I think I'm in love with your nephew but…"

"Bec," Rob sang her name in a warning.

"Hush, let her finish." Rebecca conveyed her own agenda with a return wave, adding a glare.

From her peripheral Melanie saw Rob shake his head and actually throw his arms up in defeat.

"Go on, Melanie," Rebecca urged, soothingly.

"Thank you," Melanie said, finally breathing. "He told me to move on but I can't seem to … not without some answers. I was hoping to find those here. I won't take too much of your time."

"Come on inside." Rebecca held the screen door open.

"Becca! She's a stalker!"

"Oh," Rebecca tsked, "look at her."

"I'm not…" Melanie started to say, but … "I don't mean to be. And it'll be just this once, I promise."

"Don't listen to him. Would you like some hot cocoa?"

"Love some."

Robert was already retreating to the barn when Melanie crossed the threshold of their farmhouse. Rebecca smelled of peaches and flour. The warmth of the house was its own invitation, causing a swell of tears to nearly break through.

"I've been baking," Rebecca said, moving into the dining room.

"Smells wonderful," Melanie said, taking in the 'lived-in' look of the house. Someone was a collector and she didn't think it was Robert. Commemorative plates hung on the walls and a china cabinet was filled with a menagerie of glasses, tiny cups with saucers and more dishes.

"Thank you," Rebecca said, pleased. "No one else seems to appreciate my baking. I displace dinner, you see," she said, as if it were possible to miss the pies that obscured the entire tablecloth. "A couple of times a year all hell breaks loose. I'm involved in a few local organizations and tomorrow is our fundraiser for victims of domestic violence. I'm in charge of the baking committee, which is basically only me."

"I'd like to make a donation to that," she said, feeling around in her pockets for a loose twenty.

"That's sweet but not necessary." Rebecca smiled with her eyes.

"I want to. It's the least I can do for taking up your time," Melanie said, holding out the money.

"Then pick a pie!" Rebecca laughed, "Or a bread, or a cake…" She opened the swinging kitchen door to a room of baked goods. "I may have gone a little overboard."

"Wow, you've been busy."

"I love to bake."

"Adam must get his passion from you," Melanie said.

"We love it when he visits." Rebecca turned and the two women looked at each other.

Rebecca's fair complexion was smooth. Dark shadows with purple crescents ringed her tired brown eyes and her gray-streaked hair was falling out of a loose ponytail.

Her smile was generous, spilling to every feature. "You look tired, dear."

Melanie felt exhausted. "I am."

"Me, too."

"I'm not much in the kitchen but I could help stir or wash dishes," Melanie offered.

"Let's relax for a bit first," she said, pouring milk in a pot and turning up the stove.

Melanie scanned the hodgepodge of pictures and papers that decorated the refrigerator; Adult children, grandkids, finger painting artwork, announcements and a reminder that water contained zero calories.

"It's an organized mess," she explained while taking cups out of the cupboard.

"You're busy," Melanie smiled, trying not to judge the chaos.

"Yeah, well, that'd be an excuse if it didn't always look like this. Have a seat," Rebecca motioned for the kitchen table tucked beneath the stacks of papers. "How did you and Adam meet?"

Melanie took the only clear chair.

"I was visiting family in San Diego this summer and..." *he swept me off my feet with one look from his amazingly green eyes.* Melanie's heart skipped like it always did when she thought about that moment in the restaurant.

"He's always been handsome." Rebecca nodded knowingly and handed her an extra large Woody Woodpecker mug. "I think he's gotten more so as he's settled down a bit." She dumped the papers to the floor and nudged them under the table with her foot.

"I know it's crazy … me being here," Melanie said, holding onto the cup. "And I feel as if I've been thinking and talking about him nonstop for days. I'm sick and tired of the questions. I needed to come here to find answers before I gave up on him." She couldn't meet Rebecca's eyes. She was embarrassed. "Do you know if it's what he does … leaves when it gets serious?" Melanie bit down on her lip. "Do you think he's capable of loving someone?" *I can do this*, she thought, her chin beginning to quiver.

"Here, let me get you a tissue."

"I'm not going to cry," Melanie answered. She'd shed her last tear that night in Spain. "He said he'd found someone who understood him." She had been unconsciously holding her breath. "I'm an idiot." She did a mental rewind to when he wouldn't say he loved her … It wasn't until after the excitement, the danger, that he told her he loved her. It was the thrill he loved. She looked up at Rebecca staring at her. "I think he never loved me," Melanie announced with a dry throat.

"You're not an idiot," she said, pity flowing from her gaze. "I love Adam as if he were my own son but he's never…" She blew out a heavy sigh. "Ah, well, he's been damaged." Rebecca covered Melanie's hand with hers. "I don't know how much he's told you of his past but there's been an ocean of pain for that boy. He runs from love. Stayed away from us for a decade. Just in the past five years he's visited us on a regular basis."

The walls began closing in on her. The heat from the oven was getting to her. "I'd better get going," Melanie said rising.

"But you just got here."

"I think I've known the truth all along. But it wasn't what I wanted…" the air, thick with aroma was stifling.

"I wish I could give you some hope or an explanation but I don't know Adam's thoughts. He's so secretive. But I'll tell you what," she stood, holding both of Melanie's hands. "You seem like a strong woman and it was brave of you to come here."

Too overwhelmed to speak, she nodded and pushed her way out of the clutter. In the living room, just off the entry hall, on the top of an upright piano were photos. One stopped her from continuing her flight out the door.

"Is this him?"

"He was 10," Rebecca said from behind her, picking up the frame. Her smile exposed a hidden set of dimples. "He was something. A gift. Our families used to vacation together every summer. A trickster of a kid, then one summer he grew tall and broad. Handsome and he knew it – boy did he know it. Suddenly he was a teenage playboy. All the girls loved him. Arrogant isn't strong enough to describe him." She shook her head as if to shake out the memories. "There were so many good times." Rebecca wasn't ashamed about wiping away her tears with the corner of her apron. "After the accident, you know about that?"

Melanie nodded and Rebecca continued, "Marie, Adam's mother was so grateful that he wasn't hurt, but there was guilt. The whole family carried blame for that tragedy." She handed Melanie the picture.

Adam's entire life pivoted around the accident. Everything. She could ask any question and somehow the conversation would wind back to that fateful night. No wonder he vanished. Surrounded himself with people who didn't know him ... then ... before. But in doing that he'd isolated and divided himself.

"I don't know why you want to drag this up." Rob grumbled from the couch, his gaze on the photo.

"Rob, your nephew broke her heart and she needs closure to heal."

Rob's eyes rolled back and Melanie distinctly heard a mumble about too many daytime talk shows. "Look, there's no one who'd be happier than me if Adam would settle down, get married, raise a family but ... he's been through hell and back. I think it's well advised if you put one foot in front of the other."

"She's trying, Rob. Don't you remember being in love?" Rebecca's tone was harsh and pointed.

"Of course I remember!"

"I'm sorry, I didn't mean to cause trouble," Melanie said, replacing the photo. Unable to control herself she picked up another. "When was this one?"

"Fourth of July. Rob, get the album, it's on the shelf under coffee table," Rebecca said, pointing to Rob's feet. "I've got to check the bread."

"Really, that's okay," Melanie said, her hand on the doorknob.

"Nonsense, you didn't come all this way to back out now. Go sit. I'll be out in a minute."

"Let the girl go," Rob grumbled.

Rebecca turned and pointed to his feet. Rob shrugged and bent down, digging beneath the oval table.

"Does she always get her way?" Melanie asked.

"The 40 years I've known her." With the album in his lap, Rob took stock of her. "Becca takes in every stray that wanders onto our property," he said through skeptical eyes. "I wouldn't want anyone to take advantage of her kindness."

"We don't have to do this," Melanie said. "I could sneak out." She knocked her thumb back toward her car.

"Nah, I'd be relocated to the dog house for a fortnight." He dropped an album on the coffee table. "Any way for you to prove you are who you say you are?" he asked, wiping a layer of dust off the discolored vinyl cover with the palm of his hand.

Melanie pursed her lips and thought before shaking her head. "I assume you've already tried to contact him. No answer or do you have an old number, too?" Below a heavy set of brows, Rob shifted his gaze at her. "I would never hurt him." Melanie said, "But I haven't got any proof."

"All right," it was his invitation for her to sit.

Melanie sat beside him and immediately dropped down a couple inches. She saw him grin as she scooted to the solid edge of the pineapple print cushion.

"His mother was my sister. I've tried to protect him for her but it's like stopping a cyclone." The book cracked when Rob opened it to the midsection. "He's the same age as my youngest, Robin."

The first page Rob stopped at was filled with a lanky kid fooling around, posing for pictures – tossing a Frisbee, burying a girl in a sand hole, doing handstands, and flexing thin arms. Even as a child, Adam's life force jumped off the page. Rob ran quickly through the pages as if the memories were too much to bear.

Adam grew up with each turn of the page, summer on a lake, the beach, camping – each year getting taller, stronger, his body morphing into the man she knew.

"He was always capable," Rob's voice was filled with emotion. "His parents were so proud. Adam could do anything he set his mind to … I often wonder who he would have turned out to be if that accident never happened. This was the last vacation we would ever take together," he said, clearing his throat and flipping to the back of the book.

"Oops, we're losing a few," Melanie said catching a handful of photos that fell out of the bottom of the album. "What are these?"

"Those," Rob said, taking them gently from her to get a better look. "He started visiting again about five or six years ago." He handed her one photo and paused, giving her a minute. Of the six pictured, two were men, and one was Rob.

"This is Adam?" She pointed to the person to the far right, away from everyone else. His hair was shaggy, shoulder length and he was bone thin. His face angled, avoiding the camera and covered by shadows.

"This was the following year." He handed her the next photo.

Adam stood ramrod straight, his smile leaning more toward a grimace.

Too affected by the dissimilarity between this man and the prankster boy at the beach, Melanie said nothing. The following pictures were less extreme.

"This was this year. He was talking about opening a restaurant, had lots of plans." Rob handed her the last photo.

"When was this taken?"

"May."

"The restaurant didn't work out," she said, her voice blank.

Rob nodded, deep in thought.

"What would you say if I told you I think Adam is in trouble again and it's my fault?" Melanie held her breath, stopping every voluntary function while her heart hammered.

"Well, … I'd say Adam is a grown man and I don't see how you could make him do anything he didn't already intend on doing." Rob's green gaze was thoughtful, steady, non-accusing.

"Thank you," she said, "for your hospitality." She moved quickly, and the screen sprung back with a slam.

Rebecca came out in a hurry. "Are you leaving?"

"I am." Melanie breathed the country air as though she'd just finished a marathon. "I appreciate your kindness."

Rebecca wore her confusion on her face as she walked toward Melanie. "Are you okay? You look a little pale."

"I'll be fine. But…" she opened the passenger side door and shuffled through her bag. "This is my card. I can do things, if you need anything or if … Adam needs…" she sighed. "Call me. I might be able to help." She scribbled her direct cell number on the back of the card. "Please."

Rebecca nodded. "Is he in trouble?"

Melanie shrugged. "I don't know. But if he is call me."

"I take it you found what you were seeking."

Rob showed up, standing behind his wife, wrapping one arm around her waist and the other across her chest, protectively.

"We're wrong for each other. He was quicker to figure that out than I was." Her voice held strong.

"Good luck, Melanie." Rebecca stepped out of Rob's embrace and hugged Melanie. "I hope you're wrong. I think you are exactly what Adam needs."

With nothing to say, Melanie slid behind the wheel and tried her best not to tear out of their drive.

Missing the airport exit, she kept driving for eight hours until 2 a.m., when she pulled the emergency brake at the curb in front of her apartment.

Smoke plumed from her chimney and a light glowed softly behind her closed curtains.

The latch dislodged loudly as she entered her apartment. Someone had been cooking and the TV was on in the living room. Snoring lightly on a strange white leather couch was Danny. Most of his blankets had slid to the carpet. Melanie kicked off her shoes, clicked off the infomercial and scooted in beside him, readjusting the blanket to cover them. She hadn't realized the chill on her skin until she felt him. He was warm.

"Hi, I didn't expect you until tomorrow," he whispered, husky with sleep. He repositioned his arm to accommodate her body next to his and draped it over her shoulder.

"Finished up early."

"You all right?" he asked, lifting up on his elbow.

"Tired and cold."

He pulled her shoulder down so he could see her face. "Mel?"

"Just hold me and shut up."

Danny lay back down, pulling her against his chest. She had dozed off when he spoke again. "I hate that guy. How big is he? I could take him, right?"

She smiled. "Easy. No contest." Melanie could feel him basking in his superiority.

"Short guy?"

"My height. And weak." She laughed.

"I'm being serious, if I ever meet him I'm going to kick his ass."

"As much as I appreciate the chivalry I'd rather you not provoke violence. Besides I'm dead tired from work, not Adam. Though I'd rather stay here with you, if you don't stop talking I'm going upstairs."

His head fell back down on the pillow and she tucked into his protective embrace.

"Good night, Danny," she said, but he was already asleep.

CHAPTER 23

"Please tell me you're making breakfast and this isn't some taunting dream."

"Hungry?"

"Starving. I think I was gnawing on the pillowcase right before I woke up." She stretched and padded her way to the kitchen. Snagging a sausage from the greasy plate, she hopped up on the counter. "When did you learn to cook?"

"Sausage, eggs and toast don't count as cooking."

"You think I could do it?"

"No offense, but I'd rather not find out."

"When did I get the furniture?" she asked, biting into another link.

"Like it?" he asked scrambling the eggs. "The sofa might be a little large, I didn't realize how small your place was ... but it works and the table and chairs fit along that wall."

She'd passed a tall table with two chairs in the passageway that connected the kitchen, living room and front door. In other circles it'd be considered a foyer but in her place it was more like a gap between areas.

"Very nice. But I can't accept them."

"What?" he asked, the eggy spatula in his hand. "Why not?"

"That couch is way too expensive."

His arched brows pulled in, confused for a second before he laughed and scraped the eggs on a plate. "I bought them for me … you thought I was giving them to you? Don't be ridiculous, that couch was over four grand."

"You are such a bad liar," she said. "Fine, you can store your crap here but it goes when you do."

"Thank you, Ms. Ward." He laughed as he carried their breakfast to his new table.

After a late start, she drove to the Agency. Most of the leaves had fallen and there was a distinct crispness to the air. Her body was functioning like usual but she felt distracted. She swallowed a cup of coffee to clear her head.

"Morning, Jane."

"Good morning. How was your trip?"

Melanie nodded. "There's a rental car in the lot, could you please see that it gets returned? Thanks," she said, hanging her jacket on the back of her chair. "And notify Ben that I'm on my way over?"

"He's having a meeting with Agent Parker." Jane glanced at her watch. "Started a few minutes ago."

"Right. I got your e-mail. Thanks."

Ben's door was open. His guarding assistant, Janet, was missing so Melanie went right in. The big three – Ben, Jack and Finn – were seated informally around the coffee table away from the desk. Jack and Finn were on opposite sides of the couch.

"Nice of you to finally join us."

Melanie didn't need to look to know the exact expression on Finn's tanned face. "I thought I'd try things your way for a change. Not much luck in California, I take it."

Finn growled a profanity from behind his hand.

"Agent Ward," Ben said, ignoring Finn, "we're talking assignments. Have a seat."

"Great," Melanie said nodding hello to Jack while sitting in the remaining chair, grateful for the distance between her and Finn.

"I've been considering this rift between the two of you." Ben's pale eyes focused on Finn before turning onto Melanie. "I want it settled."

The air hung heavily.

"I'm sending you on a team-building exercise."

Melanie looked at the other blank faces, confused. She was the first to speak. "Wait, you're sending Finn with me on an assignment? Together?" *Was that possible?* "Is that what you mean by 'exercise'?"

"Yes."

"What?" Finn asked Jack, whose face had contorted into a scowl. Getting no answer Finn turned to Ben. "An assignment with Ward?"

"Why not?" Ben asked, searching each of the expressions. "We are all on the same team. We have the same goals and you two need to realize that."

"I couldn't agree more," Melanie announced. *Anything to put an end to the continuous anxiety of being pursued by a hit man.* Keep your enemies closer.

Ben hooked onto her acceptance with energy. "Okay! I'll get on the arrangements."

"Hold it," Finn jumped in. "You want me to work with her? No way! Ward is certifiable. I don't want my life in her hands, she's crazy." His breathing was getting faster. "Send me out with a wacko, great idea. I don't think so – she falls into a pit, dies and then it's my fault."

Melanie gritted her teeth at that scenario. More likely was him having paid someone to dig the pit, place vertical steel rods at the bottom before shoving her in. "What'd you have in mind?" she asked, keeping up appearances.

"I'll let you know as soon as I iron out the details." Ben grinned. "I feel good about this. It's going to work."

"Well, I'm not doing it," Finn said.

"You don't even know what we're doing. Give it a chance" *you fucking loser.*

Finn's glare was full of hell fire. "I'm going to speak with my father."

Melanie avoided Jack's gaze, not trusting her ability to maintain a straight face. Instead she turned her attention to the muted television. CNN. She watched as Ben spoke.

"You speak with your father. In the mean time I'm going to get your cover story and flight arrangements going."

"Hey, have you got the remote?" Melanie asked Jack. "Turn that up, please?" Salvador Luhan was stepping up on a platform as her phone rang. "Yeah, I'm watching." She ended the call as another was coming in. "I'm watching, Mom, can I call you back? Carla knows – she just called."

Sal, in a rich navy suit, smiled at the crowd assembled outside his dealership. The podium was equipped with a semi-circle of microphones.

"Good morning," he said and the cheering began. Sal raised his hands in an effort to control the outburst. "Easy," he laughed. "I wanted to make this short and sweet. I realize there has been much speculation as to the intention of this announcement, so let me get directly to the point." The overstretched grin faded, replaced by pleated valleys along his forehead.

"I'm deeply saddened," he said, his tone dropping a decibel, "to announce … I am withdrawing my candidacy for Congressman of this fine district."

The buzz dropped to a dead silence as the collective media absorbed the news. Then competition to get the first question out erupted and the swarm of reporters attacked.

The loudest slammed down the rest. "You are double digits ahead of Bradley. Why throw in the towel?"

"I can only say that the reasons are personal and will stay that way." Sal glanced back into the eye of the camera. "I wish to extend my congratulations to Congressman Bradley, who ran a formidable race. I hope that my supporters will lend the kindness and generosity they've shown me to Ted Bradley. Thank you. No more questions." He paused, leaned back toward the mic. "But," his face broke out into a full Luhan grin, "if you need a car, remember Luhan Motors." Sal winked, raised both hands in a wave to the audience and walked off the stage as the reporters continued to bark out questions.

Melanie sat for a moment in awed silence, watching Sal get into a black limo as a voiceover commented on the race. Conflicting emotions of regret and relief were battling for dominance.

"Well," said the CNN correspondent, "that was Salvador Luhan of San Diego County pulling his name from the race. Mr. Luhan gained notoriety when he thwarted the Fourth of July bombing of Nimitz base …"

Finn's phone rang. "I'm watching it now," he said in a low voice and hurriedly walked out of the office.

"Ward, tell me you didn't have a hand in this," Ben said, splitting Melanie's attention.

Melanie stopped halfway out the door, looking at Ben ... he'd aged. "Let me know when and where. I'm willing to mend fences. See ya, Jack." Around the corner she moved quickly to catch up with Finn, hoping to catch the tail end of his conversation.

She hit the hallway jogging toward Finn's opulent office.

"Finn," she said, barging into his office.

"I'm sorry, Mr. Parker," his gorgeous assistant said, teetering on her stilettos as she tried to catch Melanie.

Damn! she thought, looking at his plush digs. *Did I really turn this down?* It looked even better in the light of day with a great view of the park. She recalled some minor thing about pride or morality.

"Want something, Ward?" he asked, waving off his assistant, "or did you come to beg me not to tell Jackson about your meddling with Luhan?"

"I came by to talk you into the assignment but if you want to discuss Luhan, I can do that. Maybe you'd like to see the evidence I have linking Sal's terrorists with your dad."

Finn looked angry but his voice was calm. "Quite a collection you're building against the Parkers. Too bad none of it matters."

"If that's how you feel, makes no difference to me ... I'll make a phone call."

Now his voice was as icy as his crystal blue eyes. "You're dead. Hear me? Better start making arrangements, there's no getting lucky this time."

"Threats I can handle."

The vein above Finn's brow began to pulse. "How about your family, can they handle it, smart ass?"

"Here's the thing." Her heartbeat was so loud in her ears she could barely hear her own voice. "Anything happens to my family, friends or the God damned neighbor's dog, I will gut the both of you. Got that?" She didn't wait for him to think of a quip.

There had to be hard proof connecting Hugh with Sal. She'd just have to find it. Outside his door she inserted the ear bud and drummed her fingers against her leg as she waited for him to make a call. She wasn't back to her office when Hugh answered his phone. The conversation was short Hugh was out of the country. His advice to Finn wasn't kind but nothing compared to what he had to say about her. *Well*, she thought, *if I didn't want to hear crap about myself, I shouldn't have been listening.*

Melanie sat back for a moment in the solitude of her office, the harsh florescent lighting subdued since she'd removed one tube from every set. It was quiet and she hated to admit it, but Finn had gotten to her. Again.

"Ms. Ward?"

Her name snapped her out of a stupor. "Yes?" She looked up into Jane's concerned face.

"Your phone is ringing."

"Oh." Melanie hadn't noticed. "Thanks. Hello?"

"There you are, hi." Danny's voice was off.

"Mel, I know you've already done so much for me but ... I need to ask a favor."

"Name it."

"Bill called. There's an informal meet-and-greet tomorrow for the candidates and their spouses. Anyway, everyone else is bringing someone … it's a day-long event at a private club in the city. Do you think…?"

"I'd love to."

"Thank you, Mel. Really, it means so much to have you there. Bill wasn't positive but he thinks only the top four were invited. It's good news."

"We should leave tonight, then." Melanie said, pressing her fingertips into her temples. He was still speaking about arrangements and what to bring as Jane's frosty voice came through the intercom.

"Agent Scott is here to see you."

The problem with office romance, Melanie thought, saying goodbye to Danny and meeting Jack in the outer office. Jack stood with his hands shoved into his pants pockets, facing the hallway as Jane clicked away at her keyboard.

"Want me to guess what you're here about?" she asked, making room for him to get through to her office.

She closed the door behind them and they sat facing each other on opposite sides of her couch.

"You can't seriously want to be partnered up with Finn. This is insane, you'll kill each other."

"Keeping him close leaves me less to worry about." She blew out a heavy sigh, tilted her face to the ceiling and ran her fingers along her scalp. She looked back at Jack, deciding how much she could trust him. "What I tell you is between us … I don't want to worry Ben any more than necessary. Okay?"

"Mel, we're friends."

Melanie decided, letting out another deep breath and raising the volume on her CD player. With a low voice she began to confide in Jack. "I try to convince myself I'm not scared of Finn but the truth is that he's a wild card. He could walk away from my murder without breaking a sweat."

"You think he's bugged to your office? Is that what the music is for?" The incredulousness in Jack's voice wiped out any hope she had of his help.

Right before her eyes he changed. Naïve. She wondered what his reaction would be if she told him she listened in on Finn on an hourly basis.

"Forget I said anything. I'm tired, my imagination is rampant," Melanie managed a convincing chuckle, one that never would have flown past Ben … but Jack was less perceptive. "Do you have any idea where Ben wants to send us?"

"Why don't you get some rest, take time and rethink the idea. You might feel differently."

"All right," she agreed, only to get rid of him. "What's with Jane's cold shoulder?"

"Oh," he coughed, "we broke up. I've been busy and," he grinned, "remember when I told you a relationship with someone you didn't have to lie to would be great?"

Melanie remembered him making a pass at her on Ben's couch – massaging her shoulders and kissing her with brute force. She nodded.

"Well, as it turns out … not so great. I'd rather lie than have someone know my every move. She's a nice girl and all but…" He shook his head.

"I hope you weren't a jerk."

"Hey! We only went out a couple of months. I was … gentle."

"That's why she's flinging daggers at your back." Melanie raised her brow.

That did it, she saw his eyes dart for the nearest escape route.

"Look at the time," he was up and out the door. "What do you want me to say to Ben?"

"Nothing. I want an assignment with Parker. I lied before when I told you I'd think about it – you approve of lying, right?"

"Women," he huffed and dashed out.

Seeking solace, Melanie took to the gym. She pushed her body until her mind surrendered to the exertion, leaving her in a pure physical mode. A salty coating of dried sweat covered her from ponytail to damp socks as she scouted through racks of costumes. She needed to play a part for Danny and she was going to use the opportunity to escape her life for a day.

By the time Marcos dropped her off at her apartment she'd showered, changed and adopted a new personality. It was odd to have to go home, to have someone waiting for her, to find the drab place alive with homey yellow lights glowing from the windows and movement behind the open curtains.

Clothing for this particular assignment was nearly weightless in her shoulder bag.

"I'm home," she called, entering her unlocked front door.

His smile caused the rest of the room to fade and Melanie's heart to cramp. Setting her bag by the door she looked away, giving herself a moment before she was pulled into an embrace.

"How was your day?"

"Mm-hmm," she mumbled into his shoulder. He smelled nice. "Marcos is waiting to drive us to the station." He also carried Danny's bag and opened the back door for them. There was no silence and Melanie eased into Danny's exuberant one-sided conversation.

"You okay?" he asked for the fifth time, his hand gently squeezing her knee.

"Yeah, I'm good. You?" she asked to redirect the attention.

"Fantastic," he said, his smile much more convincing than hers. "Did I thank you?"

"Yes." This time her laugh was genuine. He'd thanked her repeatedly.

"It never occurred to me to study for that first interview. God, it helped, otherwise I would've been just another dumb jock," he said as Marcos pulled to a stop in the loading zone and popped the trunk. "Thanks. Marcos, right? Very nice to meet you," Danny said, his hand extended, "I got the bags." He picked up hers. "Jeez, what's in here, a toothbrush?"

Melanie watched him. He'd already made friends, greeting a couple of the uniformed employees by name and waving at other passengers.

"How do you know everybody?"

He shrugged. "I've taken this train a few times ... I don't know, I talk to people."

Melanie accepted that, though in 11 years she'd never met that many strangers. The train was packed and Danny gave their seats away twice, first to a pregnant woman and then to an elderly couple.

"Should I settle in?" she asked, crammed up against a woman with an oversize purse that flowed off her lap and into Melanie's space. Not willing to fight for the armrest with the man to her left she kept her eyes down on Danny's shoes. He was seated in the row facing hers.

"Melanie," his voice was soft in the din of the cabin. "Are you mad at me?"

"No," she said in a hushed voice, aware of their surroundings.

"Then why won't you look at me?"

Startled by the question she looked up. He was leaning forward, concern etched across his face ... she inhaled, her heart in mid-summersault. "You got a haircut."

"Yeah, two days ago," the concern lightened by a faint smile.

"Sorry," she said. "I've been having a rough ... day,"

"It's okay. I know I've asked a lot of you lately and I'm to blame for what happened with Adam. I feel bad, Mel."

Danny's usual grin gave way to a tense expression of guilt.

"That wasn't your fault," she said, pushing aside the queasy feeling she got each time Adam was mentioned. Melanie desperately wanted to alleviate his doubt, but not in the center of a cluster of people she didn't know. Reaching to touch his leg, he took her hands in his.

"I love you, Melanie."

She glanced at him with a severe look of warning.

"No, Mel," he said, moving his head to recapture eye contact, "doesn't matter who knows. I lost you once before and I'm not planning on making that mistake again. When you're ready..."

She stared for a long minute, her heart racing. He'd taken her breath away. Leaving her wordless, her brain had stopped processing.

"Did I just freak you out?" His smile was returning as he shook her limp arms in an effort to rouse her.

She saw his lips move, saw the slight overlap of his front teeth as his grin took hold, but barely heard the words. Sitting across from her was Danny, her Danny. She felt his hands, no longer calloused but with a familiar scar along his thumb.

"Danny," she said as if seeing him for the first time.

"Yeah," he nodded, tightening his grip and looking straight into her. "You all right?"

"I feel like I'm waking up from a very long, very strange dream."

"You look a little pale. Do you want something to eat? I could find us some food."

"I need air," she said, starting to feel sweat drip down her back.

Her nausea stuck with her until they got off the train and walked the four blocks to his apartment.

Melanie breathed in the smells of the city: pavement, metal, exhaust – like wine, the flavors exposing themselves. Carried along with the pace of the sidewalk traffic, lights from the storefronts inviting them in despite the late hour, walking hand in hand with Danny – was unreal.

"Did you say something?"

"I thought I was just thinking," she said, undisturbed, "that maybe I'm lying in a hospital bed somewhere – in a coma, maybe," her voice drifted off.

"Well, then I'm in the hospital with you having the same dream."

"No," she shook her head, "I'm making you up. You're off living your perfect life somewhere."

Danny stopped, pulling at her arm. Letting go of her hand he cupped her face, tilting it up to look at him. "We found each other again. This is real, Mel."

"I know," she sighed. "It's just that sometimes I wish I could jump ship, start over, make different choices, and being here with you feels like I got that wish. That I was able to bail or stop time."

"Let's get home," he said, taking her hand again.

He guided her through streets she didn't recognize to an old building with ornate stonework above decorative columns with burgundy and gold-striped awnings.

"Swanky," Melanie said as they strolled through the lobby to the elevators.

"You think?" Danny asked, surprised. "You should've seen the place Lauren retained." He snorted. "Legal term."

"Well, you don't seem to be suffering."

"Not anymore," he said as the elevator door slid soundlessly closed. "Anyway, I hope you like it."

Danny's apartment was a large, hardwood-floored, three-bedroom, two-bath corner unit with a view of the city. It was furnished in a modern, artsy motif, with shaggy rugs under small, stiff, uncomfortable-looking chairs. A large Pollock-esque painting covered one wall.

"Did you ... do all this?" she asked halfway through the tour.

"No, I bought the place fully furnished. I think the previous owners skipped town because they left everything. I had to call the Salvation Army to collect their clothes and stuff." Danny stood in the middle of the living room. "One of these days I'll change it up." Smiling, he added, "My new couch could go along that wall."

"Whatever you put there would be better than those ... are they chairs?"

"And they're as painful to sit in as they look. But it beats a bean bag."

Melanie laughed. "Believe me, if we're in a dueling apartments competition you win, hands down."

"Come on, there's more," he said, nodding toward the hall.

It was his bedroom. Boxes were stacked in the corner with a couple inside the closet. Frames leaned against the wall and next to the bed was a weight bench.

"Haven't had the energy to unbox my shit and I guess I haven't gotten used to the place, so I keep everything of mine in this room." He shrugged and dropped her bag on the bed.

"This is your room," she said, looking at her bag at the foot of his king-size bed.

"I know, but it has a bathroom and I thought you'd be more comfortable here." He smiled. "I'm taking the guest room."

"That's not necessary," she said, looking around and feeling less at ease in his room than in the rest of the funky house. "Besides, I just threw you on the couch."

"The floor, actually," he said in phony thoughtfulness, "until I bought my own things."

"I'd feel better in the guest room."

"Anything you want," he said, his gaze holding an intimacy she'd forgotten. "Come along, then," he said, breaking the stare. "The cleaning lady refreshed all the sheets when I first got here – so, it should all be good for you."

The guest room had a bed with a beige leather headboard, a pair of straight back wooden chairs and a plastic dresser.

"I think it's supposed to be art," Danny said with a shrug. "There weren't any clothes in it when I got here. As for the mirrors" – all over the room tiny mirrors were glued to the wall – "I think they thought of the entire place as a living piece of art. Whatever. You sure you're okay in here?"

"Positive."

"You know where to find me if you need anything." He glanced around the room and back at her. "Goodnight, Mel."

"Night, Danny."

Melanie sat on the firm bed, checked beneath the bedding to make sure there was a mattress and it wasn't art. Then she laid flat on her back, fully dressed, fully conscious.

You're going to need to suck it up, Mel. You don't have time to sulk.

It hadn't been three minutes when Danny knocked on the door. "Can I come in?"

"Yeah," she said, sitting up.

"I'm lonely and was wondering if you wanted to hang out," he said with a cocky grin. "Or I thought *you* might be lonely and were wanting to hang out with me. Either way…" He sat on the edge of the bed, frowned and tried to bounce. "What the hell is wrong with this bed?"

"It's firm."

"Firm, hell, did they throw a couple of blankets over a slab of granite? You can't sleep in here," he stood. "Avery has a perfectly comfortable bed."

His daughter's room was all pink with a canopy bed and unicorns soaring above the crown molding.

"I always wanted a bed like this when I was a kid," Melanie said, grazing her fingers over the soft fabric overhead. "And look at all those stuffed animals. She's a lucky girl."

"Yeah, her parents are split up and she's with her mother on her honeymoon. Does a room filled with crap fix that?" He picked up a polar bear and tossed it into a corner to join its fellow animals.

"We're a great pair," Melanie said, testing out the bed.

Danny lay down and stared up. She pulled the extra fluffy pink pillows off the bed and stretched out next to him.

"Danny," she said, rolling to her side to look at him.

He mimicked her position so they were lying face to face.

"I'm not ready for all of this," she said, noticing the sweeping length of his lashes.

"I'm not pushing you," he whispered back.

"But you're ready to move further, faster and I … I don't want to disappoint you."

"You won't have to," he said reaching to brush back a strand of her hair from her cheek.

"Where were you five months ago?" She wondered, not for the first time, how life would've turned out had they run into each other sooner.

"Five months? Is that all you've been with him?" His head lifted slightly off the pillow. "That's like, June?"

The bitterness flashed briefly before he rolled onto his back. "That would mean you were together three, four months, since he hasn't been around at all the last four weeks."

Melanie remained silent, staring at his profile as he worked out the chronology of her relationship.

"Tell me," he said, turning his head. "Did you really think you were in love with him?"

"I'm still under that delusion."

His gaze flicked across her face. "Was it something corny like love at first sight?"

Melanie's heart beat a rapid session of warnings. "No," she lied. "We actually didn't get along in the beginning. He had a girlfriend…" She looked away from his prying eyes. It was hard to lie to Danny, but even more difficult to deny her feelings for Adam.

"Don't tell me he dumped that girl for you. No, you don't have to say a thing … I can read it all over your face. Oh, Mel, the guy's an ass." He squeezed her shoulder in a patronizing way, suddenly sparking a flare of emotion.

"He's not. I can see your point," her voice maintaining a calmness. "It's over. Done. And I'm not willing to talk about him or justify his actions. He didn't purposely hurt me." It was as much as she could get out before her throat closed.

"Do you honestly believe that?" There was no malice in his question, no sarcasm.

Melanie turned to the ceiling where the unicorns flew above the pink shade of the canopy. "I want to believe everything that's conspired is beyond his ability to control. It's easier than thinking what we had was all a scheme. Though, if you're looking for honesty, I have to say – I don't know if it was real."

"It was real for you."

"Yes."

"Okay, then I won't go around calling him a dick, but be sure, I'm going to be thinking it."

Danny could always make her smile. "Fair enough."

⤫

It felt early when she awoke, her back nestled against Danny's chest, his arm over hers and their fingers linked. The last thing she could recall was falling asleep holding his hand after arguing into the night.

This isn't bad, she thought, his steady breathing lulling her back to sleep.

⤫

"Sweetheart," Danny said, an annoying beeping piercing the air. "The limo will be here in an hour." He was grinning that crooked grin when she opened her eyes, "Ah, she lives."

She yawned, stretched and rubbed her eyes. "An hour?"

"Yeah, and Bill sent over the names of the other candidates."

"Really?" She sat up, awake, running her fingers through her hair, pulling it into a manageable ponytail. "Who are they?"

"I don't remember, I just woke up and checked e-mail."

"Come on, then," she said, jumping out of bed and jogging to his bedroom, where she'd noticed his laptop on top of one of the boxes.

He was laughing as they reached the computer. Bill had sent over bios of each of the three candidates.

Darien Drake, 28, motor cross. Injured last year in an accident, likely not able to ride again.

Matt Krogen, 47, tennis pro. Multiple awards, considered the best in his sport when he spiraled out of control due to substance abuse. Wrote a best-selling memoir last year.

Timothy Herald, 34, swimmer. Three-time Olympic gold medalist.

"What do you think?" he asked, reading over the brief introductions.

"I think there isn't anyone on this list more qualified than you, no one with more charm or appeal and no one who knows more about sports than you." She looked up at him. "Go take a shower, I'm going to look over this a little more."

"Thanks," he said, kissing the side of her head. "Mel, have you ever wanted something so bad that you can't imagine not getting it?"

Melanie had a flashback of standing in the hallway outside her apartment, 21 years old and almost out of college, the first time Danny asked that question. It was the first time she'd experienced heartbreak.

"You'll get this job."

"I wasn't talking about the job."

A rush of blood filled her cheeks. *Fortunately*, Danny already had his back turned. She was flushed and wondered – not for the first time if everything doesn't happen for a reason.

Treating the day as she would any other mission, Melanie prepared. She read over the bios, dressed for the part and built up Danny's confidence.

"You're fast," he said, buckling his belt at the front door.

She fixed his collar and running her fingers through his hair, loosening the hairspray. "You're going to be great." Her pulse raced from the touch and the glint in his eyes.

"Thank you."

The limo was double parked, the driver standing by the open door.

"Good Morning, Mr. Ashe," the driver said, opening the door. "May I help you with your bag?"

"Morning." Danny stepped aside, allowing Melanie to go in first.

Feeling the presence of others, Melanie blinked to adjust her sight to the reduction of light. Danny was right on her heels and greeting the two other couples before she'd sat down.

Picking up the last couple on their way to the club, the limo was filled with excited chatter. Melanie sized-up each person, while smiling and engaging in conversation.

The entrance to the club was from the alley through unmarked doors in a building without a hint of signage. *Nice*, she thought, feeling comfortable in her surroundings.

"I've been here with Lauren's dad," Danny whispered in her ear, taking her hand. "The clandestine atmosphere is just for show. The real exclusivity of this place is the price."

"I've never heard of it," Melanie said.

"It's only for the uber rich."

"Lauren's family is uber rich?"

Danny nodded.

He'd been right about the covert façade of the place. The doors opened up to a bright landing that overlooked a sunken lobby. The candidates and their guests gave a gasp that echoed and received questioning looks from the scattering of people. Gold banisters swept from the entrance to the greeter's station beneath chandeliers dripping with sparkling crystals.

"Good morning," all heads turned to a big man standing a few steps up on the staircase. His smile broke as he saw he had their attention.

"That's Paul, the CEO." Danny whispered.

"Are you as excited about today as I am?" He asked. The response was a weak, conservative, throat clearing affirmative. Unimpressed, Paul repeated the question a bit louder and got a better response. "That's better." He laughed. "We at Sports Nation are a family. It's the reason we're consistently voted Number One by our fans and" – a booming laugh erupted from the man – "My wife is giving me the wrap-it-up signal. She has this notion that I'm long-winded. Sugar, wave hello to everyone."

In unison the group turned to the back of the room where a woman in a bright pink velour tracksuit, smiled and waggled her fingers. "Hi there. Paul, could we please have breakfast before ya'll get down to business?"

"You heard the boss," the big man laughed again. "We've got one killer of a buffet set up for you. So, grab a plate, grab a seat ... nothing formal here."

Paul led the way through a set of double doors, talking and shaking hands the entire way.

Melanie piled scrambled eggs, with a few too many strips of crispy bacon and two slices of thick, whole-grain toast on her plate. Settled in at the first two available seats and poured out two cups of coffee.

The atmosphere was casual and the chatter grew louder as the food on the plates diminished. Danny, enthralled by the Olympian was completely forgetting these people were his adversaries. Leaning away from his discussion, toward her, Danny placed the softest kiss on the side of her face. "I forgot to tell you how beautiful you are."

The spot where his lips brushed was still warm when he returned his attention to the gold medalist.

"How long have you been married?"

Melanie took in a deep, meditative breath before realizing the question was directed at her. "Oh, um, not married."

"That explains it." The woman sipped her coffee, holding the cup with two hands. "Matt and I've been married for five years, but it feels more like a thousand."

"I hear that can happen," Melanie nodded sympathetically.

"I'm about ready to spike his coffee with arsenic."

Not too many things could surprise Melanie or render her speechless. She glanced at the pregnant woman next to her, to confirm what she'd heard. But she was texting beneath the table.

"Then I'd have to find another rich husband and with the economy and the competition … I'm better off staying put."

"And prison food might be bad on the digestion," Melanie added, still not convinced the bottle blonde wasn't somewhat serious.

"Right," she snorted.

By the end of the meal, Melanie had interacted with half of the people at the table.

"Danny," she said, pulling him aside as the men prepared to leave for a racquetball game. "Listen, the best I've got so far is Matt and his wife are having marital problems, infidelity is my guess." She thought of the coldness of the woman's eyes. "And there was more in her cup than just coffee."

"How do you know?" He shot an obvious look in Matt's general direction.

"I just do," she waved at him to refocus. "We've only got a few minutes. Timothy is –" Danny shook his head, cutting her off.

"I don't want to know all this … I don't even want to know how *you* know."

"Information gives you the upper hand. It's how you win."

"Win?" his smile was careless, lopsided as he caressed a strand of her hair, winding it around his finger. "I don't want to get the job because of someone else's misfortunes. I want the job because I'm the best."

"But…" *Oh*, she wanted to argue, to slap him with years of her own experience of being held down. Being the best doesn't get you what you want, out-smarting does.

"Relax, enjoy the spa day. Be yourself." He ran the back of his hand along her jaw before placing a kiss on her forehead. "I love that you are so determined … on my behalf. Thank you," he said, his expression changing from a calm friend to a nervous candidate. "I haven't played racquetball in years. Wish me luck."

"Good luck."

Watching the brave, innocent man, her pride was mixed with sorrow. He was walking straight into an old-fashioned ass-whooping. Melanie sighed. *There'll be other jobs*, she thought. *At least I didn't corrupt him.*

"He *is* something to watch."

"Agreed," she said, knowing without needing to look that the voice came from the male with a creamy complexion who'd raised an eyebrow at the generous portion of eggs she'd served herself.

"I'm Patrick," he groaned. Neither took their eyes off Danny until he rounded the corner, then Patrick gave Melanie his full attention. "Grant is my life partner." Grant had been introduced as one half of the team that would anchor the show. "My silver fox would look outstanding sitting next to your rugged athlete."

"Dan isn't officially mine," she said. "I'm Melanie."

"The girl with the metabolism," he grinned.

"You make me sound like an X-man, Metabolism Girl."

Patrick laughed. "Women all over the world would kill for that power. We'd better go or we'll be late to fight the crime of poorly painted toenails."

CHAPTER 24

By afternoon Melanie was exhausted from all the relaxing. The massage had pushed her over the edge and now she was grateful for Avery's comfy canopy bed. Danny had looked overjoyed when the group met for a heavy lunch. While the men were still being appraised the women had been released to primp for dinner.

Damn it, she thought, her eyes snapping open. Right on the edge of sleep she remembered it was Election Day. Grumpily she kicked off the covers and went in search of her phone, first leaving a message for Carla and then dialing Trish.

"How are the numbers?"

"No clue. But last time I spoke with Car she was talking legal mumbo-jumbo – and Ted was a shoo-in. I cannot believe what happened with Salvador Luhan." She mimicked Carla using his name with dead-on accuracy. "I'm dying to know why he would pull out when he was going to slaughter Ted. That panther of yours, what was his name?"

"Javier."

"That's right, he works for Luhan, right?"

"He does."

"Call him and ask, would you?"

"Dream on."

"Fine. If you're content letting me suffer."

"I am."

"Bitch." Silence softened the moment. "Anyway, what's up with you? Heard from anyone special?"

"If you mean Adam, I'm not expecting to hear from him."

"We're allowed to say his name then? Things must be going well with Dan."

"He's exactly as I remembered him."

"Total asshole who broke your heart?"

"No, sweet, affectionate and gorgeous."

"Hmm. You have a very selective memory."

"Are we going to go through this each time Danny gets brought up?"

"Until I get used to the idea. You have no idea how bummed out I am about you and Adam. Seriously, it breaks *my* heart."

"Get over it." Melanie exhaled a pent-up lungful of air. "Gotta go. Call me when you've come to your senses. And Trish," she added to make her point clear, "I suggest you get used to the idea of me and Danny, quick. Because he's going to be around for awhile."

She disconnected with Trish sending a childish raspberry to her from across the country.

Feeling anxious, she gave up the hope of sleep and wandered around Danny's living art apartment. Trying out the plastic furniture and appreciating the paintings as if she were in a museum, most of the wall art had a fanciful theme, part mythical, part science fiction.

Nothing but his bedroom held any trace of his personality. Bored, she peeked into boxes, flipped through the frames leaning against the wall, ran her fingers along the clothes hanging in the closet and lay on his bed.

The shampoo scent lingered on the pillows.

"Wake up, Sleepyhead." His voice sounded like it was coming from a great distance. She smiled as his cool fingers traced down her bare arm. "I like seeing you in my bed."

She smiled through a giant yawn and stretched. "I didn't realize I fell asleep. How's your day going?"

"I don't want to be too optimistic but... We each got to spend a little one-on-one time with both Paul and Grant. They're great guys, competitive, but Grant and I hit it off right off the bat. And thanks to you I knew my stuff with Paul."

"I hope this dinner tonight is formal because I only brought one dress and, in a word, it's slinky."

The dress had less fabric than expected. Melanie cringed at her reflection. Though the hem swept the floor, even with heels ... it was the back that made a statement, plunging to a near-obscene level. Fortunately it passed the sitting and walking tests. *Oh well*, and with nothing else to do she left the sanctity of the bathroom.

"Dear God," was Danny's reaction before even seeing the back.

Melanie looked down, panicked. Her front was fully covered but she hadn't considered visibility through the gold mesh fabric. "Good dear God or bad dear God?"

"Very good."

"Are you sure it's not too much?" She twirled.

"Definitely not too much," he said, undressing her with his X-ray eyes. "We'd better go," he choked after taking another look at the back of her dress.

Paul and Sugar were hosting the party at their home. Paul mixed drinks in the living room that opened out to a veranda with a view overlooking Central Park.

"Sugar is going to be thrilled." Paul bumped Melanie with his elbow handing her a glass of white wine. "She was worried about going formal. It's a shame people have forgotten how to dress. Don't you agree?"

Paul went back to his Mixology Bible and Patrick waved her over. "You are bold," he said, his cold fingers on her bare shoulder, swinging her around. "My guess is that you won't be alone when that thing slips off tonight."

"Patrick," Grant reprimanded. "They're friends."

"Not after tonight," Patrick said, brushing a piece of lint off Grant's lapel.

She and Patrick had spent the day primping together. He was the kind of person you wanted on your side. But Melanie was about to counter his last observation when Sugar stepped out in a dazzling fuchsia, skintight, strapless mini dress. Her rhinestone stilettos brought her to Melanie's height but the up-do of her bottle-blonde hair added an additional three inches.

"Now that's a wow," Melanie breathed as Danny appeared at her side.

"Mel, have you seen the back of your dress?" he asked, leaning in with a low voice. She felt his glance behind her shoulder. "I'm sort of afraid to put my arm around you … after I promised to behave myself." He placed a soft kiss on the crook of her neck.

"Stop that," she scolded lightly, pushing him to try hiding the involuntary shiver that began at her toes. The cocky, arrogant grin he had worn throughout college appeared. "I'm going to mingle," she said.

"You can run, Ward, but you cannot hide."

Melanie gave him a teasing look and grabbed a second glass of white wine before returning her attention to Patrick.

"Did Grant appreciate the pedicure?" she asked, unable to ignore how his black tux and black hair accentuated his blue eyes. They were so clear it was almost difficult to look directly into them.

"He finds me ridiculous. Sometimes he doesn't remember how to have fun. Now I understand why you had yours painted metallic red." He lifted the hem of her dress to admire the contrast. "Really, the gold would've been too much. Did Dan notice?"

Melanie smiled. "Always. He catches details without trying – a haircut, a new blouse." A wave of embarrassment washed over her and she turned a shade or two pinker. "Danny started me off blushing earlier and once I start …"

"It's endearing," he said with a flick of his hand to his forehead. "I sat us with Sugar for dinner. She's fabulous fun." His tone was conspiratorial as the doors to the dining room opened.

The room oozed with flowers. Petals dyed in shades of orange and arranged around the tables and the chandelier.

"I think Sugar is sleeping with the florist," Patrick whispered. "I hope no one is allergic."

Danny at her side, pulled out her chair for her. "I can't take my eyes off you." His fingers wisped over her shoulders as he angled into the seat next to her.

At times Paul would break through the individual conversations and ask a question across the table in a booming voice. Unable to resist, the entire table would be pulled into the topic. Paul excluded no one. Melanie wondered if everyone was dreading their turn as much as she was.

"Melanie," he bellowed, "Dan tells me you two met in college." Giving her an instant to acknowledge, he moved right to his question. "Is he much different today?"

Having learned that he respected speed of response she didn't hesitate. "He's exactly the same: charming, dedicated and devastatingly handsome." *Shit*, she thought, hating the rush of blood to her cheeks. She felt Danny's cocky grin as he ran his thumb over her bareback.

Like a gentleman, Danny jumped in to rescue her. "Mel was my first love," he said, "and my first broken heart." The people around her let out a sigh of pity for him as he kissed the back of her hand and she eyed him curiously. This was the first she'd heard of a broken heart.

Melanie waited for the spotlight to shift. "How could I have broken your heart," she asked with a confused smirk, "when you broke up with me?"

Danny's face pinched, his brows pulled in close. His eyes were mere slits as he stared for a long moment. "I know you've got to be kidding but you look completely serious."

She felt the blank stare. She hated when people looked at her with the clueless, dumb expression and now she could feel that look plastered on her face. *What the hell was he talking about?* She tried to be quick, to understand in a flash but she got nothing.

"Mel, it was you who ended things," he said, angling his head with a bewildered expression. "It was a dark and rainy night…" pausing for her to react. He'd used a theatrical voice but when she didn't respond his expression grew somber. "You really don't remember?"

"I have no idea what you're talking about."

Danny let go of her hand, leaned back in his chair and stared dumbfounded at her. Danny absorbed every ounce of her attention as her mind raced to make sense of his behavior and the double lines forming between his brows.

"I can't believe you don't remember." His gaze drilled in, the muscles in his jaw contracted and the corners of his mouth pulled downward. "I've thought of that night more often than I'd like to admit and you…" He sighed, ran his fingers through his hair. "Come on." Danny stood, his hand gentle as he pulled her to her feet.

Her heart was pounding as he stooped to whisper an explanation to Paul.

"Can we just leave during dinner?" she asked, almost hoping he'd change his mind. Pressing her hand to her stomach, a real fear was building over the peppered filet mignon.

Jogging to keep up, Melanie followed as Danny ushered them out onto the balcony. The cool air cleared the wooziness out of her head and raised goose bumps on her arms.

"I have to tell you, you're scaring me a little." He didn't smile and she gripped a handful of fabric from the skirt of her dress.

"It was February 9th – I remember because I'd just bought you a Valentine's present." He stared and waited. "I keep thinking you're going to tell me you're kidding or you'll remember, but no?" He sighed. "Okay, it was late, like 2 a.m. – you were banging on my door, that was when I still had roommates. It'd rained that night and you were soaked, standing outside my door. You wouldn't come inside. You were having a bad time at work, some guy was harassing you … you used to talk about him but that night you didn't explain." She could feel how difficult it was for him to speak even these choppy sentences. "You were crying when you told me we couldn't see each other anymore. I chased after you when you ran but lost you at a corner." He waited a moment, looking at her expectantly.

It began as a flicker, either his description was vivid enough for her to see or she was remembering Danny in a pair of jeans, shirtless and barefoot chasing her through cold, wet streets.

"I did break up with you in college but then we worked it out and we did the long-distance thing for awhile. Remember?"

"Of course," she snipped.

"Okay," he eased. "Let me get this straight, you think I broke up with you a second time?"

"Yes. Well, no," she tried to stop the commotion racing through her head. "I thought we grew apart. That you went one way and I another and we never officially ended we just faded. And now you're telling me that isn't right that I..." as she was speaking the impact of a memory knocked the wind out of her lungs. It'd been Finn. The beginning of their power play ... she was new to the Agency and he was her mentor when he tried to blame her for one of his mistakes. She'd been crushed. Learning the truth about Finn Parker had been devastating.

"It's okay," he said, quickly enveloping her up into his chest and holding her jellied body hard against him.

It was minutes before she could speak again.

"All this time. How could I have forgotten?" she said, her body shaking. "Oh, Danny, all this time I've ... I can't believe." She pulled away to look up at him, his expression full of sorrow. "This was because of me."

"It's all right," he said, dropping his face to press his cheek to her forehead.

Her memory felt more like a dream. But she knew it was true. Over the years she'd gotten good at pushing away inconvenient emotions. And that she chose to forget this particularly painful event shouldn't be surprising. She knew exactly what she'd done – absorbed herself in work. She became a better agent, worked longer and harder than anyone. And was never going to let Finn, or anyone else, railroad her … ever again.

"Danny, can you forgive me?"

"Sweetheart," he tilted her chin up, "There isn't anything to forgive. It was a long time ago. I'm just happy we're together now."

"I guess," she agreed, though it felt too logical. "I never moved on, every man I met I measured against you. In all these years I've only been with three men and two were basically one-night stands. And it was all my fault."

"It wasn't anyone's fault," he said, holding her tightly.

"I love you, Danny." She looked up and they shared a silent communication. Holding her breath wasn't a conscious decision but it was becoming a habit.

Danny's breath was hot along the side of her face starting at her temple, slowly dropping from her cheek to her jaw. He hesitated long enough for Melanie to grab hold of his jacket and draw him closer.

His lips were soft and they moved over hers with the expertise she expected from Danny Ashe. His hands felt as if they were on fire where he touched the bare skin on her back. Then up into her hair, cradling her head without breaking contact.

"I love you, too," he said, his fingers grazing lightly over her ear then down her neck.

Everything is going to be okay, she thought, swooning from the lack of oxygen.

Danny bent down, again, clearly intending to continue as Melanie waited in anticipation. He pulled back. "Mel, why are you vibrating?"

"Oh," she blinked, realizing the sensation. "It's my phone."

"Where on Earth could you be carrying a phone?"

She smiled, unclipped an earphone from the fabric just below her breast. "It's in my bra." The slim, receiver fit neatly on the side of her breast.

Danny sucked in a breath. "To be jealous of a cell phone," he mumbled as she answered the call.

"Yeah?" She tried to sound normal but the pitch was too high and the word came out sounding like 'yipe'.

"Melanie? It's Jack. Ben's got the assignment correlated. You need to be ready in an hour."

"Um, no can do. I'm in the city. Can't it wait until morning?" She felt shy, turning her head away from Danny.

Jack clicked his tongue. "Not that long. Be at the helipad at the dock. I'll pick you up at midnight."

Not meeting his eye, she twisted Danny's wrist to check his watch. "See you at midnight."

"Work?" Danny asked, watching her every move as she tucked the equipment back in its place.

"I'm sorry."

"It's okay. You look a little dazed. Maybe work is a good thing, give you time to catch your bearings." He closed the gap, their bodies lightly grazing, his fingers tangled in her hair. "It's like a fairy tale ... We have until midnight."

"I don't think this is exactly what the Grimm Brothers had in mind."

"Modern version." His kiss was gentle. "I am at an interview, right?" He took in the view over her shoulder, through the windows, then back to her. "Better get back. Ready?"

"You're not mad that I have to leave, are you?"

"Never. I know how important your job is to you. Besides, it adds anticipation."

"You're a bad liar."

He laughed. "I'm not lying … I'm … going to need a very cold shower. Come on," he tugged on her hand returning to the party.

At a quarter to twelve, the cab pulled up to the gate in the chain-link fence. Danny slid out of the back seat first. "I think they're waiting for you," he said, gesturing toward Jack standing watch beside the dormant chopper.

They'd been back to his condo, where she'd changed into jeans and left the gold dress hanging in his closet and her toothbrush in his bathroom. The feeling of complete exposure on the balcony had been fleeting, the kissing giving way to holding. The feel of his warm skin lingered long after his touch was gone.

"You'll call?" Danny asked, tracing the lines of her face with cool fingers. "I don't want you to forget about me while you're gone."

"I can't believe you're joking about that!" She smiled and snuggled into his arms.

"Too soon?"

She closed her eyes, taking in the scent of the cologne on his neck and the smoothness of his chin on her cheek. His hands moving along her back didn't help the spark that had taken root in a very low spot of her abdomen.

Whew, she panted, breaking contact. "I better go while I still can."

"Probably a good idea." He swiped a stray hair off her forehead. "It's going to be torture for me until you get back."

"I don't know when that'll be." She bit the inside of her cheek.

"Obviously I'm a patient man. I've waited this long for you."

She had to get away, the sexual tension was churning her stomach. "I'll be thinking about you." Quickly she placed a peck on his lips and darted to the gate. "Bye, Danny Ashe," she called to him.

"Bye, Melanie Ward," he waved, still standing beside the cab.

The chopper blades started and Melanie had to duck to reach Jack.

"You're having a good night," Jack said, opening the door for her and motioning to the pilot.

She jumped into the back seat beside … Parker and turned to wave at Danny.

"New boyfriend?" he hissed.

"Old boyfriend, actually." She smiled at her reflection as they lifted off.

"Hope you checked his background."

She didn't miss his implication. "Not even you can ruin tonight for me." She slid the headphones in place, tucking her hair behind her ears. "Okay, Jack, spill – what's the assignment?"

"Can't. I don't know. Ben's been real particular about keeping it under wraps." Jack's voice came in crackly through the speakers.

Shit, Melanie thought, *what the hell could he be thinking? This is such a bad idea.*

"I've got a folder for each of you … once we get to the jet."

"This is ludicrous. I never agreed to such a fucked-up mission. Where the hell is he sending me?"

"Arizona. That's all I know," Jack stated simply. "It's nowhere foreign or remote, so just calm down."

"Arizona?" Melanie thought out loud. It had been a hot spot recently – shootings, border crossing, racial tension, boycotts. *Okay,* she thought, *how bad could Arizona be, one state away from home?* Leaning back, sucking in recycled air, she closed off the world.

A single jet was parked at a dark airstrip just outside of the city, fueled and ready to take off.

"This is where we part," Jack shouted at Melanie over the roar of the blades. "You going to be okay?"

"I hope so," she smiled.

"Jane packed a bag, it's there by your feet. Your packet," he handed her a manila folder. "Be safe, Ward," he whispered, the pulse at his neck clearly visible. Without sentiment he handed Finn his copy.

Melanie patted Jack's shoulder as she grabbed the luggage and ducked out. Keeping her head down, she jogged over the tarmac and up the lowered steps. The age of the aircraft showed in the chipped paint and lack of technology inside the cabin. Five rows of two large, enveloping seats took up the entire fuselage with three tiny, retractable televisions in the ceiling of the center aisle.

Her bag secure in the back compartment, she plopped down into the third row aisle seat. Finn glanced over the empty plane, his blue eyes blazing through her, and sat in the first row window seat – guaranteeing no accidental eye contact.

Sliding her finger beneath the seal, Melanie eagerly cracked open the assignment. She and Parker would be guests of the Quail Canyon Ranch, a relationship-building resort along the U.S. – Mexico border. Posing as a married couple they would participate in the weekend couples retreat and marriage counseling activities.

Melanie had to reread the last part.

"No fucking way!" Finn shouted and repeated. Several times.

In her experience anything that brought out such a negative response in Finn couldn't be all bad. Grinning, she continued to the second page; Ben was sending them to couples therapy. *Genius*, she thought with a mixture of humor and nausea.

Reading over their profile, she learned they were a dysfunctional couple, married nine years with no children. He even kept their first names the same, a tactic to bring reality to their sessions – Melanie and Finn Fowler. She retreated inside her head to envision the possibility. After several tries she gave up. Reclining her seat all the way back, she slept.

The sun was rising over the very distant horizon when they touched down at a small airstrip outside of Tucson. The weather was colder than she'd expected and she searched her bag hoping Jane had planned for the weather. The airfield operated mostly as a flight school, though as Melanie stretched her legs she saw various alternative methods of flying. Bicycles with colorful fabric wings, unmanned aerial flyers and low-flying crafts.

"Excuse me, Mrs. Fowler?" asked a college age man.

And so it begins, she thought before answering.

"A car has been arranged." Holding out a set of keys he gestured toward a gravel lot.

"What are these?" Melanie asked, stepping into the shade of the hanger.

"Experimental, mostly for research. This one is mine," he said, his hand grazing the handlebars. "My dad thinks I'm nuts but … look around. Some of these will be the next wave of air transportation and others are already being used to catch drug smugglers. Over there," he pointed to another group, "are auto pilot weather aircraft. Crazy, huh?"

"Yeah. Thanks." Melanie turned toward the car. Finn was leaning against the passenger door of their vehicle. The urge to talk vanished.

"I don't feel like driving," he said, sliding his designer aviator glasses over his eyes.

"Good, 'cause I wouldn't trust you behind a wheel," she murmured, unlocking the doors.

Finn pretended to sleep from the instant his butt hit the fabric. *Asshole*, Melanie thought, glaring at his slumped, limp carcass. Fiddling with the stations she stopped on talk radio, just to be annoying. Crossing to the southeastern corner of the state was a four-hour drive. For the hundredth time she wondered what Ben expected to change with this experiment. At least Finn had the dignity to give her the silent treatment.

The two-lane highway sliced through acres of untouched desert before expanding to four lanes that contoured around the outskirts of Tucson. Stopping twice for coffee and searching the satellite radio for something, Melanie missed Danny but was she ready for a relationship?

He is a good kisser, she thought causing herself to blush. Her heart hammered as her mind continued, *once it happens you'll be fine and you'll wonder why the hell you were so afraid of having sex with him.*

She bypassed the GPS to swing by Allen Street, the sight of the famous Shootout at the O.K. Corral in Tombstone. She'd seen the movie in high school and had fallen in love with Doc Holliday. The main drag looked just like the film. A wide street with block long wooden porches linking the dusty trinket shops with saloons and banks.

"What are we doing here?" Parker groused without lifting his head.

"On vacation, remember? From Ohio ... a real couple would stop to check out the landmarks."

"You check it out, then. I'm going back to sleep."

"I hate you."

"Ditto."

When the pavement ended there were still ten miles left to cross to reach the ranch. Directing the wheels at shallow ruts in the dirt road, she knocked Finn around a little. He conked his head on the window but continued to feign sleep.

It was nearing noon when she pulled up in front of an old brick ranch house. Quail Canyon Ranch was built on a strip of grassy flatland about a quarter of a mile from the foothills. Beyond the dozen or so small cottages was open field with free-roaming horses and farther out were gray-blue mountains.

Leaving Finn in the car she headed toward the house with smoke billowing chimney. "Hello, anyone home?"

A man in a white jumpsuit with shoulder-length hair came to the door.

"Hi," Melanie said, stepping back from the screen door.

"Welcome to Quail Canyon. You must be one of my couples, I'm Dr. Seymour."

"Yes, we're the Fowlers."

"Wonderful. How was your trip?" The man smiled, his grin chemically altered to a beaming white.

"Uneventful."

He cocked his head like a bird, sidestepped Melanie. "Let me see you to your cabin." She followed and noticed him gaze at the sleeping figure in the passenger seat. "Perhaps we should include him."

"Nah, he'll keep."

Dr. Seymour had the air of a commune leader, a hippy throwback who'd lost track of time out in the wilderness. He led her on a brief tour of the meeting rooms, chow hall, stables and finally to the cabin she would be sharing with Parker.

"Got anything with two beds?" she asked, cringing. Parker was such a priss there was no way he'd sleep on the floor. She was going to end up in the tub and be the one to smash wandering scorpions. *Terrific*.

"In order for therapy to be effective you must come with an open mind."

"That may be true with others … but it's taken Finn and me years to build up to this level of distrust." Melanie eyed the doctor with his unruly mange of bushy dark hair streaked with white at his temples. "Actually, you wouldn't have a cabin I could rent separately, would you?"

"I have a cabin with twin beds." His words were clipped with disapproval.

"Anything is better than this," Melanie said, grateful to be avoiding the awkwardness of fighting over a bed with Finn.

The car was empty when they returned.

"Why don't you go and get settled? The kitchen will be open in an hour and after that the rest of the couples will have arrived and we can have our first discussion." His gaze fluttered around the grounds, possibly searching for Finn.

"See you in an hour." Melanie had already popped open the trunk and was retrieving her bag. *Hopefully I'll get a shower in before Finn's directed to the right cabin.* The possibility added purpose to her pace.

He hour was about up and Finn still hadn't made an appearance.

Her luck ended when she opened the door and found him rocking on a porch chair. She could feel the tension radiating out of him. *Let him simmer*, she thought walking past him toward the ringing of the dinner bell.

The main house was a large, one-room solid stone building with an open mouth fireplace large enough for her to stand upright. A gentle fire gnawed peacefully on a large mesquite log. Decades of burning timber blended with the distinctive scent of fried chicken, giving the room a comfortable feel.

As they entered Melanie felt all eyes swivel toward them, including the glass ones from the small herd of deer mounted on the walls.

"I can't believe I have to do this shit," Finn grumbled, his first words since Tombstone.

"Too bad Hugh's out of the country. He could've gotten you out of this." She raised her shoulders over exaggeratedly. "Oh well, what'cha gonna do?"

"Eat," he said, giving her a look that could kill before slithering up to the counter to grab a plate.

Melanie's blood rose, nearly choking her. It'd been weeks since he'd had that effect on her, when she'd woken in a cold sweat with his red, devil eyes burning her. Mentally she was back in the barn, chained to a beam, fear and hatred sweating out her pores, searching for an ounce of humanity in Finn's eyes. Feeling his fist make solid contact with her jaw, saliva had flowed inside her mouth with the metallic taste of blood.

She stood frozen, abating her instinct to leap at his throat.

What is wrong with your life? she asked herself, turning away from the assembly of food. A light sheen of sweat had built up along her hairline. *He nearly killed you*, her heart rate spiking, *and you're here pretending ... pretending that he isn't actively seeking ...* her hand trembled as she wiped her face with her sleeve. *Calm down.* She blew out a lungful of stale air.

"Not feeling well, Mrs. Fowler?" Dr. Seymour inquired, a concerned crease between his dark eyes.

"I'm fine," she answered, picking up her act.

"Water?" His warm hand took her elbow and guided her to one of the cow skin love seats in front of the fireplace.

"Yes, that would be nice." Sitting was a relief. She'd known she was under strain but the abrupt onset of the anxiety surprised her. Unfortunately she didn't have long to recover. Ten minutes. Dr. Seymour invited the entire group to take a seat in the circle.

"I'm going to ask that you sit beside your partner," Seymour clarified when Finn tried to take a vacant couch. "Why don't you start, Mr. Fowler – tell us your name, where you're from and why you're here."

Finn squirmed slightly as he eyed the couch and dropped in as far away from Melanie as possible. "I'll tell you, *Dr. Seymour*, first that I don't want to be here. It's bullshit. All I want is to be rid of this witch ... but because of some egocentric Mother Fucker I've got to sit my ass down on this repulsive cow skin couch and tell you my fucking name."

Well, that was one way to do this, Melanie thought with an insane urge to laugh. "Counseling is part of the divorce stipulation that was set up prior to the marriage," Melanie explained as Dr. Seymour took control of his opened jaw.

"Are you of the same opinion, then, Mrs. Fowler?" he asked.

"Our hatred for each other is the *only* thing we have in common."

"How did you let it come to *this*?"

"He's an asshole."

"She's a self-serving wench."

Dr. Seymour appeared mystified. "But in the beginning ... there must have been something."

Melanie thought for a minute on how to proceed. "For a couple of months I thought Finn was fairly awesome but that was before I knew who he really was."

"You don't know anything." Parker said, sliding his gaze to her.

"I know you're a lazy, pathetic liar who hides behind your father's authority – but everyone knows that. And I know that rather than getting the job done you jack off and let others take the blame." Her low voice came from the back of her throat, her teeth clenched.

"You bitch," he rumbled, the vein on his forehead protruding slightly.

He's still in control. Melanie calculated how far she could push him before he forgot his surroundings and broke cover.

"You're such a fucking goody-two-shoes, always perfect, never having any fun. Pissing all over everyone who has any sort of life, dissecting every little detail. Then running to tattle like a spoiled brat."

"Tattle? Jesus, Finn. We're not talking about smoking behind the bleachers. Lives are at," she cut herself off, took a deep breath and stopped talking and looked at Seymour.

"That is what I call progress." The doctor smiled, "my assignment for you both is to think over your partners feelings. Think about what you can do to make life better for the other." Without further ceremony he turned to the couple in the next repulsive love seat. "Your turn, Mr. and Mrs. Reading."

Melanie considered what Finn had said, crumpled it up and threw it in her mental trash, never to revisit it again as the Readings floundered for something to complain about.

As the discussion ended each couple was given exercises to perform before dinner. Melanie went back to the room, changed into a pair of hiking boots and zipped into a windbreaker. With both cell phones – her usual satellite phone and a Fowler decoy – a bottle of water and her pistol she planned to survey the immediate area.

The compound felt deserted as she kicked up the dirt beneath her boots. Curious about the vacancy of the ranch, she peeked into the main house and followed the sound of the soft, shy giggling.

It was Finn, of course. He had one of the young staff pressed up against the Sub Zero freezer, his finger twisting around a golden lock. The girl didn't look to be in need of rescuing so Melanie escaped out the back door.

At the bottom of the hill the terrain changed to igneous rock embedded in tall weeds and finally flowing into a grove of oak trees. Stomping recklessly for the first hour, she found herself out of breath, her heart beating in an irregular, rapid rhythm.

She sat on the remains of a fallen tree to sip some water and regain perspective. "You cannot live your life around Parker," her voice cracked. "You can't manage his movements … You're on your own and it's too much." She pressed the heel of her hands deep into her eye sockets to think.

Okay, she thought, *let's start with the positive. No matter how it ended with Adam, he'd never hurt you.* She let out a calming breath. It was a start. *That Parker has hired him is a good thing.* There was a sort of logic there, somewhere.

Particles swam before her eyes as she removed her fists, noticing for the first time her surroundings. She was at the edge of a wasteland, a corridor for illegal immigrants where they left a literal garbage pit –

plastic water jugs, old clothes, shoes and whatever else they couldn't carry or didn't need. Kicking aside a discarded backpack, she walked the perimeter. *The area hadn't been used in some time*, she thought, noticing the top layer of biodegradable substances had already broken down.

A hundred yards away the rock face jutted straight up with a ledge shaped like box seats about a quarter of the way from the bottom. With the right gear, the climb would be a cinch. But her feet were laced into ankle-supportive boots and the climb took more time. The tips of her fingers and the back of her knuckles were raw and bloody when she reached the outlook. From her vantage point she could see for miles. A well-trekked path led straight from the border fence to the heap of rubble below. Beyond that the terrain was flat between the mountain ridges that stretched out beneath a gray sky. Somewhere out there was the barbed wire fence that separated them from Mexico.

The first splattering of rain came slowly enough; big, fat droplets taking their time descending to her forearm and then splattering on the lens of her sunglasses.

The chilly breeze through her sweaty clothes caused her teeth to chatter as she made her way back to the ranch. *Damn downpour*, she swore, remembering the blue sky from the morning. The path between the cottages and the lodge was a giant puddle, but the rain had stopped as she ducked beneath the dripping eaves.

Finn and his luggage were still absent from the room. She threw the security latch before washing off the salty layer of mud that was caked on her skin. Her clothes were a mess from the countless slips and skidding down the cliff and through the trees. Her elbow was scraped and her jacket torn.

Close to dinner time the rain had slowed to a drizzle as she did her best to avoid the pond in the road. Dinner was pleasant. Finn was still AWOL. Sitting alone on her loveseat, listening to Dr. Seymour analyzing the exercises of the couples she sipped a cup of bootlegged whiskey purchased from the cowhand unloading groceries. She didn't even mind paying the outrageous surcharge.

At the end of the session, Dr. Seymour pulled her aside. "I have my staff on full alert searching for Mr. Fowler," he said through the thinnest lips she'd ever seen. "I really can't imagine where he could've gone to."

I could wager a guess, Melanie thought, the image of the blonde crossing her mind. "I'm sure he'll turn up when he's ready."

Waiting out the hours in the 'diversion free' cottage felt like an eternity. No television, no radio, and though her satellite phone worked – being on assignment it was for emergency use only – there was no cell service. Guests at the Quail Canyon Resort were prisoners with nothing but each other to occupy their time.

She planned on another trip out to the worn strip of ground out in the desert. The storm had broken, leaving a patchy sky as the clouds blew across the bright moon. It was undependable lighting. But the stars were out in abundance.

Unlike the previous trip out she moved quietly, making good time without disrupting her surroundings. She climbed the tallest of the low trees and perched. Leaning back into the trunk, her legs crossed at the ankles, as she settled in to think. Lulled by the musical pattern of the wilderness, she stabled herself and listened.

It was the first calm moment she'd had in months. Reflecting, she decided she was jet lagged and haggard, racing across the country for friends and across the globe for work. But avoidance was how she dealt with her troubles.

Maybe I should engage more, she thought picking her way through the brush back to the ranch.

At the base of the hill were the staff bunkers, and in the crisp night a giggle carried through the canyon. Changing her direction, Melanie headed to the back of the building, toward the sound.

"Finn!" she barked at her partner who had the girl sitting in his lap. "What the hell do you think you are doing?"

"What does it look like?" he asked, continuing to nuzzle at the girl's neck while she stared at Melanie from over his shoulder and tried to jump off him. "It's okay, baby."

"No, that's your wife," the girl whispered, dodging his kisses and freeing herself from his grasp. "I'm sorry," she said to Melanie.

"Stay away from married men."

He was on his feet. "Ward? Seriously, get over yourself," Finn grumbled, shaking his head and passing by her. "Now I've nowhere else to sleep. Happy?"

"You realize this isn't a vacation." She fell into step behind him. "I'm talking to you," she said, grabbing a handful of his shirt and yanking him backward. "Do not walk away from me."

"Get your hands off me. Or do you need a reminder of that beating I gave you a few months back?"

Melanie sucked in a tight breath. "Don't even go there, you bastard."

"Why? What are you going to do?" he asked calmly, but his telltale vein throbbed from his eyebrow to his receding hairline.

Engage. Her fists flew without warning, catching him off guard and knocking him down. Her boot was in his ribs, when he grasped her foot and twisted. She lost her balance, hit the wet ground and bounced right back up. She took a step to the right. He mirrored her actions.

Reaching into her waistband she retrieved her gun and there was moment of agreement as they locked eyes. She tossed the gun to the dirt, out of the way. His blue eyes raged as he tugged a small pistol from his calf sheath and skidded it toward hers.

"You and me," he gargled like a character from the Godfather, his fists clenched. He lunged.

Darting out of the way, he slammed into her shoulder and his punch made impact with her side. Melanie threw her knee up, missing his groin but hitting close enough to scare him off. Each giving the other room, the circling began. Her first few blows had dented his pretty face, giving her motivation to continue.

He punched and she blocked, the loose dirt making it difficult to keep her footing. Her arms ached, and her knuckles were already scraped from the climb. But it felt good to finally beat on him.

Throwing herself into an attack, Finn was on the ground, when she felt the restraint of hands clamped on her biceps, dragging her off.

"Let go of me!" she ordered, twisting and tearing away from the ranch hand with an elbow in his ribs. Looking down, no one was holding Parker. He was flat on his back and they were ringed by a few of the ranch employees.

She'd never seen a more beautiful sight. Gratified with him bleeding pitifully on the ground, Melanie regained her composure. Standing above him she reached down to offer her hand. He kicked at her.

Dr. Seymour was naked under his untied robe as he ran to the bunkers.

"You don't happen to have a medic around here?" Melanie grimaced at her tender knuckles.

"What is going on?" his wide eyes darted from the blank faces of his men, then to Finn before landing squarely on Melanie.

"We kind of got into a marital spat. It was great, you should consider offering it in the brochure."

"There's blood."

Melanie grinned and rubbed a small nodule that was forming on her forehead – right at her hairline. Taking stock of her injuries, pressing at tender spots … *not bad*. She'd protected her face and ribs, which had been through enough recently and was completely satisfied with her efforts. Finn was down and she was up.

"We have a nurse on duty," Dr. Seymour said, gritting his teeth and pointing toward a door at the end of the main house. "I'll meet you there in a few minutes." Turning to one of his handymen, "Get him in there, too."

The nurse was a heavyset woman with pudgy, soft hands.

"Heard you were in a scuffle," she said, her tiny eyes peering out from behind a thin pair of glasses. "Husband, was it?"

Melanie took in the woman's drawl. "Something like that," she said as the nurse dunked Melanie's hands in an iced, stinging solution. "Ouch."

"Husband a cad?" She asked, Melanie nodded, more concerned with the fizzing of her hands. "I had one of those, too. I'll wait a few minutes to give him pain reliever."

Dr. Seymour entered, tugging Finn along and pointing to an empty chair and sucked in a big, exaggerated breath. "I don't appreciate being woken in the middle of night by one of my employees because my guests are brawling in the yard. Never in my 20 years of counseling have I ever encountered a couple like you. You behave outrageously and have given me no choice but to remove you from the ranch."

Melanie shot a glance at Finn, who smirked from behind a blood-streaked mask.

If Seymour expected someone to say something he was disappointed. He continued, "You are disruptive and my professional recommendation is an immediate divorce before someone is killed."

"Great. You did a fabulous job, Dr. Seymour – I feel wonderful." Drying her hands with a paper towel, Melanie stood. "Finn, how about you find your own way back home? I'm taking the car." She was out of her seat and on the phone in an instant. "Jack, it's Mel. Has the jet left the airpark in Arizona?"

"Um, it's scheduled to return in the morning."

"Hold it for me – I'll be there in four hours." Melanie fastened her seatbelt as she gunned the vehicle over the slick road.

"What? You're on your way back? You just got there."

"I know, but we were asked to leave." She waited for Jack to stop laughing. "I'll explain later … just make sure that the pilot waits for me."

"What about Finn? Never mind. Just tell me he isn't dead."

CHAPTER 25

The box beside the access doors into the Manor was different. A retina-based security system had been installed. Melanie dropped her face down to the screen and was rewarded by a flash of blue light.

"Welcome, Melanie Ward," the box said in a pleasant female voice. "You must establish a pin number. Please do that now." The screen changed to a keypad.

But the door swung open before she could tap in her universal code.

"Mel, how's it going?" Mike beckoned her in. "I was just walking by when the computer announced your arrival."

"Really? You happened by at that exact moment?" she laughed. "How many times did you have to walk past for that sort of timing?"

"About 40 minutes worth," he grinned.

"All right, but first tell me what's up with the new security."

"Not sure," he said, frowning at the door. "Mr. Jackson got a memo and the next day the installers arrived. I think some of the other departments are getting this same upgrade. Seems like a nice system." He turned back to her. "End the suspense, what happened in Arizona!?" he exploded.

Melanie was heading toward the kitchen for a bite before seeing Ben, but stopped to eyeball her friend. "Mike, have you always been such a gossip?"

"Yeah, and you know it … but you forget when the information is benefiting you."

"True enough."

"What does he look like?"

Melanie tilted her head and pursed her lips, to prevent the smile. "I've got to see Ben. Is he around?"

"You fought with him, physically?"

"I totally kicked his ass – like in hand-to-hand combat – and we were told to leave the ranch."

"No shit!!" he shouted, slapping his legs.

"No shit. Look." She held out her battle-wounded knuckles. The swelling was down and the bruises had lost their vibrance.

"And you've got that bump on your forehead," he pointed out.

"I thought if I arranged my hair it wouldn't be noticeable."

"Well, I've got to go and spread the word that you beat the crap out of Parker."

"Go easy on that one for a minute."

"Why?"

"Because I'm going to get a cup of coffee and a donut and I don't want Ben to have heard about it before I reach his office."

Ben was less enthusiastic with her account of the day.

"It was a bad idea," he said, leaning forward in his chair, shaking his head. "I'm sorry, I shouldn't have forced the issue."

"No, really, for me it was an awakening. For months I've been walking around paralyzed and I don't feel that way anymore."

"Well," he rocked his head back and forth. "I suppose that is something. Ward, tell me." He paused. "How badly did you hurt the man?"

Melanie sucked in a breath. "He's bruised and he'll be sore for a few days." She smiled. "But I'm sort of hoping the mental embarrassment lasts a hell of a lot longer."

"He called, he's taking a few days off. I don't know if he's out of Arizona. I think he's waiting until Hugh gets home."

She felt smug, enjoying the fact that Parker needed days to heal. "The bad news is that you've fanned the Parker revenge flame. Hugh called right after Finn and … well, I won't go into it … you already know the routine."

She did. "I'm not worried."

⌘

The gossip frenzy lasted two days and Melanie got through them by camping out in her office talking on the phone. There was a lot to deal with at home. Olivia Rachel Marie Ward arrived perfectly healthy. Ted was embattled with lawyers. Trish was holding Jason and his engagement ring at bay. Two days, and Melanie was ready to pull her hair out – until finally an agent got shot and the spotlight was diverted.

Mike's actions were like clockwork, and on a day with so much scandal to relay, he was sure to take extra time. Rounding the corner to the men's room he didn't notice Melanie slip into the control center. Inside, Ed was at his computer, headphones on and completely absorbed in a virtual war.

Mike kept his 'items of intrigue,' as he called them, in the supply room. Some of his collection was built from pieces of technology acquired by agents on assignment and some he bought from websites of questionable suppliers. Others were outsourced technology, foreign and CIA – untraceable and state-of-the-art. Along the back wall Mike had meticulously labeled shelves with categories: audio, visual, viral. The shelves were further sorted and boxes labeled with contents, actual equipment, computer systems, diagrams. She'd bought him the label maker for his 35th birthday. He'd gone nuts, labeling everything until agents complained and the label maker mysteriously disappeared.

On the second and third shelves she found what she needed. Rubbing her palms together she compared her options, loaded her messenger bag with equipment and stole out of the room.

It was difficult in a world of professional spies to find locks secure enough to keep out intruders. *But I'm going to have to up his safeguards* Melanie decided, passing by Ed and his virtual avatar blasting through a building.

On the floor in her office she set out the assembly and tested that the items were fully charged.

"Oh, Ms. Ward," Jane said, returning with a cup of steaming coffee. "I didn't know you were here." She looked down at her cup, "I'll be right back with your coffee, and you've had seven calls this morning."

"Thanks, Jane," Melanie said, reaching into her back pocket for her phone. It was off, she turned it on and before she could check voice mail it rang. she smiled and answered.

"Hey, there you are."

"Danny," her heart fluttered with each syllable.

"Happy Birthday, Sweetheart."

Melanie looked around for a calendar. Was today her birthday? Shit, that would explain the voice mails and seven messages with Jane. Those could be from her mom alone.

"I'm calling to remind you to be home by five. Dinner, remember?"

"Stop with the memory jokes. Are you in town?" her voice quivered. She'd been thinking about him – she breathed in through her nose, remembering how good he smelled.

"On my way. Avery is with her mom and I'm all yours."

"Sounds intriguing." Was she ready to go there with him? *Can't tonight, Mel,* she thought with a sense of relief.

"Great. Should I call at 4:30?"

"Maybe."

She was already on her bike when the reminder call came.

Her messenger bag was light. The protective wrap weighed more than the cameras and added bulk that would otherwise fit into the pocket of a pair of loose-fitting jeans. The sun had set, its soft, autumn rays giving way to a cold, gray mist.

Happiness kept her warm as she rode. She had returned phone calls all afternoon. Baby Olivia was doing well. Ted's lawyers were filing complaints while Carla was kicking The Triad out of her sunroom. Trish and Jason were going to St. Bart's for Christmas and her parents were excited about Thanksgiving.

And Danny was waiting for her. She pedaled faster.

"Finally!" he said happily when she opened the door.

Her greeting was muffled in his shoulder as he drew her into an embrace. She wrapped her arms over his shoulders. He smelled of eucalyptus soap. His hair was soft and he was freshly shaved.

"Have you had a nice day?"

"A wonderful day, thank you." Still in his arms, "Have you heard about the job?"

His squeeze tightened. "I got the job!"

"I knew you would," she jumped excitedly out of his embrace.

"I can't believe I got such a terrific job."

"I can," she said, serious and meeting Danny's gaze.

"I've been dying to tell you. Now we have two things to celebrate. I made reservations at an Italian restaurant. I thought it might be nice to walk … it's a couple of blocks but, if you're too cold. I did rent a car," he said, dangling a set of keys.

"I like to walk. Let me change and grab a warmer coat – I'll be right back." She took a long glance at him as she went up the stairs and blew out a deep breath to reduce the shivers.

Dropping her bag in the closet she dressed quickly. Downstairs he was bringing her bike inside. She wasn't used to having someone do things for her and the kindness stabbed straight into her heart.

Get a grip, Melanie, she growled silently, stifling the urge to fan herself. The chill of the evening air balanced with the heat radiating from Danny's hand. His adding a swing to their laced fingers as they walked was a childish luxury that was pure Danny.

"Let me tell you what happened on the train today." He laughed so easily she couldn't take her eyes off him. She felt like a schoolgirl gazing up at the rugby star. "I got up to get some coffee and you know how narrow the aisles are. Well, this little, almost nothing of an old woman was coming the opposite direction and as she passed she lost her balance." He shook his head. "Anyway, I caught her before she fell."

"That was very kind."

"What can I say, I'm *that* guy. But you're messing me up, shhh," he said, his eyes sparkling. "Anyway, get this – I got her back up on her feet and as I was leaving the old broad grabbed a handful of my ass."

"No way, you bumped into something."

Danny tilted his head and arched a brow. "Mel, please, I know it's been a long time since someone made a pass at me but … she grabbed my ass with those tiny, bony hands."

"What did you do?"

"What could I? I grabbed her back."

"You did not!" Melanie gasped.

"No, I didn't grab her, what's the matter with you?" he asked, grinning, tugging her forward. "I didn't do anything but maybe let out a little shriek … I think the old man she was with caught the whole thing. It was embarrassing. And you know what the worse part is?"

"I can't imagine."

"That's the most action I've gotten in a while."

"Shut up."

"Seriously." His face twisted as he thought back. "Months, unless you count our kissing."

"Think of it this way," she said, blushing and sidestepping his remark. "You made that old woman's day, maybe her month. Besides, I really can't blame her." She didn't stop to think about what she was saying. "You've got a great ass."

His smile crinkled the corners of his eyes and blood rushed to her cheeks.

"We're here." He cocked his head toward a little restaurant tucked on the ground floor of the building.

"I've never seen this place," Melanie said, pulling her gaze from Danny to the awnings above the big windows. From the sidewalk, if she closed her eyes at least one of her senses could be transported to Italy. Her mouth watered and they were led to around intimate little tables to one in the back where a bottle of wine was chilling and a beautiful antipasto had already been prepared.

Danny held out her chair and all of a sudden it felt like a date. Her toes tingled in response to her nerves.

"You still bite your lip," he said. "I thought that habit was gone."

"Me, too."

She poured the wine and the task of sipping distracted her from the knots tightening in her gut.

"I have something for you," Danny said when dinner was ordered and plates brought out. "I hope you like it." He handed her a rectangular box wrapped in pink paper with a red bow.

"Thank you," she balanced it lightly in her hand. "It's my first gift, though my parents sent flowers." Sliding her finger on the inside of the seam she tore open the paper and lifted the lid off the jewelry box. It was simple, sweet, and the sight of a heart charm dangling from the clasp of a gold rope bracelet caused a lump in her throat. "It's beautiful."

"I'm glad you like it because I've been waiting eight years to give it to you." His voice cracked and when she looked up his eyes were glistening. "That," he said, arching his brows and gazing at the bracelet, "was going to be your Valentine's Day gift – way back when."

"Danny…" She didn't know what to say … He'd kept her present, wrapped and waiting. The lump in her throat swelled.

"I want us to work, Mel," he said with a shy smile then arching his brows, "Did I tell you what Paul said about the show?"

"No," she handed him the bracelet and her wrist. He fastened the clip as he clarified the details.

By the time her birthday spumoni arrived Danny had consumed most of the bottle of red wine. She'd been taking one sip to his gulp and rotating their glasses. There was a bright ring around the moon as they walked home, his arm draped heavily over her shoulders.

"You know," he slurred slightly, "I have your real birthday present back in my suitcase." He bent the elbow that was draped over her shoulder and brought her cheek up to his lips. "I love you," he said before tripping.

"Whoa," she called out, stumbling while grabbing a hold of his jacket before he banged his knees on the concrete.

"I swear I saw you sharing that bottle with me," he said, his hand against a brochure kiosk for balance.

"We're almost home." She bowed beneath his arm and wrapped hers around his waist, nearly carrying him to the leather couch. "I'm going to get us some water," she said placing a pillow behind his head and waiting to verify he wasn't going to roll off.

She already felt a pang of guilt for the headache he was going to have. *I'll just have to make it up to him*, she thought sending a ripple through her body. His snore echoed into the kitchen. *Just not tonight.*

He was asleep. She sat, lifting the pillow gently and laying his head on her lap. She ran her fingers through his hair, along the outline of his face and his lips curved up in a smile.

"What are we going to do?" she whispered.

CHAPTER 26

The feeling of importance never lost its appeal when Finn sat in his father's study. This was Hugh's personal space, where he'd held his business meetings for 30 years. Finn remembered sneaking down stairs, in his pajamas, the chill of the marble floor on his cheek as he lay flat outside the door. The desperate need for his father's approval had begun in childhood. He'd wanted to belong, to be included – and now, as he sucked in a lungful of cigar smoke with a drink in his hand, at last, he had it all.

"Where are you with this Ward problem?"

Finn shuffled uncomfortably, in his seat. "I've been in communication with the assassin but he's moving slowly. Have you had contact with him? Did he accept your offer?"

"He will." The malice in Hugh's smile was unmistakable. "We may not need him."

Finn pushed forward to the edge of his seat. "Tell me."

"I got a call yesterday from a friend at the CDC." He raised his brows delightedly. "Apparently there's been a few cases of a deadly bacteria that cause oozing, painful lesions. It got me to thinking," he said, extending Finn's tension by puffing on his cigar and tapping the ash into a tray. "I'd like to test the affects and an assassin seems … crude."

"Crude," Finn repeated, absorbing the word as if delivered from heaven. "More painful sounds good. Yes," he said, though Hugh wasn't listening.

"We cannot underestimate Agent Ward. She was manageable before … I wish you would've finished the job when you had the chance. Well," he waved his hand, "what's done is done. No benefit in regret."

"We'll make her suffer. Should I cancel the hit? But he still owes us a kill." The question was meant to distract from his failure, and it did. Finn took Hugh's grin as a good sign.

"No, don't stop a thing. I haven't made up my mind, yet. Besides, should the opportunity present itself … I'm not morbidly opposed to a bullet through her brain." He stood, indicating it was time for Finn to leave.

The smell of a wood fire was a symbol of autumn, and Finn's good mood was running high as he left the Parker Estate. A Beatles song looped in his mind as he drove home, unconscious of the melody he whistled.

CHAPTER 27

Her birthday wasn't over. She was giving herself a present, a night out.

Danny was passed out on the couch and she was dressed in black leggings, a long-sleeve thermal shirt and a pair of sleek, black climbing shoes that were designed with traction. With the bag full of Mike's technical goodies she fished out the rental car key from Danny's jacket pocket. Shrugging into a navy pea coat, she shoved a black beanie cap into her bag and checked on Danny one last time.

Her heart knocked impatiently against her rib cage as she covered him with a blanket and softly kissed his forehead.

"Goodnight," she whispered.

She used the keyless remote to locate the car. Traffic was light and Melanie took extra precautions as she wound her way around the outskirts of the city, past the Oak Hill Cemetery, to Finn's gorgeous and completely inappropriate family home. The expansive park across from the wide street felt gloomy, barren trees with their crippled branches reaching upwards. Melanie parked a block away. His car was nowhere to be seen and there was no garage. She'd been to Finn's only once, but that time she'd been invited. This time she had to disable his alarm.

His front door opened to a narrow passageway with all the doors leading to the left and a flight of stairs to the right. On the second floor was the room where none of the high-powered eavesdropping devices from Mike's technology closet could ever penetrate.

Melanie inspected the outside the room for an electrical security system but in the end all she needed was a simple pick. Cautiously she let the door swing inward and listened for a moment before placing her foot on the patterned carpeting that she swore she'd seen at a casino in Las Vegas.

As a rush of stale air blew through her, she realized that the room was hermetically sealed. It reeked of stale cigar smoke and last week's booze.

Flicking her light around the 12 X 12 room, it was not as ominous as she'd imagined. Not the secret laboratory of a mad scientist; more like he transported a room from his fraternity house.

In the center of the room were six mismatched chairs around a felt poker table, with dirty glasses set on cork coasters. Unemptied ashtrays were scattered around the various surfaces and a cabinet loaded with half-filled liquor bottles was shoved in the corner.

After a look around she went to work, installing cameras. Three, equipped with microphones, was enough to cover the small room. Directing the lenses on the seating area away from the windows and the glare, she adjusted the angles, sitting in each chair to verify the integrity of the hiding spots.

She checked out the rest of the house. The rooms meant for

company were well decorated but the rest were completely empty, cold with white walls, just like Finn himself. She was on the third floor in his bedroom when car headlights passed across the window. Finn was home, and he was whistling.

Melanie blended in with the shadows, easing down the hallway and into an upstairs bathroom. She could hear Finn and his off-tune rendition of Yellow Submarine, coming up the stairs.

Softly clicking the door behind her, she examined the room. Her only route to freedom was a small stained-glass window in the shower stall.

The crank of the old casement window was stiff and Melanie used all the force she believed the old glass could handle. It didn't budge. *Please*, she begged and firmly pushed on the iron brace, half expecting her arm to go right through.

After the loud creak there was a solid pop and frigid air rushed in. She stuck her head out the window. It was an eight-foot drop to the second-floor balcony. Melanie yanked herself up, sucked in her gut and twisted, hoping she wouldn't get stuck. Gripping the ledge with her fingers, it took all of her upper-body strength to quietly lower herself down.

She hung, one-handed from the base of the window and reaching in with her free hand, pulled the glass shut. She dropped and landing crooked the impact sent jolts of shock up her legs. She grabbed the railing to stop from falling. From the second-story balcony, a good five feet separated her from the skeleton arms of a massive oak tree.

No choice.

Pushing off, she hurled through the air, reaching out for anything to hold onto. The branches were solid beneath her weight, and she fell through the limbs. Grabbing onto a thick branch, she flipped around, secured her balance and skipped along like a gymnast on a beam. The leafless tree offered no concealment. Swinging to lower branches she hit the ground sprinting and bounded over the fence like it was no more than a hurdle.

The night was tranquil. Other than the occasional porch light it was a dark street, the neighbors tucked into bed. No one noticed the figure darting between houses on the calm November night.

She hopped into the car, cranked up the heat, drove past Finn's and made sure she wasn't being followed.

The fire was a pile of glowing embers and Danny was in the same position he'd been in when she left. *He could sleep through an earthquake,* she thought, running her fingers through his hair and settling a soft kiss on his forehead.

Upstairs she yanked off the black beanie she was still wearing and awakened her computer. She linked the cameras to a secure site, routing through two international companies before returning the images to her. These were extras steps Mike had taught her to shield herself from hackers, like him.

"Great job on the placement, Mel," she chuckled so low she could barely hear her voice. Leaning back in her chair, she felt the exhaustion seep in. *I could fall asleep right here ... but then I'd have to get up later.*

Her legs moaned as she ambled into the bathroom, squinting from the harsh light and willing to skip the floss for a few extra minutes of sleep. *It's my birthday.* She stared into her scrubbed face, looking for subtle changes of age. Her bump was the size of a quarter and looked worse than it felt. "Oh well," she sighed, ignoring the bulge and making one last effort to smooth out the skin beneath her eyes before flipping off the lights.

"Relationship issues already?"

The voice cut into her thoughts, jolting her awake and electrifying the hair on her body.

Without missing a beat she answered, "You need to learn to knock."

"I didn't want to wake anyone," Adam said.

She wanted to look at him, to dissect his expression. But her heart was already nearly bursting and all her strength was set on maintaining her cool exterior.

"You kicked Ashe to the couch? I'm surprised that you have a couch." He leaned on the dresser, attention drawn to the gold heart bracelet. "Pretty," he smirked, the chain dangling from his finger.

Snatching the bracelet from his hand she brushed over his skin. The touch happened in a flash but ... her fingers had grazed over the battle wounds from kitchen knives ... along his trigger finger.

He stopped grinning, seizing her chin with two fingers and angled her face toward the light. "What happened?"

"Walked into a door."

The muscles in his neck tightened and twitched. "Who did this to you?"

"I told you, a very angry door." She twisted out of his grasp. "Is this why you're here?"

"No." He let her go but watched her through narrowed eyes. "Where were you tonight?"

"Is this multiple choice?" she asked, reaching into her back pocket for her phone. If they were going to talk business she needed to protect them from prying ears.

"Okay," he started. "Why were you ... can we speak?" Tapping in the final bits of code, she nodded and ran a playlist for added security.

"Why were you at Parker's?"

"Are you tracking me or him?" she asked with annoyance and resenting the awful beard that still covered his jaw.

"The house."

"From assassin to security guard, interesting career path." She wasn't meaning to be hostile but couldn't help herself. Adam ran his hands up from his chin, over his face and through his short hair.

"You must have entered from the front. I was watching the back ... didn't know you were in there until you almost brought down the balcony. What were you thinking?"

"That I had to escape. Besides I was graceful." Melanie sighed, *fine*. "Finn has a room I haven't been able to penetrate – soundproof, high-tech. It's like a giant vacuum ... and, well, I wanted to know what he's up to."

"Parker's house? What happens when he finds ... what did you plant?"

"Cameras and sound," she smiled. "And he won't find anything."

"But," he began to complain.

"But nothing. They aren't detectable, he can't trace them back to me ... he's arrogant. Didn't even have additional security inside the room. Besides, who cares if he does know it's me? Can't prove it and ... I've got nothing to lose."

"Melanie, you're rattling his cage."

"He makes most of his big mistakes when he's unnerved. I know what I'm doing."

Scratching at his beard, his gaze locked onto hers. "I don't like it."

"Doesn't matter," she said softly.

His voice lowered to match hers. "God, you are frustrating."

"Good thing you don't have to deal with me anymore," she said, turning away.

"How are you?"

"Don't. Don't act like I mean anything to you," she said, facing him as he shifted from one foot to the other.

"Why is Ashe on the couch?" The muscle at his jaw twitched.

"It's where he sleeps."

"Why?"

"I'm not sure how any of this is your business," she said, studying his blank expression as he tried to read her. She didn't bother to mask feelings she didn't fully understand … a mixture of wanting him to know she'd been forgivably faithful and ashamed that she was too weak to move on.

His body tensed as she watched a veil lift. "You're not…?" An intense moment passed before he stepped, soundlessly to the nightstand. Pulling on the small brass ring, the shallow drawer nearly fell to the ground as he roughly knocked around the contents.

Realization dawned. "They're all there," she said, letting him count. He'd bought the box of condoms and though she knew exactly how many were left she wasn't sure he'd remember.

With his back still turned toward her, her ragged breath held, she watched him. He looked big, his shoulders broad and she knew that beneath his long-sleeve shirt his muscles were rock hard. Her heart beat erratically.

When he turned back around there was a burning in his eyes and for an instant Melanie thought he was going to kiss her. But the thought lasted longer than the glint.

"This changes nothing," he growled.

"I didn't think it would," she said, her teeth aching from being clamped together.

"What the hell is wrong with you?" he barked, straining to control his rage, his fists opening and closing.

"You," she answered absently. His mouth was moving but she could only hear the thoughts swirling around in her head. "Did you ever love me?" she asked, searching her memory of him, trying to remember what he felt like. What she missed were the spicy scents that used to linger at his shirt collar.

"We've been through this." His voice deepened and the edge was clear.

"I know." She surrendered her position. She'd already lost this argument but the unsatisfactory answers still nagged at her. Melanie knew he was about to bail and there were things to say. "I am sorry … for everything."

"What do you have to be sorry for?" he asked, interested enough to cut the distance between them.

Her mouth went dry. "For screwing up your plans, for getting you in this mess, for pulling you into my train wreck." She'd counted out her faults on her fingers and would've continued but the memory of his uncle Rob's photos overwhelmed her into speechlessness.

He stared for a long, uncomfortable moment, the gray of his eyes cooling.

"I've got to get some sleep." She cranked the doorknob, twisting it the way she felt her insides were being constricted. "I realize you don't want to hear this but … I do wish things had worked out differently for us. I know … move on. Trust me I am, this was my last look back." It was only when she stopped talking and the silence engulfed them she felt self-conscious of how much she'd said.

His fingers folded around her wrist. "It wasn't you who fucked up my life."

"Right, thanks." He meant well but the heat of his touch was searing her skin, marking her.

"Be careful with Finn. I'm not joking about this."

"And I thought you were." She couldn't stop the sarcasm.

"I'll do my part but quit pissing him off."

"Adam," she sighed, "that I'm breathing pisses him off. But I promise, I won't purposely antagonize."

"Okay," he sounded satisfied. "We'll talk."

"Sure," her answer, directed to their shoes. He was inches away, the tips of his leather loafers pointed toward the door.

She felt the grip of his fingers cup the base of her neck. He was rough, pulling her to him but the act held compassion. The right side of her face pressed to the fabric of his black overcoat. His heart pounded ferociously through the thick wool and she wanted to melt into the fibers. His clutch tightened as she felt the pressure of his lips on the top of her head, his nose buried in her hair – able to count the length of time she clung to him with a handful of heartbeats.

Then he was gone. Adjusting to the darkness as if he had night vision, avoiding the creeks and groans of her apartment.

She stood at the landing long after the slice of streetlight had vanished from the opening and closing of her front door. All he left behind was a feeling of oppressive emptiness. His escape had been so smooth that if she hadn't known where to look she could've easily missed it.

"Move on," he'd said. *That's what I'm going to do*, she thought, her heart expanding as she watched Danny, blissfully unaware, curled on his side and breathing heavily. *What's wrong with you? What are you scared of? Just do it. Close your eyes and leap.*

Minutes passed.

This is not a big deal. You can do this. Though her definition of *this* was broad. *You can have sex. You can change you life. You can give up on Adam.*

She lifted the blanket carefully. He was wearing a faded Pink Floyd T-shirt and plaid boxers.

She bit her thumbnail still debating – tossing and turning all night in her empty bed or allowing Danny back in.

"Brr," he shivered, adjusting his position to give her space.

"Sorry."

"You okay?" he asked, groggily.

She didn't answer. She just nestled in, her back against his chest. His arm moved protectively over her as his leg draped over hers, sending goose bumps down her spine.

I'm not alone, was the last thought to cross her mind as she drifted off.

❧

Consciousness came delightfully slowly. A gentle morning glow, soft blankets. She yawned and tried to reposition. Locked in, Melanie peered out of one squinty eye.

"Hi," she twisted around to face Danny, who was up on an elbow grinning down at her.

"Too much room in your bed?"

"Something like that." She smiled and rested her cheek on his chest. "You smell nice."

"Mel, what happened to your forehead?" he asked, caressing her bruise.

Damn. "Walked into a door."

He smiled, bent to kiss her injury. "You really need to be more careful."

"I will." She grinned, promising.

"You falling back to sleep?" he asked, his fingers pulling her hair away from her neck.

"Mm-hmm."

"Okay, but can we change sides?"

Hours later she lurched out of sleep to gunfire.

"I'm sorry – didn't mean to wake you," Danny said, grabbing the remote and frantically reducing the volume of the surround sound.

"What time is it?"

"Almost three."

"In the afternoon?" Melanie sprang to life, jumping off the couch and hunting for her phone on the coffee table. *Shit, it's in my room.*

"I already talked to your assistant Jane. She called hours ago." He twirled her phone between his fingers like a magic act. "Told her you were sleeping in."

"Oh, thanks. They get worried if I don't call in," she stammered. "How long have you been up?" She scooped her hair in a big ponytail, noticing he was dressed in jeans and a rust-colored, long-sleeve shirt with opal snaps down the front.

His brown alert eyes were untroubled and his casually tumbled hair showed that his confidence was back.

"A while ... I had some work to do and I ordered in, you hungry?"

"I think so." She tore her gaze away from him to stare longingly at her phone.

"Call," he laughed. "I'll get your lunch." Danny nuked the beef with gingered broccoli as she checked in with Jane and skipped through voicemail.

Danny set her plate on the table. "Everything okay with work?"

"No casualties. At least not until Jane starts to prod me about you and sleeping in," she said, unable to reverse the upward curve of her lips.

"What will you tell her about us?" he asked, leaning against the table, facing her.

"What do you mean? I'm not telling her anything," she declared, stabbing a bright green floret.

"Give me a break!" he chuckled, and turned her chair away from the food, lowering himself to her eye level. "Last night when you came to the couch with me ... was it because you were lonely or cold or because..." his smile broadened. "You're ready?" He cradled her face in his hands, tilting her head up. She scooted off the chair to stand tiptoe before him, resting her forearms on his shoulders. It was natural to hold the back of his head, to rub the back of his neck.

Taking in one heavy breath, she took the initiative, sliding her lips along his jaw. Danny didn't move. Looking up at him, his eyes were closed – she smiled and kissed the corner of his mouth.

His arms tightened around her. His lips were soft on hers, delicate as he barely touched her. Somewhere from the back of his throat she heard her name. The kiss turned, heating up as he pressed harder moving down from her mouth to her neck, gently pulling at her skin with his teeth.

Squirming at the sensation she pulled back and yanked on his shirt until the snaps gave. She grasped his face in her palms and kissed him, jumping to wrap her legs around his waist. He carried her up the stairs, slipping on the fourth step. Catching her before she hit, he landed on top of her. Melanie tugged his shirt off his shoulders. She worked fast but Danny was quicker, pulling off her T-shirt and lifting her into the bedroom.

Then life became a blur of mouths, skin and clothes flying.

CHAPTER 28

Dressed in a towel, Melanie opened her underwear and sock drawer and found a wrapped, rectangular box. She smiled. *Danny had said there was another present,* she thought, eagerly lifting the heavy package and setting it atop the dresser. She poked her head out the door, wondering if she should wait for him to return from the kitchen. But the shimmery silver paper and big orange bow were calling her name.

The thick wrapping threatened a paper cut as she wedged her finger under the tape. Ripping off the first strip of the shiny material, Melanie knew this black metal box wasn't from Danny. Carefully she released the fasteners and gently raised the lid. Snuggled in dark grey foam was a beautiful, compact .380.

The pistol was cool on her fingertips, its black pearl handle reflecting back an iridescent green. Melanie wrestled it out of the foam. It was light ... constructed out of some kind of polycarbonate. She'd never seen anything like it. The weapon felt good in her hand, an extension of her arm. She caressed the trigger, softly applying pressure, and smiled. Laser trigger.

She popped out the extra clips, inserting and releasing them inside the handle and stroked her gift before toggling it back into place.

How had he known it was her birthday? She closed the gun case, secured it behind the loose paneling in her closet and dressed for work.

It doesn't change anything … his words.

CHAPTER 29

The three days following her birthday, Melanie rushed home from work on time, leaving Spy Melanie at the office to become Danny's girlfriend. The simplicity of it was mesmerizing. Dinner, curling up on the couch, telling stories – Danny had taken to reading her sports articles, romanticizing the plays and adding innuendos that had no place in the story.

She was startled awake the first night when the alarm on her phone sounded. Easing out of Danny's embrace, pulling on a sweatshirt and flannel pants, she sat by the dying fire with her laptop. The motion sensor had been activated in Finn's Victorian secure room.

Swiveling in the chair behind his desk, Finn was on the phone. She could hear only his side of the conversation; it'd been too risky to bug the landline.

"You haven't done anything. It's been months and has there been progress from you? No. I'm tired of the delays. Think it over, Amigo, then give me a call back." Finn leaned way back in the chair, tipping so his head nearly touched the wall. "One more thing. My father's offer isn't open ended. If you want in … I suggest you let him know, like pronto."

He was speaking to Adam. Melanie would have loved to hear Adam's response. Finn didn't look worried. He swallowed the last inch of liquid in his glass, cracked his knuckles and killed the lights as he left the room.

The following night she anxiously waited, all night, at her computer.

It was 10:30 on the third night, Danny asleep. Lying beside him, she placed a hand on his forehead. He felt feverish, radiating heat that caused her to keep a window cracked open in the middle of November. Moving her head to the pillow she watched him. His chest was lightly dusted with hair that narrowed to a strip down his abs.

She was cold the instant she dragged herself out of bed, having grown accustomed to Danny's 100-degree heat. Raising the thermostat on her way downstairs, Melanie threw a log on the fire and settled down in a blanket; Finn was hosting a poker party.

Melanie dozed as Finn poured cheese balls and pretzels into bowls and gathered the dirty glasses from around the room, emptying the contents out the window. Of the five men that arrived, two were agents – no surprise – and the others were sons of politicians and a local businessman.

For an hour she observed their game. Texas Hold 'Em … of course, unoriginal and trendy. The game was dull – she'd expected more from agents, even if they were Parker's friends. The below average performance was a let down. Only one could lie with any aptitude.

It was chilly in her living room and when the subject turned to wives, Melanie considered giving up for the evening. Just as she was about to close her computer the conversation got interesting.

"If you're seriously interested in getting rid of her ... I might have a name for you."

"Forget it, I'm done with women. Besides, she'd squeeze my balls so tight I doubt I'd be able to get it up again."

Melanie opened one lid to look at the man, the son-in-law of the Speaker of the House. Handsome, but they all were in that generic, perfect kind of way.

"I'm not talking about another woman – I'm talking about getting rid of the one you've got." Parker continued dealing, wickedly grinning at the Queen of Spades.

"What do you mean?" Melanie asked with the men, simultaneously.

He looked up. "Let's just say I've got a friend that owes me a favor and," he flipped a card, "I might not be in need of his services."

"What kind of friend?"

"What kind of services?"

"Professional. Ante up, men." Each tossed in a chip, without breaking focus from the questioning. "All right," Parker laughed. "I won't name names, but I've come across a less *crude* way of liberating myself from a nuisance. Something more befitting, and by that I mean excruciatingly painful, over a prolonged period of time." Checking his cards, barking out another howl of laughter, "God, this is my lucky day."

He means me, she thought. *He's not going to use Adam ... another method, more painful*. Her throat constricted. Her mind raced to the cool attitude he had with Adam. *It's because he knows he doesn't need him anymore*. She thought of her parents. It took hours but damp with sweat she decided there was a lot to do before her terrible death.

"Good morning," she said as she trudged into the kitchen.

"Hi, beautiful." His smile was brilliant as he pulled her into his arms. "Didn't sleep well?"

"Not really." She dug her fingers into Danny's shoulders, drawing him as close as possible.

"I love you, Mel," he said, never missing an opportunity to tell her. "So," he said, lowering his voice. "I've been wanting to ask you something." She nodded, loosening her grip and taking one step back to examine his expression. "We haven't talked about it in a long time but I was curious about your feelings regarding marriage."

"It's only been three days!" Her astonishment was clearly plastered on her face.

"Eleven years and three days." He laughed. "Okay, enough said." His eyes sparkled as he kissed her cheek.

"No, wait. You caught me off guard. The truth is I haven't had reason to think about marriage in a decade."

"What about Adam?" He couldn't say the name without contorting his face.

"I realize that compared with 36 hours he and I were together for a lifetime but no we never spoke about it." She took care choosing her words. "Besides why would you want to?"

"One mistake won't scare me," he said, running the back of his hand along the side of her face. "I liked being married. But you're right, we have plenty of time."

Grief clamped onto her heart, nostalgic for the family she may never have.

"You're not supposed to cry."

Melanie swallowed, choked up. "I'm just really happy." She couldn't tell him the truth.

"Oh, Sweetheart, me, too."

Closing her eyes she leaned into him just as his pocket began to ring out Lauren's song.

"She can wait," he said, not letting go.

"No, you'd better answer. It might be about Avery. You pick her up tonight, right?"

"Yeah," he huffed. "What's up?" he asked, the resentment loud in his voice.

Giving him privacy, Melanie headed upstairs to get ready for work. Ignoring the arguing, she occupied her mind with the list of tasks she needed to complete. Danny was leaving for the weekend and she'd have time to set her affairs in order.

"The call went that well, huh?" she asked sarcastically, when he slammed down the phone. His shoulders were tense and raised to his ears.

He rubbed from his forehead down to his jaw. "I'm not a violent person but right now…" he growled. "I'm thinking about it."

"Can I help?" she hopped to sit up on the counter.

A low rumble came from his throat as he looked up at her. "She wants Avery for Thanksgiving. Since I'll be alone, she thought it'd be more fun for her to spend the holiday with her new family."

"What did you say?"

"I said no fucking way."

"Good for you."

"Right before I relented and said okay."

Melanie laughed. "Seriously, Danny?"

"God, I'm pathetic." He ran his fingers through his hair. "But to be honest, Avery doesn't want to spend Thanksgiving with me … She'd have more fun with the other kids." His eyes were moist when he dragged the back of his finger beneath them.

She stretched, reached the collar of his shirt and pulled him to her. "You are the best father ever," she said, scooting to the ridge of the counter and wrapping her legs around his hips. "You, my sweet man, will come home with me." She nuzzled the corner of his mouth. "You said you wanted to come the next time I went," she said, nibbling over to the other side of his mouth.

"Think it'd be all right?" he asked, rubbing her thighs.

"Are you kidding?"

"I get Avery on Friday night, after Thanksgiving," he breathed, the tension leaving his shoulders.

"That's perfect. You can fly home Friday morning. Come with me, Danny. You can sleep in Bruce's old room."

"What day do we leave?"

Melanie threw her arms around him and squeezed. "Early Wednesday." She plastered his face with rapid kisses.

He laughed, catching her face and holding it still. "Thank you." He caressed her back, rubbing the sides of her breasts. "Do you have time?"

"For you? Always." She kissed him and checked her watch. "Are we at the stage where I can ask for it to be quick?"

⌘

Danny was a wonderful distraction, but she wasn't displeased to have her privacy back.

"You're going to miss your train," she said, adjusting his bag on his shoulder and tiptoeing for one last goodbye kiss.

"I'd love to stay with you but Lauren would murder me." His words were interrupted as his lips made contact with her skin.

"See you Tuesday?"

"I can't wait. I'm actually glad it worked out this way. Don't tell Avery I said that." He smiled and bent to kiss her.

She waved as he pulled from the curb. Within that same minute she was on her bike pedaling toward the office, and she didn't return to her apartment until the following Monday.

She'd worked nonstop, compiling and arranging data for the various media outlets. Evidence collected over 10 years rolled into one digital file and embedded into a single photo.

In the end her fixation resulted in a five-page expose, photos, audio and video material implicating both Parkers with facts, dates and times that, when assembled, couldn't be ignored. *Hopefully.*

She replayed the file for the 10th time. Satisfied with the results she realized, *The only way this gets seen is if I'm dead*. She blew out a heavy sigh. Morbid thoughts had caused two days of headaches.

The top bar of her computer stated MON 8:23 – a.m. or p.m.? Melanie pulled back the curtain to the orange glow from the streetlights illuminating the slanted track of falling rain in the dark evening sky.

It was still early in California.

"Oh, Honey, I can't talk right now. I'm at the grocery store and it's a complete zoo. One would think we were back in the depression … fighting over a bird. But you haven't changed your flight, have you?"

"No, Danny and I will be there tomorrow. Late, I think." Rita was humming and Melanie knew her mom was only partially listening. "I'll let you go. You've got someone helping you with Thanksgiving dinner, right?"

"What? I'm sorry I wasn't listening."

"Bye, Mom."

Trish's number went straight to voicemail and Carla was in the middle of a state dinner. Melanie debated on calling Jen. She never called Jen – for a reason.

Tapping in the code, her stomach knotted and her fingers trembled. The small gathering on the balcony of the South American palace zoomed into focus. She couldn't help but scan the women – judging which one would be the next to suffer an Adam heartache.

They always seemed to be having a party with beautiful women. No wonder Adam didn't want to come back to her. She found him alone, stacking logs in a copper fire pit. The sleeves of his green sweater were pushed up to his elbows as he arranged the wood.

Melanie dialed the number she had for him, waited for the delay and felt the rush of nerves when he stood and pulled the phone from his pant pocket. *Answer,* she commanded, seeing his reluctance.

"Hey," he said, snapping his fingers to someone seated and pointing to the unfinished fire pit.

"Hi," she said, giving him a minute before continuing. "I'm sorry to bother you."

Adam walked to the far side of the pool, his back turned to the small crowd. "What can I do for you?" he said, politely.

"A favor." She ignored her body's reaction to his voice.

"Shoot."

She smiled at the assassin humor. "I'm going to send my mom a document with an embedded file. I'll have her forward it to everyone on a list. I need you to look for the file and follow the instructions."

"What's this about?"

"It's just a precaution. *If* Finn is successful, I won't go down without a fight." Her throat clamped up, again, but the fear had vanished. "I'm not saying he'll get to me but I can't pretend that there isn't a possibility." Adam was silent. He gripped the railing and leaned over slightly, staring out at the ocean. "There's no one else I trust," she added, her mind already calculating what to do if Adam said no.

"Nothing is going to happen to you." He pushed away from the edge and glanced at a woman warming her hands at the fire pit.

"You can't be sure. I'll feel better knowing they won't get away scot-free. Look, I know you have another life filled with parties and friends and I don't want to mess that one up, too. But…" She was about to tell him how important it was to have him professionally in her life. That she needed him and there was no one else she could be honest with.

Adam's gaze shot up, his eyes narrowing as if he were looking into deep space.

"Jesus Christ. Are you spying on me?"

"It's sort of what I do, spy on people." She smiled.

"How's the view?"

"Pretty good except for the beard. I'm not a fan."

"I'll keep that in mind." He cleared his throat. Getting back to business. "Fine. What is it you need me to do?"

"Thank you. The file will be embedded in a photo I'll have sent to my mom the minute I'm confirmed … anyway." At this Adam dropped his head so she couldn't see any sign of his emotions. "I don't know your e-mail, so, I'm counting on you keeping in contact with Jason. They'll make you aware of my…"

He sighed. "I'd be aware. But it's not going to be necessary."

"Okay," she said, feeling heartsick.

"This isn't a license to be reckless, to do something stupid," he growled. In a chance gaze he seemed to be looking directly at her.

"I'm rarely reckless. I would think you'd know that by now."

"I think you have a judgment lapse when it comes to the Parkers."

He scanned the sky. "Mel, be careful, they don't play fair."

"What about you? Are you playing their game?" she asked, thinking about the one-sided conversation she'd heard between him and Finn.

"I'm doing what I have to."

"So am I."

"I hate this." He rubbed a hand over his eyes.

"Adam, no matter what happens … it wasn't your fault. I think my number was up this summer. I've been living on borrowed time ever since and I thank you for that."

"Did something happen? Is there something I should know?" His chest heaved as he turned away.

"Nothing. I just can't let them get away with what they've done. At the very least they might regret."

"Babe, if they get to you, which they won't, they won't have time for regret."

"Now who's being reckless?" She breathed. Melanie couldn't help but gaze at the woman behind him.

"I'll be in touch." He icy tone was back as he clicked off the phone and made a wave gesture to the heavens.

"Bye." Melanie couldn't cut him off as easily. She lingered. Terese turned, giving Melanie her first good view of her face. She was older than Melanie expected. There was a pulled, plastic look to her and Melanie thought the slight movement of her face was a smile when Adam draped his arm over her shoulder and kissed the side of her head. She cut off the feed and left her office.

"Mikey," she smiled, rolling a chair next to his.

"What's up?"

"I have a vital task and you're the only one I trust."

"Yeah?"

She held out the flash drive. "I need you to e-mail this to my mom in case I fall into trouble that I wasn't able get out of."

That got his attention. He gaped at the drive. "Are you already in trouble?"

"Maybe. Take it, it won't bite." He didn't, so she reached for his hand, turned it palm up, balanced the small device in the center and closed his fingers. "Don't freak out, agents do this all the time."

"But *you* don't. Holy, holy, holy shit! Melanie, no."

She laughed to ease his mind. "I'm fine, Mike. It's just last summer when I thought my time was up … I wished I had explained stuff to my parents. It's only if I'm," she was about to say murdered, "killed. This is a precaution, one worry I can forget about."

"Promise?"

"I promise," she lied, as the fear slowly faded from his eyes.

"Okay. Maybe I should take precautions, too."

"Probably a good idea." She clapped his shoulder as she left. "Thanks, Mike, I knew I could count on you."

Melanie headed to Ben's office, trying to kick off the morose feeling of everything being the last.

"Just the agent I wanted to see," he grinned, rising from behind his desk to pour a scotch. "Would you like one?"

"No, thanks," she said, pleased to know it would do no good. "So, why'd you send Finn to Mexico? His Spanish is fair but…"

Ben grinned and handed her the glass. "You waste no time getting to your point."

"Drug family retaliations aren't usually our thing."

"Yes, but assassins are."

Melanie studied Ben to verify he wasn't joking.

"You sent him to delve into a band of murderers?" A small gurgle of a laugh escaped. She couldn't tell Ben her secret. First, there was no proof. Second, he was tired of the Melanie vs. Finn fiasco.

"You're thinking he'll irritate one and they'll shoot him," he said, sipping his drink. "I don't think you give him enough credit. He might be a walking disaster but he can be charming when he wants to be, which unfortunately isn't often."

"I thought the murders down in Mexico had been brutal, unsophisticated blood baths."

"Completely separate situations."

"Ben, I need an assignment. Something that takes me away for a few months, deep cover." Her heart pounded. Finn was getting to her and though she hated the idea she needed to distance herself from Danny, for his safety.

Ben's blue eyes were sharp and he examined her. "I'll see what I can do. But you're not the only one who hears things. Are you sure you aren't trying to run away?"

That was exactly what she was doing, running away from Finn.

"I heard you were seeing someone."

That wasn't what she was expecting. "I'm distancing myself from potential disasters, Finn being enemy number one. Nothing to do with," she smiled, "with the boyfriend."

"Oh," he nodded. "Well," he said, slowly. "A new option has recently landed on my desk. Truthfully, I can't decide if it is a good thing or not."

Melanie didn't breathe, blink or shift her gaze an inch.

"There's a position open at the CIA … It's a good job, high but not so high that there'd be much inquiry. And, well, all they need to move forward with Finn is a positive recommendation from me." He stared right at her. "He's Hugh's son."

"Wow." She mouthed the word. "He'd be out of here?" Ben nodded. "Do they know he's a complete fuck-up?"

"Not yet." He raised his brows. "We'll keep that under our hats for the moment but are you okay with this?"

"Hell yeah!"

"It's a promotion for him. A step up to … God only knows how high."

It was the short-term gain vs. the long-term travesty of Finn becoming a powerful voice that was bothering Ben. He would be responsible.

"It's a good option." She sipped the drink.

"I know it's not fair but … I'll submit the paperwork in the morning." Ben tilted his glass between his fingers, sloshing the liquid from side to side. "I wish..."

"I know." She swallowed her drink in one gulp.

"Have a happy Thanksgiving, Agent." Ben smiled.

"You, too."

CHAPTER 30

"You missed the turn off," Melanie said.

"We're not going directly to your parents."

"You know I don't like surprises."

"Relax and enjoy. We're on vacation."

"Hmm. I never thought of my parents house as a vacation." She said.

Danny pulled into the parking lot of a hotel.

"Aren't you staying with me at the house?" Melanie asked, reading the La Jolla Inn sign above her head as the tires sprang back from the curb.

"I am, and I'm guessing you won't allow me to be affectionate with your family under the same roof."

Melanie laughed nervously. "If by affectionate you mean screwing around, then you are absolutely correct."

"Thus the need for the hotel."

"So, we're going to sneak back and forth?"

"I like it, sneaking sounds illicit," Danny grinned. "I requested our old room ... I wonder if it's changed much." The tingling feeling started at her toes and shivered its way up her spine. "Please tell me you remember we stayed here."

"Of course." She remembered clearly that night of celebration, madly in love with Danny and expecting to spend the rest of her life with him. Sliding out of the passenger seat, she grabbed hold of the moment. "I did tell my mom we'd be getting here late."

❦

Losing track of time, she watched the ocean from the balcony.

"We'd better go," Danny said, striding up behind her, pulling aside wisps of hair to kiss her neck.

"It's peaceful here."

"I know, but your mom is going to start worrying."

Melanie spun to face him. "Thanks for this."

"Ha," he chuckled, caressing her face, "I should be thanking you. I really didn't want to be luring you out to the backseat. I would have. Definitely. But this is more comfortable." Searching over her shoulder at the horizon, he said, "Next time we're here I'm bringing a wetsuit and a board. Think I can still balance?"

❦

Dropping her bag at her feet, Melanie bounced on her bed. The lilac bedspread smelled of fabric softener. It was good to be home.

Danny was right down the hall. It was strange, uncomfortable and she knew her dad would be getting very little sleep for the next two nights. Melanie smiled despite the turmoil.

"How's it going?" Danny whispered, peeking in from the hall.

Melanie couldn't control her incessant grin. She sat up. "Fine. And you?"

"Did you see the way your father looked at me? Jeez, Mel, it's not like you're a teenager."

"Yeah, we'll see how you handle things with Avery."

Danny pondered for a moment, still not venturing into her room. "Good point. I definitely have to get used to his perspective. I think your mom wants us down to help with the preparations." Danny leaned his head on the door jam. "Mel, I thought you said she was ordering dinner from someplace."

"I thought she was, too. Although she was at the grocery store when I spoke with her on Monday."

Danny shivered. "I can't even imagine."

Melanie stretched her legs. Even in heels she still had to look up to meet his eyes. "We'd better see if we can preempt the salmonella. You aren't afraid?"

"You know I love your mom, Mel, and I will gladly digest poison not to hurt her feelings. But you can't stop me from being frightened."

"She's going to hear you," Melanie cautioned. "Oh," she remembered, "be sure not to drop any buzzwords that'll send her off to her church friends." At the top of the stairs, Danny was still working on her meaning. She whispered, "Ring, wedding, marriage, kids."

"What about proposal? Is that an alert word?"

"Ha-ha. Don't even try to be funny." Melanie lightly punched him in the arm as he laughed at her and raced downstairs. "You have no idea the damage," she continued, talking to herself as Danny disappeared into the kitchen, "the infliction, the anxiety you'd cause by your lack of humor." She stopped. Hearing Danny and Rita chattering on the other side of the swinging door was unnerving.

Too many times her mom had embarrassed her, thinking it was all in good fun.

"Whatever you two are laughing about … I'm here now." Arching a brow at them both, "I'd forgotten how you liked to gang up on me."

"We weren't laughing at you, Dear." Rita winked at Danny. "Not much, anyway."

Melanie rolled her eyes. "I thought you were ordering in for Thanksgiving," she said, cringing at the pots and pans lined up, freshly washed and waiting to be put back in the cupboards.

"Oh, well, that…" Rita stammered. "Danny, dear, would you mind helping Roger with the leaves for the table? I think we're going to need both, and the extra chairs are around the house."

"I'd be glad to." He smiled at her but sent Melanie a sideways grimace as he passed.

She smiled, watching Danny go and search out her father. Roger would warm up, eventually. He had liked Danny – before the broken heart, anyway. *How necessary, is it for her to fess up that she'd caused her own pain?*

"Your friend Adam sent a man to…" She scrunched up her forehead. "Well, he called it 'prep work.'" Rita leaned in close, speaking in a low voice, raising her brows and nodding animatedly. "His name is Brian, and he helped me at the grocery store and came by yesterday morning. He'll be back tomorrow, 5 a.m., to bake the turkey and set up for the mashed potatoes and stuffing."

"Adam? Did you speak to him?"

"Yes, it was very sweet of him to think of us. Even after … well, you broke up with him."

"He said that?"

"He didn't have to. Why else would he still want to be involved with our family? Such a wonderful man."

"Yeah, he's a charmer. What else did he say?"

"Only that he wished he could be here but he had somewhere else to be. Which is a good thing, don't you think? Yikes, that would be an awkward meal." Rita fixed her perfect hair. "Anyway, he knew how important it was for me to have all of you here and that's why Brian is helping out."

Hmm.

"I don't mean to pry but…"

"Yes, you do. And I don't want to talk about it."

"I like both men, dear, but have you chosen one? I thought it was Dan but … Adam was so considerate. I just think you'd better settle on one. It's hardly appropriate to have a back-up boyfriend."

Melanie couldn't help but laugh. It started out as sarcastic but turned genuine. "I'll keep that in mind. Oops, saved by the phone," she said, lifting her ringing phone.

"So, are you here?" was Trish's greeting.

"I am."

"Come over for dinner. I've gotten really good at dinner parties. Do you have a car? No, I'll send Jason over to pick you up. How about early, I can't wait to see you."

"Hold on, Danny's with me." Melanie waited, dreading Trish's reaction.

Silence.

"You still there?"

"Yeah. I know how you feel about Dan but … well, you know how I feel, too, I suppose. We're still picking you up, both of you."

"We've rented a car … so how about we meet you at Jason's at eight?"

"Wow, Dan Ashe is back and you've *rented a car*." She repeated the comment with a note of amazement. "I'm not being rude, it's just that renting a car is so couple-ish."

"I know, isn't it great?"

"Fabulous. Anyway, eight is too late. Seven. And please don't snack because I want you to be hungry." Melanie was about to end the call when Trish called out, "Mel, I am happy for you – only a little worried, too."

"Thanks."

By six-thirty Melanie had to pry Danny and Roger apart. Heads bent over a sports diagram. "What've you got there?"

"Fantasy football." Roger said, not bothering to look up.

"Danny, we've got to go."

"Five more minutes," Roger was marking the page.

"Can't. We're meeting Jason and Trish for dinner."

She had to name drop to get her dad's attention. All the Ward men were smitten with Jason.

"Great. Okay, go. Jason and Bruce will be here tomorrow and we can add them."

"I see you two worked things out." Melanie said, taking the driver's seat.

"You're driving?"

"You don't have a problem with that, do you?" she asked, watching him from the corner of her eye … in dare mode.

"I love it, gives me a chance to relax. We're having dinner with Trish and her boyfriend … like I've time-traveled back to college."

"Weird?"

"In a good way."

Following the purple line on the GPS, Melanie pulled into the long driveway of Jason's energy-efficient, green home. A bottle of wine in one hand and Danny's fingers entwined with the other, he rang the doorbell.

"Danny, two things." She raced to relay the information she hadn't wanted to discuss in the car. The first she'd held onto purposely as a decoy to distract him. "One, do not tell Trish that Rita is cooking. And two, Trish might be holding a grudge toward you for breaking my heart."

"I didn't break your heart."

"You sort of did ... anyway she's protective."

"She's pissed at me?"

No time to answer. "Yay," Trish clapped, "you're here." She squeezed Melanie in a tight hug, then tossed Melanie aside to give Danny the once over. "God! I cannot believe it!" she said, taking a slower head to toe review. "And you're still hot."

"You, too," he said appraisingly, leaning to get a better view of her backside.

"Really?" Trish asked, rotating to show off, then stretching her leg from beneath her short skirt, to pose her foot in a point.

"Exactly the same." Danny eyed the long leg.

"Come inside, Jace is doing something with a slab of cow," Trish cheered, grabbing the bottle and pulling on Melanie's free hand.

Jason was in the kitchen, spicing up a tray of steak.

"Angel." He smiled, rinsing spices and blood from his hands. "It's good to see you." He covered the distance in a few long strides and lifted her in a big hug.

"Jace, this is Dan," Trish interrupted.

"Hey, nice to meet you," Jason said, carefully lowering Melanie and extending his hand. "I've got the BBQ going out back." He smiled broadly. "How about we get ourselves a couple of beers and sear some rib eye?"

"What's with Jason?" Melanie asked. It was no secret that he held Melanie at least partially responsible for Adam's absence.

"I told him that if I had to put up with Adam's girlfriend, Gigi, last summer he could put up with Dan."

Melanie nodded her approval. "Nice argument."

"I wasn't exaggerating, Mel, Dan looks good. Really good." Melanie followed Trish to the bar by the fireplace, where Trish mixed vodka martinis. "He's smoking hot, got that whole sexy thing going," she said, worming her body down in a twist as her hands rubbed her hips.

"He's always had that – well, not exactly *that*," she gestured to Trish's funky moves. "Just regular sexy." Melanie took a sip. "You're getting scary good with that shaker."

"Have you seen the price of beverages at the clubs?" Trish led her to the open living room. She curled her feet under her and settled down on the couch, facing the big window. "How is he in bed?"

Melanie slipped off her shoes and sat beside Trish to enjoy the view of the men grilling. "Why do you always do that to me?"

"It's fun. You're cute when flustered."

Melanie shook her head, ignoring her friend as she watched Danny getting along with Jason. "It's oddly easy with Danny."

"Unlike Adam?" Trish asked bitterly.

"Exactly."

"Adam's out?"

Melanie took a sip to give her extra time to think – Trish was going to relay everything she said to Jason, and Jason in turn could inform Adam.

"Adam's out. Before you risk a wrinkle with that creased, judgmental face, stop. We're not having this conversation. I love you but, enough. I need another drink, please."

"I'm glad you're an alcoholic again." Trish said, skipping to the shaker.

"Only on special occasions."

"I really wanted you and Adam to end up together," she said, refilling the glasses.

Melanie shrugged.

"And you're seriously okay with Dan?"

"Better than okay. It's fate that he's back," she said as he turned to notice her staring, and raised his bottle of beer. "Trish, I need you to be on my side. And, frankly, I don't want to waste any more time worrying or dissecting the hidden meaning of each sentence. Danny is wonderful and he makes me laugh, he's handsome and kind and we're good together. I really need you to at least pretend to be excited."

Trish stared. "I can do that. I mean, I *am* happy for you. I really wanted us to grow old together."

"That would be nice," she said, before catching the wistfulness in her voice. "We still can. Look at them getting along out there."

"It's possible. Do you swear you'll try?"

"I swear." *I'm doing this a lot lately*, she thought about all the promises she'd been making. *God, I hope I can keep them.*

Absently Trish said, "I better get the salad ready."

Melanie followed Trish back through the big house to the kitchen. She opened the stainless steel fridge door, pulled out a bag of lettuce and dumped the contents into a large wooden bowl.

"Have you moved out of your apartment?"

"I let the lease expire in September." Trish's gaze held for a beat longer than normal. "Can you keep a secret?"

Melanie grinned. "I think so."

"It's still vacant and I was thinking about signing another lease."

"I think you should let it go," Melanie advised. "You don't want to lose his trust."

The muscles in her face tightened. "He's still talking marriage. I change the subject every time, but I think he's ready," Trish said, dropping the wooden salad fork. "I swear, I break out in a cold sweat each time I think about ... you know."

"Saying 'I do'?" Melanie filled in the gap and chuckled.

"I'm freakin' scared to death! What the hell am I going to do?" Her voice shook in desperation.

"Talk to Jace." *I'm a great one to be counseling*, she thought, climbing up on a stool to listen to Trish's complaints.

"Here's my little cook." Jason, tall and lean, entered the kitchen.

Danny grinned as his gaze traveled from the salad bowl to the empty, ready-made salad package and back to Trish.

"Dan's been filling me in about the college years." Jason's eyes twinkled and Trish squeaked from his pinch.

"He'd better not be," Trish teased a little too exuberantly. "You can't believe a word he says, he spent the entire last semester with his head up Mel's skirt. I can't tell you how many times I walked in on them humping."

"Trish! That is so not true!" Melanie blushed.

"Oh, I was discreet," she laughed. "Caught them in the kitchen one time."

"We *never* did it in the kitchen," Melanie exploded.

"Um, Mel?" Danny squished her hand. "Every room in that apartment, remember?"

"But the kitchen?"

Danny nodded.

"I don't know what the big deal is … Jace and I do it in here all the time." In unison all eyes went to the food on the granite. Trish huffed, "It's not like we're eating right off the counter."

"That was fun tonight," Melanie said, her head resting on his chest with his arms around her waist. Leaning against the railing from their hotel room balcony. The wide, black ocean was peacefully melodic and made her feel wonderfully insignificant.

"It's cold out here," Danny shivered, pulling her inside.

"Let's keep the doors open – the sea air reminds me of home," Melanie said, wiggling out of her jeans to crawl under the goose-down comforter. "How do you get so warm?" She scooted over, pressing against his muscular body.

His kisses ran over her skin until they were both out of breath and sweaty.

"We're getting really good at this," Danny said, getting up to pull on his pants.

"You got along well with Jason."

"Were you worried?"

"No, but you know Trish. There's no telling the things she'll say." She sighed, reluctantly sitting up and fixing her disheveled hair. "I can't believe I'm meeting my niece tomorrow." Melanie pulled on her sweater.

"They'll be here by noon," Danny said, mimicking Rita. "Your mom is in love with that baby. She told me a dozen times Bruce was in Temecula visiting Cheryl's family."

Melanie felt his eyes on her as she dressed. "If you keep staring at me we won't make it home by dawn."

CHAPTER 31

To Melanie it seemed unlikely they'd be able to slip in without her father hearing. Still, before Danny tramped his size 11s down on a single step, she masterfully pointed out each creek and moan of the old wood.

Her goodnight wish was carried soundlessly on her breath, while his was transferred through soft lips and strong hands. Releasing her with a final kiss on her forehead, he slipped inside the guestroom.

Melanie woke to the scents and clatter of Thanksgiving.

"Good morning," she said, heading for the coffee. "Smells great in here."

"It does, doesn't it?" Rita placed a motherly kiss on Melanie's cheek. "I'm so glad you're here, we're going to have a wonderful day. Look," she lifted the lid off a big pot of peeled potatoes, boiling. "For the mashed potatoes. And over there," she pointed at fresh green beans, "a salad. This is going to be the best Thanksgiving."

"Where's Brian?" Melanie said, sniffing a bowl of pumpkin.

"He left, had his own dinner to prepare."

"How can I help?" Melanie asked, waving her cup of coffee under her nose before taking a sip. "Good coffee. I want to help early so when Bruce and Cheryl get here I can play with the baby."

"They'll be here around noon," Rita said, reminding Melanie of Danny's imitation. "There's a recipe by the pumpkin. You can finish the pies if you'd like." She handed Melanie an apron. "You got home late last night."

"Mm-hmm," she answered, concentrating on the amount of condensed milk needed for two pies.

"What did Trish make for dinner?"

"Trish," Melanie said looking up from the mathematical complexities. "She made the salad. Jace grilled steaks and zucchini. Trish's new fad is dinner parties. We played charades and Pictionary. It was fun until Danny and I kept winning and Trish's ultra-competitive gene emerged, angry and spiteful."

"You should let her win a few times. No one likes to keep losing."

"You're crazy. If they want to win – then they'd better be better than me," Melanie said, turning back to her task. "Stop that tsking."

By noon, she'd turned out four pies, emptied a bag of frozen corn into a microwavable dish and appealed to Danny for help with the 10 pounds of potatoes.

"What's wrong with them?" Melanie asked, knowing all her mother had done was boil them. "They taste funny."

"Dan," Roger barked from the doorway, "pre-game is starting."

"I'll be right there."

"You cannot leave me with these," Melanie gripped his bicep. "I'll be blamed."

"For bad potatoes?" he asked.

Defensive and panicked, she shot out a reply. "You think I'm overreacting? They're just potatoes, right?"

"Go, take a shower, get ready for your family to arrive. I'll take care of this." Both hands on her shoulders, he turned her toward the door.

She hadn't reached the stairs when a car door slammed outside. "They're here," she called out excitedly, as her foot caught on the corner of the area rug. Her ankle twisted and she collided with the wood planks.

Rebounding, Melanie sprang back up. Her mother stood in the dining room with concerned, twisted eyebrows gazing at her.

"That," Melanie pointed to the wipe out spot, "did not just happen."

"Whatever you say, dear." Rita said, amused as Bruce, with a baby carrier, opened the front door.

"Finally," Melanie breathed, giving her brother a sideways hug to look at the baby. "Oh, she's beautiful. Great job, little brother."

"I did all of the work," Cheryl piped in.

"Well, congratulations. She's perfect."

"Bruce, in here," Roger hollered from living room. "Happy Thanksgiving, Cheryl."

"I swear, he's a fanatic," Rita declared with a shake of her head. "Let's set the playpen up in the dining room."

"Annie, where's Dan?"

"Kitchen."

"Don't shout, you two ... It's Thanksgiving." Rita scolded loud enough for both to hear.

"What's he doing in there?" Roger griped.

"Helping out," Melanie replied. "You want gross mashed potatoes?"

"What do you mean *gross potatoes*?" Rita piped in.

"I messed them up, not sure how, but he said he could fix them," Melanie admitted before seeing Danny at the door.

"There wasn't anything to fix. Bruce, good to see you again," Danny clasped Bruce on the back.

"Wow, Dan, I thought you'd escaped a long time ago." Bruce stretched out his hand. "Good to see you, man."

"You ladies going to hang out in the hall all day or are we going to watch some ball?" Roger grumbled.

"What's with dad?"

"He's got a bet riding on the game," Danny whispered, kissing Melanie's cheek as her father continued to harass the men into the living room. "I'll tell you later."

Cheryl and Rita were quick at setting up the collapsible playpen, snapping hinges and locking the wheels in place. She felt out of her league as the women aptly handled the baby, feeding and changing. Her first experience with her niece, Olivia, was when Cheryl placed the crying baby in Melanie's awkward arms.

"I'm your aunt Melanie." She said, introducing herself to a powerful set of lungs. "Mom!" Melanie called out, handing the baby back to a capable adult.

"Hello!" Trish sang out opening the door – as she felt no need to knock. "We're here."

"Jace!" Bruce shrieked, giddy at having Jason in the house. "We're back here."

Little Brother was star struck.

"Happy Thanksgiving," Jason said, having to lean way down to hug Rita. "Thanks for inviting us. Angel," he placed a kiss on her cheek.

"What are we doing?" Trish asked, looking around at the empty dining room table.

"Playing with the baby."

"Oh," Trish said, lifting the bottle of wine she'd brought. "We may need a couple more of these."

"Corkscrew's in the kitchen."

"Sounds like my kind of place," Trish winked. "I don't think Cheryl likes me," she added as they exited and the murmurs began behind them.

"She might be a bit jealous."

"I guess I can't blame her ... I mean she's like twenty-something and already saddled with a kid."

"I take it back, she's not jealous. You're offensive."

Rita broke out two more bottles of red wine before the bird was set at the head of the table.

Roger stood with a battery-operated carving knife. "I'm not much on ceremony. How about we get this show on the road?" The knife buzzed in his hand.

Rita objected and Roger delivered a prayer before slicing the turkey.

"What a great day," Melanie leaned her head on Danny's shoulder as they shared the afghan and mindlessly watched TV. "Exhausting, but terrific." Sleepily she smirked, "Our football game was close."

"Your dad is a maniac. Did you see him knock me to the ground?"

"I did, and I kind of feel bad about Bruce twisting his ankle."

"Don't. There was no way he was going to catch you, I can't

believe he tried."

"He was showing off for Trish or Jace, I'm not sure which." Melanie grinned, remembering. "And how about that cheer Trish made up? God, she's embarrassing."

"I wish I didn't have to leave so early. Roger offered to take me to the airport." Danny lowered his voice. "He wants to get to the casino to collect his winnings."

"I knew he and Bruce were into the game but that Fantasy Football thing is nuts. Mom said they're glued to the TV for hours. Thank you for not having fanatical tendencies."

Tightening his grip around her, he whispered, "Speaking of which, I wish we still had the room."

"Were we always this bad? I don't know if I can make it up the stairs but I know if we could find a place..."

"Sweetheart, there's no doubt you'd find the energy." He pressed his lips to the side of her cheek and took the remote. "Bed time." He clicked off the television, took her hand and pulled her to her feet.

She sunk down into the soft pillow-top mattress with the clean scent of home, comfortable and safe. Her bare legs felt delicious between the cool sheets as she extended them out and drifted off.

No light glimmered in her window, but something alerted her out of a dead sleep. Slowly, she slid her arm off the mattress and reached between the box spring where she'd stored her gun.

"No need to shoot, it's me."

Her muscles loosened at the sound of his voice while her anger flared. "What the hell are you doing in my bedroom?"

"We need to talk."

"Is my family in danger?"

"No."

"Then come back tomorrow. My dad is a *really* light sleeper."

"Can't wait. Meet me somewhere … at the cove." When Melanie exhaled, he continued. "I wouldn't be here if it wasn't important."

"Okay," she thought, *fair enough.* "The cove," she said, holding the covers over her. She wasn't naked but her camisole was sheer. "You need to go … I'm not … dressed."

"You're not a mystery," Adam replied in a bored tone, sending a pang to her core. "Fine. I'll be waiting." He stared at her for an uncomfortable moment before darting out the window.

The wind blew through her room. Jumping out of bed to shut the casement window she grumbled as her skin met the chilly air. Quickly she dressed in a pair of black yoga pants and a large sweatshirt. In silent socks she crept down the stairs, grabbing her tennis shoes and a wool beanie as she passed the kitchen door.

"Want a snack?" Roger asked, without turning from his raid of the refrigerator.

"Sure," she sighed, slipping on her shoes before pulling clean plates out of the dishwasher. "Couldn't sleep?"

"I hear every noise within a block." A stack of containers littered the counter. "Where are you off to?" he asked, nodding at her attire.

"To get some air." She hated deceiving him while he was at the simple task of piling sliced turkey onto a roll.

"I thought I heard voices in your room," he said, with a disapproving look. "It's not right, Annie. You can't go leading those men on."

"I'm not," she blurted out, horrified at what her father was thinking of her. "Adam isn't in the picture. He's moved on…"

Roger stopped dabbing cranberries on his sandwich to ask, "Aren't you running off to see him?"

"We have business, it's not romantic. He's moved on and so have

I. I wouldn't hurt Danny like that."

Roger nodded. "If you have it under control. Keep in mind that a man who sends for you in the middle of the night and helps with Thanksgiving might not be a man who has moved on."

"We have a working relationship. Nothing more."

"Better take him a sandwich." he finished off the snack with a spoonful of steamy gravy. "Do you need me to drive you? It really isn't safe to be out alone in the dead of night. Tell me you don't do this in D.C."

"I don't, not usually." She weighed the damage that would be done if she showed him her gun, conveniently hidden inside the pouch of her hoodie.

"I'm going to bed."

"'Night, dad."

The wind had picked up and the lack of light gave the neighborhood an ominous feel. Narrow shadows clung to the corners. Melanie felt exposed, and jogged in the side of the road.

The rhythmic pattern of her footsteps joined the cacophony of the tempest winds that limited her ability to sense danger.

The waves were high and crashing well above the normal breaker level. From the overlook she scanned the sea lion cove for any sign of Adam. In the darkness the only light at the shore 20 feet down was the phosphorus glowing from the whitecaps. She couldn't be sure there was any life in the protected cove. She moved to the opposite side of the ranger station and followed the gritty concrete stairs to the beach.

He wouldn't have left, she knew. But it was possible that he grew impatient and was waiting in the comforts of her bedroom. The wind whipped through the soft cotton of her pants and flared out the loose strands of hair that hung below the cap. She pulled the hood of her sweatshirt over her cap.

This is stupid, she decided and headed back toward the steps. If he wanted her he'd have to make another attempt. She was going home.

"Giving up already?" Melanie turned back, and closer than she'd expected was Adam. "I told you I'd wait." His voice added to her chill.

The pair moved close to the cliff wall where the noise wasn't deafening and the wind kept their conversation private.

"What is it you want?" she asked, his face camouflaged by the wavering shadows. She'd thought they'd gotten over the anger.

"I need access to the surveillance you installed on Oak Street."

Parker's Victorian. She nodded, this was business. "Has there been a change in circumstances?"

Adam nodded.

"You'll memorize my code?" He nodded and she repeated the 15 digit numerical sequence twice. "Finn is up for a promotion, CIA. I'm hoping this solves most of my problems. The more I think about him moving on the better I feel about it."

"When is this to take place?"

"I don't know – I suspect Ben will do what he can to rush it through. Why?" Her nerves spiked. "Has Finn's timeframe been shortened?"

"He hasn't been forthcoming. Hence, the need for your surveillance."

"When he gets this new job I'm done worrying about the Parkers," Melanie stated.

"Meaning you're done with our secret meetings." His smile was forced.

"I am. The next time you come over – use the doorbell."

"Babe, I'm just trying to save your life." His expression was concealed by the darkness. "How was your holiday?"

"What was the point of Brian?"

"To help, I like your mom. I would have been there myself if it were possible." He stepped in closer.

"You kind of screwed that up," Melanie said, anger causing her heart to beat harder.

Adam shook his head, his eyes distant and searching the cliff behind her shoulder. "It was inevitable anyway."

"What does that mean?" Her words were clipped and biting.

"It means nothing. What's in the bag?" Adam raised his chin.

"My dad made you a sandwich and there's a slice of pie."

"You told your dad you were meeting me?"

"I told you, he's a light sleeper." Melanie's eyes burned from the tears that were about to fall. Her jaw was clenched and her entire chest constricted. "Is there anything else?"

"No."

"Great." She turned hastily to rush the flight of steps.

"Melanie," he called. Questioning him with her eyes, it was Adam who spoke. "Could I hold you for just a minute?"

With nothing to read visually, she replayed his words, felt the force in his hands. "Are you in danger?"

"Not like you think." He sighed, "Not physical."

"And you don't want to tell me?"

"No."

It was all so confusing. The outside of his jacket was cool as she cautiously held her breath. She wrapped her arms around his waist and patted his back. Startled when his chest convulsed, she wanted to pull back but was restrained in his embrace. "Adam?"

"I'm all right," he whispered tensely, lowering his head beside hers. "I'm sorry. I'm, I'm only lonely."

Not breaking the hold, Melanie adjusted her arms over his shoulders like she normally would have held him.

"Thank you," he swallowed. Even in the darkness she knew he was controlling his emotions. "I'll be in contact." He cleared his throat. "Thanks for the food."

"You sure you're all right?" she asked, uncomfortable about leaving him.

"Go."

Melanie jogged home, her mind spinning. It must be Terese. *Doesn't matter, Mel,* she chided herself every 10 minutes until it was time to get up to take Danny to the airport.

"I'm going to miss you," she said, rising up on her tiptoes. "You sure you don't mind if I don't take you?"

"I'm fine," he squeezed, "I'm going to miss you, too." The crinkles at the corner of his eyes deepened with his smile. "Monday we're starting to film promos and brainstorm about featured stories, stuff like that. You wouldn't believe how excited I am." She could believe, it was plastered all over his face. "If you can't come up – I'll get to DC as soon as I can." He brushed the hair from her forehead and his brows pulled together slightly.

Roger buzzed around, anxious to get to the casino.

"Seems like a long time. I know I'm being silly," she tried to sidestep out of his arms.

"Then I'm silly, too. Because I was thinking that same thing." He kissed her cheek as they parted.

"We better get going, Ashe."

"Dad, stop with the coach attitude or I'll have a chat with mom."

His smile flashed. "Oh, Annie, you are tough. I was only thinking about Dan, but it's okay by me if you want him to miss his flight."

"He's right," Danny laughed. "I love you, Mel."

"Me too, you."

She balanced on the curb and waved until Roger turned the corner. Melanie let out a strained, pent up breath, blowing out her own loneliness. There was that word, it brought back the heaviness from last night.

"I'm going for a run." She called into the house to her mom.

Her eyes ached behind her polarized sunglasses, but the cool breeze felt good as she headed toward the row of shops on Prospect Street. Starbucks was bustling as usual. Melanie kept it simple with a large vanilla coffee and a raspberry scone, breakfast on her feet she headed home. The caffeine and sugar gave her the energy boost she needed.

Instinct kicked in at the steps to the porch. Melanie turned to look up and down the street and saw a couple of unfamiliar cars at the neighbor's curb.

Her father was gone, but her mom was home. Melanie felt the familiar, cold sense of calm. Placing her coffee cup on top of the banister, she reached for her .380 secured to a belt at her waist.

Cursing the rickety screen door as she slipped inside. The furnace was running and the hot air was fierce as she opened the front door.

"There she is," she heard her mother say from the kitchen. "In here, dear."

Melanie transferred her weapon to her pocket.

Adam and Rita were seated at the kitchen island, piping-hot tankards of coffee between them.

"Look who's back," Rita smiled. "Isn't this nice?"

"Unbelievable." Melanie searched Adam's expression. He was

difficult for her to read but there looked to be a grin playing at the corners of his mouth. "What are you doing here?"

Rita coughed her admonishment while rinsing out her cup and leaving it on the rack to dry.

"You told me to ring the bell next time I came over, so I did."

"Honey, why don't you offer Adam something to eat? I've got to run, I'm already late." Rita hurriedly gathered her glasses and purse before kissing Melanie on the side of her head and whispering a command to be nice.

"Late for what?"

"Black Friday. Shopping."

"What's going on?" Melanie asked, taking over Rita's stool at the counter to face Adam.

"How do you like the .380? It's custom. Laser with a fingerprint lock and a black pearl handle."

Laying the gun across her palm to admire, she said, "It's amazing, beautiful. I meant to thank you before … but with everything else I forgot."

"Handles well?"

"It does. It's so light that I wasn't sure how it would absorb the impact but … I love it, thank you."

"I realize it isn't a bracelet," he said, sarcastically, "but I thought it might suit you."

"Don't. We're getting along fairly well and if I'm not breaking out in a jealous sweat than neither should you."

"What if I can't help myself?"

"I really don't want to hear about your troubles with Terese."

"Who said I was having trouble with her?"

"Adam," Melanie sighed. "I'm really tired. Whatever you're doing here … you need to go someplace else. I'm finally okay with how things are. You're obviously not angry with me and I'm not angry with you. Stop trying to be a Boy Scout."

"I've never been accused of that," he laughed and was almost the man she remembered.

Chaos erupted with that one look. Knowing she was about to blush, she said, "I'm moving on with my life, just as you suggested, and I would appreciate if you didn't pop back in when ever the mood suits you."

"The mood? You called me last week, remember? I needed the codes and today … I didn't come to intrude."

Adam was changing. Each time she saw him, he was leaner, his bone structure more exposed. He was in black cargo pants and heavy boots with a dark blue, plaid, collared shirt. An Army jacket hung on the hook by the front door. The beard still covered half his face. His hair was shorter than she'd seen it in awhile and the purple streaks beneath his green eyes more noticeable. The wear of the past few months was evident.

"Is there something more?" she asked.

"Your mom offered me breakfast."

"Seriously?"

"Can I get you a plate?" he asked, rising to open the fridge and pull out the leftovers.

"I wish I could read you better," Melanie said, unabashedly staring. If he could ever seem at home, it was in the kitchen. *You've never seen him in his other job.* The thought sent a shiver down her spine.

"I'm just hungry."

Adam fixed two plates with as much precision as he had handled her weapon. "I don't like yams," she volunteered and he scraped them off onto his plate. "How's your life?" she probed. "Making friends?"

"Always." He stuck both plates in the broiler to warm. "Everyone loves me."

She wasn't satisfied. "You did a nose dive into Hector's life, was it too much? Taking over the business, his house, his wife."

This stopped him and he looked directly into her eyes. Was it for the first time? Had he been avoiding eye contact? Or had she?

"Is this our conversation?" he asked.

"The best we can do, I guess." Melanie said, looking up at him. "Your life?"

"Complicated."

"Can you walk away?"

Adam took in a long breath. "It's possible I don't want to. Let's eat. Would you like a shot of Bailey's in your coffee?"

"Why the hell not?" Melanie said, following Adam to the dining room. "You realize you confuse me."

"I don't mean to."

"That your strange car out front." Melanie said, twirling her fork. "Like it?"

"What happened to the BMW?"

Adam shrugged. "This one's faster."

"The new you?" She couldn't keep the disapproving tone out of her voice. "Fast cars, faster women."

"I thought you didn't want to do this."

"I don't. I think this whole breakfast was a bad idea," she said, setting the napkin on the table. "What are we doing?" Melanie dropped her face into her hands. They were cool and her face felt warm. *Let him go, Mel.* "You were right," she stated simply, teetering between what was best for her and what was right.

"This should be interesting." His smile was kind when she looked up.

"We don't know each other. I thought we did because of our secrets, but the truth is that I knew only who I wanted you to be."

"When did I generate that pearl of wisdom?"

Melanie smirked, he didn't remember. She remembered every second, replayed every conversation and he didn't remember. "It was when you told me about Terese. You said you'd chosen her because she understood you in ways I never could." The words were easier to get out when she didn't focus on their meaning.

His lips were pressed into a thin line. "I'm a prick. Do me a favor and forget everything I've ever said to you."

She tried to nod but was afraid any movement would give away her very delicate emotional balance.

"Since we're bonding, isn't there news you want to tell me?" His throat caught in mid-question.

Melanie blinked back the confusion. "I can't think of anything you don't already know."

"Was your fantasy guy as perfect as you'd hoped?" He shrugged casually as if his remark didn't matter.

The heat rose to her collar and she felt the anger and guilt rush to her cheeks. He was leaning back in the chair, looking over at her with a demeanor of superiority. Melanie erased her emotions from her face.

"I can't believe you're doing this." She looked at the man and realized, "I guess I never really did know you. Because the Adam I fell for wouldn't have put me through all this ... then throw it back in my face." Melanie stood. "Finish your meal and then I don't want to see you again. I mean it."

"Mel," he said, the request for redemption in his voice, but she was already shaking her head. "I'm jealous, okay?" He said, standing. "I knew I would be."

"You're jealous?" It was such nonsense she couldn't stifle the laugh. "That's a good one because in order for you to be jealous you'd have to have human emotions and I'm not sure you do." She felt another surge of guilt as the words hit her ears and his chest sunk as if she'd punched the air out of his lungs.

"I deserve that," he said after a tense, silent moment. Then taking his time he shifted the chair in place before looking directly at her. "It must seem like I don't have feelings ... but I do. I never wanted to be a monster." He brushed past her as she stood motionless.

I'm not going to let him make me feel bad! She thought, measuring the slant of his shoulders, the angle of his head and the depth of his forearms into his pant pockets. *I don't feel guilty about hurting his feelings*, she scolded herself as she listened for his silent footsteps to hit the porch.

Damn it!

"Adam wait." She called out, flinging open the front door and jogging down the steps. He was at the curb when he turned and she slowed. Melanie looked up at him and held her breath until his smoldering emerald eyes looked back at her. "I didn't mean those horrible things. I know you're not a monster. I know you have feelings." She sounded stupid, she knew. "I'm sorry. But, Adam, I am so angry with you. And a part of me *wants* to hurt you. To get back at you for not loving me. But," she sighed, unable to purposely cause him pain.

"It's okay. I deserve it." He attempted to smile but the curve of his lips was wrong and it made her feel worse.

"No. I'm mad at you." She stopped, feeling the prickle of tears behind her eyes. Tightening her lips to a single, distraught line she nodded at him – deciding there was nothing more to say, even if she could – and turned to leave.

He moved fast, facing her as she moved to the door. His arm around her, pressing her back while a hand scooped up the hair behind her neck. The kiss came without warning. His mouth was gentle and firm and for a fraction of a second she'd gotten lost in him.

Pushing him away, with little force, her palms against his chest. He pulled her in tighter, kissing harder.

"Stop." She broke away, gave him one glaring look and darted inside. Melanie raced to the back of the house before returning to the front door. He was gone. She flipped through her list of possible distractions and called Carla.

CHAPTER 32

Forty minutes after her flight landed, Melanie was scanning her retina at the back entrance of the Manor. The halls were quiet. It was Sunday night; Jane was gone and Mike had left two messages while she was in flight.

"Ben, you here?" Melanie tapped her knuckles against the solid metal door to his office. "What's with the ghost town?"

"Ah, Agent Ward, how was your holiday?"

"Confusing." There was something in his voice that caused her to falter, her smile masked her rapid pulse.

"Should I ask?"

"I wouldn't if I were you."

Folding his arms over his chest he leaned back in his big brown leather chair. "We're entering in a major political dilemma. Homegrown terrorists are what they're being called, Americans who are aligning with the anti-American forces. I've been given a list of 30 names. All potential suspects."

"Are we hauling them in or did you have something else in mind?" She asked, overcoming her concern for his state of mental health.

"I wanted to go over the details with you and Jack before we submitted our proposal to the Board."

"Proposal? Since when do we have to submit paperwork?"

"This mission is being requested from the top." He lifted his brows in a gesture of intrigue. "Very hush-hush. Americans being investigated by the government for their political views." Ben shook his head. "Could come back and bite the administration."

"That kills bringing them in by force."

"Let me give Jack a call, he'll want to be included," Ben said, pressing the intercom for Judith.

"She's probably not here," Melanie called Jack from her cell. "He'll be here in a couple of minutes, he was in his office. He's a good agent."

"Yes, dependable." Ben poured three glasses of brandy. "This you've got to try." He handed her one.

Melanie took the glass, jiggled the ice and looked up at him. "I'm sorry for the problems I've caused these last six months."

"What about the 10 years before that?" He was laughing.

"I'm serious."

"Me, too. You've been a pain for far longer than six months. You're just too damn good to let go." He looked at her with fatherly eyes. "Every agent goes through a rough patch, yours was a long time coming. You're already rebounding. I can see it in your stride." Ben fished a file out of his drawer and spread the papers over the rectangular coffee table. "Here's all the information I've been given. I'm concerned about rushing in – if this is a network, we don't want to scatter off the others." Ben flickered his gaze up as Jack entered.

"There he is. Have a seat, we've been waiting for you."

"Jeez, Jack, you ever go home anymore?" Melanie asked.

"Not much point, lost another girlfriend over the weekend."

"You really should keep better track of them," Melanie said.

"Nice try, Ward. But you can't cheer me up." Jack shrugged. "Oh, well, gives me more time here and less time being nagged about how much time I spend here."

"We're on a deadline, Agents," Ben said, spreading out the photos of suspects. "We'll review the facts, and from there we can formulate a game plan – something tangible I can sell to the Board. This is big, people."

The process was therapeutic, late hours examining evidence and plotting an effective strategy. She and Jack argued over tactics while scouring histories until sunrise, when Ben returned with breakfast.

"Did you notice he was gone?" Jack whispered. "Ben never struck me as the sausage-egg biscuit type, he's more of an oatmeal man."

Stifling her laugh, Melanie choked on a mouthful.

"I do hope you two didn't fool around all night." His back stiffened, startled, "What I meant to say is…"

"I don't think I've ever seen you red faced," Melanie grinned.

"Breakfast and a show," Jack raised his meal in salute.

"Gone are the good 'ole days when agents showed a sense of maturity and respect."

"Mature or not, we solved the puzzle. Want to know the solution or do you want to keep blushing all morning?" Melanie chuckled.

"What do I have to do to stop the harassment?" he asked, removing his eyeglasses to rub the bridge of his nose. "And why do I allow you to tease me?"

"Because she's your favorite," Jack stated simply.

Melanie bullied through the awkwardness of the comment by explaining their tri-fold plan.

"Mike will check on links connecting the suspects, organizations, web-browsing habits, social media outlets ... Then comes the blitz, sending two agents to each location to evaluate the degree of potential danger, and finally handing back the information to the FBI so they can facilitate a raid."

"Time frame?" Ben wanted to know.

Melanie and Jack gave each other *the look*. They'd been disagreeing about this point ... "Three weeks from beginning to round-up. Four weeks, tops."

"Cut that down to two and I think we've got a start."

The agents shared a silent high-five. They'd overestimated the time to get the full two weeks needed.

"We'll do what we can, just know that I want to be involved in the team phase," Melanie announced.

"I like that, you back in the field, training exercises. Partner the young agents with seasoned ones ... good. But Ward I'd like for you to stick close to home."

She slid the pages of photos, shifting them until she found the college student from NYU – "I'll take him."

CHAPTER 33

"I can't believe it's been over a week since San Diego. I'm dying over here." Danny sounded tired.

"We're both busy," she said. "You can stop sending flowers."

"Then the same goes for you. I got the roses today, they look great in my dressing room. No one's ever sent me a bouquet before … all the women in the office thought they were for them."

His smile radiated across the states, and she returned the giddy grin. "I'm going to be out there tomorrow or the next day but I really don't know if I can pull away from more than a few hours." Holding the handset away from her ear, she could still hear him loud and clear.

"Anything. Talking over the phone has been great but I want to feel flesh in my arms." He stopped to laugh, "That sounded weird, didn't it? I had a dream about us last night," Danny began.

"Okay, I'm at work right now … If this story is going to get hot and sweaty you'll have to keep the details until later."

"Fine, it'll hold." Danny's voice was soothing. Her mind traveled with his thoughts as she swiveled in her chair to face the window.

His words flowed into a pocket of her brain, close enough to her conscious that she could remark without hesitation, but letting the details fall through the cracks. The arrangements for the mission looped through her thoughts.

"I'm going to hang up now." Threatened the king of long goodbyes.

"Bye Danny." Melanie smirked.

"I really am."

Jane's voice came over the intercom. "Agent Ward, your meeting is starting in the conference room."

"I really do have to go."

"Have a safe trip and call when you get in. Love you, Mel."

She grabbed her disc and headed to the final meeting before the launch of the operation. The room was alive – it was the first time all the agents had been pooled together. Melanie and Jack met at the door. "It's go time," she said, the energy from the room spilling out into the hall.

"Let's do this." Jack said to her. "Please take your assigned seats," he called over the clamor. "The dossier in front of you contains everything you'll need for your task tomorrow." Melanie made her way to the other side of Jack, where her file waited. "You will be paired up, an experienced agent alongside a freshman," Jack continued. "Go ahead and take a few minutes to meet your partner if you don't already know each other."

"Hi, I'm Melanie Ward," Melanie said, introducing herself to her new partner seated to her right.

"I know that," said the girl with short brown hair and the look of a tough Natalie Portman. "I'm Logan Holland."

"Well, it's nice to meet you." Melanie said, forcing the pleasantry.

Logan's attitude wasn't a new phenomenon. Young, ambitious agents – usually female – often targeted her with a spirit that came in either the form of worship or hostility. Logan saw competition.

"I'm really glad we were partnered, we can learn a lot from each other," Logan smiled.

Melanie looked at Jack and forced her thoughts onto him.

Jack laughed and said loud enough for only her to hear, "You want me to repeat your precise words?"

"God, never mind. I don't want to hear. Can we just move this along? Please?"

"All right," Jack said loudly, taking back control of the room. "Remember you're a team, so senior agents let the novices carry their share of the load. Lunch will be delivered in the next few minutes. Find a quiet spot to go over the game plan. Agent Ward and I will be around to answer questions or to help out in whatever way needed. Are there any questions at this point?"

"Agent Holland, let's go over our objective before I go help the others," Melanie said, taking in a big breath of patience.

The long afternoon gobbled up her evening, leaving her weary and dreading the days ahead.

"She couldn't have been that bad."

Melanie, moving only her eyeballs, looked up at Jack from the comfort of her couch. "Worse."

"Don't you remember being fresh out of training? She's excited."

"She told me," Melanie sat up, making room for Jack, "that she planned on using me as an example of what not to do."

"You aren't serious," he said, taking the seat next to her.

"Well," Melanie rolled her eyes, "her exact words were closer to … I plan on not making enemies of the other agents and keeping my personal life, personal."

"She's got a set on her, you gotta give her that much."

"All balls and no brains doesn't make for the best agent."

"I talked with Logan," Jack said. "She was really excited about working with you. She was probably trying too hard to make a good impression. Give her a chance."

"Bright and early," Melanie said. "We're flying out together."

Bright and early turned out to be bleak and cold.

They spoke little on the flight but Melanie could feel Logan sneaking glances as she tried to catch a couple of extra minutes of sleep.

At the hotel Melanie cleared her room and knocked on Logan's door. "Ready?"

"Do I look like a professor's assistant?" the young agent asked, smoothing invisible creases in her navy blue pencil skirt.

It was the first glimpse she'd gotten of Logan's vulnerability. "You look fine."

The mid-afternoon journey to Tim Harmon's theology class was cold. Melanie twisted her scarf up under her hair and tucked the ends into her jacket.

"I need a cup of coffee," Melanie said, walking through the cloud of her own breath. "How about you?"

"Agent Ward," Logan started... "I mean, Melanie."

"Inside," Melanie ushered them into the corner coffee shop. "How do you take your coffee?"

"I don't. Hot chocolate."

Melanie ordered, paid and was out the door with Logan jogging to keep up.

"Um," she said, touching Melanie's sleeve. "I'm nervous. This is my first assignment, and…" she bit down on her bottom lip.

The gesture gave Melanie an extension on her tolerance. "You're ready. We're playing a role, I'm the substitute professor and you're my assistant. We watch Tim and you make a connection. If you can't, we bump into him someplace else and try again."

Logan nodded. "What if he doesn't like me?"

"He's a 20-year old-college boy … He'll like you."

"Thanks."

They opened the door to an auditorium and Melanie began.

"Hello, class," she said and set her bag on the desk at the front of the room. She had prepared a lecture from the syllabus and before she was ready the bell rang and the students were up out of their seats. Scanning the room she saw Logan was leaning on a seat talking with Tim. *Good girl*, Melanie thought, giving them space but keeping an ear open for any sign of need from her young partner.

"Bye, Tim, I'll see you tonight." Logan waved and blushed as Tim raced up the stairs. "I feel sick," Logan said, wiping her brow. "Is it always like this?"

"You did great." Melanie was changing her opinion of the girl. "Where are you meeting?"

"Dinner date … A vegetarian restaurant or some crap like that. Did you know he was a vegan?"

Melanie grinned. "Does it matter? I take it you're a carnivore. Well, I tagged the collar of his jacket. We'll follow his movements from a quiet spot on campus."

"When did you mark him? I thought I was watching every second," Logan said. "Will you show me how you do that?"

"Someday."

"Is there somewhere we can eat? I'm starving."

Melanie watched the girl, Logan was buzzing with nervous energy. "There are a couple of fast food restaurants around the corner."

"Actually, I think it's the vegetarian thing. I'm ravenous for meat." She said, gazing at the open sign above the door of an Asian diner. A small pyramid of orange chicken was set on a bed of fried rice and Logan was already eating as she carried the tray to the table.

"Wow, is it always like this on a mission? Like a drug. I swear, I think, I'm addicted."

"We need to prep you for tonight," Melanie said, eyeing Logan closely.

"Do you want some?" she held up a fork full of food. "I'm so sorry, Melanie," she said through half an egg roll. "I can't believe how rude I was to you … It's the rumors. I won't ever pay any attention to them again because you are *awesome*. So confident. Shit, you had me believing you were a professor and I knew the truth. The way you walked in there … It gave me courage and I was scared to death. I'm talking at rocket speed, aren't I? It's the adrenaline."

"I know. Did you bring running shoes?"

"Is that what you do? You run off this … this feeling?"

"Until I'm so exhausted I don't think I can take another step, and then I go one more mile."

"I can see that. Let's run."

Logan had the speed and endurance of a sprinter, blasting off 200 meters in 20 seconds before slowing and wheezing by the end of the first mile.

"Come on, we're not done," Melanie said, passing the girl on the jogging path beside the park. There was no sound for the first few paces and Melanie was ready to rail into the girl when the heavy, clumsy tread of Logan's non-rhythmic beat sounded behind her.

"Did you bring casual clothes?" Melanie asked. "You need to seem natural, trustworthy and sexy."

"I don't know if I own anything that can do all that. I brought black pants and a white sweater."

Along the way to meeting Tim, Logan insisted on eating again. The cold air and her nerves gave a rosy tint to her cheeks and made her look young and innocent.

"It's a date, Logan. Don't push the direction of the conversation – let it flow. I'll be listening and though you won't see me ... I'm watching. Don't go into his apartment or be alone with him in any tight quarters, and do not confront him. If he gets upset or makes you uncomfortable... walk away. And keep your phone on. Got it?"

She nodded and released a sigh of tension. "Is it normal to feel dizzy?"

"Yes."

Melanie turned a corner and disappeared, leaving Logan to walk the final two blocks on her own. Melanie felt nervous for the girl but jumping in was the only way for her to learn.

The ear bud fit snugly. She'd decided against a two-way transmission ... Logan wasn't experienced enough, she was nervous and if Melanie needed to talk to her she could use the cell.

Eavesdropping on their dinner prattle was painful. Melanie rolled her eyes at the silly, uncreative flirtations as she took in her environment, the backseat of a parked car. *Of course it's a piece of crap car with a nauseating smell of pungent-onion-body odor.* She shoved a stack of mail off the stained upholstery. It was the only vehicle with a direct line of sight on Logan.

After the vegan meal Logan and Tim strolled to a small coffee shop with posters plastered on the windows and artistic graffiti painted on the brick walls. Melanie considered a description. *Filthy eclectic*, she decided, already writing her report. The side of the street with the coffee shop was shabby and drab, unwelcoming. *Extra vigilance* were the words that disrupted her consciousness. Melanie crossed the street to one of the dozens of specialty coffee shops that seemed to have popped up all over the city. Ordering an espresso flourished with latte art she took a seat facing the big window. Hiding behind the hand-painted advertisements on the glass, she stoked up a conversation with the barista as the woman transformed foam into a beautiful representation of maple leaves.

"How long have you been here?"

"A year," she said casually.

"How does that place across the street make it?" Melanie asked, dropping a couple of bills in the tip jar.

"No idea. They're weirdos over there." Her eyes narrowed. "Sorry. I mean, we get some customers who say our place was too crowded so they went across the street and were refused … Well, they were told they were out of coffee." The barista shrugged. "Look at this," she boasted, carefully sliding the cup to Melanie.

"I almost hate to ruin it."

"I hear that all the time," she laughed. "Enjoy."

"Thank you." Melanie carried her cup to an absurdly small table, thinking about the grungy shop across the street. Why would people choose that infested locale instead of this bright and tasteful coffee house? The questions were piling up. She tuned back into Tim and Logan's conversation.

"How do you like the coffee?" Tim was asking Logan.

"Great. Delicious."

His 'hmm' interrupted Melanie's thoughts. Her heart raced and her finger flew to the redial button, about to save Logan with a phone call.

"Truthfully," Logan sounded guilty. "I have no idea … I hate coffee but I worried about telling you."

Tim's laugh echoed in her ear canal.

"Good, because this is the worst coffee ever. This place is more about the company."

Melanie called Jack. "I need you to check out the other suspects … any local hangouts, spots that don't fit or places that seem a bit off. I've got Logan here in a mess of a coffee shop and I'm about ready to sneak over there to have a look around."

"Will do. Call me."

Outside, the sidewalk was dotted with people. Melanie ducked between patches of light to the side alley. Stale coffee grounds overpowered the stench of rotting consumables at the bin by the door. Adjusting the collar of her coat and maintaining a downward profile, Melanie picked her way through the lock.

Cracking open the metal door, the musty aroma brought back the memory of Disneyland's Pirates of the Caribbean ride. Inside there were two choices: forward to a descending crumbly cement stairs or right to the sounds of the kitchen and spicy smelling coffee. Her curiosity was too strong a force and she took the first cautious step down the decaying flight.

Steadying herself on the steep slope with her gloved hand on the wall, Melanie's senses were heightened. A single bulb lit the corridor to the brick wall at the base of the steps. At the corner she listened to the emptiness before entering an open room with rectangular tables and folding chairs.

The room was as dingy as the rest of the building, with a large

American flag nailed to the wall. Homemade banners hung about the room from the low ceiling. Cell phone in hand, Melanie snapped photos: *Revolution = Patriotism*, *Stop America's Tyranny* and *What can you do?*

On one of the tables were flyers and sign-up sheets. Delighted, she ripped off the two completed pages and stuffed them in her pocket. *Amateurs*, she thought. *But violence has to start somewhere and this looks like a recruitment center.* Taking two steps at a time, she climbed the old stairs and was outside in the alley, pulling the metal door shut when she was interrupted.

"Hey! Who are you?"

Shit! She sighed, she'd hoped to get away without being noticed. "I'm sorry, what?" she asked, turning toward the man who'd spotted her.

"What are you doing here?"

He wasn't very tall, *another two steps* ... her foot almost reached his windpipe, but it was good enough to drop him. His head to the pavement was what knocked him out. Just to be certain, she yanked the glove off with her teeth and jabbed two fingers to his throat confirmed he was still alive. An alley mugging would go unnoticed, so she pushed aside his jacket and snatched his wallet.

Picking up her pace, she dialed Logan. The girl needed to get away from Tim and they'd rehearsed the phone call.

"Logan, this is Professor Ward. You do realize that you were to stay put in your room."

"Um," was the nervous reply. Melanie grinned, enjoying her work and glad to be out of the dirty alley and onto the main street, "Sorry, Professor, I know. I got hungry. I'm on my way back."

Melanie ended the call and took a quick glance over her shoulder to watch Logan rise to her feet. In her ear she heard Logan explain and apologize.

"I could walk you back to your hotel," he was offering.

"No, if she saw you…" Logan drew a line with her finger across her own throat.

"Can I see you again?"

"I'd like that." Melanie could feel the heat rushing up Logan's neck. "You have my number … Bye, Tim."

From the rustling of fabric, Melanie guessed she must've kissed him before flying out the door and hailing a cab.

"I'm out," Logan whispered into the mic.

Melanie waited a minute to make contact. "Good job. Go back to the hotel, pack and catch the late train back to D.C."

"Did I do something wrong?"

"Not even close. We'll talk later," Melanie answered, distracted. She leaned against a niche in the masonry to watch the congregation at the coffee shop. "See you back home."

"Okay, you're not just saying I did a good job, right?"

"I'm not here to stroke your ego, Logan. If I said it – I meant it. You were fantastic. We got what we needed. I'll fill you in later … I promise."

"Thanks, Melanie."

Melanie spied the commotion as her victim was found sprawled on the pavement. He appeared conscious, his feet were moving along as he was carried inside the café. Reading his hand gestures, he pointed out location of the attack, the size and height of his assailant, the realization of his missing wallet. She'd taken the five dollars, wiped it down on her pants and tossed the nylon casing by the trash.

No police came.

It was the most action they'd see for the night. Melanie packed up her things at the hotel before heading to Danny's.

"It's dawn, Mel." Danny said, his arms circling her waist.

"I know, go back to sleep." The side of his face felt warm and bristly on her lips.

"I don't want to." He said, working to stay awake. "Before I forget. Would you be interested in going to a party with me on Saturday?" he asked, rubbing his eyes with the back of his hands before pulling them through his unruly hair.

"What kind of party are we talking about? Work?"

Danny shook his head. "Friends." Melanie raised her brows in inquisition. "Lauren can't make it so ... I was invited."

"That's sad, Danny."

"Not really, Adrienne is Lauren's closest friend and it's her party. I want to show you off."

"I'd love to go. What should I wear?"

"It's black tie. Adrienne thinks she's posh," he said, drifting back onto the pillow.

She scooted in closer, resting her cheek on his shoulder. *This is nice.* She closed her eyes and slept in Danny's arms.

Too soon she had her bags in hand, made sure he felt her kiss goodbye and reminded him she could find the way out when he mumbled an offer to walk her down along with a complaint about her schedule.

A party, she mused, *with every detail about her and Danny recited directly back to Lauren.* Her abdomen squeezed in response to the flare of jealousy. She was going to have to look better than good.

At the station the holiday garlands and wreaths swayed above her head. Melanie slid the five-dollar bill from the wallet she'd taken, along with a bill of her own, into the red kettle and wished the bell ringer a Merry Christmas.

∞

Jack was deep in concentration when she knocked on his office door. "Conquered the world yet?"

"On my way," he said, the purple crescents bunching beneath his eyes.

"Have you considered a nap?" Melanie dragged out the chair from his desk and settled in. "Did the hotspots pan out or was Tim's coffee house an isolated incident?"

"Still have work to do to answer that. But…" He lifted his index finger, "Mike did find a connection. Over 20 suspects belong to the same social networking site."

"Is that a lot? I thought millions of people wasted time online."

"They're fans of a particular organization … It matters."

"If you need me to go out, I'll travel to any or all of those targets," Melanie offered. "I like being out there on the streets and let me tell you, Logan was excellent. I had my doubts – she needs training, but there's potential."

"She came back yesterday raving about you like you were some sort of goddess who could free the planet of evil."

"Impressionable kid," Melanie grinned. "Well, break out the data. We've got work to do."

CHAPTER 34

The tavern in the heart of the village was the unofficial meeting spot for Adam and his crew. A neutral place to relax and unwind outside of the palacio. The building was a single, large room – built from painted, unfinished cinderblock. Everything the tavern served was fried and the smell of grease moistened the air. Along the walls graphics depicted a variety of striking, detailed and unusual sexual positions.

Adam lit his cigar as he made his way to the back of the room. He felt the responsibility of having to protect these men who called him 'Jefe.' Tonight they were celebrating a productive quarter and from the sounds, the party had started without him. The hoopla that greeted him was loud, and immediately a drink was rammed into his hand.

"There he is!"

"Speech!"

Adam raised his glass. "Salud, dinero y tiempo para gastarlo."

The uproar resumed and Adam found himself at the center of the applause. The men expressed their pleasure with pats on the back, embraces and punches to his arm.

"You made us a lot of money, my friend."

"It was a good season," he laughed. The season for gun-running was year-round. "What's Bobby doing here?" Adam tilted his head toward a young man who'd recently joined the ranks. He wasn't yet a full member and so wasn't invited to private events.

"Terese," the old man said, flipping his brows to the wife of his former boss. "You should've done something about her when you had the chance. She's going to cause trouble."

Adam rolled the cigar between his fingers. "You know her as well as I do. What would you suggest?"

"Scramble her brains with that famous cock of yours." He pounded Adam on the back with a howl.

"I like your colorful suggestion but I can't do that."

"I don't know where those highfalutin' morals came from. None of the rest of us ever said no to her."

"Morality had nothing to do with not sleeping with her," Adam said, watching Terese settle onto Bobby's lap as he covered her neck with his mouth. "She asked me to take a meeting with him." He lifted his chin and gestured to the boy then turned his head, opting for a more pleasing view of a waitress with a tray full of drinks.

"He wants us to break into the drug market."

"He's crazy." Adam said.

"He has some good ideas. He's worked with two families already and he thinks he can form alliances."

Adam turned to his old friend. "You don't seriously want me to consider trafficking drugs!?"

"They make a shit-load of money."

"And have less time to enjoy the profits." Adam turned back to Bobby, who now had his hand up Terese's dress.

"Just hear him out."

The old man shuffled away, relying on a cane in his left hand. *Unbelievable*, he thought. "Terese, if you've got a minute … we need to talk."

She whispered something in the boy's ear before meeting Adam at a table.

"Look, I don't judge your behavior," Adam started.

"My behavior!" Terese gasped. "What could you be talking about … having fun? Because, you certainly made it clear you weren't interested in having any."

"You want to talk about being interested? That kid is only interested in making a name for himself and doesn't care who he uses to get there. Terese, he's no good for you."

"My bedroom door is always open to you, if you have a better idea."

"That's not what I'm saying."

"No, you just want to control me. You're just like Hector."

"Yes, we both care about you."

"Bobby is a genius. All the other men see it. He can make us a super power, a family to be reckoned with. Rich beyond belief."

"We have plenty of money. More than we can spend in a lifetime. Why the greed?" Adam asked.

"Why not?"

"Because drug-trafficking is deadly."

"Bobby has connections."

"I'm not going to argue this with you. The answer is no."

"Maybe it's not up to you," she retorted, not bothering to hide the innuendo.

"What are you implying?"

"Simply that you are a temporary replacement for Hector ... not permanent."

He took a puff of his cigar and blew the smoke out of the side of his mouth before answering. "We made more money these months than ever before."

"With a great deal of effort ... we could make 10 times as much without an ounce more work."

The threat in her voice vanished and she was back to pleading. Adam studied her ... measuring how far she'd go or had already gone.

"Okay, I'll have a sit down with Bobby. My office. Tomorrow. But, no promises."

Terese's broad smile was what made her beautiful. "That's all I wanted. Once you listen to his plan, you'll change your mind. He's determined."

That's what I'm afraid of, Adam thought, finishing off his drink.

CHAPTER 35

There was no guilt about leaving for two days. Her part in the homegrown assignment was over. Jack had taken the lead and was on top of the situation. Though he'd bitched all week about not having a life and being alone, this was her turn to live and she was going to take advantage of the opportunity.

Posh was how Danny described Adrienne. The ripple of dread from that one word had caused Melanie to break out in a cold sweat. She needed the perfect dress. Not like that mistake she made at the interview party. Though it'd worked out okay, a naked back wasn't the impression she wanted to give Danny's friends. She was going to be judged by his ex.

The wardrobe closet was packed with costumes ranging from kilts to kimonos laid out by size and theme. Melanie's hands moved deftly as she sifted through the hangers with gowns her size. On the final rack, she nearly gave up hope … until her fingers touched the fabric and she knew she'd found the one.

Gripping the rugged garment bag, she made the trip north to Danny's apartment.

"There you are, gorgeous," he greeted her, standing in the center gap of the gliding elevator doors.

"Danny!" she sprang into his arms, her legs encircling his waist.

Staggering only a little, he caught her. "Hi." His words were muffled by her hair. "God, you feel good."

"Finally," she answered, her arms around his neck, the garment bag hanging from her wrist behind his back. Unhinging her legs, she dropped down, still holding on to him. "We have two days," she said, her face rubbing against his neck, taking in the subtle scent of cologne on his smooth skin.

"We should go inside." She looked down the empty hall and into the open door to his apartment.

He took her bag and replaced it with his hand. Her body felt electrified. He was always taking care of her. Finding reasons to touch, Danny would take hold of her fingers, her hand or arm. At a table he would touch her thigh or link his foot with hers. Melanie hadn't realized how much she missed being cared for, and with that came the awareness that she was happy.

She followed him to the kitchen. His every movement sent her heart into commotion. The horizontal line of his shoulders, the way his shirt draped over his chest as he opened the refrigerator door to retrieve the tomatoes. Melanie sighed and stared.

"I get Avery on Monday for the few days before Christmas," he said, slathering the bread with mayo. "What day do we leave for San Diego?"

"Twenty-third," she said, leaning around the counter to check out how nicely his pants clung to his muscled thighs. "You're the gorgeous one, you know," she said, interrupting his sandwich building and raising her gaze.

"Mel, you can't do that. I'm trying." The tendon in his jaw flickered and a look of determination tightened his face. In one concentrated stride he reached her, lifting her on to the counter, to stand between her legs, his hands on her thighs. "You said you didn't want our limited time together to be solely about sex. Then you give me that smokey look."

"Maybe I was being rash."

"Really?"

Her nod was all he needed to sweep her off the counter, toss her over his shoulder and jog the short distance to his bedroom.

⊰⊱

"Sweetheart, you about ready?" he asked, freezing as she moved out of the bathroom. "Oh, Melanie." His hand covered his heart, his eyes welling up. "I cannot believe how lucky I am."

"We're lucky," she whispered. He'd taken her breath away, like that very first date in college. Dating Danny had been a dream come true. She felt the same way staring at him in his crisp black tux.

"Melanie," he said, gently, "I've fallen in love with you all over again. I can't explain how you make me feel. These weeks apart from you I've never felt so lonely and so totally happy. Jesus," he said, swiping his fingers through his hair and clasping onto her fingers with his.

Melanie didn't dare to breath.

"I wasn't going to do this here…" He forced out panting breaths, bent down on one knee and smiled up at her.

Her thoughts were slow but the panic was fast.

"I know you think it's too soon but I've waited almost a decade to ask this," he stuttered. "I'm nervous." He shook out his arms and breathed out. "Okay. Mel, we're right for each other. When we're apart all I can do is think about when we'll be together again. I don't want to go another day without you. Melanie Ward," he said reaching in his breast pocket with one hand.

Oh my God, help, she thought, frozen.

"I promise to always love you, to make you happy and to be your best friend. Will you marry me?"

"Yes! Oh, Danny, Yes!" The words flew out, she was accepting and suddenly there wasn't any doubt.

"I haven't showed you the ring." Danny's laugh trembled as he lifted the lid of the little box and removed a diamond ring set in platinum. His fingers were cold as he took the ring and glided it onto her finger, too easily. "We can have it sized."

"It's perfect," Melanie grabbed Danny's sleeve for support as she looked at the diamonds on her hand. "It's perfect."

Her eyes were glued to her finger as she pressed the button for the elevator, the diamond glinting as she hailed a cab and again in the mirror as she checked her makeup. She could feel the intensity of his stare with every move she made.

The weight felt odd on her left side, out of balance as she teetered on her stilettos on the uneven sidewalk, interlocking her fingers with Danny's.

"You okay?" Danny asked, stopping them away from the windows of the party. "You've been so quiet."

"Shock. I'm in ... a happy shock." She looked over at the wide storefront where the party was underway. "Do we tell people?"

"I want to, do you?" His deep brown eyes held her captive.

Melanie bit down on her lower lip and took a leap. "Let's tell the world." Her body quivered as she walked through the door. "This is an odd place for a holiday party," she said, trying to behave normally.

"Adrienne's husband owns property around the city and currently quite a few are vacant. This party is basically a real estate venture," he said, giving his coat to the coat check girl and helping Melanie out of hers. "This place used to be a floral shop and before that a boutique – one of those cursed locations that seem like a good spot but nothing lasts."

"There you are," a heavily made-up woman in red satin rushed in. "I've been waiting."

"Adrienne," he said, hugging her as her arms were already around him. "You haven't been waiting for me," his voice was teasing. "You've been dying to meet Melanie."

"Daniel, you can't give away all my secrets," Adrienne said, patting his shoulder while her eyes crawled over Melanie and stopped at the ring.

"Nice to meet you." Melanie smiled warmly.

"Is there news, Daniel?" she asked as if the two were alone in the room.

"The newest." His grin lit up the space around him. "Melanie," he took her hand, "has agreed to marry me."

"Oh," she gasped with eyeballs the size of golf balls. "Well," Adrienne swallowed. "Congratulations. And I heard you got a show on Sports Nation? Wow, Daniel, you're on fire."

"No, I'm on top of the world," he said, pulling Melanie closer to him. "We're blocking your entrance ... Would you like a drink?" he asked Melanie.

"Where are my manners? Of course … Melanie, is it? There are waiters with cocktails and nibbles all around the room. Make yourself at home."

Pulling away from Adrienne, Danny leaned into Melanie's ear. "That was fun. You do realize we've informed the town crier."

"You're okay with Lauren finding out through the grapevine?"

"I don't owe her a thing."

Danny led her to one corner of the room where the crowd was divided into clumps of threes and fours.

"These were our friends." He said, under his breath.

These people, with their jewelry and designer clothing called him Daniel. And Daniel behaved differently. His voice deepened, his chuckles were throaty and he rested his hand lower on her hip than usual.

Melanie was fascinated. She'd never seen him pretend. She didn't even know he had it in him … he was looking cool on the surface while beneath he had to be writhing.

The word of their engagement was the talk of the evening. She received a few glares and a couple of cold shoulders but … she drank her wine, nibbled on appetizers and enjoyed frequent glances across the room to find Danny, looking incredible.

"How are you holding up?" He asked in her ear with his hand on the small of her back guiding her to a broom closet. Stepping over the buckets he locked the door behind him.

"I'm good. How are you?" she smiled at his impression of her, so mild as to be affected by comments or frowns.

"Ready to ditch this place." His hand was already cupping her face and leaning in to kiss her. "You're staying all day tomorrow, right?"

"Mm-hmm."

"Do you think we have to say goodbye or can we just leave?" Danny asked, his tongue following the line of her collarbone.

"If we say goodbye," she closed her eyes, his touch making her forget what she was saying. "It will be another hour before we get home."

⚮

"Mel," Danny said, on the pillow beside her. "Tonight was really weird for me. The whole thing felt wrong, like I didn't belong."

"It didn't show."

"I doubt we'll be getting many more invitations but if we do … could you remind me about how much that sucked?"

She caressed the side of his face as she promised to remind him.

The next day Danny showed off the studio that was being redesigned to house his set for his segment.

"Come sit in Grant's seat." He said patting the chair beside him. "I know this place isn't finished but can you see it? It's going to be great! Over there," he pointed out the production side with eagerness and introduced her to everyone who passed by as his fiancé.

"We haven't set a date yet." She said, a dozen times.

"But soon," was his reply.

Dinner was a prepackaged stew, that was heated in the microwave, and a wedge of multi-grain bread. Simple.

"Do you think Avery will like me?" She asked. It'd been on her mind all day.

"She's going to love you and I can't wait for you two to meet. You'll see how awesome she is."

"Okay," she said only slightly moved by his huge grin. But then remembered him saying something about Avery being Lauren's clone. *You can survive terrorists, Mel, you can surely befriend a six-year-old girl.*

Danny was incredible.

She completely forgot her problems for ninety minutes. But as she drifted to sleep, she conjured up schemes of how to make Avery like her.

"Danny, someone's at the door," Melanie said, nudging his chest to wake him up. "I think Avery's here."

"Too early for Lauren," he grumbled, rising and pulling on a pair of flannel pajama bottoms and a T-shirt. "Don't move, I'll be right back."

Melanie checked her watch. It wasn't early at all. She had to commute back to work and it was almost seven. She should've been up and out already, but the bed was warm and ... she leisurely stretched. Outside the bedroom came shouts with little footsteps running down the hall and a slamming door.

Rushing out of bed, she dressed as she shoved her clothes into the suitcase. Hell was breaking loose and Melanie cracked open the door an inch to peek. She felt like a villain sneaking out through the brothel window – with her pants around her ankles.

Lauren and Danny were arguing and Melanie understood Avery's need to run. She groaned, debating between the right thing to do and the thing she wanted to do. She wanted to disappear and call Danny later ... But the right thing was not to slink away, like the guilty party, *introduce yourself and then exit ASAP.*

Tiptoeing her bag down the tiled hall ... the voices amplified. Reaching her escape hatch without being seen was too much of a temptation. She'd call Danny from the station.

No way am I barging into that, Melanie thought, clamping the front door knob, her new ring sparkling. *Chicken.*

The ring didn't fit with work life. Too distracting. An hour outside the city Melanie called Danny, left a message and shoved the engagement ring deep into her pocket.

CHAPTER 36

The days after her weekend with Danny were hectic. The holidays were in full swing and the usual increase of activity had made three days feel like a month. She was sitting in on one of the ten meetings scheduled for the day.

"Excuse me," Melanie whispered, reaching into her pocket to silence the melody from her cell and turning her back on the table. "Hello?" she asked in a hushed voice, curious about the unavailable description of the caller. "Who is this?" she asked, uncomfortable with the labored breathing on the other end of the line.

"Mel." Adam coughed out her name.

Activating the trace, she nodded to Ben and made a quick exit.

"Where are you? Are you all right?" She couldn't wait for a response. "Speak to me," she commanded, while his breathing remained unsteady. "Stay with me," she said, sounding in control even though her brain felt too big for her skull and blood rushed to her eyeballs. "Where are you?" He didn't need to answer as the purple, pulsating dot zeroed in on her map, trace completed. He was in D.C. – only a few miles away. "I'm coming to get you … Stay where you are … Do you hear me?" There was no way he didn't, she was yelling. Without ending the call she put her phone in her pocket and raced to the garage.

First row parking was reserved for Agency vehicles. Taking seconds to hotwire a sedan, tires squealing, she floored the gas, checking the address from the trace.

"Adam," she said over the hacking. "What's happening? Come on, talk to me," she urged before the dead silence. "Please, God, no! Adam," she raised her voice into the vacuum.

Driving faster she weaved around pedestrians and vehicles until she was in the approximate location of his whereabouts. Nothing. A touristy part of town with shops, eateries, street vendors, people walking, a homeless guy on a bus bench, a woman with a stroller … Slamming on the brakes she spun the car in a U-turn, her blood rushing at the recognition. *That wasn't a homeless man!*

The jolt from jumping the curb without slowing knocked her teeth together. Biting down hard on her tongue, the pain flooded her eyes and blood oozed from her wound. She jerked to a stop, the passenger side only feet from the bench where Adam was sprawled. Running to him she wondered how she'd recognized him. His face was ashen white, his lips were colorless and his arm hung limply with his knuckles scraping the concrete. Melanie swallowed down a lump.

Christ! "Adam, it's me, Melanie. Come on," she scolded angrily, grabbing hold of his face with both hands. He felt cold. Opening the passenger door, she lugged his dead weight, folding him into the seat and strapping him in with the seat belt, talking at him the entire time.

Running stoplights she hauled ass to the only place she could think of ... Dr. Andrew.

"Doc," she said, bypassing the pleasantries and aiming the heat vents directly at Adam. "I need your help, are you home?"

"Yes."

"I'm on my way ... five minutes. Be ready, I'm bringing in someone. It looks like ... Jesus ... I don't know," she stole a glance at Adam's slumped body. No blood but she couldn't be sure. "Gunshot, maybe. More like something internal ... I don't know. Just please be ready, he's having trouble breathing."

"Okay, but I need you to take a breath."

"Four minutes," she said, ending the call. "Okay, Adam we're getting you to a doctor," she talked without looking over. She could still hear him panting. "He'll fix you up. Please, Adam..." Melanie crushed the steering wheel, shaking with the mass of energy she'd built up under her skin – she'd push the god-damned car if she had to.

Dr. Andrew lived in a two-story attached house 10 minutes from the center of town. He had been employed by the Agency's clinic and Melanie trusted him.

Her tires screamed as she drove recklessly, turning too quickly, stopping abruptly inches from the doctor's garage door. Andrew, who'd been waiting by the door, ran to help carry Adam inside, each taking an arm over their shoulder, his feet dragging across the flagstone walkway. His head was slumped to one side and there was no sign of life. His hand in hers felt cold as death.

"Put him in the dining room. I prepped it the best I could ... lay him on the table. Count of three, all your strength." Andrew had draped a sheet over the table. "Help me get his clothes off."

A cart with sterile supplies had been rolled beside the table. Melanie grabbed the scissors and began cutting off Adam's shirt while Andrew checked his pulse. Holding the little flashlight with his teeth, he scanned Adam's eyes and mouth.

"How well do you know this guy?"

"Well, I guess. Why?"

"I'm thinking he's been poisoned." She felt Andrew's gaze. "You're not surprised?"

"Little surprises me."

"Okay," he said, refocusing, moving to the sideboard and picking up a syringe. Melanie was pulling the remnants of a shirt from beneath Adam when Andrew tapped the needle and injected a clear substance into Adam's arm. "Get the bucket." He motioned for a trash can and tipped Adam onto his left side. "This usually works pretty fast."

She hadn't expected the convulsions. Bracing against the table she held him as his eyes opened and rolled to the back of his head. "Andrew?" she said just as the yellow fluid started spewing from his mouth. "Andrew?"

"Hold him, don't let him fall." Andrew ordered. She threw her shoulder into the effort until the puking stopped and the coughing took over. "Here, cover his mouth." He handed her a cloth.

"Is this normal?" Melanie asked, the tension in Adam's body relaxing as his seizure subsided.

"Clear out his mouth and throat, use a clean cloth. Wrap it around your hand – whatever he took you don't want to get it on your skin."

She did as she was told. Andrew checked Adam's vitals.

"How is he?" Melanie asked at the first opportunity.

Andrew's reaction was not encouraging. "We'll have to wait and see," he said, sticking electrodes to Adam's bare chest. "Wipe off any substance that might have splattered on him and yourself. His breathing is stabilizing," Andrew shook his head. "I'm going to try and flush his body with fluid. He's dehydrated."

As the doctor inspected Adam, Melanie breathed, the first breath she'd taken in minutes. She held onto the table for support.

"We're doing the best we can," Andrew said, noticing her fragility from above a pair of magnifying glasses.

"I'm responsible for him. If he dies, I'm responsible." She shored up her emotions and left to fetch clean water and towels, shutting the kitchen door to collapse in silent agony.

You're not doing any good here squatting on the ground, she chastised herself. *You can breakdown later.*

"You're going to be fine," she told him, repeating his name and reminding him that it was her, Melanie, with him and that she wouldn't leave. Brushing back his sweaty, matted hair she wiped down his forehead with cool cloths.

"Should he be sweating like this?" she asked, exchanging the damp blanket with a heavier, dry one. As she did she noticed something she'd overlooked in the mayhem: a tattoo. Looking up, she met Andrew's concerned gaze. "Was this here before?" she asked, with an embarrassed chuckle. "I swear I didn't see it."

"You were pretty focused." His eyes shifting from Adam's shoulder, he bent to examine his neck. "The poison was probably administered orally." He laughed nervously. "I was just thinking about those old spy movies, where an injection was administered from the tip of a cane or an umbrella."

"Ah, the good old days," Melanie agreed, too concerned to be distracted. "You think he's going to be okay?"

"His fever is high and I don't have the proper equipment. I'd like to pump his stomach to make certain he's –" Adam began to seize and Andrew rushed to hold him down. "Grab his shoulder."

For hours she and Andrew watched over Adam.

"Is he looking worse? Or is it my imagination?" Melanie finally voiced her silent worry. "He's not holding down the fluids, his fever is still up and…" She stopped to breathe.

"You need to rest."

Melanie threw him a glare. "Just worry about him. I'm fine."

"Melanie, it's not over. He's healthy and putting up a fight. Vomiting is good, it's the body's way of ridding the toxins. And," this part he made certain she met his eyes, "you aren't responsible for everyone."

"For him, I am." She turned back to Adam lying on the table. Andrew was doing his best and she knew that … "Andy, I'm sorry," she said, dropping into a chair and looking up at him. "I'm sorry. He'd have died without you."

"There's no need to apologize," he said softly. "I get it. You're afraid."

Melanie's lips tightened into a thin line as she nodded.

"I'm going to make us some tea. We have a long night ahead of us," Andrew said, patting her back as he passed.

For hours Melanie paced, spoke to Adam as Andrew checked vitals and his supply of medicines. Time ticked slowly.

"He seems to have stabilized," Andrew said, taking Adam's pulse. "I think he's rounded a corner. We should move him to the bed where he'll be more comfortable. I've prepared the guest room and the bed is on casters."

Together they lifted Adam onto the bed. He seemed to be sleeping peacefully but the weight still clung heavily to her shoulders.

"All right, Melanie, if I keep going I'll be of no use to you tomorrow. Help yourself to anything you need. My room is just down the hall."

Alone with Adam, having no idea what time it was, she pushed the sweat-caked hair from his forehead, smoothing out the curl. "You cannot do this to me," she said, caressing his fiery skin, her hand sliding down the side of his face. *He really is a perfect specimen.* Memories swirled. Still stroking his face she tried to ignore the increasing need to inspect his tattoo.

Melanie looked over her shoulder. The hall was empty … there was nothing to feel scandalous about. Still, she held her breath, folding back the covers to release a current of heat. He was too hot. Throwing off the entire set of blankets, she began wiping him down with a cool, damp cloth.

"What were you thinking?" she asked wiping down his fevered skin.

The tattoo began on the left side of his chest. The skeletal hand of death tearing through flesh and gripping Adam's blackened heart. Squeezing the charred organ so it oozed out between death's fingers.

A white-capped wave created by the artist picked up again at Adam's side, just below his pecs. The water flooded in, a torrential, violent storm crashing upon his eight-pack abs and churning into a raging river by the top of his Levis. The images played out like a graphic novel over flesh. The work was beautifully sad and the pain evident as she stroked his hot skin, following the path of the river. Riding the fierce stream was debris of what Melanie feared to be symbolic pieces of his broken heart.

It was the story of pain and loss and there was little doubt the flood was formed from an ocean of tears.

The horrible illustration of Adam's anguish continued below his Levis. Leaving the final chapter hidden. His jeans were loose and had slipped down to his pelvic bone. Even unconscious his muscles were defined. He was chiseled. His shoulders broad and the veins over his biceps were pronounced.

God Adam, what happened to you?

Covering him with the blankets, her fingers brushed his neck ... The man was too damn sexy, asleep or awake. *The scary thing*, she thought, was that he had a piece of her she could never regain.

"Please," she whispered, feeling uncomfortable about craving him. "You need to fight harder, Adam. Please fight."

Melanie wiped the moisture from her eyes with the heel of her hand and rinsed the cloth in fresh water. If she could've washed away the wrongness of her emotions, she would've.

Melanie felt as if her eyelids were glued shut and her muscles were unresponsive. She hadn't planned on falling asleep when she settled on a thin strip of unused mattress beside him. Now her body was rejecting her command to wake. He felt solid and warm; She was sure his fever had broken.

Forcing her legs over the side of the bed, Melanie sat up and rubbed her eyes. Adam was still unconscious.

"Good morning," Andrew said and Melanie squinted in the direction of the door. "I'm glad you got some sleep," he said, handing her a cup of coffee.

"Thanks." Just looking into the dark java improved her state of mind. "He looks better."

Andrew nodded. "Much."

"What time is it?"

"Noon."

"Jesus, I feel as if I've been drugged."

"Go home, take a shower. I'll call if there are any signs of change."

Melanie shook her head. "I'm not leaving him until…" she snorted out a laugh.

"Until when?"

"Until he's just about ready to wake." Melanie stood, watching the gentle rise and fall of Adam's chest.

"I suspect that won't be too long," Andrew said, adjusting his stethoscope.

"Really?" Melanie asked, surprised. "He was in such bad shape."

"I'm not guaranteeing, but…" Andrew knocked his head back and forth. "My Magic 8 Ball says, 'All signs point to yes'."

"That's not comforting coming from a doctor," she chuckled.

Andrew dragged two chairs from around the room and stationed them by the bed. "I took a couple of vials of his stomach contents. I want to send them to the lab for analysis."

"Could I have one for our lab?" Melanie's interests were peaked.

"Certainly, I'll get it to you before you leave." Looking back at Adam, he added, "That guy's been through a lot." Melanie nodded. "There're major scars all over his body."

Most are on the inside, she thought. "This is good coffee," she said, changing the subject.

"I've been a bachelor a long time. I make a mean cup of coffee and killer scrambled eggs – and that's dinner about thee times a week."

"I'm no doctor or anything," Melanie said, with teasing concern, "but aren't you supposed to throw a vegetable in there somewhere?"

"Ever hear of a coffee *bean*? Wait," Andrew said, standing.

Adam had opened his eyes, Melanie was at his side in an instant.

"Hi there," she smiled, holding his hand. In return he applied pressure to her fingers and tried to lift her hand. "No, you need to rest," she protested, he closed his eyes but his weak attempt continued. "What is it?" she asked, moving her hand for him – he carried it to his lips and placed a kiss on her palm. "Sleep." It was all she could get out of her clamped throat.

He would be up soon. And there was no way she wanted deal with an alert Adam. Melanie drove her stolen sedan back to the Agency.

"Ms. Ward, there's a meeting in the small conference room," Jane said as soon as she entered.

"Thanks," she sighed, turned and headed back down the hall. "Heard there was a powwow going on with all my favorite people." She grinned at the three men.

"Great. I was hoping you'd make it back in time," Ben said from the head of the table. "Cut the lights would you? We've got a surveillance video and a couple of other items to go over."

"What happened to you?" Jack whispered when she took the seat next to him. "Looks like you've been on a bender."

"Later. Hey, Mike."

Melanie struggled to stay awake during a gory slideshow. The light, the hum of the machine and Ben's droning voice were the perfect combination for a spy lullaby.

"How are you doing?" Melanie asked Jack as the meeting broke. "You look sort of happy."

"I am." His grin was wide and there was no sarcasm in his tone. "What?" he asked, questioning with his palms up. "We're going to have some major ass to kick now through New Year's. Aren't you excited?"

She looked at him with the probing stare.

"All right, Jane and I made up. I don't know what I was thinking before," he said, shirking off the thought, his grin creasing the skin around his eyes.

"Be nice to her ... I don't want to have to hurt you," Melanie warned. "By the way, what'd you get her for Christmas?"

"Get her? Ah shit, I forgot."

"Jack!"

"Take a joke, Ward," he laughed. "You leave in a couple of days, right?" His hand patted her on the shoulder. "Have a good trip and stop worrying."

She was grumbling to herself, walking briskly down the corridors as her phone rang. It'd been days since she'd heard from Danny.

"Hello."

"Melanie, it's Andrew."

"Oh," she stopped short.

"He's gone," Andrew's voice was grave and Melanie felt the Earth open up beneath her feet and swallow.

"What?"

"I tried to tell him it was way too soon for him to take off. I still don't know what chemicals he consumed. But he wouldn't listen."

Tears of relief washed over her eyeballs. "Not your fault, you couldn't stop him – I actually think that's good news. Oh, I just got that sample to the lab ... I'll let you know what we find out as soon as I know."

"I've got a vial ready to send to the tox-lab I use at the clinic."

"Thanks again, Andy. Really, I can't express..." Melanie overextended her lungs. "I can't ever repay you, but if there's ever anything I can do for you, you just name it."

"After all the times you've helped me out ... consider this partial payment."

Melanie smiled, forcing back any sign of weakness that might be showing through the cracks. "He won't collapse out there, will he?"

"He'll be weak." Andrew paused, then began timidly, "His main concern was you. He seemed affected when I told him you'd stayed up all night with him." Speechless, she tried to work out Andrew's purpose to that particular observation. "I thought you should know," Andrew picked up after a moment of silence.

"You aren't substituting your stethoscope for a matchmaker's shawl, right?"

Andrew's words broke through his chuckle. "Hadn't thought of it that way ... but you both were emotional about the other ... I just thought..."

Melanie interrupted, "Forget it. Stick to doctoring. Thanks, Andy."

"Anytime."

"You didn't happen to ask him about who might've been behind the poisoning, did you?"

"I know better. Bye, Melanie."

"Yeah, bye," she said, gazing down at the pattern on the hall carpeting. *Who?* The question frightened her. *Before you leave, find a gentle way to remind Mike about that e-mail to your mom.*

Melanie showered, wolfed down a burger and went directly to the gym. Now that the question had entered her mind, she was forced to play out the scenarios. There was no escaping her personality, goal-oriented and zeroing in on a new objective was all-consuming.

"Crap," she said, having missed Danny's call while steaming out her pores from the brutal workout. She hit redial and went straight to his voice mail. Melanie cursed her phone – with communication these days, there wasn't supposed to be telephone tag!

CHAPTER 37

Dreams invaded her restless sleep, fragmented dreams that lingered for only a hazy instant after she'd woken and then were gone.

In gray pants, a ruffled white dress shirt and high boots she took the stairs down to the communication room. There was work to be done and Mike was first on her list.

"You sure you want to be this hands on?" Mike asked after an hour of sifting through data. "Or are you gunning to get your seat back from Jack?"

"Don't be ridiculous," was her answer. "We need to find one connection, one detail that will unfold this entire terrorist cell. If we find it Jack can take the credit. I just really need to keep mentally busy," she said, her eyes blurry. "Off the subject, do you still have that flash drive for my mom?"

"Of course," he said absently – his mind as preoccupied as hers. "I was thinking..." he rattled off a few of the names on the list.

"Do you memorize all of your reports?"

"Don't you?"

Rolling her eyes and about to comment, her chiming ring made her jump. "Hi handsome, finally!"

"Hey, how are you?"

"Better now."

"I'm sorry I haven't called much lately, but … well, I'm in your lobby and I … do you have a few minutes?"

"For you? I could carve out some time. I'll be right down." Stowing her phone in her back pocket she turned to Mike to tell him she was leaving for a few minutes.

Melanie raced to her room, grabbed her long wool coat, opened her top dresser drawer and slipped the ring out of the velvet box and onto her finger.

Danny was staring out the window when she entered the no frills lobby with plastic chairs. His golden hair covered the collar of his silver metallic jacket.

"Hi," she said, wrapping her arms around his waist and kissing the back of his neck.

"Hi." He squeezed her hands before unlocking them and turning to face her. "Beautiful."

"Are you okay?" She asked, reading his mood.

"Can we take a walk?" he asked, his head down and shoulders slumped.

Melanie looked outside. The cold front predicted had arrived and without the benefit of snow. She buttoned up and coiled the scarf twice around her neck. Walking side by side, she reached into his pocket, withdrew his hand and entwined their fingers. The day wasn't as cold as she expected, the low clouds holding in the warmth.

Across the street from the Manor was a park frequented by joggers and dog walkers. The center path was wide, clear of trees and lined with brightly painted green benches. In spring the cherry blossoms were gorgeous with the green grass and abundant flowers but winter had claimed all of nature's color.

Melanie stopped at the first available bench and sat angled to face him.

"Danny, what's this about?" His mood was miserable and she was already thinking about other networks, other opportunities for him. "Did something happen with the show?"

"No, the show is fine. But there is something." His chest deflated with the exhaling of air. "You know how much I love you."

Melanie studied his tightly knit brows, the droop of his eyes and the heavily weighted corners of his mouth. There was no wind, no birds, and the movement around the park slowed as her heart pounded.

"What's going on?" she asked, puffs of misty air escaping her lips in quicker succession.

He looked down into his empty hands. "I meant every word I've ever said to you."

"What are you talking about?"

"Lauren. Mel, it just happened." Danny looked up at her with puppy dog eyes. "I never thought ... we were arguing, like we've been for months, when..."

As words fell out of Danny's mouth all she could do was stare. She fixated on the slight crookedness of his front tooth as if he were speaking in slow motion.

"I'm so sorry, Mel. I never meant to hurt you. If there is anything I can do..." He stammered, coughed and looked bashfully away.

Swallowing hard didn't dislodge whatever it was that was caught in her throat.

"We have a child … it makes sense for us to work on … to not throw away all the years we've been together. And she's changed. She sees how important our family is." He was breathing rapidly. "We're getting back together."

The final words were a sharp slap to her face, startling and stinging. Mentally she replayed them. Her heart was beating fast and hard as she pushed the words out. "She's married." The lump was rising, evident by its foul taste.

"It's not working out," he defended. "For her and Paolo, it's not working out." He reached out for her hand, covering hers with his dank one.

She ripped it away. "Don't."

"I'm so sorry, Mel."

"You can't be serious about this." She searched his face for any sign of humor, feeling sick.

"I love her and she regrets … you don't understand how bad she feels about how our marriage ended. Mel, these last days with Lauren … we've yelled, fought, screamed and cried. Passion like in the begin…" He snapped off the end of his statement and held his breath. "I mean it's different now. Like it used to be."

"Stop. Trying. To. Explain." She gritted her teeth as she felt her head ready to explode.

This isn't fair! She wanted to cry out. *What do I do?* She struggled to answer. Her mind was in a thick fog … her fight instinct ready to kick in. To rip him and Lauren to shreds, to defend what was hers, to, to …. *What, Melanie?*

"It's not just about Lauren," he continued, not knowing he should keep quiet. "There's Avery to consider, a kid needs a mother *and* a father."

Dizzy, she felt the earth sway beneath the bench. A wave of nausea washed over her and then was gone. Danny's voice still rang in her ears but she felt nothing else. Empty. There was no anger. No cold. He was leaving her.

"This is yours," she wiggled the ring off her finger.

"No, keep it. I gave it to you."

"Why would I want it?" She shoved it into his damp palm.

He shrugged. "You could sell it."

She looked away, giving herself a moment to sort out what was happening. The emptiness had been fleeting and now the swirling was making her feel woozy. She couldn't focus.

Danny beside her on the bench, miles away, was hunched over, elbows on knees, twisting the ring between his fingers.

"I had plans for us, a future." His head fell into his hands. "I feel bad about this. You were so good to me, so good for me. I can never fully thank you."

"Enough. Just," she shook her head, blowing out the anger. "You're unbelievable."

"I never thought she'd be back. I can't help it, Mel, I'll always be in love with her." He looked up. "I wish it were different. I'd rather…" Reaching inside his coat he pulled out a blue envelope. "I want you to have this. It's the trip I booked last month. A celebration for us."

"Take Lauren."

"It was supposed to be our romantic getaway. I wouldn't feel right … please take it, as a thank you. I would never be where I am if it weren't for you." Danny folded the envelope in half and stuck it in the pocket of her overcoat. "You're going to be fine, Mel, you're so strong."

"Am I? I'll survive because that's what I do. But you don't *know* that I'll be fine."

"I never meant to hurt you."

"You've said that already."

"Please."

"Please what?"

His brown eyes were red-rimmed, she hadn't noticed earlier. "Please tell me you forgive me."

"I can't do that."

Time stretched, as she stared at Danny, wanting to bolt and at the same time never wanting to leave.

"Danny, I'm not ready…" about to push aside her pride and give in to her desire to cling – the air above her was disrupted by a whizzing sound.

Reacting on impulse she threw her body over Danny, knocking them both to the ground as the second bullet sounded. She waited the length of a heartbeat before moving.

"Are you hit?"

"What the heck!?"

He's fine. She relaxed infinitesimally. Her thoughts shifted from defense – to Adam. Could he have recovered enough to be the shooter? With no other shots fired, she carefully raised her head to survey the situation and ordered Danny to stay down.

Across the wide path, one bench over, a man was leaning oddly … *Holy shit!* Melanie was up, running in a crouched position to the fallen man who'd nearly been decapitated.

"Oh, dear God," Melanie gagged, as a pair of blue eyes rolled around to look at her. "Finn?" Swallowing back a mouthful of bile she lied, "It's going to be all right." She lifted his head back to a natural angle and pulled off her scarf. His blood was everywhere, gushing out of the cavern that had once been his neck. "Call 911," she yelled over her shoulder at a passing shadow. Applying pressure, the stain of his blood was swelling rapidly, absorbing wickedly into the cream-colored fabric of his coat. Hopeless. "Don't you die, you stupid son of a bitch."

Oh God, oh God, oh God. He stared, his eyes filling with blood, his shoulder warm and wet. Melanie felt for her phone and speed-dialed Ben.

"Jesus, Ben, Finn's been shot – we're at the park. It's bad, Ben. Someone is calling 911 – we can't wait for our ambulance. It's bad."

"Okay, we're on our way."

Melanie nodded, her hands drenched in blood. She looked up at wide-eyed, panicked faces.

"I called the clinic," the tall man in the center said. He was an agent, she knew, but at the moment his name eluded her. "They're on the way."

The others around him were agents, too. "Good," she said, aware of someone kneeling by her side. Danny was holding Finn's wrist, feeling for a pulse. He looked up at her and shook his head.

Danny! She had to get him out of there. With her he was in danger.

"John," the forgotten agent's name flashed. "I need you to take over for me. Don't let anyone else touch Parker, understand?" As she spoke she grabbed one of his hands and pressed it to Finn's neck. "You have to hold his neck together." Before exchanging spots with John she looked at her enemy. "Finn, if you die, I win. Don't let me win."

Nodding at John she took a quick scan above their heads in the direction the bullets came from. If it was Adam she was safe, but she doubted he'd have taken the shot with her in the crosshairs. Gripping

Danny's hand, she pulled him out of the crowd.

She was pushing Danny into the back of the cab as the ambulance turned on the dirt path.

"What was that?" Danny asked, his pale expression filled with astonished confusion. "Did that really happen? It was like a movie. You knew that guy?"

"Parker." It was all she could get out, her throat constricted.

"That was Parker? Wow!" He twisted to catch the shrinking scene. It took a long time for him to process, the length of the ride to his hotel before he spoke again, "You've got his blood all over you."

Melanie looked at her hands, the cuffs of her shirt and coat, her chest, arms, everything was drenched in red.

"What can I do?" Danny asked, looking helpless and taking her saturated hands in his.

"When we get to the hotel walk briskly to the elevators, don't run and don't stray." It wasn't what he meant.

Inside his two-bedroom suite, she closed the drapes and instructed him to keep them shut. Nothing was out of sorts, except her.

In a trance-like daze, she noticed how strange Finn's blood looked all over her hands. The water flowed and colored the basin in a large swirl down the drain. Impossible to imagine that it recently pulsed in Finn Parker's veins.

"Mel." She looked up, her stupor dissolved. Danny was leaning against the door jam. "I can talk with Lauren – she's going to need time for her divorce, anyway. I'll stay with you until you feel better."

"I don't need you, Danny." She put up her hands to ward off the intended embrace as he moved closer. "Thanks," she added, softening her tone and drying her hands. "But I doubt Lauren would appreciate your offer. I'd better go."

"I suppose so," he said, following her to the door. "Take care of yourself, Mel."

Her was hand on the knob. "You know you can't come back. When she changes her mind, again … and she will … you can't come back to me."

They both took a few seconds. She gazed at him, her body aching. It took all her strength to close the door behind her as she entered the hall and pressed the down arrow for the elevator. Fortunately, she only had seconds to stare at her bedraggled reflection before the metal doors opened and out flounced a blonde woman who strutted by without noticing Melanie standing a foot away.

Melanie held the doors for an extra second as Lauren knocked roughly on Danny's door. Sighing, she felt too fragmented to feel the pain.

Outside the light had faded, the clouds so low she could reach up and grab a piece of sky. The temperature had dropped and beneath her cold skin her blood flowed like ice. She slid into the first in a line of cabs in front of the hotel, ready and waiting.

Melanie slid as far back into the seat as possible, her thoughts jumping from what had happened to what she was going to find. Unconsciously, chewing her lip. From the street the one-story building was non-threatening, no bars on the windows, no ambulance wailing out front – just a No Parking sign on the curb that ran the length of the building. Nothing about it said medical clinic.

Melanie ran her badge and pass code. *Damn it!* She cursed the eye scan. "Come on," she urged the release of the doors and threw them open when the lock popped.

"They're all downstairs in the crypt," said the nurse behind the counter. "Unless you're here to be seen?"

She shivered at the sound of those five letters, "crypt."

"No."

"Would you like me to take you down?"

Melanie shook her head and rushed on.

The morgue was usually a quiet place. Today, however, when she rounded the third set of stairs the conversation hummed feverishly. She eased past a group gathered along the stairwell. Another handful were in a tense circle outside the door. The voices turned to whispers and ceased as the group parted, silently opening a path for her to pass.

The milk-glass window was coated enough to allow the sight of shadowy figures but she couldn't make out their identity. She stared at her hand as she pushed open the door. She wasn't thinking, she was surviving.

The room was cold and the chemical scent of sterilizing fluid filled her senses as she took the first crucial step inside. The men standing around the stainless steel table turned, clearing a direct line of sight to Finn.

He lay still. His dress shirt had been sliced open, exposing a slab of pale skin and a purple-ringed cavity where a bullet tore off his shoulder. Even with that gore, it was his neck that she was terrified to see. Concentrating to the point of pain she forced herself to look. The hole was the size of her fist – exposing vertebrae. She stared a long while before she was able to lift her eyes to Finn's face. His eyes were closed and his colorless lips were stretched into a grimace.

There was no peace in his expression, which bore only a slight resemblance to the Finn she knew. Melanie covered her mouth to fend off a wave of nausea.

"What is *she* doing here?"

"Agent Ward was at the park when Finn was … assassinated."

Ben's voice cracked. It was the first time she could recall that ever happening.

"I don't want her here."

Melanie swallowed. "Senator Parker, I am sorry for your loss ... I did the best I could to keep him alive. But the wounds were ... too much." She glanced at Ben before turning to leave. The man had just lost his son and no matter who he was she didn't want to upset him more.

"Get out." Hugh's foul breath penetrated her skin.

She raised her gaze to the grieving father. She saw the shift from rational to insane. It was the direct eye contact that triggered his loss of control. He lunged at her with outstretched arms reaching for her neck. Melanie tried to deflect the attack but she couldn't without doing damage to the old man. She could feel Ben, Jack and a board member tugging and pulling at him. But his bony fingers curled around her throat, cutting off her oxygen and she was left without options. She lifted her knee with as much force as she could muster and Hugh dropped like a bag of sand.

Melanie gasped, her hands protectively covering her neck as she staggered to the wall, coughing and sputtering.

From the ground Hugh moaned, "You killed my son!"

"No."

"You wanted him dead," Hugh whispered.

Ben ushered her out before she could retort. Her spirit was gone and she was grateful to be removed. She pulled out of Ben's grip, rushed up the stairs and burst outside into a frigid drizzle. The rain had turned to sleet, making the sidewalk slippery.

"Melanie." His voice was by her ear, soft and clear. She slid to a wobbly stop in mid-stride. Reaching out, he grabbed her and set her back on her feet. "Oh," he gasped, pulling her under a low-watt bulb on the side of a building, "You're hurt! Melanie," his hands were frantically searching for chest wounds.

"Not mine," she answered, exhausted.

"You're all right?" he asked, the glint in his eyes suspicious as he removed his hands and took in her blood-stained clothing.

"Finn."

Adam let out a sigh. "I've been going crazy with worry." The streetlight deepened his gaunt appearance. "I'm so sorry I wasn't there." His grip on her biceps tightened. "When I think…" Losing the battle to hide his emotions, he dropped his forehead to her shoulder and pulled her into a tight hug, her cheek against his chest. He was warm and she was too stunned to move. "Babe, it's cold out here, where's your coat?"

She pulled back to show him her wool calf-length coat … It was missing. "I don't know."

He was covering her with his coat before she could protest.

"Finn is dead," she blurted.

"I know," he said.

"Was it you?" she asked, already accusing.

"No."

"There's no reason to lie."

"I'm not." His gaze was focused as the muscle in his jaw twitched. "I want you to know I tried to stop this, I went to Hugh." Adam took her hands. "I need you to know, I'm not a monster."

That word stood out as she listened, *he's used it before.* It was something she meant to remember.

"This was going down and it was either him or you." Adam was still explaining. "Finn cut me out of the circle, hired a punk he met off the street. We were lucky I found him – paid double but there was no guarantee with a guy like that. No scruples."

She knew she was missing every other word but … "Hugh knew what?" she thought of the senator standing over Finn's corpse. Her breathing was labored as she sorted through the information.

"I went to him a couple of days ago. After I refused to join his organization he wouldn't listen … told me to do what I had to do. But, Mel, what the hell were you doing at the park?" He let go of her hands to tug his fingers through his wet hair, dragging the curls off his forehead.

"I…" her heart panged and she couldn't bring herself to explain. "This is too much, I can't. I've got to go."

A new pain reached his eyes. "I'm so sorry, but there's one more thing I need to tell you."

What more could possibly be piled onto this day?

"Apparently I'm strong … so just let me have it."

"It's Ashe."

The air escaped her lungs as if she'd been punched. Her body clamped into a tight knot and her voice held none of the shake that was raging through her body.

"You had better not touch him. Do you understand, one hair on his head gets bent and I will…" she poked her finger into his muscular shoulder as she threatened.

"Stop," he said, his body as rigid as hers. "You think I would hurt that asshole? If I wanted him gone, Mel, he'd be gone." Adam snapped his finger to show the speed and ease of the effort.

It was the first time she'd ever seen him angry and it scared her. "What, then?" she tore her hand from his.

The vein in his neck pulsed but the anger in his voice faded. "He's been *cheating* with his ex-wife."

Melanie's tension was released, laughing out a snort and feeling borderline crazy. Adam watched without a hint of judgment.

"I thought you knew everything," she accused, pushing off his jacket.

"I'm not making this up," he said apologetically.

"I already know. Danny told me today, *that's* what I was doing at the park." She grunted, "He was breaking up with me." Melanie bit down on her lip. "I guess I should be happy to know that even you can be surprised."

"I'm sorry I got rough with you."

"I've got places to be," *after I figure out where the hell I am*, she thought looking around for some familiar guidepost.

"I cleaned out the equipment from Oak Street."

"Oh." She hadn't been able to think two minutes ahead and had forgotten about the surveillance at Finn's. "Thank you."

Adam's smile was rueful. "Mel," he said, nervously.

"What?" she asked, looking out at the soggy night.

"If you need anything."

Melanie nodded. "Take care of yourself. You're free. Go live a good life."

The cold had cleared her head some and she managed her way back to the Manor.

"So, it is true!" Mike said two minutes after she'd entered. "Jeez, Mel." His eyes were huge. She must look terrible, she realized – everyone was giving her the same wild expression.

"Where are you going?" he asked, at her heels.

"My office, I've got things to figure out. How'd you know I was here?"

"Are you crazy? You need a hot shower. You're practically blue from the cold and you're shivering. You may never have listened to me before ... but tonight you are."

Melanie stopped. *Am I losing control everywhere?*

"Don't make me force you," he said with a slight quiver to his voice.

She smirked. "Very frightening, Mike. Take me to my room," she said, turning to the elevator. *Besides*, she thought, massaging the tips of her fingers, "I seem to have lost feeling in my extremities."

"Why aren't you wearing a coat?"

She couldn't remember having taken it off. It had to be at the clinic ... she'd felt claustrophobic ... The nightmare in the basement rushed back.

"Could you try and find it for me? I think I had it in the cab but..." she said, unlocking her door.

"You going to be okay?" His eyes drilled into her.

"Yeah, thanks."

"I'll get you something to eat and be right back."

"I'm not hungry."

"I'm in charge, remember?" Mike smiled from the doorway.

She nodded. "Enjoy it while you can."

He left and she walked by the empty ring box, exactly where she'd left it a lifetime ago. She threw it in the trash on her way to the bathroom. The steam came off her body as she dried and slipped on a pair of cotton pajamas.

"Hi," she said opening the door to Mike, still wearing the unnatural smile.

"I brought soup."

"I can smell it from here. Clam chowder. Yum. You can stay if you stop gawking at me," she said, taking the soup to her faux pine table for two.

"Don't want to talk about it?"

"Nope."

Mike leaned back in his chair. "Did I tell you I went out on a date last Saturday?"

Melanie felt drained but willing to go with the diversion. "The girl from R&D?"

"Naw, she doesn't talk to me anymore. This new girl works in IT in Charleston. Cute, too. I had to travel for this date."

Melanie breathed in, "First, what happened to the goggle girl and second, how'd the date go?"

"Well," he squirmed in his seat, "I don't want to talk about Goggle Girl. I still like her."

"I can't even begin to describe … I could really use a good story."

Mike twisted his lips into a grimace. "I wouldn't call it a *good* story. Awful story, really. Well," he squished his face as if he were in pain, "she sort of … I sort of … she accused me of stalking."

"Were you?"

"Protecting."

Melanie smiled at the thin line.

"She lives in a really bad part of town. I planted, I mean … placed cameras in her front yard for her safety."

"Thank you, Mike. Seriously, I'm laughing on the inside. So, how was the date?" she asked, looking down at a drained bowl of soup. *Did I eat it all?* She couldn't recall but it was gone – her mind traveled with Mike as he detailed his date with the IT girl from Charleston.

"I'm talking too much, you should get some sleep. I'm a phone call away if you need anything. Or if you decide you want to talk."

"Sleep is a good idea."

"Where's your phone?"

"My coat pocket, I think."

"The same coat you lost?"

"Mm-hmm." She was already eyeing her bed.

"I'll find it. You get some rest."

Melanie pushed the image of a purple Finn out of her head. Her mind raced in reverse. Adam, Finn, flipping back to the park bench with Danny. Stuffing her face into the pillow, choking on the sobs, she fell asleep.

CHAPTER 38

The banging on the door jerked her out of a peaceful unconsciousness, twisting her insides and wrenching her heart out of place. She sprang out of bed and was at the door when the previous day rushed over her.

"Agent Ward, your presence is requested by the Board of Executives."

"Who are you?" she asked, the thick necked brute.

"I've been hired as your personal guard."

"Hired to protect or to keep tabs on me? Never mind. I need to dress," she said, the base of her door bumping his large shoe. She stared into his dark, dull eyes until he moved his foot. "I'll be right out. Kill anyone who tries to enter, will you?" Melanie put on the first thing she could find and called Ben. "I've got a body guard waiting in the hall who wants to haul me in front of the Board. Do you know anything about this?"

"Only that Hugh was distraught. Go with him. And Ward, mind

your temper. I'll see what I can find out. I'm sure they're going to have you issue an official statement."

"Ben," she asked, "did yesterday really happen?"

"It's going to be okay," his soft tone answering her question. "But Ward, I don't have to tell you to watch what you say. I'll be there as soon as I can."

Melanie settled the receiver on the charger and picked up the phone again. "Hello, Mom," she tried to sound chipper as she canceled her plans and disappointed her parents. "I love you, too," she said, sighing … hoping to make good on her promise to reschedule her trip.

She opened her door to the wide, fatty back of her security detail. There was a certain amount of humiliation being escorted out of the building to the back lot.

The guard sat beside her in the back seat as Marcos drove to Headquarters. Her nerves were on edge as she walked the familiar path through the halls to the cavernous room where all the members, except Hugh, had already assembled. The conversation halted as she and her shadow entered. He left her at the door and Melanie strode to the sole chair set before the panel.

"Hello," she said into the newly installed microphone. Some of the senior executives were having difficulty hearing and decided it was an acoustic problem.

The interview began mildly. Everyone expressing their sorrow over Finn's horrific death.

"We're investigating what happened to Agent Parker," an old man started. "We understand you were at the scene when the incident occurred."

"Yes," Melanie answered during his pause.

"Please, Agent, if you would recount the events that led up to the assassination for us."

"Okay," she said, through a dry mouth. "First, may I ask who the gentleman with the recorder is?" She tilted her chin to the suit in the corner.

"This is Mr. Rogers, he's our attorney."

"In that case, I would feel better about speaking if I, too, were represented."

"Agent, when I said he's *our* attorney, I was including you. We are a team. Mr. Rogers is here for you as well as for the Agency. Besides, this is a preliminary meeting, completely unofficial."

"Even so, I am uncomfortable with this situation. You don't mind if I call my own lawyer?" Melanie said, knowing the answer.

The exchange behind the bench was charged, as they shuffled about. Making out the gist by the few words caught in the microphones. The convergence broke and the collective set of Executive Board eyes fell upon her.

"Agent Ward," the oldest of the members spoke. "You are welcome to confer with any one of the attorneys we have on staff. Our internal affairs department is dedicated to defending the equality for all of us."

"And if I want one not on *our* payroll?"

"That request will be denied."

"I see," Melanie said.

"No, I don't believe you do," said a man at the end of the table. "We aren't denying you a fair shake, we are concerned about this tragic situation being leaked to outside sources. No one can know what we do here, Agent."

"We also can't allow a murder to occur to one of our own and not punish the accountable person." A third man jumped into the discussion.

"Simply tell us what you know or what you saw."

"Then, I would like Agent Jackson to participate as a witness." She was starting to feel the prickles of nervousness creep up her spine. "I mean no offense but I've been treated less than fair by this very Board and I have reservations."

The melee started up again. The argument between the men continued. She wasn't being unreasonable and the only reason she had a chance was because of the absence of Hugh.

"Agent, this is more complicated than we expected. But we are discussing the death of a high-ranking spy." The old man, from beneath a heavy curtain of brows, made eye contact with security standing behind her.

"Am I being arrested?" Melanie asked as the oppressive presence of the guard behind her caused the hackles on the back of her neck to rise.

"Not arrested. Detained."

"I don't understand why. What reason do you have to conclude that I'm a flight risk?"

There was coughing before a voice sounded over the speakers.

"Senator Parker stated that he has compelling evidence. You will be comfortably kept at one of our detention houses for women."

Melanie's involuntary muscles constricted. "No. Some of those women are there because of me. No way." The guard's chubby hand weighed down her shoulder.

"She's right," one man said, gazing at the others over his bifocals. His face filled with concern.

"There are secure apartments in the Manor."

A few others agreed, offering alternatives and Melanie watched as if it were an episode on television.

In the back, behind the big chairs of the Board, the door swung open and a cold stream of air blew in, carrying away her hopes. Hugh stood, red-faced and imposing in his pinstripe suit, snarling out questions and flinging accusations. Each member of the Board turned at his booming voice but not a soul was willing to take him on.

Melanie stood alone across the room, staring at the tip of Hugh's extended finger.

"You murdered my son!" His deep, throaty sound reverberated against the marble floor.

"NO!"

"She's spinning her lies. Fooling us for years, having us believe in her loyalty. Now my son is dead and she's to blame. We all know it!"

She tried to speak, calling for Ben's cloak to shelter her from Hugh's storm but there was no one listening. The forest green walls were closing in as Hugh yelled. She looked to the Board members who only minutes ago were siding with her ... their faces were cast downward.

"Arrest her!"

"No," she said, with her back against the wall.

Panic bolted to her legs and she was on her feet when the guard tightened his grip on her shoulder, his sausage fingers digging in hard enough to bruise.

Hugh's beady eyes glaring at her, daring her ... she reached up, grabbed the guard's pudgy hand and twisted, snapping at least a quarter of the twenty-six bones. She rotated his arm behind his back, threw him to the ground and ran out the double doors, down the narrow corridors and fell into the bright winter day.

Dazzled by a light dusting of falling snow, Melanie stalled. *What the hell just happened?* No time to ponder the ramifications. She ran, caught a cab and fled to Bethesda.

"May I help you?" the Asian woman behind the counter asked when the bell above the door alerted her.

"Suzie, hi." Melanie smiled, her best mask. They'd been neighbors for a short time years ago when Melanie first moved out of the Manor. Suzie had been her only friend and Melanie had felt the loss when Suzie married Rex and moved to run the market. "It's been a long time."

"Melanie," Suzie called out and dashed around the counter of the small produce market to give her a hug. "How are you?"

"Fine. How are you?" Simultaneously Melanie relished and was tormented by the waste of time for the bit of normalcy.

"Oh, you know, barely staying afloat." She shrugged at the boxes of apples and pears. "Rex and I haven't killed each other yet so it's not all bad. Would you like a cup of coffee?"

"I'd love to catch up, I'm sorry but I've come for my things."

"Sure." Her brows were a prelude to questions as she ducked into the storeroom for a lock box. "I've kept it safe, just like you asked," she said, opening the box and handing Melanie the 5 X 8 goldenrod envelope.

"Thank you," she said, embarrassed about having to run. "We'll go out for lunch," she promised, creasing the envelope in half and slipping it into her pocket.

"Take some oranges," Suzie said, grabbing a couple. "These are delicious."

"Thanks. It's great seeing you again." They hugged goodbye at the curb.

"Is there anything I can do?" Suzie asked as Melanie climbed back into the cab.

"You just did." She waved through the window and gave the driver the address to her second stop.

❧

The last time she'd been inside this bank was when she rented the safe deposit box. The customer service rep in the center kiosk greeted her, verified signatures and led her to the big vault.

Melanie removed the key from the envelope she'd gotten from Suzie and turned one half of the locking mechanism while the representative's unlocked the other.

"I believe all of the rooms are available. Whenever you're ready I'll be at the desk." She left Melanie alone with her box.

A quick inventory: bundles of cash, two passports, a wig, glasses, contacts, a bulky 9 mm that left her nostalgic for the slim birthday gift she'd surrendered at the Agency's main office, and a canvas duffle bag. She flipped on the safety latch of her loaded gun, stuck it in the top of her jeans and filled the bag with the rest of her contingency material.

She'd chosen this branch because of the convenience to a Metro station. Descending on the steep escalator, keeping her head down, she slipped into the restroom and refashioned herself. With her new blonde hair smoothed and her lips a bright shade of red, she chose a middle-aged man standing on the platform and borrowed his cell.

"Ben, it's Melanie. Before you start – I've only got a minute."

"What is going on? Where are you? I've gotten 10 calls from Board members and the picture they're painting doesn't look good for you."

"I can explain."

"It'd better be one hell of an explanation." He was nearly yelling.

"Hugh wants to send me to one of our detention centers. Ben, there's no release date in those centers – no outside intervention. At best I'd get my ass kicked but more likely I'd wind up dead. I'm not going to let them drag me there without a fight."

"The Board would never have allowed that."

"The Board cowers to Hugh. I've got to go … see what you can do for me. Otherwise I'm out here on my own trying to clear my name." She halted. "You know I wasn't involved in this, right?"

"I know."

She stopped to buy a disposable cell on her way to a low-budget hotel. She needed to disappear while she figured out her next move. Running may not have been the best decision but...

The hotel was run down and in a seedy part of town that city officials didn't want the tourists to see. The carpeting was worn down to the pad by the bed, the shower showed signs of mold and the television remote was bolted to the nightstand. Still it was 100 times better than the women's prison from which she might never escape.

The bed creaked beneath her as she laid back and closed her eyes. Her mind worked diligently in her otherwise motionless body. First, she decided, Adam was out. It wouldn't be possible to involve him without jeopardizing his freedom.

And link me with an assassin, bad idea, she thought.

Though she didn't want to, she forced herself to travel back 24 hours. Starting with the phone call … Danny's voice. She felt the resentment building – they should be in San Diego now. *Instead, I'm sweating it out in a crappy hotel.* Alone it was easier to be mad at him … and remembering his face caused her blood to pulse.

Melanie choked back the rising ache and moved through her

memories. Back and forth she played the scene, rewinding and searching … the fact was Finn hadn't been on that bench when they arrived at the park.

I need my cell phone to check Finn's calls. Someone notified him of my idiotic location. Jesus, what had I been thinking? A sitting duck.

She needed Mike and there was no way to get to him. It was no secret he was her go-to-guy and no doubt they'd be monitoring him. Opening the drapes a slit she looked beyond the streetlamps and overfilled dumpsters to the setting sun. If Mike were still at the office, and he most likely was … she shook her head. With retina scans and high security she wouldn't get anywhere near the place. She was going to have to wait and catch him outside of the Manor.

Melanie turned on the TV.

By morning she couldn't tell for sure if she'd fallen asleep at all. Already dressed in the only clothes she had, she left her room, ready to kill a couple of hours to get to the Manor by lunch. If he were to leave the building for anything, it'd be food. And it was likely he'd be seeking her out, especially if he had her phone.

Drumming her fingers on the wall she leaned against, Melanie spied on the patrons entering the café two blocks from the Agency. Her leaning turned to pacing out in the cold as she waited, praying Mike had the sense to abandon the confines of his secure world.

Twenty minutes after noon she recognized the bounce of his step from a block away. The glow of his fiery-red Hawaiian shirt made her smile. She called the café.

"Lady it's lunchtime," the guy who answered whined at her request. "I don't know any Mike, they're all chubby with thinning hair," he said of her description.

"He's third in line."

"Fine. Yeah, I see him." Through the muffle of a hand covering the receiver she heard the employee complaining to Mike about not taking too long. "It's a business line, not a 1-866 number."

"Hello?"

"It's me. We need to meet."

"I knew you'd find me," he whispered. "I've got your coat."

"Bring it … tonight at the Air and Space, an hour before closing."

"Is that a good idea? I mean, what if someone's following me?"

"Go home early, put the radio on and sneak out your back door. You still have the key to your neighbor's?"

"I do."

"Go through their house and exit the door farthest from your place. Call for a cab and have them pick you up on the corner. Then take the Metro, it leaves you about half mile from the museum. Walk briskly but not enough to draw attention, make sharp turns and keep your eyes open."

"Great. Anything else, wrestle an alligator? I cannot do this."

"You can. See you at 4:30."

Melanie hung up and went shopping – she needed clean, suitable clothes and a laptop. By 4 p.m. she'd secured everything, but the computer, in a locker at the Metro station and was on lookout for Mike.

We're going to have to do something about that walk, she thought as he bobbed up and down in the crowd. His head jerked from side to side as he exploded on to the sidewalk, making Melanie laugh. *I love that guy*, she thought, gazing at his adorable awkwardness. She followed him at a distance.

After a few minutes she knew he was alone, but he didn't. His pace slowed and quickened at whim, he turned at every corner and backtracked half a dozen times. It was good, though she was certain he never spotted her as she maintained a smooth gait across the street from him, sometimes ahead and sometimes falling behind.

He got to the museum first. She'd forgotten the barren, wide-open space at the glass entrance. *You're slipping. A spy on the run can't afford to make a dumb mistake, Mel.*

Mike had moved past the counter and deeper into the museum when she tracked him down in the Looking At Earth exhibit.

"Thanks for coming," she said, noticing the satellite reconnaissance images.

"Crap, stop sneaking up on me," he panted.

"You're waiting for me, how could I sneak up on you?"

"My nerves are frazzled but I don't think I was followed," he whispered.

"You weren't unless you count me." She smiled. "Have you got my phone?"

He set it on the plexiglass description plate and walked away.

"You're getting good at this," she teased, approaching him at the Tour the Universe gallery.

"It is kind of fun, when my heart isn't palpitating. Remember not to turn your phone on until you're ready to get caught. If they haven't placed a sensor on that frequency yet, they will. Hugh is out for your head."

"What else is going on?" she asked, pressing buttons to light up different qualities of the artifacts.

"The usual. They confiscated your computer, swept your office and your apartment, too, I think. The Board is interviewing agents, your boyfriend and get this … even some of the couples on that retreat in Arizona."

"Not wasting any time, are they?"

"This was in your coat as well." He handed her the blue envelope.

Her brain, packed with essentials, had forgotten this one completely. A romantic trip for two to Italy with a cruise around the Greek Isles. Melanie sighed. "Do me a favor and ask Jane to change the reservations to my parent's names and send it over to them."

"Will do. You know I'd kill to find out what's on your cell." He looked over at her guiltily. "But if they torture me I know I'd spill everything."

"No one is going to torture you, Mike."

"The only reason they aren't following me is because they haven't thought of it. They're too consumed with gathering information on you and breaking your security codes."

"Did they get through?" She grimaced.

"I did but..." he looked around, guiltily. "I transferred appropriate information to another hard drive and gave them that one. I didn't look through your stuff but what I did see..."

"Thanks. I don't want you to get in trouble." She spoke in a low, library voice. He needed to know what he'd gotten himself into. "I've been recording Finn's calls and e-mails." She felt his eyeballs snap. "I don't know why you're surprised. Finn tried to kill me a few months ago and then he hired a hit man and I'm supposed to do what? Nothing?" She walked away agitated and continued, calmer, as he caught up. "I would appreciate it if you would check surveillance around the park. Finn was not there when Danny and I arrived."

"Sure, that's fairly simple, what else?"

"Can't think of a thing." She gave him her new cell number and turned to leave.

"Mel," his fingers curled into the arm of her new jacket, "I don't believe you had anything to do with Finn being taken out. And I'll do whatever it takes to help clear you."

Melanie nodded her thanks. Her vocal cords were clamped and she didn't know how to express her gratitude.

Melanie hailed a cab and traveled to the most populated place she could think of … the shopping mall. Night was overtaking day in their endless chase. The snow had stopped, leaving a muddy mess as people sloshed through the parking lot loaded down with bags.

"What day is it?" she asked the driver.

"Twenty-fourth. You been under a rock?"

The food court was a zoo and she ended up at a counter in a coffee shop. Her laptop was charged and ready as she fitted the cell with its battery and tried to upload Finn's final conversations. Her hands had been shaky as she opened her computer and typed in the codes to retrieve Finn's calls. An hour later she was slamming down the keyboard, frustrated. She was lacking a program and it was impossible for her to upgrade without linking to the internet.

Everything is going wrong, she snarled inside her head as she loaded her few possessions into her bag and headed out. The night was cold and the air thick with moisture. Drawn to the sound of carolers she stood back, mixed in a crowd of bundled people to enjoy the spirit of the song.

I should be home with my parents and Danny. Her eyes burned, loaded down with too heavy a burden and not enough sleep. *Nothing will go right until you get your head on straight*, she thought, stepping away from the song.

She wandered until near midnight when she found herself at the scene of the crime, the park. Seated in Finn's unfortunate spot she calculated the trajectory of the gunshot. She'd felt the bullet above her head from across the path. Her eyes adjusting to the dim light, she focused in the general direction.

"Waiting for Santa?"

It was only years of training – and laughing at Mike, when he made the ridiculous gesture – that prevented her from clutching her heart and yelping in fright.

Adam slid in beside her on the bench.

"I don't believe anymore," she answered, wondering if he could hear her heartbeat against its protective cage.

"What are you doing here?" His head mimicked the angle of hers and looked in the direction she'd been scouting. "He was in that tree, third one back. It's kind of dark now, we could walk over there if it'll help."

"Oh, no," she answered, surprised. Her job was all about probability and it was oddly uncomfortable knowing actual facts. "I was only curious. Hmm," she said, mindlessly. "Sort of a let down ... the knowing. It isn't as interesting as the challenge of figuring it out."

"Sorry."

Melanie felt her grin rising. "What are you doing here?"

"Looking for you."

They sat in silence, her shoulder to her knee pressed against his, staring off into the darkness. If she'd been anyone else, she thought, she'd rest her tired head on his shoulder and let him take care of her.

"Hugh is gunning for me," she said finally.

"I figured," he covered her hand with his. "He won't get to you."

Her throat tightened. "I feel helpless. It's Hugh. And," she took her hand back to swipe at her nose, "I've got stuff but it's not enough ... He's crazed now that Finn is gone. I'm running circles around things that won't make a difference and for the first time that I can remember…" She looked up at him and admitted, "I'm scared."

"Babe," he began.

"No. I'm only telling you because … I don't know why." She set her mind and shook her head. "I don't want your sympathy or anything else from you."

"I want to protect you."

She stood. "Go home where it's warm. Terese is probably waiting for you in one of those thong bikinis."

"That's not my home."

"Well, wherever it is … go," she said, suppressing a nagging lure of curiosity.

"Mel, this may not be the best time to tell you…" he said, standing beside her.

"It's not," she said, her breathing returning to its rapid state. "I can't deal with one more thing."

"Okay," he nodded.

Hating herself, she inhaled slowly. "You aren't dying or in immediate danger, right?"

"Right."

"Okay," she exhaled. Clearly there was no way to leave him with something looming over her head. "Do I need to sit for what's coming?"

"Forget it."

"Shit," she said, looking around at the frost bitten world. "Just give it to me." She braced herself and waited as he judged her mental state. "Come on, it's against the rules to bring something up and then not follow through."

"It's about Terese." His words came out slowly, gauging her reaction.

Melanie shrugged. *Nothing new about this topic*, she thought. *No sweat compared to a bullet through Finn's neck.*

"There's never been anything but a business relationship between us." He stopped again, allowing the meaning to catch. "I lied to you."

"Why would you have to lie about not having an affair?" She felt the scowl on her face, the tightened brows working to comprehend – like grabbing smoke. And then it was gone.

"Finn was asking too many questions about us and I needed to throw him off track. That was around the same time Ashe came into the picture. It seemed logical."

She shook her head. "No. If that were true you would've included me and..."

"Couldn't risk it. If Finn knew how I felt ... feel about you it would never have worked."

"But," she couldn't form the right questions. Her brain was tangled. "You never loved me."

"I've always loved you. I thought he was safer, better for you."

Melanie looked up into his gray eyes and ... slapped his face. She felt the burn on her palm as she forced his face to the right. He didn't look at her until she started talking.

"You have no idea the damage you've caused." Angry tears threatened to spill over. "Did you know he asked me to marry him? For real, ring and all – I said yes. That was last Saturday. So, Adam, was I safer with him? I watched you with Terese ... you tore me apart and I turned to Danny and..." she coughed, breaking up her rampage. She could feel the strain on her facial muscles, dragging her expression down. "You know," her body slumped, "after everything that's happened, maybe a bullet would've been better." She pushed her way past him, bumping into his shoulder.

He gripped her arm, forcing her back to face him. "Don't even joke about that."

She felt the rage in his tone and in the strength of his fingers. She hadn't been joking but she didn't know if she was serious, either.

His clutch eased and his voice mellowed. "You're going to be fine. I've taken care of things."

"Like you did before? No thanks." She looked down at his white knuckled grip. "Let go of me." Melanie said before yanking herself free and with a slight uneasiness walked away.

"You would've chosen him, anyway." Adam's voice came softly.

Melanie switched back, furious. "Never. I don't know if you ever loved me but I loved you and now I can barely look at you. And it's not because of what you'd done in the past, it's what you did to me now." She kept walking as her phone rang. Only Mike knew this number, she fumbled with the unfamiliar buttons – leaving Adam to the night.

"Hello," she said, her hands shaking so badly she couldn't keep the phone to her ear. "Slow down, Mike. What did you say?"

"I said ... Hugh had a stroke. He's at the hospital!"

"Oh my God," she replied, glancing over at the Manor.

"Ben wants you to get back ASAP. You're safe. The Senator is temporarily out of commission and the other Board members are uninterested in you."

"I'll be right there," she said, already disconnecting from Mike and looking over her shoulder. Adam was still at the bench, sitting, rubbing his hands together, blowing on them for warmth. He looked up as she approached. "Word is, Hugh had a stroke."

"He's been under a lot of stress the last few days."

Her knees gave out as she sat, staring at Adam, her heart skipping beats. His dark hair was hidden by a gray knit hat pulled down to cover his ears.

"He probably won't die," he said, his left brow arched.

"How?" She coughed, the cold air freezing her open mouth.

"I went to see him, again. Thought maybe he'd be reasonable but … damn, that man is evil. I've met a lot of people, Mel, and never has anyone chilled me like him. I don't believe in heaven or hell, the devil or God, but I do believe that Mr. Parker has too much. Too much money. Too much power. Too much influence. And that abundance has made him corrupt beyond imagination."

It was like hitching her wagon to a freight train – her mind bouncing around behind him, picking up phrases and meanings long after they'd passed.

"It wasn't a stroke. Tonight he may have taken *too much* heart medication with his brandy." Adam shrugged. "Unless he added a third element … he should survive."

"I better go." She stood again, not understanding the emotion running through her: happiness, relief, gratitude, horror. "When were you going to mention this to me?"

"I didn't think I was ever going to tell you." His head was cast down so that an inch of his neck was visible between his jacket collar and the short curls of dark hair winding above his cap. "All I wanted was to keep you safe."

She placed her hand on top of his head. "You need to get away from me. I'm dangerous for you."

"I have no place else to go."

"Find one," was the last thing she said to him.

CHAPTER 39

Her code still worked. She entered the Manor without wailing alarms or flashing red lights. She cautiously pressed the up arrow on the elevator, ready for the assault. Glances filled with confusion were the deadliest weapons thrown her way.

Anxiously, she knocked on Ben's door, ready to be arrested.

"You heard," he nodded, waving her in. "I think we all could use a stiff drink." Ben rose, filled two glasses of amber liquid and handed one to Melanie. "Thank you for coming in."

She couldn't sit, her instincts still on flight mode. Swirling the whiskey in the tumbler before tossing back the contents in one swallow. The consequence – momentarily blurry vision.

"It's the fugitive," Jack laughed, patting Melanie's shoulder as he entered Ben's office and accepted his glass. He took a seat on the couch and motioned for her to join him. "It's really all right," he said with a serious tone she'd only heard a few times before. "I spoke with the senior member of the Board. No one believes you were involved with Finn's death. Have a seat, you're making me nervous."

Ben refilled her drink.

Melanie sat. "Don't either of you find this strange? Twenty minutes ago I was running, trying to figure out a way to prove I didn't kill Finn and now we're having drinks."

"The entire event is strange," Jack said so casually that it did nothing to remove her concern.

"We should be getting news on the senator's condition at any time," Ben said, reclining in his desk chair. "I'm not surprised he had a stroke. He's been frantic since ... well, you can't blame the man."

"What exactly do we know about Hugh?"

Ben shifted in his seat. "According to his personal assistant, he'd had been racing around all day but despondent at night. The assistant checked on him before going to bed and thought he was fine, asleep. But noticed a spilt glass of water on the nightstand, which caused him to take a closer look. When the senator wouldn't wake up he called 911."

The three sat in silence. Melanie's mind was on Adam. *He's rescued me again*, she thought, feeling the coarse fiber of his cap on her hand before remembering she was mad at him.

She and Jack both behaved as if they weren't eavesdropping on Ben's phone call. It was the update they'd been waiting for.

"Hey Mel, I was sorry to hear about..." Jack stalled. "You know, about the breakup."

"Yeah, well, those things happen." Melanie could feel the fire burning in her cheeks. "I was hoping to keep that part of my life private." She looked over at him. "No such luck, right?"

Jack shook his head. "The word is already out. If there was a company website you'd already have gone viral."

"Terrific," she grunted as Ben set down the receiver and held her breath expectantly.

"You've had a shitty year." Jack observed.

"One breakup compared with your what? Twelve?"

"Something like that, but I can't remember half their names." Melanie smiled.

"He's alert but there's been some nerve damage." Ben set his pale blue eyes on her. "That's all I've got for now."

"I hate to be self-absorbed but what does this mean for me? You spoke about assignments … am I able to throw my name in the hat?"

Ben plopped down heavily in his seat, removed his glasses and pressed the bridge of his nose. "I will admit with Hugh down your future is significantly brighter." He set the wire rims on his desk and looked over at her. "Even before the events of tonight, the Board had decided to overrule him. His behavior has been erratic – especially when it came to you."

Melanie breathed and thanked the God she'd been praying to.

"And I do find myself suddenly overrun with cases and not nearly enough agents. It all seems to materialize at the same time. When this business with Finn has been settled I will have assignments for you. But I understand if you're not up to taking on a big role."

"I am. I want to work. I'll take whatever you've got," Melanie practically leapt on the desk, overjoyed. "And," she said, feeling the sense of normalcy return, "I'd like to start mentoring the junior agents, starting with Logan Holland. She showed promise."

Ben read her mental state with one scrutinizing gaze. "That's a great idea. Okay," he nodded. "What about you, Jack?"

"I'm wrapping up the home-grown terrorist plot with the FBI. So, you can count me in on any new project."

"I'd be glad to help you out with that," Melanie said, not knowing how to be subtle. "That is, if I'm fully understanding what's happening – that I'm done worrying over ... everything?"

Ben sent her a wink and a nod. "With the statement given by Daniel Ashe as to the circumstances that brought you to the park that afternoon, there are no suspicions about your involvement. We've surveyed tapes and you were clearly preoccupied."

She didn't wonder what Danny had said. She knew – the truth. He was naïve and couldn't lie convincingly. "I see." She looked down at the glass in her hand. "You don't have to worry," she said, seeing the shadow of sorrow pass over Ben's expression. "I'm fine," she cleared her throat so she could speak. "It was a shock at first and then with Finn..." She swallowed. "But I can manage."

"Of course you can. You're Melanie Ward, strong and fearless," Jack said as a way of encouragement.

"So I've been told." She smiled back at him with an empty grin.

CHAPTER 40

Her fingers knocked the gravel off a slim ledge as she used her feet to brace against the mountainside. It was April in Africa and the world around her was a monotone shade of gold. She'd abandoned her few possessions back at the village and the lightweight backpack was like nothing at all. Three months in Niger had brought her back to center but now her climb was leading her home. The assignment had been identifying corruption in the mining industry, uranium being the main target. Teaching English and building the school had been on her own time.

Rocks scattered down the side of the cliff to the sandy floor, the dry grassy plains far beneath her as she pulled herself up. *It's always my last bit of strength*, she thought, heaving her body over the side to lie in the burning sun at the top. Protruding rocks stabbed at her back as Melanie sat up, pulled off her ball cap and ran her fingers through what was left of her sweat-soaked hair. The shortness still felt strange, but dealing with the head lice had been worse. And finally having had enough, she took a pair of rusty shears and cut off all but an inch from her scalp.

She felt the tingling burn of the rays on her exposed skin but the moisture of her sweat acted like an evaporative cooler in the arid breeze.

Drinking down the last swallows of water and using her sleeve to wipe the sweat off her face, she hoped nothing had stalled Jack. How long could she survive in the African desert without water? The only water source, a river, was half a country away. Melanie stood at the edge of the bluff, shading her eyes from the blinding sun. Gazing out miles over the harsh environment she smiled at the puff of dust being kicked up by the all-terrain tires.

Moving 10 yards in from the ledge she turned back to face the open expanse and took a deep lungful of baked air. She ran, her soles grinding down the gravel, as she pushed off from the edge of the cliff. Falling at nearly 200 mph she refrained from celebrating as the barren land quickly rose to meet her.

With not much time to enjoy the flight, Melanie pulled the chute and was yanked back as her fall was slowed. Gliding, she crossed the open desert-scape and toward the dust cloud that was Jack.

As the ground approached Melanie prepared, releasing the chute at the moment of landing. She ran as her feet touched ground and jumped into the open Jeep, catching her ride home.

"You know how to make an entrance," Jack laughed, stepping on the gas.

"I did offer you this part of the assignment," she reminded him.

"I wasn't speaking out of jealousy. I like my feet firmly on terra firma."

The hot air rushed through the vehicle. She leaned back and smiled. "God, don't you love this job?"

❧

EPILOGUE

"Mother Fucker!" Melanie jumped up, banging her head on the tin disc that covered the single hanging light bulb. "Did you see that!?" She pointed to one of the nine monitors as she looked back into the on site Command Center. Two other team leaders were on their feet, too.

"What the hell was that, Heintz?" One yelled rushing at Heintz.

"Tell me," Melanie started turning directly toward Heintz, her arms out separating the two men. "Did your people pollute the well or poison it?" She'd gotten the words out through clenched teeth, her heart pumping. Heintz's casual smile was all too reminiscent of Finn's.

"I guess that's what you'll have to decide." He said, face to face with Melanie, peanut butter lingering on his breath. She felt the others grouping at her side but Heintz kept his casual tone. "If you believe that I am capable of risking the lives of your recruits, then by all means, go down there and warn them…" he shifted his gaze to look at the other agents. "But that'll cost you a penalty, and at this point in the challenge that would surely eliminate you from the finals. Besides maybe your teams won't pass by this water source at all."

"You can't do that!" The shouts were building.

Melanie pulled herself out of the fray as it exploded. She'd calculated every movement of her team, and they were three miles away with empty canteens. Heintz was an old timer, he wouldn't kill an opposing team. But she knew his conscious would forgive a good old-fashioned stomach pumping.

She turned to the monitors, keeping an ear on the quarrel behind her.

"The wells are supposed to be off limits!"

"If there are no rules, then there is no integrity."

"Dahl," Melanie's voice cut through the gruff threats Heintz was enduring. "What are the options?"

"Well," Dahl, a tall pasty stick of a man was rocking from one foot to the other. "What he said is true. If you warn your team, then you incur a fairly harsh penalty. I'd have to look it up exactly but…"

He was still listing the possibilities as Melanie searched the other screens for her people. "Wait! Dahl. You said if I warn *my* team then I get dinged … what if I warn everyone? Then we all benefit equally. Loophole?

Come on, quickly!" She snapped her fingers.

"Yeah, I suppose … but I'd have to check."

No time. Melanie tossed through the supply cabinet, stuck two cans of spray paint into the pockets of her cargo pants and lifted the trap door. The on site Command Center was located in a tree house twenty feet from the soft fertile ground. The window of opportunity was tight, her team wasn't far from the well and she had hot, sticky jungle miles to cover. About to forego the rungs of the ladder and slide down ... "Damn it Heintz, this sucks!"

"Ward, wait. You're people are already at the well."

Shit!

"What'd you tell her for ... she could've been eliminated?"

"Turn up the volume!"

Melanie elbowed her way to the front. Her three young agents surrounded the stone structure that had been specifically dug for the ITC, Intelligence Training Challenge. There was no way to reach her team, Melanie prayed as she watched her recruits approach the well.

She'd been tough on them. Working them nonstop for months, drilling in lessons of mental agility, while taking them to their physical limits. There were times when they hated her, said it to her face twice, but this was more than just a game ... it was going to be their life and the better prepared, the higher the chance of survival.

Melanie chewed on her bottom lip watching her three students. Somehow, they looked much younger than when they were in her care.

"Look at those tracks," Logan said, "Another team was trying to hide that they'd been here."

"And why would anyone do that?" Ma asked, his voice clearly sarcastic.

"Lift the lid, let me take a whiff." Lasota dipped his head deep into the well. "There's a faint scent of..." he growled, "Some type of chemical but I'm not sure, sorry."

"That's okay." Logan said, looking around. "What would Melanie tell us to do?"

"Not drink this."

"But these marked wells are supposed to be fresh, and we need water."

"The next source is probably miles away."

Come on, Melanie thought hard trying to mentally send the answer their way.

"We should spare one of the purifying tablets."

"Yes!" Melanie called out throwing her fists in the air and exhaling a huge breath before turning on Heintz. "You pull crap like this again … I won't bother going to the board. Understand?"

She didn't really expect him to cower, but with three other challenges left to win the coveted trophy, Melanie wasn't about to take it easy.

Agent Melanie Ward
Returns in Book Three

ACKNOWLEDGMENTS

First, I would like to thank my family. Without their support, completing this or any other story would be impossible. Thank you Syd and Sam for being absolutely awesome! Brent for ... everything. My mom and dad for taking care of me and for not giving me away. Thank you to Frank, Ralph and Steve, who have the common traits of being generous, kind and completely ridiculous. I'd like to thank Linda, Kris and Mercy for being great additions to this family.

Huge Thank You to Jill Jorden Spitz for being a wizard with words and grammar. Your help is greatly appreciated and no one can truly know how much better this book is because of you.

Thank you Angie Chiara for your keen eye and being the first to read Second Chance (sorry it took longer than expected). You are an important part of the process and a valuable friend.

A special thanks to Amy Anderson for being my sounding board of reason and a patient Social Media Guru.

Thank you PowWow Publishing for your dedication and always taking my phone calls.

I'd also like to acknowledge the Gallardo and Vasquez families, Sharon Schaum, Allyson James, Joyce Mathis, Jessie Montano, Steve Rosenberg and Bonnie Lewis all of whom have played a roll – whether they know it or not. To my nieces and nephews who keep me entertained.

And to the wonderful readers who've emailed me – caught me at a writing spot or at a book signing to say they enjoyed *Living Lies* – your words are lifting and give me motivation to continue ...

Thank You!

Kate Mathis on Facebook
http://www.facebook.com/pages/Living-Lies/228205853872791

Kate Mathis Blog
http://book-writing-tips.blogspot.com

Kate Mathis Website
http://www.KateMathis.net

or scan the image above with your smartphone
go to getscanlife.com to get the free mobile app

Kate Mathis

is also the author of Living Lies, Book One in the Agent Melanie Ward Novels. A graduate of the University of Arizona, Kate is a native Tucsonan, where she lives with her husband and twin daughters.

Second Chance

AN AGENT MELANIE WARD NOVEL

In a world of espionage and deceit, Agent Melanie Ward's life is rocked by scandal. She returns in Second Chance, Book 2 of the Agent Melanie Ward Novels, ready to reclaim the life she once had. But her rival, Agent Finn Parker and his father, Senator Hugh Parker, have very different plans for her future.

Adam Chase, the chef with the ability to assemble a rifle in seconds, has rejoined the crew of mobsters that followed him on his rise as a professional assassin.

Melanie throws herself into the work she loves – life is all about the mission, sanctioned or not.

Danny Ashe, her college obsession and first love, is back and going through a divorce. Her friend, Trish, hates him, her mother makes Thanksgiving dinner and Carla can say Salvador Luhan three times in one sentence (and that's before breakfast).

In Second Chance, Melanie is caught between two worlds, two loves and a decision that will change everything ... or nothing at all ... but in the end, someone has to die.

Mystery, romance and humor fill the pages of this fast-paced adventure.

www.ingramcontent.com/pod-product-compliance
Lightning Source LLC
Chambersburg PA
CBHW050900250626

47155CB00001B/43